Penguin Books
A Fringe of Leaves

The author was born in England in 1912, when his parents
were in Europe for two years; at six months he was taken
back to Australia where his father owned a sheep station.
When he was thirteen Patrick White was sent to school in
England, to Cheltenham, 'where, it was understood, the
climate would be temperate and a colonial acceptable'.
Neither proved true, and after four rather miserable years
there he went to King's College, Cambridge, where he
specialized in languages. After leaving the university he
settled in London, determined to become a writer. His first
novel, *Happy Valley*, was published in 1939, and his second,
The Living and the Dead in 1941. Then during the war he was an
R.A.F. Intelligence Officer in the Middle East and Greece.
After the war he returned to Australia and is currently living
in Sydney.

His other novels are *The Aunt's Story* (1946), *The Tree of
Man* (1956), *Voss* (1957), *Riders in the Chariot* (1961), *The
Solid Mandala* (1966), *The Vivisector* (1970), *The Eye of
the Storm* (1973) and *The Twyborn Affair* (1979). In
addition he has published two collections of short stories,
The Burnt Ones (1964), and *The Cockatoos* (1974), which
incorporates several short novels. His autobiography, *Flaws
in the Glass*, was published in 1981. In 1973 he was awarded
the Nobel Prize for Literature.

Patrick White

A Fringe of Leaves

Penguin Books

Penguin Books Ltd, Harmondsworth, Middlesex, England
Viking Penguin Inc., 40 West 23rd Street, New York, New York 10010, U.S.A.
Penguin Books Australia Ltd, Ringwood, Victoria, Australia
Penguin Books Canada Ltd, 2801 John Street, Markham, Ontario, Canada L3R 1B4
Penguin Books (N.Z.) Ltd, 182–190 Wairau Road, Auckland 10, New Zealand

First published in Great Britain by Jonathan Cape Ltd 1976
First published in the United States of America by The Viking Press 1977
Published by Penguin Books 1977
Reprinted 1979, 1981, 1982 (twice), 1983, 1985

Made and printed in Great Britain by
Richard Clay (The Chaucer Press) Ltd, Bungay, Suffolk
Set in Monotype Times

To Desmond Digby

A perfect Woman, nobly planned,
To warn, to comfort, and command.

William Wordsworth

RAT-WIFE	Humbly begging pardon – are your worships troubled with any gnawing things in the house?
ALMERS	Here? No, I don't think so.
RAT-WIFE	If you had, it would be such a pleasure to rid your worships' house of them.
RITA	Yes, yes, we understand, But we have nothing of the sort here.

Henrik Ibsen

If there is some true good in a man, it can only be unknown to himself.

Simone Weil

Love is your last chance. There is really nothing else on earth to keep you there.

Louis Aragon

1

As the carriage drew away from the Circular Wharf Mr Stafford Merivale tapped the back of his wife's hand and remarked that they had done their duty.

'No one,' Mrs Merivale replied, 'can accuse me of neglecting duty.' She might have pouted if inherent indolence had not prevailed, and a suspicion that those acquainted with her must know that her claim was not strictly true.

So she smoothed the kid into which her hands had been stuffed, and added, 'At least we were, I think, agreeably entertained. And that is always compensation for any kind of inconvenience. Miss Scrimshaw,' she asked, looking not quite at her friend, 'weren't we entertained?'

'Oh yes, *most* agreeably,' the latter answered in a rush, which transposed what must have been a deep voice into a higher, unnatural key. 'Living at such a distance nobody can fail to be refreshed by visitors from Home. The pity is when their visits are so brief.'

Mrs Merivale decided to appear satisfied, while Miss Scrimshaw, obviously, was not. An atmosphere of unconfessed presentiment was intensified by the slight creaking of woodwork and friction of leather in the comfortably upholstered carriage. Rocked together and apart by the uneven surface of the street the occupants were at the mercy of the land as seaborne passengers are threatened by the waves.

'Short visits make no demands,' Mrs Merivale consoled herself. 'Don't you agree?' Mr Merivale being a man, there was no question but that her remark was intended for Miss Scrimshaw.

'Oh yes,' she answered as expected, 'there is that about short visits.'

In all the large circle of her acquaintance it was Miss Scrimshaw's duty to agree, which was why her voice sounded only on some occasions her own. In exceptional circumstances, however, she would express an opinion, and it was this, together with her strong nose, long teeth, and Exalted Connection, which caused the Mrs Merivales of Sydney to glance not quite at their companion and hope they were accepted.

'Who can guess,' Mrs Merivale ventured to pursue the subject, 'from exchanging a few friendly words, with strangers, on a ship's deck, what demands a longer visit might entail.'

At that point the carriage lurched.

'Oh no, people can be frightful!' Miss Scrimshaw asserted, rather flat, but surprisingly loud. 'I do not believe one will ever arrive at the end of people's frightfulness.'

This was an exceptional circumstance, and it made Mrs Merivale quail inside her fur palatine.

'I don't know,' her husband began, who had been content until now to leave it to the ladies, and to sit staring in transparent pleasure at whatever object presented itself the other side of the carriage window; 'I don't believe I've ever come across a fellow in whom I didn't find a fair measure of good.'

There was so much that his sex and nature must always prevent him understanding, the two ladies were at once reduced to a collusive silence.

Mrs Merivale looked in some detachment at her husband's hand as it rested against the window-jamb, the skin altered inexorably by those first years in a harsh land into something almost part of it. Mrs Merivale shuddered to remember a lizard which had once stared at her, through bleached grass, from a scorched earth.

Mr Stafford Merivale was of that stamp of English gentleman, not so gentle as not to be firm, not too positive, yet not altogether negative, who will transplant reliably from his native soil to the most unpromising pockets of the globe. Engaged by the Crown as a surveyor, he had already investigated vast tracts of the colony of New South Wales, and on one occasion pushed as far as the more recent settlement at Moreton Bay. His strength lay in his capacity for enduring boredom, his wife suspected, quite overlooking the possibility of a relationship with a landscape, an unprepossessing one at that. By now Mr Merivale was as tanned as leather, as chapped as canvas, practically a fitting of his customary saddle.

Mrs Merivale traced a seam, enjoying the texture of her newly imported merino gown. For a brief, unhappy period after joining her husband in the country of his fate or choice, she had been persuaded to follow him into its surprising hinterland. She had jolted sulkily behind him on a dray, and made a somewhat unwilling effort at bivouacking. There had been the episode of the lizard, and many others too awful to remember. Mrs Merivale was an adept at closing her mind to awfulness. Divine mercy, besides, had blessed her very soon with a delicate state of health, so that she was able to retire to a villa at the Glebe, and have the girl draw its curtains almost as at Winchester. As for Mr Merivale, he was too absorbed in his man's world of levels and distances, of soil and water, to notice her absence overmuch, but when released from official duties, would make his way to the villa at the Glebe to fulfil those other duties of a husband. His wife submitted, while the washstand-set unpleasantly rattled, and a foreign skin caught in her satin coverlet.

Now as Mrs Merivale sat tracing her seam, she tried to think of the answer she would make to the man she had elected to marry.

'Miss Scrimshaw did not mean,' she explained with ever such patience, 'she did not mean that *all* people are *wholly* frightful.'

But for some reason, for the moment, her friend refused to collaborate.

'Almost all!' Miss Scrimshaw persisted.

Mrs Merivale was taken with a laughter, which would heave itself up at times, in wheezy, but fairly refined bursts, out of the depths of her stays, shocking in anyone normally so placid. 'Oh, my dear,' she cried, 'it is the north-easter! It has given you a liver!' But at once she wondered how she had dared, remembering Miss Scrimshaw's Connection: the Honourable Mrs Chetwynd of Saffron Walden.

'When I proposed this little expedition to *Bristol Maid*, to speed the Roxburghs on their way, I didn't expect we should be plunged in gloom,' Mr Merivale remarked, his own good humour protecting him from becoming more than superficially involved.

'How you misunderstand, Stafford!' his wife protested and frowned.

It was her favourite expression for use upon her husband, although if asked to elaborate, her own understanding might not have stood the strain.

As for Miss Scrimshaw, she fell to contemplating her lap, and answered with recovered meekness, 'Almost everybody, I imagine, is subject to their fits of gloom.'

She was dressed entirely in brown, with an aureole of brown moiré roses parcelled into the scuttle of her bonnet. It made her complexion, if not livery, browner than it should have been.

Mrs Merivale thought she recognized, below the hem of her friend's mantle, a skirt she herself had discarded, and was at once rewarded by this glimpse of her own generosity.

'Miss Scrimshaw, like myself, probably felt most deeply for those poor souls in their wretched little tub, and all the miles of tedium and danger between them and what they love.' Mrs Merivale in her enclosed and comfortable carriage allowed herself the luxury of pity. 'Much as I dislike my present surroundings I would not undertake the voyage home except in some fast-sailing barque equipped to accommodate passengers. I cannot endure discomfort, as you know.'

She might have been accusing her husband, but was in fact frowning through the window at a carter who, in the effort to turn, had jammed his dray across the street, threatening to bar their passage.

Mr Merivale cleared his throat. '*Bristol Maid* reached Hobart Town in passable time – I have it from Captain Purdew – and without undue incident. With the same good seamanship, there is no reason to believe she'll come to grief on the return voyage.'

Nobody spoke at first.

Then Mrs Merivale reiterated, 'Had it been myself, I should have waited for a passage in some fast-sailing barque.' Her head swayed tragically, not so much for the fate of her new-found acquaintances as for the tactics of the offending carter struggling to manoeuvre his dray.

'It must have been the brother,' Miss Scrimshaw decided. 'It is embarrassing – as I know – to depend indefinitely on the good will of a blood relation.'

Mr Merivale laughed. 'Austin Roxburgh and his brother Garnet have always been devoted to each other. That is why Austin, in spite of failing health, decided to make the voyage out to Van Diemen's Land – to enjoy the pleasure of seeing his brother – I don't like to say it, but must be candid – for what could be the last time.'

'With such an affection for his brother it is all the more extra-ordinary that an ailing man should hasten to sail in a brig the size of *Bristol Maid*.' Miss Scrimshaw was ferreting after something. 'Perhaps,' she hesitated, 'it was *Mrs* Roxburgh who made the decision.'

It was enough for Mrs Merivale to lose interest in the carter and his dray. 'Why ever now should Mrs Roxburgh?' She looked to Miss Scrimshaw for some revelation of a stunning nature.

'Mrs Roxburgh may not have been so affectionately disposed towards her husband's brother.' Miss Scrimshaw's voice slurred, and she blushed for what was more sibylline inspiration than solidly founded reasoning.

Mrs Merivale rounded on her. 'There was no hint today that Mrs Roxburgh and her brother-in-law had fallen out.'

'That may be,' Miss Scrimshaw confessed, staring, and not, into the street. 'No,' she ejaculated, as though about to disparage her own instinct. 'Nor do I wish to cast aspersions of any kind on any of your acquaintances. *You* must realize, Mr Merivale, it was a mere theory, regrettably flimsy, which formed itself in the course of conversation.'

Mrs Merivale was all admiration for her friend's agility in ex-tricating herself from possible blame; her own lips moved like those of a ventriloquist in time with his knowing doll's pro-nouncement.

While Mr Merivale might have withdrawn behind a curtain of the past: when he spoke, his speech had slowed. 'I can't say I was close to Austin. His wife I never met until today. The brother, Garnet, was my friend.'

For a moment it seemed as though this honourable and un-complicated man had grown disgruntled too, for the way fate had dealt with him. If his mouth had tightened, his ordinarily gaunt, erect head lolled softly on his shoulders, the eyes half-closed on a deeper than antipodean shade, his memory apparently dwelling on images more convincing than any the present had to offer. Each of the ladies was conscious of a change of climate, although neither received the same sting of wet oak-leaves on parted lips.

'Garnet and I rode together over half Hampshire when we were boys,' Stafford Merivale recollected. 'First, on shaggy ponies. Later to hounds. Often when we were grown, we would hack just for the fun of it, over the downs, and along the Roman road. I can remember Garnet putting his horse at a hedge as wide as a hay-wain, somewhere this side of Stockbridge. One moment, there he was, beside me on the sunken road. The next, I heard him laughing the other side of a thorn wall.'

'And you?' Miss Scrimshaw inquired. 'Did you follow him?'

'I was always a plodder,' Mr Merivale replied.

Nor was the spinster's respect diminished.

'Austin now, was of another temperament – a different strain, one might say,' the surveyor continued. 'Always had his nose in a book. I scarcely saw him, excepting when he would come outside, poking about in the garden. Not *working* at it. He was delicate, you see. At one stage he was thought to be sick of a consumption. Then, his heart was bad. And the strange part was, it seemed to draw him closer to his very unlikely brother. As though he hoped to borrow some of Garnet's health and strength. I think I was jealous of Austin.' Stafford Merivale smiled, and paused. 'He studied law. But did not practise. His health would not have permitted. And married this devoted young woman we have just met.'

'Mrs Austin Roxburgh,' Miss Scrimshaw gravely asked, 'was she also Hampshire born?'

'I never heard of her,' Mr Merivale replied, 'anywhere round Winchester.'

'I understood Mrs Roxburgh to be from Cornwall.' Mrs Merivale never missed reminding her husband of anything he happened to forget.

'A *remote* county!' Miss Scrimshaw was perhaps reinforcing her 'theory'. 'Of dark people. I cannot remember ever having been on intimate terms with any individual of Cornish blood. All my own family,' she added, 'were fair. Both brothers and sisters. Especially the daughters of cousins. With faint tea-rose complexions. I was the only brown one.'

Mrs Merivale might have felt chilled had she not realized at once that Miss Scrimshaw's mind had strayed to her Connection, the titled lady of Saffron Walden. In the circumstances, Mrs Merivale warmed to poor Miss Scrimshaw, youngest of a clergyman's protracted family. None had heard tell how she had reached New South Wales, nor taken her deep enough into their hearts to call her by her first name. (Whether out of wariness or cruelty her parents had in fact christened their tenth Decima.)

Miss Scrimshaw, her inward eye fixed on fair estates, might have elaborated on the darker side of Cornwall had not Mr Merivale chosen the moment to propound something most unexpected.

He sat forward, hands clasped between his knees, the better to accuse, it would have seemed. 'I don't believe you ladies formed a high opinion of the Roxburghs.'

'Oh, Stafford!'

'I wouldn't go so far as to say you actively *disliked*,' the vexatious man allowed, before his prosecution was interrupted.

The carter ahead of them had succeeded in bringing round his dray to a point from which his sweating Punches could strain past them down the narrow street, and the carriage surged forward, throwing the guilty females together in a tangle of chains and ribbons and a spray of protest.

'Only that you didn't take to them. At all,' their accuser unkindly insisted, himself bobbing like an uncontrolled marionette.

'I will not be persecuted, Stafford – so very horridly!'

'Such a distinguished gentleman and admirable character as Mr Roxburgh appeared to be!' Mr Merivale's charge of what amounted to injustice had made Miss Scrimshaw breathless. 'And such an enjoyable experience. The little brig – the captain – Purdew, was it? An obviously open-hearted fellow.' The spinster had a weakness for the sea, and suffered a cruel blow as a girl when a lieutenant of the Royal Navy was carried off by a fever at Antigua.

Now the carriage was settling itself into its regular roll, and the ladies might have recovered their balance had not the relentless Mr Merivale fired a further shot. 'At least *Mrs* Roxburgh, I could tell, was not to your taste.'

Which was tasteless on his part, not to say strange in one so innocent.

'What can possess you, Stafford?'

Miss Scrimshaw, on the other hand, was silenced for the present.

13

'And she as pretty as a picture,' Mr Merivale declared with a courtliness which came naturally.

'Pretty? Oh, well, *pretty*!' his wife conceded.

'And elegant besides,' the gentleman added.

'She was wearing an unusually beautiful shawl.' Mrs Merivale hankered after material things.

'A pretty woman, yes. But Mrs Roxburgh is not what I would call beautiful,' Miss Scrimshaw announced after giving the matter deepest thought. 'Beauty is something grander, nobler,' here her head was invisibly tossed, 'and is in no need of a fancy shawl to remind us of its presence.'

'Mrs Roxburgh is a woman, not a marble statue.'

Mrs Merivale was pretty certain that her husband's vision was un-draped.

Miss Scrimshaw must have realized too, for she blushed and quickly added, 'What I meant to suggest was that true beauty is spiritual. There was nothing spiritual in Mrs Roxburgh.'

Miss Scrimshaw herself had composed verses when a young girl and wreathed them in watercolour violets and pansies.

'Would you say she is a lady?' Mrs Merivale ventured.

'I would not care to give an opinion,' Miss Scrimshaw discreetly answered.

Mrs Merivale at once recoiled as though it were someone else who had asked such a vulgar question.

'She was a very quiet, well-spoken person. Or so it appeared to me at least.' Mr Merivale by now hoped to end what he had started.

'Still waters, as they say.' Launched into philosophy, his wife felt justified in looking languid.

But Miss Scrimshaw had begun to kindle. 'For my part,' she announced, enveloping the others with her air, 'I would never trust a silent woman.'

'I should have thought it a distinct virtue.' Mr Merivale's throat made it sound the drier.

'Mrs Roxburgh holds her silence at moments when people in general would offer candour. There are silences and silences, I mean.'

Although Mrs Merivale was not at all sure what her friend did mean, she nodded her head in vigorous support.

'Mrs Roxburgh is something of a mystery,' Miss Scrimshaw added with a sigh.

'If you want my honest opinion,' Mr Merivale said, 'the ladies haven't left her a leg to stand on.'

Miss Scrimshaw hung her head. 'It is not possible to practise charity every hour of the twenty-four.' Then plaiting her gloved fingers, 'Please don't think,' she begged, 'that I exempt myself from criticism of the faults I share with Mrs Roxburgh.'

It was certainly one of her days. They did not know what to make of her.

Mr Merivale's present intention was to drive round by the Brickfields and call at the house of one Delaney who had undertaken to collect a leg of pork from a Toongabbie farmer.

'I do hope I shall not put you to any inconvenience,' Miss Scrimshaw remarked.

She had begun to fidget, and arrange herself, and sigh for Church Hill, where she lodged with a widow, a decent soul, though not a lady.

'No inconvenience at all,' assured the blander Mrs Merivale, who could find little uses for people, and had not finished with Miss Scrimshaw yet. 'I took it for granted you would dine with us. We have a pigeon pie.' She had, besides, her *mousseline de soie* which needed letting out. 'And spend the evening, agreeably. At cards. Or music.'

'That would, indeed, be agreeable,' Miss Scrimshaw replied with heartiness enough to suggest that she was unaware of the catch.

Amongst her extensive acquaintance her needle was in almost as constant demand as her tongue, for which she accepted remuneration, usually in kind, though preferably in envelopes, turning her head the other way.

This evening, however, it was less Miss Scrimshaw's needle than her subtlety that Mrs Merivale hoped to encourage. The thought of it started her nervously coughing and rummaging for a pastille, if she had one.

'The window, Stafford!' she complained, as though a particle of dust might have affected her precious throat; for they had begun to approach the Brickfields in the neighbourhood of which the fellow Delaney had chosen to live.

This Delaney, an emancipist, had become finally a man of substance from being engaged in the carrying trade and whatever other gainful ploys nobody was altogether certain. In any event, he throve, though his house, neat and substantial enough behind its whitewashed fence, remained complacently countrified rather than pretentious in the urban style. As the carriage approached, a brace of speckled pullets could be seen fossicking at the entrance to a yard, and an old, matted sheepdog lifted his head from out of the dust to hawk up a few rheumy barks.

Mr Merivale began to grunt and unfold his long legs. Since the raising of the window, the enclosed carriage was more than ever its own world; to leave it amounted to an emigration.

'Will you come in?' he asked his wife, lowering his head as he trod out backwards.

The coachman had clambered down, though the master was not of those who accept assistance.

'Oh dear, no!' Mrs Merivale's nature made it short rather than emphatic.

'*She* will be disappointed.'

'She would stuff us with plum-cake. Before our dinner. And get us tipsy on her ginger wine.' Here Mrs Merivale looked to Miss Scrimshaw, who responded with a wicked pursing of the lips.

'She will be disappointed,' Mr Merivale reminded fruitlessly.

Mrs Merivale watched with scorn as her husband strolled towards the rear of the house with that elaborate informality gentlemen in the colonies assumed for their inferiors. At the same time a hand, bunching the holland curtains, disclosed *her* face at its post, a desperate, mulberry-tinted pudding.

All this occurred during only a matter of seconds before Mrs Merivale's ordinarily sluggish mind was sucked back by her intention into the stuffy, confessional gloom of the box in which she and Miss Scrimshaw were seated.

Now that the moment had arrived, her throat was contracting, bloodless; her heart went *fut fut fut* inside the layers of fur, merino, caoutchouc, and flesh.

Mrs Merivale wet her lips for a start. 'To return, Miss Scrimshaw, to the subject of Mrs Roxburgh.'

That her companion appeared not to have heard made Mrs Merivale tremble.

'I would be most interested to know,' she faltered, 'in what

16

way,' placing her words as though they had been ivory chess-pieces, 'this Mrs Roxburgh struck you as being – as you said,' Mrs Merivale became aware of the heat of her own breath, 'a mystery,' she heard herself practically hiss.

Now that it was out, her own inquisitiveness left her feeling distressingly exposed, a situation intensified by Miss Scrimshaw's continued failure to express either interest or approval. But no professional pythoness can afford to remain indefinitely silent, and turning at last in the direction of the suppliant she trained on her a pair of eyes, normally piercing and lustrous, but now so far shuttered by the lids, they might not be prepared to illuminate more than half a secret.

'I cannot give you an exact account, Mrs Merivale,' she said, 'of the impression Mrs Roxburgh made on me. Unless – to put it at its plainest – she reminded me of a clean sheet of paper which might disclose an invisible writing – if breathed upon. Do you understand?'

Mrs Merivale did not.

And Miss Scrimshaw said, 'If I were able to explain away a mystery, then it would no longer be one, would it?'

Such horrid logic confounded Mrs Merivale. 'Ah,' she murmured, and her lips hung open in a manner she herself might have found vulgar in anybody else.

'But,' she pleaded, 'can you give me no *inkling*?' Mrs Merivale's 'inkling' tinkled piteously inside the carriage.

'I will tell you one thing,' Miss Scrimshaw vouchsafed. 'Every woman has secret depths with which even she, perhaps, is unacquainted, and which sooner or later must be troubled.'

Mrs Merivale was terrified, who had never, ever, been 'troubled', unless during the journey on a dray into the interior of New South Wales; and would not have dared ask Miss Scrimshaw whether she suspected her too, of having the invisible writing on her.

'But this Mrs Roxburgh!' she could not suppress what emerged as a wail.

'Ah,' Miss Scrimshaw replied, 'who am I to say? I only had the impression that Mrs Roxburgh could feel life has cheated her out of some ultimate in experience. For which she would be prepared to suffer, if need be.'

17

Perhaps it occurred to the sibyl that she was unveiling herself along with Mrs Roxburgh, for she hesitated, then hurried on. 'Of course, as we all know, any of us may suffer, at any moment, worse than we ever bargained for. And will continue to offer ourselves, out of bravado.'

Mrs Merivale might have remained confused, not to say alarmed, by her friend's esoteric confidences, had not her husband, in company with the emancipist Delaney, appeared round the corner of the latter's house. As always when in any way rattled, Mrs Merivale was materially reinstated by the presence of the man she had married, though she would have preferred not to have him carrying the Toongabbie pork, inelegantly, by the ears of the sack in which it had travelled.

The two men approached. The emancipist, a reddish, freckled individual, might have behaved obsequiously had he not done so well for himself. Bull-shaped, he was none the less got up in cloth of superior quality with a flash of gold across the waistcoat. If the rim of his neckcloth was soiled, as it was soon possible to observe, it went to show that the habit of acting had survived that of giving orders.

When the two had shared the last of some masculine joke, and put it away, and Delaney had made his last grab at the sack, the weight of which he only half-intended to take, they arrived at the carriage, where the emancipist stuck in his head, and asked somewhat rudely, Mrs Merivale thought, whether the ladies would step inside for a bite of something.

'Oh dear, no,' she replied, 'and the girls waiting to dish up our dinner!'

From her throne she returned the stare of this preposterous subject, too round-eyed and solemn for the size of the favour he was asking. But the emancipist wasn't Irish for nothing: foreseeing how he would be received, his mouth had shut in a saucy grin as he reached the end of his proposition.

'The ladies are in low spirits,' the surveyor thought to explain, 'after taking their leave of friends on a ship homeward bound.'

'Not I! And scarcely friends,' Mrs Merivale protested. 'Nor can I waste sympathy on those who needlessly risk their lives.'

'Then, Miss Scrimshaw is sad,' her husband would not be put

off. 'My wife is more practical than sentimental. But Miss Scrimshaw too, must leave us soon.'

Delaney, his eyes grown smaller in concentration, examined these two females, the fat, soft, satiny thing, and the stringy, craftier one in brown whose beak was raised to parry what was only a playful blow on the surveyor's part. They would never admit him to their world, but it amused the emancipist to regard them as being of his.

'Miss Scrimshaw is for the Old Country? Good luck to her then!' He laughed softly, and let them interpret it how they pleased.

Mrs Merivale simmered, not because her friend's sensibility might have been offended by the interest of a rough, common man, but because a convention had been flouted.

'Far from it,' Miss Scrimshaw answered with a return to that meekness which did not altogether go with her.

'Miss Scrimshaw is leaving us,' Mrs Merivale condescended, 'on an extended visit to Moreton Bay – to Mrs Lovell, the Commandant's wife.'

Invested by her patroness with grandeur, Miss Scrimshaw should have risen to the occasion, had not all Sydney known (or anyway, its politer circles) that the Commandant had engaged a companion for his wife, exhausted by bearing children in quick succession, and isolated from refined society in a remote and brutal settlement.

In the circumstances, Miss Scrimshaw was not comforted by the probability that this Irishman was unaware.

The latter at least realized something was amiss, and had not enough control over his natural propensity for cruelty to resist ruffling the feathers of the two foolish birds before him. He began to look cunning, and to wet his lips, and to turn to the surveyor only half in confidence.

'I did not mention,' he lowered his eyelids, and clicked his tongue, 'that Mr Isbister arrived but recently from Moreton Bay, after calling in on Mr McGillivray of Murrumbopple, where they told him a tale – not unheard before, worse luck, in the country we live in.'

The ladies sighed, and smoothed themselves, and prepared for endless men's talk.

19

Mr Merivale would have nodded to the coachman to start for home. Instead he smiled, out of politeness, into the sun, which was lowering itself by now in a cloudless winter sky.

'Yes?' he felt bound to encourage, though the colour had gone from his voice.

'It appears,' the emancipist informed them, 'that two shepherds in a remote corner of the run had fallen foul of the natives. Some matter – excuse me, ladies – of women.'

The ladies pricked their ears, but hoped it had gone unnoticed. Weren't their eyes so decently lowered?

Delaney cleared his throat; in other company he would have spat.

'Well,' he said, 'to cut a story short and come to the point however tragical, the two men – honest fellers both of 'em – had just been found, their guts laid open (savin' the ladies presence). Stone cold, they were, an' the leg missin' off of one of 'em – a mere lad from Taunton, Somerset.'

Mrs Merivale might have been impaled; Miss Scrimshaw on the other hand, continued distantly watching a scene, each detail of which filled her with a fascinated horror.

She said finally, 'It is what some – not all of us – have chosen. To live in this country. Suffering is often a matter of choice.'

Her friend Mrs Merivale was rasping with disgust. 'Tell him to drive on!' she asked, or more precisely, ordered her husband. 'Loathsome savages!' she gasped.

As her husband closed the door behind him, Mrs Merivale was fumbling in her reticule for her little silver vinaigrette.

Delaney waved, not exactly laughing at his disappearing audience.

As the vehicle lurched on its way, Mrs Merivale and Miss Scrimshaw seemed united in what could have been contemplation of a common fate; only Mrs Merivale continued to protest by never quite exhausted spasms, 'I don't understand! I don't understand! Not where human nature is concerned. Such a world as this is not fit for a decent person to live in.'

'There, there, Alice! Everything has always been against you. Can't you accept it? Then we shall enjoy the pie waiting for us at home.'

It was a proposition material enough to have appealed to Mrs

Merivale had she not chosen to indulge herself in the luxury of hysteria.

When Mr Merivale, for the second time that afternoon, launched an unexpected remark. 'I wonder,' he said, 'how Mrs Roxburgh would react to suffering if faced with it?'

Mrs Merivale's mouth fell open. 'Mrs Roxburgh?' she almost hiccuped; then was still.

The occupants of the carriage were rolled on into the deepening afternoon, and finally, like minor actors who have spoken a prologue, took themselves off into the wings.

2

On waving good-bye to her departing callers Mrs Roxburgh went below. Though much of what she brushed against in her descent felt corroded, and all that she smelled was acrid and stale, she had grown attached on the short voyage from Hobart Town to the texture of worn, sticky timber and the scents of rope and tar in what they must accept as home during the months to come. Arrived between decks, she was now groping through a musty gloom towards the quarters which Captain Purdew's compliance and her own efforts had made snug and personal. Hands outstretched, she touched the door she knew to be there, and after rallying herself an instant, entered the narrow saloon where her husband had taken refuge even before their guests had moved in the direction of the gangway, his excuse being a hastily contracted sciatica.

Mr Austin Roxburgh was seated with his back to the door, reading the book for which the tedium of a formal visit had soon started him hankering. On top of his other clothes he was wearing a twill overcoat, which the winter air, sharpened by the sound of water lapping against the vessel, made practically obligatory for anyone not exerting himself.

Without looking round, he spoke up on hearing the creaking of the door and the motion of his wife's skirt. 'Well, are they safely – *sped*?' he asked while apparently continuing to read.

'Yes,' she replied, and laughed. 'Oh, yes,' she repeated, more subdued. 'They are gone.'

'And did you extract some last-moment grain of wisdom?'

'They were full of doubts and suspicions, I could tell, but too Christian to come out with them.'

The Roxburghs' whole exchange was familiarly and pleasantly low in key.

Still at his book, Mr Roxburgh laughed through his nose and said, 'I don't believe those two women were in any way satisfied.'

'Mrs Merivale and Miss Scrimshaw would like to be thought ladies.'

Corrected, Mr Roxburgh began again, 'The two ladies would have preferred to find us unhappy, in ourselves and our ventures.'

'I expect, on leaving us, they discovered every reason why we should be feeling desperate,' Mrs Roxburgh answered, 'and will entertain each other this evening going over our wretched prospects. It's their profession, surely, to scent unhappiness in others.'

The voice might have sounded complacent had not its tone also suggested the recital of a set lesson. In any event, Mr Roxburgh must have felt re-assured: he glanced at his wife with an expression verging on gratitude. As the light through the porthole showed it, his face was sallow, fine-featured, a glint in the deep-set eyes implying fever, or fretfulness, or both. If Mr Roxburgh were not recovering from a recent illness, he looked experienced in ill-health, and would always expect to be victimized afresh.

His wife had not thought to return his glance. They appeared a couple whose minds were known to each other and whose conversation would run along well-worn grooves. Instead, Mrs Roxburgh had gone inside the cabin partitioned off from the end of the saloon, and presently reappeared with a shirt she had been mending earlier and put away on the boy's announcing company.

Mr Roxburgh had erased the expression which confessed a weakness, and was making a show of concentrating on his book.

It did not prevent him murmuring rather irritably, 'Do you think there is so much wear, Ellen, in that old shirt, that you should keep on fiddling with it?'

'This is *my* occupation,' Ellen Roxburgh replied, 'and I thought you would have approved of it. To keep you clothed, my dear, during a long voyage.'

Seated the other side of the table, her shawl fastened tighter against the draughts, she resumed her work of accommodating the torn shirt. The attitude she had adopted might have made her seem over-virtuous had she been less amateurish and awkward. At one stage she pricked her finger, and sucked the wound, before approaching her task from another angle. She did not appear to care for the old but still wearable shirt, but would persevere. Perseverance could have been a virtue Mrs Roxburgh had brought with her from another field to press into more finicking service.

23

She was a woman of medium height, not above thirty years of age, which made her considerably younger than her husband. Without the cap she would have been wearing if discovered at home, the head looked rather larger than suited the proportions of her form, but presented without ornament or undue art, in the last of the winter afternoon, it had the unexpectedness of one of the less easily identified semi-precious stones in an unpretentious setting. She wore her hair parted straight, and encouraged it to hang in the flat sleek loops prescribed by the fashion of the day. In contrast to the dark complexion deplored by others, the eyes of a grey probably bred from blue, were candid or unrewarding according to the temper of those who inquired into them. This no doubt was what had aroused suspicion in the ladies whose visit was just past; or it could have been the mouth, on which circumstances had forced a masculine firmness without destroying a thread of feminine regret or its charm of colour.

Mrs Roxburgh laid aside the mending, which either she had finished, or else could no longer endure. Her mouth grew slacker and any hardness of the eyes dissolved perceptibly in thought. A lonely childhood, followed by marriage with a man twenty years her senior, had inclined her mind to reverie. Perhaps her most luxurious indulgence was a self-conducted tour through the backwaters of experience.

Clasping herself still closer in the unusual though practical woollen shawl which had so enchanted Mrs Merivale that same afternoon, Ellen Roxburgh half-smiled to recall the accents of envy.

'How I do admire your pretty shawl! It caught my eye before anything,' Mrs Merivale admitted, and shook the small, perfect ringlets with which the underside of her bonnet was too generously loaded.

The caller was a composite of tremulous feathers, discursive fabrics, and barely controlled greed, her glance travelling from the shoulders of the individual she had condescended to patronize, over the intaglio brooch, the bosom (very discreetly here), eventually arriving at the fringe. Here Mrs Merivale had not been able to refrain from lifting and submitting the goods to close examination, as though on a progress through one of the stores she favoured with her custom.

'Would you care to try it on?' Mrs Roxburgh inquired, already preparing to disvest herself.

'Oh dear, no!' Mrs Merivale recoiled. 'Of course not! You must forgive me.' The shallow eyes flickered in search of someone who might accept blame for a *faux pas.*

Mrs Roxburgh stood arrested, and fell into one of those silences, the gravity or 'mystery' of which, the two ladies afterwards discussed. All the while the tones in the shawl had continued fluctuating, from sombre ash, through the living green which leaves flaunt in a wind, the whole slashed with black as far as the heavy woollen fringe. This too, was black, relieved by recurrent threads of green.

Mrs Roxburgh re-arranged her warm shawl. She sank deeper into it; until forcing herself to break her regrettable silence, she remarked, 'It was hard to decide what to bring – how much for summer, how much for winter – on a voyage to the other hemisphere. My husband was all for restricting us to garments practically ready to be thrown away. But I insisted on bringing my very particular shawl!' She laughed, and stopped.

Was she affected? frivolous? or did they detect an echo in her voice? The two visiting ladies were puzzled to the point of mild hostility; they turned to the woman's husband for confirmation of all that is solid and practical in life.

This suited Mrs Roxburgh, for it had been her intention to draw him in.

'Ellen is notoriously vain,' he sighed, with a weariness or lack of interest which dismissed the whole situation.

In thus condemning his wife Mr Roxburgh might have gone beyond what the visitors' sense of propriety allowed. But Mrs Roxburgh accepted her role as one of the several allotted to her; while the two ladies disguised their views behind a rattling social titter.

'She decided that I was condemning her to rags to mortify her,' Mr Roxburgh continued with a candour which confused, 'when it was her intention,' he added in a burst of irony, 'to make a conquest of my brother on our visit to him in Van Diemen's Land.'

It stimulated interest at least.

'Mrs Roxburgh had not made her brother-in-law's acquaintance,' the brown eagle inquired, 'before?' But so discreet.

Mrs Roxburgh replied, 'Never,' and lapsed again.

She stood looking down, slightly smiling as she played with the fringe of her shawl. The whole scene might have been pre-arranged, superficial though the details were.

It was only in the darkening saloon that the incident of the afternoon assumed greater consequence. While the images recurred and floated and dissolved, her husband's material form remained obstinately upright throughout, like a sense of duty, as he sat and read, or attempted to give her that impression. She was not altogether convinced; when he turned a page he did so absently, fraying an edge with a fingernail, making a dog's-ear of a corner.

On and off, the native flower would blaze and intrude. They had found it the day before on one of their enforced rambles round the water's edge at Sydney Cove, waiting for the breeze which would carry them home.

There were times when Mr Roxburgh held Captain Purdew responsible for the defected wind; at others he all but accused his wife; he had grown so devilishly irritable.

'Yet nothing would satisfy you,' she had to remind him, 'but that we should set out on this voyage across the world.'

'Yes,' he gasped, for the rocky slope robbed him of his breath and made him stumble, 'it was my idea – and a bad one. I'll go as far as to – admit – *that*!'

Each listened to the ferrule of Mr Roxburgh's stick striking the adamant colonial stones, in some case scarring them, in others driving them deeper into barren sand, where the activity of ants illustrated in parallel the obtuseness of so much human endeavour.

Back turned to him as she climbed, Mrs Roxburgh's voice whipped over her shoulder, as did the fringe of her loosely draped, mazy shawl. 'Is it too much for you? There's no need to follow, but I'm determined to see whatever lies beyond this knoll.'

An infernal wind blowing from the wrong quarter caused her voice to flicker like the landscape; the latter in no way appealed to him.

'I am not impotent!' he protested, his cheeks sunken as he worked at sucking on the air through blenching nostrils.

They struggled on, asunder and in silence, until he stood beside her on the rocky headland it had been her intention to conquer.

In their common breathlessness they made a show of peering out at the scene spread before and below them.

'I've not made you ill?' she asked from between her teeth.

He did not answer, but accepted her fingers in his free hand.

'A fine prospect,' he remarked, 'for the future inhabitants of Sydney'; and added, 'How happy I should be to wake, and find ourselves at home at Cheltenham.'

'Oh, my dear!' she exclaimed. 'We are back where we began! When I thought the sight of this blue water would cure you at least temporarily.'

Disappointment made her withdraw her hand, to pick at the twigs of a bush which drought and wind had not prevented from putting out flowers: golden harsh-coated teasels alongside grey, hairy effigies of their former splendour.

In her distraction, Mrs Roxburgh's fingers dwelt indiscriminately on the live and the dead. 'You can't deny that the visit to your brother made you happy.'

'And you scarce at all.'

'My whole concern was not to come between two brothers parted for years, who have a great affection for each other. So I went my own way. I discovered another world. Which will remain with me for life, I expect. Every frond, and shred of bark. My memories are more successful than my sketches. I know your opinion of those, and there I agree with you.'

In her attempt to lighten the situation colour must have flown into her cheeks; she intercepted that expression which suggested he would have drunk up every drop of an elixir he liked to believe might be his salvation.

'Weren't you a little jealous?' he accused.

Her lips swelled with answers, unutterable because immodest. 'Mr Roxburgh,' she managed at last, 'you sometimes ask the unkindest questions.'

There was no trace of archness in her addressing him thus: the austerity of his Christian name, together with the difference in their ages, discouraged her from using it.

'You were, in fact, more than a little jealous,' he persisted in baiting her; 'and your riding off alone amongst tree-ferns and over mountains made it appear more obvious.'

Resisting the moan of protest she could feel rising in her throat, she tore one of the tassel-shaped flowers from a gnarled branch, and directed her attention at it. 'I wonder what they call this extraordinary thing. We must try to find someone who knows.'

For the moment she was only conscious that his eyes continued looking at or into her; the stab of misery she experienced could not have been sharper.

'And he went after you. To bring you back.'

'Your brother Garnet could not have been kinder. Everybody was very kind. It was unfortunate – foolish of me – to lose my way – and let myself be thrown. Poor Merle was on other occasions the gentlest creature.'

'But Garnet found you. And brought you back.'

'Oh dear, yes! Yes!'

She almost threw away the flower she was twirling between her fingers, for it had grown sharp-toothed and vicious.

'Won't you look at me?' he asked.

She did so, with the result that they were forced simultaneously into a bungling attempt to prove their love for each other, their lips as bitter-tasting as the leaves they had torn from exotic trees on arrival in an unknown country, their cheeks freshly contoured to fingers which might have been exploring them for the first time. She prayed it would remain thus; she was afraid of what she might find were she ever to arrive at the depths of his eyes.

When he had mumbled a few last fragmented words, she who usually took the lead when it came to practical moves suggested, 'We should go back, don't you think? Perhaps we shall hear we are to sail. Otherwise I'll begin to suspect that Captain Purdew and Mr Courtney are in league against us.'

'Two such honest men,' he murmured, his conscience still bruised; and followed her.

Conscience for conscience, her own had been stricken to discover she disliked her brother-in-law on sight: his cleft chin, the rather too full, lower lip. In addition to aggressive health and spirits, Mr Garnet Roxburgh paraded the assured insolence of a lapsed gentleman.

'I hope you will be happy at "Dulcet", and consider it your home as long as you are here.' The exertion of opening a jammed window turned admirable sentiments into a command.

As the window shot upward she was again conscious of wrists

which had repelled her as he sat holding the reins on the drive from Hobart Town. But she must not continue in this most unreasonable dislike. Beyond the window an orchard, its green fruit glistening amongst leaves transparent in a western light, showed every sign of expert husbandry. Again she experienced a twinge, from contrasting in her mind this opulent scene with another in which damsons racked by winds from across the moor clustered with an ancient, woody pear tree at the side of a cottage, in rough-hewn, weather-blackened stone. Her hands might still have been red and chapped. She hid them before realizing her foolishness, then resolved that in future her heart would have no room for unreasonable dislike and envy.

Until now, far removed from the fat pastures of Van Diemen's Land, leading her husband over the stony ground of this other, more forbidding landscape, Mrs Roxburgh could only bitterly admit that she had failed in her resolve, and that the moral strength for which she prayed constantly eluded her.

Thus chastened, she continued stubbing her boots against the stones, until able to turn and announce to Mr Roxburgh, 'See, my dear? There she is! It was not so far after all.'

Since a wind from the right quarter proved as elusive as the moral strength for which Mrs Roxburgh prayed, they resumed their life of waiting in the narrow saloon and the improvised cabin at the farther end, and on the evening after the visit of the surveyor and his two ladies, there was only the native flower to trouble the memory, or illuminate human frailty. Mrs Roxburgh was inclined to wonder at herself for keeping the golden teasel, but Spurgeon the lugubrious fellow who acted as their steward had provided an earthenware jar in which she had stubbornly arranged her spoil, and there it stood, as stubbornly, its blunt club throbbing with the last light reflected off the water outside.

When Mr Roxburgh, without interrupting his reading, inquired, 'Did somebody identify your specimen?'

Although unprepared for this sudden interest she was not altogether taken by surprise: she had grown to accept his intrusion on her thoughts, or those of them which lay closest to the surface.

She replied, 'I didn't think to ask,' while examining with displeasure her rather too broad, if not unshapely hands.

'Like all the flowers of this country – or the few we've seen on our walks – it is more strange than beautiful,' Mr Roxburgh pronounced.

'I haven't made up my mind. Memorable, certainly.' She wondered whether her voice sounded as hard and dry as she felt it become in her throat. 'Whether beautiful, or only strange, I doubt I shall ever forget their flowers.'

Yes, her voice sounded ugly, doubtless due to a constriction of the throat, as her locked hands sped their becalmed brig, her thoughts in tow, till she was again seated beside the silver kettle, behind brocade curtains which the servant had drawn, listening for some indication that her husband would join her at the tea-table, or whether she would conduct the silent ritual of taking tea alone.

When Mr Roxburgh spoke again she was not immediately conscious that they were aboard a berthed ship, or that he was reading aloud from the book in his lap.

> '. . . felix, qui potuit rerum cognoscere causas,
> atque metus omnes et inexorabile fatum
> subiecit pedibus strepitumque Acherontis avari . . .

Splendid stuff! Did you hear, Ellen?'

'Yes. I heard. But shall not understand unless you have the goodness to translate. I thought you would have known that.' Now she merely sounded like a peevish woman.

'As you are in almost every respect admirable, one tends to forget that you don't always understand.'

While he gave the lines his renewed consideration, humming to himself from behind his moustache, drumming on the page with his fingertips, she was forced up from her chair to fidget restlessly in the narrow space in which they were confined.

'Perhaps this will satisfy you,' he ventured at last, 'without doing justice to the original verses. "Happy is he," ' he no more than muttered, ' "who has unveiled the cause of things, and who can ignore inexorable Fate and the roar of insatiate Hell." ' Mr Roxburgh coughed for his own efforts on concluding them.

Then he said almost immediately, 'The light which prevails in Virgil makes that black streak seem blacker.' There followed a sweeping of the page as though to rid it of crumbs. 'I don't believe he feared death.' Again a scratching or a sweeping. 'For that

30

matter – although I've been threatened several times – and am prepared to be gathered in by – our Maker – death has always appeared to me something of a literary conceit.' His laughter came out as a high neighing, so that her heart, turning to water, lapped against the timbers of the stays in which she was boarded up.

'I should modify that, I suppose,' Mr Roxburgh conceded, 'by adding: in connection with myself.' Once more the desperate neighing of some gaunt-ribbed gelding.

She had halted close behind his chair, and leant, and put her arms around him, as though attempting to cleave to him as she had sworn. 'It's my loss that I can't share your pleasures in the way you would wish.' Her hot mouth drove her regret into the crown of his head. 'It was too late when I started to learn. I shall only ever know what my instinct tells me.'

'I would not have it otherwise.'

She suffered him to twist the rings on her fingers.

'There is almost nothing,' she sighed, 'which cannot be changed for the better.'

But in her own case, a kind of sensual apathy intervened as often as not between the intention and the act. Or, in the beginning, life to be lived.

He had indeed lent her books, first of all the little one he called his 'crib' to the *Bucolics* when she brought the tray to the room. She had scarce read it, for it made her nervous to have a gentleman's book in her keeping, and herself with little enough of education. Her hands were rough besides, from working in the fields, and milking when the wind blew from the north, or driving the cart to market at Penzance.

'I'll read 'n,' she promised rashly, 'but not while there's daylight, and the hay not in.'

She went away, proud if fearful of the book he had lent her.

Mr Roxburgh must have felt incommoded by her leaning on him; he started fretting, and shrugging her off. 'Why then, Ellen, don't they weigh anchor?' he asked as though he had never wondered at it before this evening.

'Because the wind is not from the right quarter,' she repeated with an equanimity she had cultivated, while settling the collar of the overcoat which her embrace had disarranged.

The flower glowing in its chipped jar had been practically extinguished by the close of day; what sounded like a rat scampered somewhere through the dusk, back to business; water slithering on the vessel's hull might have created an illusion of motion for any two souls less experienced in listening for it. The Roxburghs' hearing was so finely tuned they all but jumped at sound of a pair of boots thudding down the companion-ladder, and when a hand rattled the loose door-knob, and a beard blundered through the slit of a doorway, and the face of Mr Courtney the mate became distinguishable, they were no less embarrassed for their shadowy thoughts.

Mr Courtney was so solidly built, anything overwrought or inessential could only expect to be skittled. It was unlikely that the mate's own mind would ever wander out of bounds, except perhaps during sleep, heaving in those more incalculable waters like one of the whales it delighted him to watch.

Mr Courtney spouted rather than spoke, 'Captain sends his compliments, but was called away, and you mustn't wait dinner for him.' As one accustomed to give orders rather than deliver speeches, the mate drew breath. 'Other news – wind is veering, and unless we're out of luck we'll sail at dawn.'

Cap in hand, Mr Courtney continued standing. The upper, whiter part of his forehead glimmered in the dusk above a leather mask fringed with whiskers, the effect of which might have made him look sinister had it not been for the ingenuous eyes. On discovering that Mr Courtney was the least sinister of men, Mrs Roxburgh had felt free during daylit moments to examine the texture of his weathered skin, for her own secret pleasure and his hardly concealed discomfiture. In spite of the broad wedding band the mate was not at ease with ladies.

But rank compelled him to make the occasional effort. 'Has the feller forgot to bring candles?' His Adam's apple jerked it out painfully.

'On the contrary,' Mrs Roxburgh answered, brighter than before, 'we've had them all this while, but preferred to enjoy the evening light and our conversation.' She patted her husband's arm, asking him to support her, not so much in a falsehood as out of social expediency.

'Nothing could have lit our gloom better than the news you've brought us,' the gentleman contributed.

Mr Courtney grunted and laughed together. 'Hasn't Sydney found favour with you?'

'I can neither admire nor dislike what irritation prevents me seeing.'

Her husband's gravity so abashed the mate, Mrs Roxburgh lit the pair of yellow candles to alleviate a situation.

His skin ablaze, Mr Courtney announced, 'I'll leave you, then. There's things to attend to. And the feller'll be fetching down your dinner in a jiffy.' It implied that himself had found good reason why he should not sit down with the gentry.

The instant after, he was gone; his great boots could be heard maltreating the timbers.

Mrs Roxburgh's spirits soared. She could have sung, and literally, but her music-making had never been admired. Instead her face reflected the joy she hoped to find in her husband, and indeed, the weight had been lifted even from Austin Roxburgh.

So much so, he was moved closer to his wife, laughing without constraint, and pinched her on the chin. She might have been a child, not theirs, certainly (he would have been more guarded in the presence of their own) but a sympathetic substitute who would not grow up to accuse him, however mutely, of the folly of bringing her into the world.

'I can't express my feelings adequately,' Mr Roxburgh blurted.

That was obvious enough as he teetered with a joy and relief to which he was unaccustomed, the long, fastidious hands inspired to gestures equally foreign to them. The husband had never danced with his wife, yet at the moment, she sensed, they almost might have begun. Given more suitable conditions, she would have guided him through a few judicious steps guaranteed not to unbalance his importance or his dignity. Nobody must see him without those.

Instead Mrs Roxburgh made the effort to control her own obstreperous exhilaration. 'Quietly! Quietly, though!' she advised. 'You might bring on one of your attacks.'

'My attacks!' he snorted.

At his moments of extravagance he wanted no one to present him with the bill; he was wealthy enough to ignore reason when it suited him.

'When you are so much improved,' she remarked perhaps imprudently.

Austin Roxburgh was so far provoked that he pouted. To be coddled was intolerable; on the other hand, to be ignored might have struck him as worse.

'Do you know where your drops are?' she persisted in her role of solicitous wife.

'Of course,' he snapped, yet was in sufficient doubt to start working a couple of fingers around inside a waistcoat pocket.

Mrs Roxburgh touched him to dispel an anxiety she could see rising. Her own eyes were filling and frowning at the same time; she too may have felt in need of some drug, tenderness rather than digitalis. But whatever the illness from which either suffered, the interior of the wooden ship shimmered an instant with stimulated hopes and tranquillized fears.

When footsteps were again heard, of a flatter, more slithery persuasion than before. The 'fellow' who waited on them had taken advantage of the captain's absence to ease a bunion by leaving off his boots. The horny feet slapping the boards gave out a sound not unlike that of a razor in conjunction with the strop.

Spurgeon the steward (cook too, Mrs Roxburgh fancied) was a somehow disappointed character whose reactions were on the mournful side. His attempts at cleanliness failed to deceive, yet in spite of it all, they had grown attached to him, and it amused Mr Roxburgh, if not Spurgeon, to tease the fellow out of himself.

'Well, Spurgeon, we're about to embark on the next stage of our Odyssey,' the gentleman launched his evening joke. 'When we reach the island I trust you'll find your Penelope has waited for you.'

Spurgeon had long since given up expecting sense from any member of the educated classes, so did not bother to rack his brains, but grumbled in undertone to satisfy the superiors he was unable to avoid. The cloth he flung billowed an instant from his fingertips before settling miraculously on the table, its chart spread for further inspection. Many an imaginary voyage had Mrs Roxburgh traced round the continents and archipelagos of the saloon table-cloth.

Sight of the familiar, grubby cloth inspired her to fresh attempts at winning their steward's approval. 'Look, Spurgeon, my flower is still alive'; she indicated the teasel in its jar as though it were the symbol of some conspiracy between them.

'I wouldn' know that,' he replied without deigning to look. 'There's a lot in this part of the world that looks alive when it's dead, and vicey versy.'

He continued absorbed by a problem of cutlery until somebody stuck his head through the doorway.

'Hey, Mr Spurgeon,' a boy called in what he might have hoped a voice the passengers would not hear, 'the chook's all but fell apart.'

Spurgeon left to perform more esoteric duties with a stateliness sometimes achieved by thin people of painful bones.

By the time Mrs Roxburgh had washed her hands and smoothed her hair, and added a pair of ear-rings to match the intaglio brooch, the steward re-appeared with a tureen.

'The captain's compliments,' he said, 'there'll be sweetbreads atop of this, and a fowl. Better make the most of 'em, because the salt tack is all you can expect from now on.'

As the passengers sat restraining with their spoons the circles of grease which eddied on the surface of the soup, Mr Roxburgh noticed his wife's ear-rings. 'I believe you would dress yourself up, Ellen, for a breakfast of yams and opossum with savages in the bush.'

'I would dress myself up for my husband,' she replied, 'if he was there.'

Downcast eyes did not prevent a certain fierceness of expression, and it pleased him to think he had dominion over a divinity, even one whose beauty was wrapped in nothing more mystical than a cloud rising out of a dish of greasy soup.

As the evening progressed the sweetbreads proved to have disintegrated; the fowl had not done likewise because held together by antipodean muscle; and excessive sugar in the bread pudding soothed the palate at least, after the bitter ale in which the diners had drowned the worst of their revulsion.

Too familiar to each other, they sat and crumbled untidy fragments of conversation.

'The brown woman – that eagle – or *vulture*, would peck out a man's liver for tuppence.'

'You are unkind to ladies on principle, but depend on them more than most men.'

'Do you think there are rats on board? I could swear I felt one run across me in my sleep.'

'In your sleep! Since we left home, I've experienced worse awake. A dream rat is nothing, Mr Roxburgh!'

'A sea voyage is recuperative.'

'Did you like the man? I liked the man better than the women.'

'He was somebody to whom I had nothing to say.'

''T isn't always necessary. There are simple, honest men who put us to shame. We ought to be silent with those.'

Silence fell on the remains of the valedictory meal.

'That is the kind of man your Mr Merivale is,' she broke in with uncharacteristic harshness. 'He has got wisdom in a hard country. He was always, I think, a countryman at heart, and most country folk are not for sellin' what they know, or else,' she raised her chin to recover her balance and her husband's good opinion, 'they dun't want to be thought soft.'

But Mr Roxburgh had neither heard nor seen, it appeared, as he rolled little pellets of grey bread. 'Merivale was Garnet's friend. They racketed over the county on horses. It's a wonder they didn't break their necks.'

In spite of the pellets he continued rolling Mr Roxburgh was far removed from his physical activity.

'Garnet has thickened. It's surprising he didn't re-marry. They say he's attractive to women, and that there are several who would accept an offer.'

'There are those who have his interests at heart. So I gathered.'

'And were you surprised?'

'Who am I to pass judgement on a man I only slightly know?'

'But surely you formed an opinion?'

'My opinion is that your brother is noticeably attached to his brother.'

'We were always fond of each other. That is natural – something, Ellen, I should have thought you might accept.'

'Oh, but I do! Indeed I do!'

He heard the exasperated swish of petticoat as she came round the table and knelt beside him. In her agitation Mrs Roxburgh had dragged the cloth askew, threatening the remnants of their bread pudding.

'I can accept anything,' she said, 'for the sake of peace – in this frightening world'; and held her head for him to stroke.

Upon realizing, he obliged.

'Listen to the silence!' Ellen Roxburgh shivered. 'To the water!'

From the moored vessel, each sounded immeasurable.

'I'll listen gladly,' he told her, 'when I hear it flowing against our sides.'

'Flowing and flowing. For months and months.'

Although their ship remained stationary, the cosmos revolved about them as he caressed her head with the short circular motions he had cultivated as a sickly boy, when a cat he owned would spring and curl up on his lap. It sometimes occurred to him on remembering Tabby that he had not been on better terms with any living being.

Possibly due to excitement over their promised departure, or the recurring taste of bread pudding, Mrs Roxburgh felt slightly sick.

3

Falling asleep she had resolved to wake at dawn, to watch their passage through Sydney Heads, and perhaps contribute something of her own strength of will to their setting out. But when she awoke the light had matured, and was flowing dappled over the timbers, like water itself. She lay a few moments to watch the light and allow wakefulness to seep back into filleted limbs and a stuffy mind. Then she realized the air too, was flowing, that the vessel was plunging and groaning, in different directions it seemed at first, and that her slippers had slithered from the place where she had stood them in a neat pair the night before.

Bristol Maid was already at sea.

So Mrs Roxburgh screwed up her eyes, and bit her lips, though not to the extent of experiencing pain. She put out her arms to embrace the cold future, for no voyage fails to provoke a sensual shudder in the beginning. Then she clambered carefully down. It had angered her husband to find the carpenter had fitted their cabin with bunks one above the other instead of side by side. But Mrs Roxburgh pointed out that such an arrangement would have left no room, and calmed him by offering to take the upper berth. It was out of the question that he, in his precarious state of health, should scramble up and down during a voyage of months, and she had soon grown adept at reaching and leaving her shelf without disturbing him in any way.

Now, while unbuttoning and divesting in the chill morning, she observed her husband. Mr Roxburgh lay stretched asleep. Always when laid to rest behind his features, they appeared the finer for it, and this, together with an exaggerated pallor on the morning of *Bristol Maid*'s departure, might have given her cause for alarm had the gravity of her own thoughts not been relieved by the expression on his face. Mr Roxburgh's chin had receded under the influence of sleep. He was blowing through his mouth with

38

an intensity verging on desperation, sucking in, from beneath a jutting lip, the draughts of air vouchsafed him. It was comical as well as touching. She might have laughed had she not toppled and bruised her thigh against one of the many corners with which their small cabin was furnished.

When she had regained her balance and taken off her nightgown, her skin appeared already to have darkened in warning of the bruise to come. It made her body look too white, too full, too softly defenceless, though in normal circumstances her figure would not have been considered noticeably ample.

She finished dressing at a speed which did not dispel a mood of faint melancholy nourished by tenderness and resignation. At such moments she was consoled to think she understood their marriage.

In the same state of conviction or delusion she climbed the companion-ladder. *Bristol Maid* was labouring by now. What had seemed a morning of limpid light in the cabin below was in fact tatters of increasing grey. The wind blowing from the south had begun fetching up fog as well; great clouts of dirty fog caught in the rigging before tearing free. The sea rolled, still revealing glints of a glaucous underbelly, but its surfaces were grey where not churned into a lather of white. She was reminded of a pail she had withdrawn too quickly from a cow's threatening heels and how the ordinarily mild milk had run as hot as the despair she felt for her clumsiness. So a shrieking of gulls in the present came closer to sounding human. Mrs Roxburgh kept up her spirits by watching the more unearthly rise and fall of their immaculate wings.

At the same time she was carried staggering across the deck, clinging, with an alarm she could not quite laugh off, to any object which offered itself. Whatever she touched, ratline or bulwark, or her own person, was drenched with salt moisture. She had battened down her bonnet with a scarf, and swathed her shawl closer to her form, and would advance of her own volition whenever it became possible, arms rigid against her sides, hands stiff as butterpats, till reaching the mainmast and comparative security.

Here she was sighted by Captain Purdew, who immediately left a group composed of Mr Pilcher the second mate, a couple of seamen, and one she presumed was the boatswain from the authority he exercised and the quantities of hair which overgrew him. Even the captain, for all his professional experience, seemed to make only human headway against the careening deck, thrusting himself into the wind, hands clutching fortuitously at holds of rope.

He reached a point where she caught sight of his teeth; then his voice arrived, but coldly. 'Are you afraid,' he called, 'Mrs Roxburgh?'

'No,' she lied, 'why should I be?' and laughed.

'Of getting wet,' it billowed back.

'No, no, no!' Against the wind, it sounded a pitiful chatter.

The captain had taken his passenger by an elbow, both to steady her, and to estimate the damage to her clothes. 'You should wait for fair weather, you know.'

'I am disappointed,' she screamed, 'not to have watched the last of the Heads.'

But her words were lost in the mewing of the gulls, although she had delivered her reply with a raucousness she had judged would carry.

'Your husband will be anxious.'

Perhaps she, too, failed to hear. Their difficulty in communicating caused them to smile at each other with exaggerated candour. Her face, she felt, must be the thinner for screaming, while his had grown more leathery from being subjected to the salt spray. Captain Purdew might have appeared a bleak man had it not been for the spirit of kindness his whiskers allowed to escape.

All around them was the sound of canvas creaking and straining. The sails which had sunk her in despair at Sydney for continuing so long furled and passive were almost frightening now that their bellies were filled and the daemon of energy possessed them. Human life was made to appear an incidental hazard, especially since the harsh-voiced gulls, at first seemingly attuned to her own earthly experience, had been dismissed by herself and the motion of their wings to another, more sublime level.

Mrs Roxburgh was surprised when Captain Purdew brought his face so close to hers that she felt for an instant a distinct tingling of beard. 'Were you born at sea, perhaps?'

'No,' she shouted manfully. 'On a moor.'

'More what?'

Had it not been for the mast and the captain's ribs she would have been swept by the rolling in the direction of her ineffectual voice.

'A Cornish heath,' she tried afresh. 'Within reach of the land's end.'

Captain Purdew, had he been less kindly, might have felt irritated by what seemed like his female passenger's desire to take part in an adventure. His own wife, during the several voyages they shared after marriage, had remained below, embroidering tea-cosies and hand-towels to give at Christmas. When she ventured above, she no more than crossed the deck to interfere in the galley. Possibly Mrs Roxburgh was only trying to test her courage in a man's world, though the captain suspected there was more to it than that. He would not have known how to express it, but in his still centre, round which many more considerable storms at sea had revolved, he sensed that his passenger had an instinct for mysteries which did not concern her.

So they continued smiling at each other, or she looked about her with an unnatural eagerness which would justify her being there. She looked at the land, still faintly visible to larboard, its grey mass founded in the predominating sea. She tried to visualize the interior, to which her presence might have lent reality, but which in her continued absence must remain an imagined country, a tangle of indeterminate scrub burning with the tongues of golden teasel.

Presently she realized Captain Purdew had begun to guide her by a forearm, and in the light refracted by a blow she received at the same moment from a sheet of canvas, she saw the image of her father, another grey, thickset man picking his way amongst rocks and hussocks at dusk to bring her back into the house, where, he said, she was needed by her mother.

It was herself increasingly who guided Pa as Pa took increasingly to spirits; his favourite, rum, announced itself without any telling.

She sometimes wondered whether she had loved Mamma and Pa. If she had in fact, memory had transformed love into pity. But yes, she must have loved them.

After her marriage, her mother-in-law had advised her to keep a journal: *it will teach you to express yourself, a journal forms character besides by developing the habit of self-examination.* (Old Mrs Roxburgh was too polite ever to refer directly to shortcomings in those whose welfare she had at heart.) Ellen Roxburgh started a journal, but had not kept it day by day, or not above the first three weeks. The journal might have decided whether she had loved Mamma and Pa, had they not been gone before she married. Mamma went first. It was Pa's death which decided her to accept what some considered Austin Roxburgh's 'extraordinarily injudicious' proposal.

Alone on a derelict farm on the edge of a moor, she would have had to leave in any case, but where to go? Into service? Aunt Triphena would not have had her on account of Will and *incestuous marriages between cousins*, as Hepzie pointed out in a book. There was, moreover, a smell of poverty at Gluyas's which appealed to Aunt Tite's nostrils as little as the midden in the yard. It pained Ellen, who loved their farm after a fashion; it was all she knew. (Then she must surely have loved her parents who, with herself, were inseparable from it, the three of them living at such close quarters you could hear one another's coughs, groans, dreams almost, anywhere inside the echoing house.)

Aunt Tite Tregaskis, married to substance and early widowed, mindful of herself and money (and of course her darling Will, not so much Hepzie because she was a girl) had despised her sister-in-law for years. The brother who shamed her, Triphena did not even despise. Dick the Hopeless and Clara the Helpless. (And Ellen – *whatever will become of Her?*) In time Triphena found she could enjoy the luxury of pitying her sister-in-law from another county, another country you might say (Kent, was it?) who followed Lady Ottering when it took her ladyship's fancy to leave London for Glidgwith. Clara Hubbard was lady's-maid, delicate-looking, of pale complexion, hands fine enough to fit into her ladyship's gloves after the powder had been blown in. Clara Hubbard met her husband by accident while visiting a common acquaintance at Penzance.

After she began taking Mamma's side, Aunt Tite used to say it was the worst accident ever befell anyone: that Miss Hubbard should have been sipping her madeira when Dick Gluyas looked in with an eye to a free glass, and that if Clara was laid in an early grave it would be on account of the pair of 'roughskins' she was saddled with.

Aunt Tite was that unjust. Ellen knew that her hands were chapped, but she wasn't *rough*. Nobody was gentler with Mamma in what became her last illness. She would carry her down the narrow stair, and sit her by the window to take the sun and enjoy the fuchsias. As for chapped hands and red cheeks, Ellen tried rubbing in milk as soon as she learned she ought to be ashamed. She smeared them with the pulp from cucumbers according to the old receipt Hepzie found in *The Lady's Most Precious Possessions*. Ellen's cheeks stayed red until they toned down, seemingly of their own moving, to look by the best light what might have been considered a golden brown. (Not until herself became a lady was she properly blanched, by sitting in a drawing-room, and driving out in a closed carriage, and keeping such late hours the fits of yawning forced the blood out of her cheeks.)

Ellen Gluyas was a hoyden by some standards. Pa would have liked a boy, an industrious one, to help about the farm and make amends for his own poor husbandry. What he got was a strong girl he did not properly appreciate, who did such jobs as she was asked to perform, and drove him home from Penzance when drunk on market day.

Sober, he was jovial enough, and she could forgive his being an idle muddler. But drunk, he became passionately abusive and unjust. Once he knocked her down in the slush as punishment for a gate himself had left open. While still a boy he jammed a thumb in a cheese-press, and instead of a nail, had a brown horn-thing growing there. It frightened her to catch sight of it.

Captain Purdew was still shouting, '. . . advise you . . . below,' as he stooped to initiate her descent by the companion-ladder, '. . . Mr Roxburgh waiting on his breakfast . . . steward bringing . . . appetite . . .'

Lowering her head she mastered a sudden distaste for the last of the flung spray. Or was it the captain's damping words? In any event, Mrs Roxburgh returned by stages to the close, and by now sickening, constriction of the cabin, where she found her husband groping for his boots and complaining a great deal.

'We got what we wanted at least. From the word go, we are at sea!' Nor could he find his shoe-horn.

When finally he straightened up, Mr Roxburgh exclaimed, 'Do you know what a sight you are? You are soaked!'

'Yes.' The crude little glass nailed to the wall for their convenience confirmed it. 'Not soaked, that is. But a sight.'

'You'll do well to change at once, and not run the risk of being laid low with rheumatic fever for the rest of the voyage.'

Mr Roxburgh spoke in the voice he used when expressing fears for himself. She recognized it at once, and its tone brought her lower still.

'I intend to change,' she assured him without enthusiasm.

But she continued standing, waiting for her husband to finish dressing and remove himself to the saloon.

Then she tore off her scarf and bonnet, which were not so much wet as limp with moisture. So with all her outer garments. Her habitually well-kempt hair, dulled by salt, had strayed across her cheeks in tails. Her skin, mottled by the imperfect glass and watery stare of dazed eyes, brought to mind some anonymous creature stranded at a street corner in a fog of gin and indecision.

But Ellen Roxburgh did not remain for long oppressed: the canvas crowded back around her, together with the sting of spray, both on the deck of *Bristol Maid*, and farther off, along the black Cornish coast.

On reaching the age of discontent it seemed to her as though her whole life would be led on a stony hillside, amongst the ramshackledom of buildings which gather at the rear of farmhouses, along with midden and cow-byre. Poor as it was, moorland to the north where sheep could find a meagre picking, and a southerly patchwork of cultivable fields as compensation, she admitted to herself on days of minimum discouragement that she loved the place which had only ever, to her knowledge, been referred to as Gluyas's. She would not have exchanged the furze thickets where a body might curl up on summer days and sheep take shelter in a squall, or the rocks with their rosettes of faded lichen, or cliffs dropping sheer towards the mouths of booming caverns, for any of the fat land to the south, where her Tregaskis cousins lived, and which made Aunt Triphena proud.

Some professed to have heard mermaids singing on the coast above Gluyas's. Pa told tales of tokens and witches, which he half-believed, and of the accommodating white witch at Plymouth. If Ellen Gluyas wholly believed, it was because she led such a solitary life, apart from visits to the cousins, flagging conversation with an ailing and disappointed mother, and the company of a father not always in possession of himself. She was drawn to nature as she would not have been in different circumstances; she depended on it for sustenance, and legend for hope. (It could not be said that she was initiated into religion till her mother-in-law took her in hand, and then her acceptance was only formal, though old Mrs Roxburgh herself was intimate with God.)

It was Ellen Gluyas's hope that she might eventually be sent a god. Out of Ireland, according to legend. Promised in marriage to a king, she took her escort as a lover, and the two died of love. Pa confirmed that they had sailéd into Tintagel. She had never been as far as Tintagel, but hoped one day to see it. Her mind's eye watched the ship's prow entering the narrow cove, in a moment of evening sunlight, through a fuzz of hectic summer green.

She grew languid thinking of it, but would not have mentioned anything so fanciful, not even to Hepzie Tregaskis, her cousin and friend.

Instead she told, with the extra care a lady's-maid cultivates, 'Mamma is thinking of taking in a summer lodger. Don't tell Aunt Tite. She'll blame it on us.'

That Hepzie told her mother was not surprising (she so seldom had anything worth the telling) and her mother did disapprove, because Aunt Triphena disapproved on principle.

'Poor Clara! I never thot to see lodgers under any Gluyas roof – like we'm tinners or clayworkers.' Aunt Tite had forgot that their father had been a travelling hawker.

It was one of Mamma's bad days. 'No ordinary lodger,' she gasped. 'Acquainted with her ladyship. A gentleman of independent means, but poor health.' Mamma had to wipe her eyes. 'A change of air was recommended, and simple, nourishing, farm cooking.'

Aunt Tite laughed. 'I hope tha'll knaw, Clara, to take a fair share of the gentleman's independent means. For sure my brother wun't knaw.'

45

Whenever Mamma met with unkindness she did not exactly cry, she trickled.

Aunt Tite would not relent. 'And who'll tend to the gentleman's needs?'

'I'm still on my feet, Triphena. And Ellen is a strong girl, and willing.'

Aunt Tite smiled her disbelief in a plan she had not conceived herself.

'The money will help us out,' Mamma dared suggest. 'And it will give the girl an interest to have someone else about the place. A gentleman of scholarly tastes, so her ladyship writes. She sent the letter over by the groom.'

Aunt Tite composed her mouth, re-tied her bonnet ribbons, disentangled the three gold chains she wore as a sign of importance and wealth, and drove off in the donkey jingle.

Ellen grew that apprehensive she was all thumbs and blushes in advance. She broke the big serving-dish and had to take it for riveting. She fetched it back only the morning of the day Mr Austin Roxburgh arrived. His luggage impressed those who saw it. Although stained and worn by travel, it still had the smell of leather about it. She stood it in his room, and went from there as quick as she could, leaving him staring out of the window at something he had not bargained for, which might have roused distaste in him. Whatever it was, he looked dejected, as well as fatigued by the journey down.

Mamma too, was nervous, in spite of her experience of gentle-folk. She could not remember whether she had put the towel and soap. Between them they made a rabbit pie, to follow a soup with carrot in it, and, for added nourishment, some scraps of bread.

Ellen might have continued apprehensive had the lodger not been hesitant, if it wasn't downright timid. His conduct lent her courage; until the books stacked in the parlour given over to him robbed her of her new-found confidence. It returned at sight of the medicine bottles arranged on the sill of the bedroom which had previously been hers. The names of the drugs and instructions for use inscribed on the labels filled her with pity once she had overcome her awe.

Mr Roxburgh hesitated, but finally asked, 'Are there any interesting walks, Miss Gluyas, in the neighbourhood?' (No one had ever called her 'Miss Gluyas'.) 'I've resolved to take up walking – for my health.'

'There's walking in all directions.' (Nobody had ever asked her advice.) 'There's the sea to the north – it's wilder op there. And the church. To the south there's a whole lot of pretty lanes. And chapel. You could walk to St Ives – or Penzance – if you're strong enough,' she thought to add.

But Mr Roxburgh no longer appeared interested, as though he had done his duty by the landlady's daughter.

Then he became dependent on her, to remind him of time (his medicines), to warn him of changes in the weather, or to take a letter on market days when she drove to Penzance.

'My mother tends to worry,' he told her; and on another occasion, 'She is fretting over my brother, who left, only recently, for Van Diemen's Land.'

'Aw?' she replied with simulated interest.

She was unacquainted with Van Diemen's Land. She had heard tell of Ireland, America, and France, but had no unwavering conviction that anything existed beyond Land's End, and in the other direction, what was referred to as Across the River.

The void suddenly appalled her, and she repeated with spontaneous fervour the prayers Mamma and Mr Poynter had taught her it was her duty to recite after undressing.

That night she did not dream, and for some reason, awoke with enthusiasm. As it happened, it was the day on which he lent her his 'little crib of the *Bucolics*'. She looked at the cover of his book as though reading were her dearest occupation. 'But not while there's daylight,' she warned.

She was wearing a coarse, country hat, the brim of which rose and fell, allowing him glimpses of a burnt face engrossed in country matters.

She told him, 'There's two lads should come for hay-making, but can never be trusted to.'

'May I help?'

'Well,' she answered, 'I *suppawse* tha could,' and at once blushed for her thoughtlessness.

Again she was embarrassed when he came upon her pulling the milk out of Cherry.

'Is this what you do?'

'Some of it.' She dragged so hard the cow kicked and grazed the pail.

They were for ever encountering each other at the least desirable moments.

On one occasion she had to halt him and lead him back across the yard. 'Not that way,' she advised, her instincts persuading her that Mr Austin Roxburgh needed her protection.

But he looked back, and noticed the calf pinned to the ground, its throat tautened to receive the knife.

'They're killing the calf!'

'Yes,' she admitted. (Will had come over to help Pa perform the operation.) 'You dun't have to watch, Mr Roxburgh.'

Without thinking, she touched his hand, unladylike, to lead him back into the enclosed existence others had ordained and maintained for him, in which death, she only latterly discovered, was a 'literary conceit'.

Soon after his arrival her own reasoning told her that books held more for Austin Roxburgh than the life around him.

He read aloud to her what he said was the *Fourth Eclogue*. 'A pity you're not able to appreciate the original, but you'll enjoy, to some extent, the crib I've lent you.'

It seemed that poetry was all, and the 'natural beauty of a country life'.

'And labour,' he remembered to add. 'Over and above practical necessity, labour, you might say, has its sacramental function.'

Yet he retired gladly to nurse his blisters after a morning with the rake, and sniffed and frowned to find pig-dung stuck to the heel of his boot.

When Will came over, as for the slaughter of the calf, he would stay on and have a bite of something with them in the evening. It was a custom which did not meet with his mother's approval. She was for ever searching her son's face for bad news, and her niece's for worse. As children they enjoyed a rough-and-tumble, with Hepzie joining in, till Aunt Tite found they had outgrown childish games. They exchanged kisses only in the presence of relatives at Christmas and New Year; nobody could have objected to that. Birthdays, marking the advance towards maturity, were more questionable. On her fifteenth birthday Will had been unable to disguise the pleasure her company gave him; he fumbled at her outside the dairy. Whether she had enjoyed it, Ellen was afraid to consider, for Aunt Triphena's becoming a too sudden witness.

'I'll get vex with you, Will, if you act disrespectful to Ellen. She's as close as your own sister, remember.'

Will grew moody, took to kicking at the flagstones, and would no longer look her way. Nor kiss at Christmas. Until, on an unofficial occasion, he gave her a cuddle which flooded her with a delight that surprised her.

It was not repeated. With the advent of Mr Roxburgh she acquired responsibilities. She must look serious and neat. Her head was full of dainty puddings.

Will inquired on the day they killed the calf, 'What's th' old codger op to – on 'is own – i' the parlour?' And chewed off a crust in such a fashion that his naturally handsome face looked ugly.

'He idn' old,' Ellen Gluyas reminded her cousin. 'An's a scholar an' a gentleman.' She was so enraged.

Pa laughed, and winked at Will. 'An' 'as got the girl stickin' 'er nawse where't never was before – in books!'

Ellen went to fetch Mr Roxburgh's tray from the parlour.

He seemed to be waiting for her; he looked anxious, and was walking up and down. 'Ellen,' he said (he had never called her 'Ellen' before) 'I've mislaid the pills which normally stand on the bedside commode.'

'Aw,' she answered, flushing, 'they was there this mornin', Mr Roxburgh.'

He looked at her so quick and startled he might have forgot the pills. 'They *were*, were they?' He continued gravely looking at her.

Did he think she had taken something she valued so little? except that he set store by them.

In the bedroom she moved the heavy marble-topped commode, and found the bottle which had fallen down against the wainscot.

'There!' she said. 'I knawed they couldn' uv gone far.'

His gratitude forgave her any possible lapse.

When she took the tray out to the kitchen Pa and Will were looking at their plates, the two of them moody by now it seemed.

The guest outstayed his welcome. The hay was made and stacked. The leaves began to turn, as a warning against early cold.

Mamma always grew tearful at the approach of winter. 'And to clean an extra grate! And fetch in wood!'

But Mr Roxburgh's cheeks became pink-tinged. He was taking longer walks, in a tweed cap, and a comforter which his mother, he said, had knitted for him. He had even walked as far as St Ives, but hired a fly to bring him back.

On an occasion when the days were drawing in, the girl remarked, 'By now you must have seen everything,' and realized that she dreaded the reply.

'Yes,' he confirmed, 'I have, but would like to be better acquainted with what I know superficially.'

It made her sorry for him: that his life should be so empty, and at the same time, complicated.

He was setting out on one of his walks. Without intending to encumber him, and in no sense prepared (she was wearing her apron, not even a cap, let alone a bonnet) she found herself bearing him company. The going was rough, for they were headed into the black north, the bushes catching at their clothes with twigs on which sheep had left their wool.

'There's a storm coming our way out of Wales.' It was not a rare enough event for her voice to lose its equanimity.

After drawing the comforter tighter at his throat, it occurred to Mr Roxburgh, 'Do you think you're suitably dressed – that is to say, warmly enough?' His ordinarily mild eyes looked almost fierce in consideration of her welfare, or was it, again, only his own?

'Aw, yes!' She laughed, her arms hugging each other against the apron. 'We're used to our own weather.'

They crossed the road and stumbled on, into the gale, when it had not been her intention to accompany him farther than a stone's throw from the yard.

As they were walking recklessly, so they had begun reckless talk.

'This is nothing,' Mr Roxburgh shouted, 'to anyone who has crossed over by the Swiss passes into Italy – or even the English Channel into France.'

'I was never in Italy'; she would not bother to confess that she had not crossed the English Channel. 'I was never farther than Land's End. And Plymouth to the other side.' She hesitated. 'It is my ambition to see Tintagel.'

'What an unambitious ambition! Tintagel is practically on your doorstep.'

'I cannot explain, Mr Roxburgh. Some of us are born unambitious, I suppawse'; when their conversation inspired her to soar amongst the black clouds swollen to bursting above them.

They walked on, heads lowered against the wind, the rooted furze streaming towards them.

Mr Roxburgh remarked that they were behaving most imprudently, but in the circumstances, could not disguise a certain tone of self-approval.

'Yes,' she agreed, 'and will come out of it with nothing better than a soaking.'

Her improvidence did not prevent her feeling much older, wiser, than this slanted stick of a gentleman. If the storm did burst upon them, she was strong and jubilant enough to steady the reeling earth, while he, poor man, would most probably break, scattering a dust of dictionary words and useless knowledge

It was the storm which broke, at that very moment. As the rain lashed out, they gulped down draughts of cold wet air.

Mr Roxburgh stumbled. 'How very foolishly,' he protested, 'a rational human being can behave!' His skin, she thought, had turned from pink to mauve; his features had grown pinched and transparent.

'Are you ill?' she called. 'Mr Roxburgh?'

Though he did not answer, she felt at liberty to ease her shoulder under his, the better to support and lead him.

'A little,' she thought she heard. 'I have these turns, but they pass.'

Providentially, her strength seemed to increase and cope with a condition akin to that of drunken staggers, as she brought him round on a curve, the wind now driving at their backs, sending her hair ahead of them, together with the tails of Mr Roxburgh's comforter.

On the lee side of a collapsed wall, originally built of the flat stones disgorged by a field, she settled her charge, and gave him the additional protection of her own body. She would have wondered at herself if, from being a man, her companion had not become a mission. His hands felt dead inside the knitted gloves. The cap had slipped askew over one fragile temple, carrying a gentleman's dignity with it.

She re-settled the cap, and fought to wrest encouragement out of her throat. 'You must take heart, Mr Roxburgh. You can rely on me to bring you back,' she almost ejaculated 'to life' before recovering herself, '*home*' she substituted; 'we'll get the fire lit, and have you a warm meal – in no time'; lame in the end.

They continued huddling, stacked against each other and the wall, and gradually the rain was pelting less; the wind might have used itself up, or gone on to aim at more distant targets. It was no longer a strain to catch the gist of spoken words.

'At least you have seen me at my worst,' he said.

'You can't be answerable for your health, as I knaw from my own mother.' Thus she tried comforting him, when it was no comfort to herself; she would have liked to see him hale and perfect, leaping from the ship as the prow beached in the cove at sunset. (She was that foolish, or 'romantic'.)

Mr Roxburgh said, 'There are those who are able to rise, at any rate morally, above their physical condition.'

He was nothing if not moral, she felt. It did not console her.

'Couldn't you get on your feet?' she asked, 'If I give a hand?'

He obeyed as though she had been the mother to whom he so frequently referred, and whom she would not have cared to meet; better Lady Ottering giving advice through a carriage window, or passing judgement on geums or phlox as she trod the garden path on visits of patronage to her former maid.

In the silence the storm had left behind, Mr Roxburgh remarked as they crossed the road dividing farm from moor, 'I admire your strength of character.'

'Dear life!' She was so embarrassed she almost choked. '*Strength* – yes! That's about all I've got to my name. And must depend on it.'

Presently they saw the roof, and then the slope gave up the house, the ramshackle outhouses, and the scraggy pear and damson trees. There was mud on their boots. She scraped it off her own at the back door and indicated that he should do the same before entering.

Dr Hicks prescribed nothing more drastic for his patient's 'turn' than the tincture of digitalis he was already taking. Mr Roxburgh lay abed, and she persuaded Mamma to wait on him. Because Mamma had experienced less of their lodger's condition and mind, she would be less likely to expect him to break in her hands.

And as soon as he was restored, Mr Roxburgh decided, 'It's time I went home. My mother will be wondering.'

Ellen Gluyas was relieved, though she would not have admitted it to Pa or Will. She would not have admitted that the smells of medicines lingered (if they did) in the room where he had slept (it was again hers) or that she could still detect in the parlour a distinct smell of ancient books. He had left behind a bottle of ink which she appropriated, for what purpose she could not think. The smell of ink was real enough when she uncorked the bottle. Between Mr Roxburgh's visit and her attendance at the dame's school where she got such learning as she could boast, the smell of ink had scarce crossed her nostrils. Now whenever she sniffed at the bottle of which she had possessed herself, she experienced a sensation as of slight drunkenness mingled with that of sober despair.

Bristol Maid's sides were shuddering as she laboured, and Mr Roxburgh called to his wife from the saloon that the fellow had brought their breakfast, which she should come and eat if she had any intention of doing so. Restored to balance, Mrs Roxburgh did as she was told.

Mr Roxburgh was sipping tea with evident repugnance. 'The same old musty stuff,' he warned, 'but hot.'

It was, as she knew, little more than a brew of sticks, yet she preferred to ignore the salt pork (more fat than lean, more conducive to nausea) and join her husband in drinking the travesty of tea.

She sipped at it, and her eyes were moistened and enlarged. Except that their surroundings were so very different, they might have been seated together at Birdlip House, Cheltenham. At least the silences they kept were the same, and the moments when he emerged from his, to complain, or else it seemed, to take stock of her.

This morning Mr Roxburgh said, 'You are looking uncommonly nice, Ellen.' This she had learnt to interpret as a compliment from one brought up to abstain from vulgar enthusiasm.

It required no answer, but she murmured, 'All of it old and familiar,' and looked down, and touched her skirt.

'I was right in advising you to wear green.'

'My aunt used to say that green made a woman look trumpery.'

'Your aunt, I noticed, didn't care for you to look your best.'

Mr Roxburgh continued examining his wife, less pointedly perhaps, more thoughtfully. As a youth he had written poetry, but even to himself, his verses had sounded well-intentioned rather than inspired. By the time Garnet was riding to hounds with the young Stafford Merivale, Austin had attempted a novel, but already by Chapter III, it was clear that his characters were rejecting him. Laying his manuscript on the fire, he watched it catch, not so much with regret as relief; it allowed him to return to the classics. Yet Austin Roxburgh, whatever appearances suggested, was not all bookish: in him there stirred with vague though persistent uneasiness an impulse which might have been creative.

He was unable to draw, or he would have sketched the farmer's daughter in her country hat, or returning from the moor, driving her ewes ahead of her to pen them for the night. Remembering her thus, after he had left for home, started him wondering whether he might also be in love. If his passion had been stronger, the obvious course would have been to make her his mistress. It was inconceivable that she should ever become his wife; and yet he continued thinking of her, standing in a light reflected off fuchsias punching a basinful of dough on a scoured table, or again, arms folded against a starched apron-bib as she crossed the yard on some undefined errand. He certainly needed someone. Perhaps he did love her. He remembered her strength and kindness when overtaken by an autumn squall which brought on one of his attacks.

That he might marry Ellen Gluyas became after all a tenuous possibility on seeing her not only as his wife, but also as his work of art. This could be the project which might ease the frustration gnawing at him: to create a beautiful, charming, not necessarily intellectual, but socially acceptable companion out of what was only superficially unpromising material. There were remedies for chapped hands and indifferent grammar; nothing can be effected without the cornerstone of moral worth.

Austin Roxburgh felt so inspired he could not wait for his mother to leave him to his studies as she did each night at ten o'clock. When at last she kissed him and he could her her groping her way upstairs, and finally trundling overhead, he sat and wrote, though with a caution to which his initial inspiration had been reduced:

Dear Mrs Gluyas,

Remembering with pleasure the weeks I spent beneath your roof last summer, it occurred to me that it would be most agreeable to repeat the experience, shall we say, from the beginning of June? if those same rooms are not already promised to somebody more fortunate than I.

My regards to Mr Gluyas, and my best wishes to your daughter, whose concern for my welfare touched me deeply on my previous visit.

Hoping to hear from you in good time so that I may complete my plans . . .

Mr Roxburgh did in fact receive a reply in good time, if not at all favourable:

Dear Mr Roxburgh,

I am sorry to inform you my mother passed on this January and my father does not feel we shld let rooms for not being able to do the best by a lodger, least of all one so particler as yourself.

I hope your health has improved since autumn last, and thank you for thinking kindly of us.

Yrs ever respectfully, E. GLUYAS

Mr Roxburgh was so put out by this setback to what he visualized that his feelings immediately became suffused with genuine tenderness, if not actual passion (he might never be capable of that). He wondered at the time what he could do, beyond compose the correct reply, just as he was still pondering over his relationship with the woman he had made his wife.

'Yes,' he repeated as the saloon was battered out of perspective, then allowed to settle back into its original shape, 'green is the colour I advised you to wear, because unlike so many women you have nothing vapid about you. That is why you appealed to me.'

He had evidently satisfied himself; whereas Mrs Roxburgh, indolently lolling in a somewhat primitive saloon chair, dangling one hand as ladies are apt to do, was relieved to hear a rattling of the door-knob.

It was Captain Purdew to announce that, if they gave permission, he would breakfast with them.

The captain was rubbing his hands together so briskly they produced a grating sound, and in Mr Roxburgh, a corresponding heartiness. 'I must congratulate you, Captain, on enjoying such health.'

Captain Purdew retaliated in similar vein. 'Your lady, sir, is the one we should congratulate – for presiding so charmingly at a breakfast of salt pork.' The captain crooked a finger in preparation for further gallantry and his tea-cup.

Mrs Roxburgh received the compliment with an air of disbelief inherited from her mother-in-law. If she was not carried over into downright boredom as she poured the captain's tea, it was because an elderly, grizzled man is entitled to pay compliments and because a certain ingratiating, cumbrousness reminded her of her late father on his less bearish days.

Jovially for him, Mr Roxburgh had begun questioning Captain Purdew on the technicalities of his calling, the state of the weather and their general prospects for the voyage, in none of which could his wife join with anything like conviction. Instead she fell to caressing her throat, as a hand which both fascinated and repelled her attacked those slabs of refractory, not to say rubbery, pork.

While she was still a little girl, he used to stroke her cheeks as though to learn the secrets of her skin. She would feel the horn-thing on his crushed thumb scraping her.

On one occasion, unable to bear it any longer, she cried out, 'Cusn't tha see I dun't want to be touched?' and threw him off.

He brooded and sulked a fair while, but it had been necessary; shame told her she was as much excited as disgusted; she grew more thoughtful as a result, and melancholy on wet afternoons.

Poor Mamma was too preoccupied to pay attention, but after her death, the two survivors were less distressed by her absence than by each other's company.

At the same time Pa grew increasingly dependent on herself to conduct the day-to-day routine, and on the blessed grog to release him, not so much from grief as the despondency which had always

56

been eating him. He would rise in the dark and fuddle through the morning at little unnecessary jobs, but sit all afternoon at the kitchen table, if he was not gone on a journey. He would invent journeys which ought to be made, only, it seemed, for the sake of motion.

That spring, a late one after an unusually bitter winter, he asked her to accompany him as far as Tremayne, needing her help with a heifer which Mr Borlase had shown some inclination to buy. Pa was driving the sprung cart, dressed in his best pepper-and-salt, while she knelt at the back attached to the unwilling heifer by a rope. It was raining a cold drizzle; a slush of dirty snow had almost thawed out in the ditches. Distress at leaving home had given the poor beast the scours. Her betrayer's hands were soon a mackerel colour from holding to the rope, at which Beat would jerk each time she threw up her head to bellow. The jolting of the cart, familiar whiffs of the animal she had reared from a calf, and glimpses of grey sea above stone walls or through the gaps in thorn hedges, increased the misery with which, it seemed, Ellen Gluyas might remain permanently infected.

At Tremayne, Pa got down and took over the heifer. His hands were trembling. She wrapped a sack about her shoulders and said she would stay behind. He cursed her for behaving unsociably, or for being an imbecile, or both, before plodding with their pretty Beat into the not-far-distant yard.

She rocked herself back and forth on the bare board on which she was seated, to generate a warmth her old drab kersey didn't provide, and as a substitute for company. Had she been able to invent journeys, like Pa, and had her belief in magic promised to sustain her, she might have gathered up the reins, and driven the rest of the distance to Tintagel, or farther still, wheels grating over pebbles before entering those grey waves.

Presently the sun showed, and she felt guilty for her wicked thoughts, as well as for misleading Mr Roxburgh into putting his trust in one who was unworthy of it.

When Pa returned it was without the heifer. As he had reckoned, Mr Borlase was unable to resist such a well-shaped beast. Pa had grown heartier, for the cash in his pocket and for having quenched his thirst at the buyer's expense. He had made so sure of this she wasted no time in taking the reins from his hands.

Thus released from responsibilities, his body slithered back and lay on the floor of the cart, his legs, in their shiny black leggings, propped and twitching on the seat beside her.

Had he but slept; instead he started shouting, 'What's taken the girl? I can see by they shoulders you're op to yer old game. Well, you ent goin' to make me suffer. I had too much, Ellen.'

'Gee op, Tiger!' She slapped the horse's rump with the ends of the reins.

They rattled home at a fair pace, but the day was drawing in as she penned the ewes; it was dark before she finished milking.

She fried him a teddy-cake, which he pushed away. He sat pouring for his own consumption. Sometimes his elbow would fall short of the table.

He said, 'You'll always hate me. I bet tha's stuck pins in me and throwed me to the fire.'

She messed the potato with her fork. 'Why would I hate you?'

'For bein' your father.'

She had no answer.

'If you dun't hate me, you dun't love me.'

Again she had no answer.

'You've no cause to. An' every cause. To love a father.'

She felt she might retch if she stayed, so she got up, and went outside, and started trapesing up and down through the drizzle which had begun again.

Once she looked his way, and he was sitting in the lamplit kitchen, amongst the unscraped dishes, sucking by now on his bottle.

She was too tired to postpone her return, whatever accusations might be preparing. Instead he stared at her, and asked in a distant, frightened voice unlike his own, 'Nelly' (he had never addressed her thus) 'was it you knocked to the door? Or was it a token?'

He might have been coming to her, but stumbled, and fell against the dresser, and was gone before she could take him in her arms.

Whether it was grief she felt or terror at finding herself alone in a silent, no longer familiar house, with a stranger's dead weight threatening to drag her under, she could not have told.

*

Captain Purdew was devouring prodigious quantities of pork, accompanied by gulps of green tea to assuage a thirst brought on by the saltness of the meat.

'I wouldn't exchange this sturdy little vessel, Mr Roxburgh, for any of your fast-sailing modern packets.'

'May I pour you another cup, Captain?' Mrs Roxburgh was still contemplating what might have been the skin of her own father's hand.

She shivered. The gale had discovered cracks in the 'sturdy little vessel', the sea too, it appeared: a thin trickle of water was advancing across the saloon carpet.

Of a sudden Captain Purdew seemed to grow embarrassed for his hands, those great cracked flippers, coarsened by hard use and weather, stiffened and knobbed by the rheumatics.

'As a boy,' Mr Roxburgh was leaning forward with an earnestness his wife recognized as the mode he adopted when indulging in confidences, 'I experienced none of the rougher pleasures of life for being handicapped by poor health. The damp winters affected my chest. From early childhood I was dressed in the thickest wool and practically suffocated by well-meant precautions.'

If his wife had at first subscribed to the theory of prevention by suffocation, it was to win over her mother-in-law. Old Mrs Roxburgh was persuaded to see virtues in one who patently observed the tradition of Austin's delicate health; humble origins and rude manners might be overlooked, to some extent, or anyway temporarily, in one who showed such dedication.

As a bride the young woman developed the habit of bringing her husband drinks of scalded milk from which she had been careful to take the skin according to instructions. The skin was the nourishing part, she protested without insisting, but he confessed he only had to catch sight of wrinkled skin on a tumbler of milk to feel queasy. On another occasion, on asking her to close a window, he made it known that open windows were a source of anxiety ever since he had developed pneumonia after an evening at whist in a friend's over-ventilated house. But on a mild evening like this, she coaxed, the air can but warm the room. Instead of obeying, she forced the sash higher by several inches, on such a meadowful of placid light and sounds of rooks settling themselves in elm-castles, he must have decided to waive his objection.

... so I was sent abroad,' Mr Roxburgh continued explaining, and leaned farther forward as his narrative took him into foreign parts, 'first to Switzerland, then Italy, in the company of a tutor, a fool of a fellow, who at least left me to my books and my own devices while he pursued the ladies. So much so, we had to forgo the Levant after he was challenged to a duel at Palermo.'

No doubt remembering his duties now that his hunger was satisfied, the captain had grown fidgety. He resumed sitting on the hands which, he suspected, offended a lady's sensibility, while he waited to seize the appropriate moment for breaking free.

Mrs Roxburgh yawned, and forgot that she ought to disguise it.

'I was sent abroad,' Mr Roxburgh repeated, 'but was cured at last, cheaply, and at home.'

If he glanced half-amused half-regretful at his wife, it was because she remained unconscious of the reference; nor could she share his momentary vision of greenish-yellow light with the sound of wasps stealing upon them as she put up a hand to test the degree of ripeness her pears had reached inside their muslin bags. *One forgets, Ellen, how much you know.* And her reply, *How much? how little is surely nearer the mark!* He might have insisted in contradicting had modesty not suited her so well, and also because a wife's modesty suits a husband.

His passengers' visible withdrawal gave Captain Purdew his chance. 'If you'll excuse me, ma'am, I'll return to duty – refreshed and encouraged, I needn't say.'

While the passengers made no attempt to restrain one who must continue foreshortened in the light of their own lives and thoughts, the captain was glad to escape for no reason that he could properly explain.

After the steward had cleared the table Mr Austin Roxburgh fetched his writing-case, extracted his journal (Morocco-bound) selected a pen which, even so, he might not have cared for, and settled down to write.

15 May 1836

he inscribed it with perhaps too reckless a flourish,

Resumed our voyage in *Bristol Maid*. A wretched vessel if ever there was. Rolling horribly since dawn. Prudent enough to rise late and find my feet, but E. must venture early on deck, with the result that she returned soaked.

From the little we have seen of this Colony after the comparatively fertile expanses of Van Diemen's Land, there was never an emptier, more hostile country (E. not altogether in agreement because of the fanciful, or 'romantic', streak in her nature).

Mr Roxburgh paused, and would have examined his wife's face, half-expecting her to have read his mounting thoughts, but she had gone from the saloon into the cabin, from which, as she moved about the other side of the partition, came the sounds of tidying. She liked to pass the morning thus, even making up the bunks, as a favour to the steward, or, her husband rather suspected, in repentance for the sin of defecting from the lower class.

Complete isolation persuaded Mr Roxburgh to let himself go. He swallowed the bitterness in his mouth, and clenched his teeth as his nib slashed the surface of the page.

Oh the blackness in which it is never possible to distinguish the outline of a beloved form, or know the wife of one's own choosing! No wonder that a state of doubt, anguish, even terror, should exist, to explore which might prove disastrous. I am from time to time the original Abyss, into which I must restrain my rational self from plunging for fear of the consequences. Happy, indeed, is he who can ignore the too substantial shadows of long afternoons at sea. The mornings can be filled with domestic details, and recall of life as we have experienced it, but not the reflecting glass of endless afternoon and evening . . .

Here Mr Roxburgh's guilt or fears got the better of him. He hesitated, then began most carefully to obliterate under an opaque hatching of India ink most of what he had written since breakfast, but could not be absolutely sure that he had done the job with thoroughness. The page was at last as good as damaged. Only then, and after glancing over a shoulder, did he reach for his Virgil.

What should have been silence was in competition with a creaking of planks, a dashing of waves, a distant, confused thunder. In the cabin adjoining the saloon Mrs Roxburgh had performed the tasks with which she had learnt to occupy herself during the mornings of a voyage. If she had neglected the bunks, she would see to them later. In the meantime she was prepared to indulge herself a little. Seated at the chest sideways because there was no accommodation for knees, she took out the journal she had kept up sporadically since her late mother-in-law advised her to form the habit.

At sea

she wrote in her improved, but never altogether approved, hand (*at least my dear no one would deny it has its individual character*).

Just now remembered overhearing conversation between Mr Daintrey and Mr Roxburgh discussing his brother Garnet R. Mr Daintrey deciding that G. R., in spite of his looks, spirit, and prospects, showed himself a 'lost soul' from birth. Did not fully understand, but felt alarmed lest somebody accuse me behind my back of being 'lost'. Mr Roxburgh, his mother, Mrs Daintrey, have all professed to find me agreeable and assured me of their approval and love. That wld not have prevented them recognizing what myself has always half suspected from my worst days at Z. It has stuck in my mind like a furze thorn in the thumb. (Had she known, Mrs Roxburgh wld have accused me of *morbid thoughts*!)

Went on deck early and was intocksicated by a sense of freedom, of pure joy. Gulls approaching, then swooning off. At moments I felt dizzy with the air I swallowed, but sad to think I will never explore this vast land seen at a distance through spray and fog. Captain Purdew bore down wanting to protect me. We smiled at each other more than necessary, because it was almost impossible to be heard, and for want, I suppose, of anything to say. Good, kind, tedjus men make me feel guilty. Perhaps it is Pa's blood in my veins. I am given to fits of drunkenness without having indulged. Unlike many others, Mr Roxburgh does not bore me I think. I am sure I do not write this out of gratitude. A husband can become one of his wife's most pleasing habits . . .

She put it away. The airless cabin had given her a head. Soon she must make up the beds, but would rest a little in the lower berth, overcome by a faintness, or languor, to which the motion of the ship contributed.

Mrs Roxburgh lay, not uncomfortably, except for a slight nausea, in the hollow her husband's form had impressed on the palliasse, and was encouraged to re-enter her maze.

'Whenever in doubt, ask, and I shall advise you, my dear, to the best of my ability,' old Mrs Roxburgh promised after her 'unlikely' daughter-in-law had won her respect and affection.

She had a soft, perished neck, and rumbled gently after drinking tea, which she took in immoderate quantities from forgetting the number of cups she had poured.

Her mother-in-law's rumbles had calmed Ellen's initial fright and roused in her a tenderness for the defenceless old thing.

The elder Mrs Roxburgh had not appeared at the wedding, which, conveniently, was 'far too far'; a pity considering Aunt Triphena had insisted on standing by her niece to show that the girl came of a respectable, not to say substantial, family. The embarrassing question of whether to produce the father had been tactfully settled by nature when Dick was carried off by the drink. In fact, by giving Ellen a fright, it was more than anything Dick's death which ensured that the ceremony would take place. Mr Roxburgh had caught her on the bounce, so to speak, after a renewal of their correspondence.

Aunt Tite had not been able to resist hinting at the bitter truth. Ellen, in her confusion, was ready to admit it, while none the less grateful to her pale, thin-legged stranger-lover descending from the coach, together with a second gentleman, his solicitor and friend, Mr Aubrey Daintrey. Mr Daintrey was the only member of the Roxburgh faction to attend the wedding and take stock of the background Mrs Tregaskis had provided. If he appreciated what he saw, he gave scarcely a formal sign. Mr Daintrey could not have been colder, steelier (steel with the slight tremor caused by inordinate tension) had he been acting as Mr Roxburgh's second at a duel.

Aunt Tite, whose charity was only ever skin-deep, showed her generosity by choosing white satin and lace, with satin slippers and kid gloves, for her pauper niece. Hepzibah Tregaskis, as bridesmaid, wore rosebud pink which went with her pretty complexion. The bride, who had spent too much time in the fields, looked the swarthier for her white.

But Mr Roxburgh appeared enchanted, and Mr Daintrey the best man raised a few fairly unrestrained smiles.

Ellen hoped she would not cry. She would love her husband in accordance with what she was promising, and not only out of gratitude.

It was decided by Mr Roxburgh and his mother to defer the honeymoon, that the bride might be initiated without delay into the customs she was expected to adopt. So, from living isolated on a poor Cornish farm, Ellen Gluyas entered into temporary purdah in a Gloucestershire mansion, the family having moved from their original Winchester in the hopes that Mr Austin's health might benefit by the mild climate and polite society at Cheltenham.

At least she rarely found herself alone: there was her gently admonishing mother-in-law; there were the servants. Most terrifying for Ellen Roxburgh was the maid who attended on her rising and her setting.

'You should put yourself in her hands,' old Mrs Roxburgh advised, with no more than an oblique glance at her newly acquired daughter-in-law. 'Vetch will brush your hair, and help you to dress – and *un*-dress.'

'But it is not what I'm used to,' the younger Mrs Roxburgh protested. 'And what shall I call her? *Vetch?*'

'If that is her name, what else?'

'But nothing more?'

The old woman preferred to ignore a question which embarrassed her by betraying ignorance of worldly manners in her son's wife, or else a regrettable perversity, for old Mrs Roxburgh was not unaware that the girl's mother had been Lady Ottering's maid.

Vetch was a trim, sour, elderly person who performed her duties according to rule, perfectly no doubt, but with a coldness which disdained one who was imperfection itself.

Ellen Roxburgh learned to lean back and enjoy the hair-brushing; she allowed herself to be dressed and undressed; but on the first occasion when Vetch knelt to peel the stockings from her legs, she put out a hand to stay her.

'Why, ma'am, I'm accustomed to do what any lady expects.'

'But I do *not* expect it. I was never so inactive. And cannot bear anyone to touch my feet. They're ticklish.'

Though she laughed to encourage her maid, Vetch failed to kindle; a lifetime of service seemed to have damped her responses to life.

Yes, her servants despised her, the young Mrs Roxburgh could tell; they suspected her of wanting them to re-admit her to a society she had forsworn without sufficient thought for the secrets she was taking with her.

Old Mrs Roxburgh, on the other hand, was convinced that this honest and appealing girl could never be admitted to hers except in theory, and her heart began to bleed for her. In an effort to make amends, the old woman relinquished a ruby necklace and a topaz collar. 'Why should you not have and enjoy what will be yours eventually?'

These were the sweets; the gall was in the copybook, because the mother-in-law was of the opinion it were best to start at the beginning, '. . . considering that your hand is not what one would call cultivated.'

So she was put to forming pothooks and hangers, until coming upon her pupil without her knowledge, the old woman sensed from the tilt of the head and a hunched shoulder the indignity the girl was warding off. Accordingly, they skipped pothooks. She was promoted to simple copying, and invited to compile inventories of linen, plate, and furniture, in spite of the fact that there was no immediate call for such records.

Then there was the journal favoured by old Mrs Roxburgh as a source of self-knowledge and an instrument for self-correction.

20 Aug 1821
I will make a start today at writing in this clean book which I hope not to spoil because I owe it to Them. My life has become all starts in every quarter – and sometimes fits as well if I wld give way to them. I must not complane, I have evrything – a house excepting it is Theirs, his Mother lives in one wing but eats with us, she is very kind. I have cloathes aplenty, servants not all of them necessary or desirable, who do not speak unless spoken to and then not always. I have a Spanish jennet. Mr R. has presented me besides with a pair of finches in a cage, and my little pug Tip, she is merry as a cricket. I ride out in my green habit though not far, Mr R. will not allow it, or I drive my own pony car, or we are driven out Mrs R. and me in the carridge, or chaise if the weather is fair. Freinds greet us, most of Mrs R.'s age. We sometimes call at some grave house and are invited to take a glass of wine or dish of tay. Unless I am spoke to in strange houses I keep quiet for fear of what may jump out of my mouth. But will learn no doubt. They have give me books to read – Bishop Taylor's *Sermons* and Miss Edgeworth, and the crib to the Latin poet that Mr R. most loves. Not being able to make much of any of it yet, I sit with my books more often than I read, and look at the toe of my shoe, or watch the wasps trying to get at the pears through the muslin bags, or my little pug to catch her tail. I wish I

would dare go inside the kitchen to make some jam, I may yet, and read a book without my eyes ache . . .

⟩ She had been encouraged early to tell the truth, but found that truth did not always match what she was taught by precept or in church: it was both simpler and more complicated.

Her parents in the past, and now her husband and mother-in-law, expected more of her than they themselves were prepared or knew how to demonstrate. It had pained and puzzled her as a child, until as a girl she too began accepting that there are conventions in truth as in anything else. As a young wife and 'lady' she saw this as an expedient she must convert into permanence, and former critics were soon applauding her for observing the conventions they were accustomed to obey.

Moral approval is all very well. Ellen Roxburgh would have liked to shine, but in the circumstances, did so only fitfully. Once or twice on coming downstairs in ruby necklace or topaz collar, her hand accepting but languid guidance from the rail, she had sensed unwilling admiration in an apathetic, if not coolly hostile, servant. A housemaid dazzled out of her thoughts abandoned the scuttle she had brought to a neglected grate and fled behind the baize door. On another, more equivocal occasion, the butler looked up with what might have been interpreted as an expression of shock.

'Did I startle you, Perkins?' she asked with that mild indifference she had copied from those who knew how to use it better.

'Not at all, ma'am. It struck me you were looking exceptionally well.'

Although triumphs of a kind, they were hardly salve for her worst wounds. A fashionable rout could become the scene of grievous torture where the truth was aimed when her back was turned. She was sometimes all but felled by what she overheard through an open doorway or under cover of an urn or column.

'Mr Roxburgh is of excellent family, I am told.' The lady visiting at Cheltenham might not have appeared to be fishing had her eyes not grown a glaze and the tips of her marabout plumes trembled with anticipation.

Mrs Daintrey the solicitor's wife confirmed that Mr Roxburgh was 'of an established and respected family'.

66

A gentleman had started making preparatory noises in his throat.

The visitor flicked her marabout afresh. '*Mrs* Roxburgh, I understand, is of quite humble origins.'

Mrs Daintrey moaned a little. 'But is doing very nicely,' she conceded out of friendship for her husband's client.

'In any case,' the gentleman who had been preparing seized the opportunity, 'the Roxburghs themselves were in trade a couple of generations ago.'

Stouter than ever in friendship, Mrs Daintrey cried, 'But never behind the counter!'

'And the brother?'

'Ah, I cannot vouch for him.' Mrs Daintrey sighed. 'Very little is known – to me, at any rate – about Mr Garnet Roxburgh. Should we, perhaps, sample the ices?'

Mrs Roxburgh wrote in the journal which from being a virtue was becoming a vice:

... I would like to see my husband as perfect. I will not have him hurt. I am better able to endure wounds, and wld take them upon myself instead. Women on the whole are stronger because more knowing than men, for all the knowledge men lay claim to. We also learn to numb ourselves against suffering, whether of the body, or the mind ...

To please and protect became Ellen Roxburgh's constant aim; to be accepted by her husband's friends and thus earn his approbation; to show the Roxburghs her gratitude in undemonstrative and undemeaning ways, because anything else embarrassed them. What she would not admit, or only half, was her desire to love her husband in a manner acceptable to them both.

Just as she was to learn that death was for Mr Roxburgh a 'literary conceit', so she found that his approach to passion had its formal limits. For her part, she longed to, but had never dared, storm those limits and carry him off instead of submitting to his hesitant though loving rectitude. 'Tup' was a word she remembered out of a past she had all but forgotten, in which her own passive ewes submitted, while bees flitted wilfully from thyme to furze, the curlew whistled at dusk, and night was filled with the badger's chattered messages. She herself had only once responded with a natural ardour, but discovered on her husband's face an expression of having tasted something bitter, or of looking too deep. So she replaced the mask which evidently she was expected to wear, and because he was an honourable as well as a pitiable man, she would refrain in future from tearing it off.

In the second year of their marriage she conceived.

... I am of course very happy and Mr R. is overjoyed. His brother Garnet has not got a child, and it is right that himself the elder brother shld pass on the name through a son and heir. (Provided it is this and not a disappointing *girl!*) The child will also *give a filip*, he says, *to our conversation.* I did not know we were in need of a go-between. But so it is!

Mrs Roxburgh miscarried after a fall from her Spanish jennet, and was forbidden to ride Dapple again; she must content herself with being driven. Even to those aware of the train of events, young Mrs Roxburgh did not look less handsome, if a trifle pale, in her violet silk, with the black, fringed pelerine. From carriage or chaise she returned her acquaintances' greetings with no more than the degree of pleasure her situation called for; the plumes only slightly rippled in her great hat.

On days when she took little walks through the grounds her mother-in-law might accompany her. Grown infirm since the tragedy, old Mrs Roxburgh hung on her arm, trembled, and tottered. 'I find it chilly, Ellen,' she murmered. 'Should we not go in?'

Alone, the younger woman sometimes roamed the house, discovering attics and cupboards hitherto unexplored, and which she doubted would ever be hers; she was to that extent bereft and restless. One evening as the light on the elms started to wane, she found herself scratching on an attic window with a diamond, as she had heard told it was possible to write. She printed on the glass TINTAGEL in bold, if irregular letters, and then was ashamed, or even afraid, for what she had done, though neither her husband nor her mother-in-law was likely to climb so high, and those who did would not connect the name with their mistress's thoughts or any part of the real world.

Two years later Mrs Roxburgh again conceived, and this time bore a child, a perfect little boy, but who was with them so short a while, she did not even record his passing in her journal. By unexpressed agreement Mrs Roxburgh and her husband decided not to mention the incident again.

Nor did the grandmother dwell on it, unless obliquely. 'Austin was the sickly child. Garnet was such a sturdy little fellow. I can see him in the firelight, sitting in front of that brass fender after Nurse had given him his bath. Brimful of life and health! Austin so pale. He developed a cough. I would not allow myself to think, because if I did, I would have believed he must die.'

On the table beside the old woman's carved chair stood a miniature framed in a garland of gold leaves and pear-shaped pearls. 'There, you see,' she would invite her callers to admire more than once in the course of the same visit, 'my two boys!'

Enhanced by Austin's sallow face and expression of anxiety, Garnet made a charming impression: his frock so cut as to reveal the shoulders, his lips as glossy as washed cherries, his chestnut hair arranged by an admiring nurse with a studied casualness which left the forehead engagingly exposed.

'Though Providence has dealt me several blows,' the old lady would maunder on, 'I should not complain. Austin was spared, and Austin has been a comfort to me. Well, we shall all soon be dead. Not you, my dear, you are far too healthy.' Here a soft white hand would fumble after a firmer one. 'Garnet is as good as dead. What use is a boy to his mother, or anybody else, living down there in Van Diemen's Land?'

Once Ellen had taken a deep enough breath to ask, 'What decided Mr Garnet Roxburgh to emigrate to Van Diemen's Land?'

The mother was so far caught off her guard that she launched herself immediately. 'He didn't decide – it was decided for him by Austin, Mr Daintrey, and several others who had his interests at heart. It was not his fault. He was headstrong and unwise, and fell amongst bad company.' Here it must have occurred to the narrator that it might be imprudent to cast more light on an incident best consigned to obscurity, for she gasped, and sniffed, and dabbed a little before concluding, 'They say there are compensations for living in Van Diemen's Land – some very quaint marsupials. Garnet himself told me about them in a letter.'

Not long after, old Mrs Roxburgh died. Her son Austin was deeply affected by her death, as might have been foreseen, and all but his wife decided to avoid his company during the prolonged period of mourning. As for the old woman's daughter (so Ellen considered herself and was considered by then) she wept as the earth was shovelled in unfeeling clods down upon the coffin. Her husband would have preferred her to restrain her grief, at least till later, because a red face smeared with tears reminded him in public of the farmer's daughter he had married, when he had begun to congratulate himself on her being buried deeper than his mother. (Stricken by his private sentiments, Mr Roxburgh wrote off to London, ordering a dozen pair of gloves of the size he had noted at the back of his journal the year he married 'Ellen Gluyas'.)

Persuaded to rest awhile in her husband's bunk Mrs Roxburgh regretted her lethargy. Within the motion of the heaving ship and the rustle of the straw-filled palliasse she remained a core of inertia. She yawned uncontrollably. Oh for her down pillows and featherbed at Cheltenham! Wishes did not prevent her ploughing her cheek deeper into the coarse slip upon which it was resting and where her husband's cheek lingered: around her there was still the scent of sleep; she was pervaded and soothed by it. Soon, she promised herself, she would make up the beds, like any under-housemaid, but until then, she resigned herself to the undulations of her feathered thoughts. If she shuddered once or twice, and chafed the gooseflesh out of her arms, it was because she knew she would be led deeper than she would have chosen, and inevitably trapped in what she most loathed.

'*Why?*' he pondered in high anguish.

They were seated on deck in a warm corner on the lee side of the barque *Kestrel*. If the breeze held, they were but a day out of Hobart Town.

The warmth, the prospect, must have gulled Mr Roxburgh into meeting his wife's disagreeable question with an uncharacteristically direct reply. 'My brother was accused of forging a signature. Oh, nothing was *proved*! The accusation was based on suspicion rather than evidence, and knowing my brother I am confident that he was not guilty.' Mr Roxburgh thrust his hands back to back between his bony knees; sunken cheeks and clenched jaws contributed to the impression that he had suddenly aged. 'Poor Garnet, he was never bad! Rash, admittedly, and too personable.

70

He had the fatal gift of attracting almost everyone he met. The wrong people led him astray.'

'When the wrong people led him astray, surely it was your brother who must have felt attracted?' For her husband's sake she would not have liked to think it.

Practically shouting, Mr Roxburgh repeated in his brother's defence, 'He is not *bad*! It was never *proved*!'

Presently they gathered up their books, their rugs, and went below, where Mrs Roxburgh occupied herself writing in her journal until it should be dinner-time.

.. asked the imprudent question and received the painful answer. Mr R. most distressed. But I had to know. If I cld only rid myself of my dislike for Garnet R. so as not to go against my husband. But I continue seeing the little boy with glossy lips, and shallow eyes determined to dazzle as he stares out of the likeness his mother loved to show visitors. I can imagine the 'personable' man grown out of this little boy – the mocking lips, the blue eyes hardened by conceit and – I shld not allow myself to write it – *unproved dishonesty*. I believe I have always detested Garnet R. for outshining his brother. I must not allow myself to think such thoughts when it wld pain my dearest husband, only that I must protect him from his innocent faith in one who I am sure was never worthy of it . . .

By the time they went in to dinner Mrs Roxburgh was entrenched in her own virtuous resolves, and wore a glow to which her husband could not but respond admiringly.

Berthed alongside the quay at Hobart Town the following morning, a shrouded mountain looming over all, Ellen Roxburgh was less confident of her armoury. She remembered she was the farmer's daughter who had married an honourable gentleman, and corrected her speech, and learned to obey certain accepted moral precepts and social rules, most of them as incongruous to her nature as her counterfeit of the Italian hand and her comments on the books with which her husband wished her to persevere. But her meeting with that husband's adored brother, a second gentleman whose doubtful honour led her to expect a subtler version of the first, could prove the severest trial of those to which she had so far been subjected.

In the circumstances, Mrs Roxburgh lingered below settling her very modest bonnet (an old one, as Mr Roxburgh had requested for their voyage), patting the carpet-bag into shape, locking her leather dressing-case (in which she also kept her journal), while Austin Roxburgh went on deck to take part in the joyful, if also unnerving, reunion with his sibling.

When she could no longer defer the moment of joining them, her confusion at first prevented her assessing 'Garnet R.' with any clearness. She was aware only of the blaze from blue sceptical eyes, an intensification of the milder, shallower stare of the child in the miniature, and a hand uncommonly hard, like that of some mechanic, or farmer. By contrast his clothes, without being ostentatious, suggested expense, even fashion. The shirt-cuff was of impeccable linen, as he stooped to retrieve a leather glove he had let fall on the deck.

Withdrawing her glance from the wrist, she listened to the unnaturally high-pitched inanities in which long separation had forced the brothers to engage each other. After the initial compliments and inquiries on Garnet Roxburgh's part, the two gentlemen mercifully ignored her.

'... Are you *well*, Austin? You *look* well, you old, creaking gate!'

'Inactivity, or the long sea voyage, has put new life in me, dear fellow. Though naturally I must always take care. My heart, as you know, is not of the best.'

Mr Garnet Roxburgh smiled absently, if it was not incredulously, at the idea that someone might suffer from a heart.

'And you, Mrs Roxburgh – Ellen, isn't it? if you'll allow me – have you no ailments – or at any rate, complaints?' he inquired as he propelled her the short distance along the gang-board on to the quay.

'None,' she answered while he was still at her back, 'unless the nervous fidgets I developed from not arriving sooner.' She was glad to hear grit beneath the soles of her boots, which not only meant she was once more standing on solid land but her first abrasive contact with it might have disintegrated a reply which could have sounded insipid, insincere, or worse to her husband's ears – indiscreet.

But the brothers were too busy organizing and explaining to pay attention to shades of meaning.

'The baggage will follow by bullock-wagon,' their host told

them. 'That is, all but your immediate necessities. Those, we can take with us in the buggy.'

Except that mud had collected on the wheels and spattered the bodywork, the vehicle wore a gloss of paint which disguised bluntness of form in an elegance matching that of the owner himself.

During the longueurs of the voyage out Mr Roxburgh had informed his wife, 'There is no actual reason for pitying Garnet, though our mother, understandably, always lamented losing her favourite son – yes, let us be realistic – to a hard and *morally infected* country like Van Diemen's Land. In fact Garnet has done very well for himself. By marrying a considerably older widow of means, his position in the community became assured. If the woman died not long after, in a regrettable accident, at least he inherited her property, from which, I gather, he has a respectable income.'

'How did Mrs Garnet Roxburgh die?'

'In the accident,' Austin replied, but vaguely, for his mind was occupied with other thoughts.

Driven by the widower through Hobart Town, Ellen returned, if only by an imagined glimpse, to the accident in which Mrs Garnet Roxburgh died.

'Do you approve?' she realized her brother-in-law was asking.

'Of what?'

'Of our neat little town.'

'It is that,' she said. 'And English. I have difficulty in believing I am being driven through a famous penal colony of the antipodes.'

He laughed. 'You will soon believe, but need not fear, or feel embarrassed if, like Austin, you are given to embarrassment. The authorities keep the wretches suitably employed, and on the whole, subdued.'

Overhearing himself accused, Austin began to protest that he never experienced embarrassment – well, almost never – and the two brothers were soon engaged in banter and laughter and reminiscence.

Excluded from this, Mrs Roxburgh was able to enjoy her view of the unassuming, while often charming houses, their general effect of modest substance sometimes spoilt by the intrusion of an over-opulent façade. Hens were allowed the freedom of the streets, and an ambling cow almost grazed a wheel of the buggy with her ribs. The scent of the cow's breath, the thudding of her hooves, and the plop of falling dung, filled Ellen with an immeasurable home-sickness. Had it not been for the uncommunicative stares of respectable burgesses and the open scowls of those who must be their slaves, she might have been driving Gluyas's cart to market.

When they had left the town and were headed for the interior, the two brothers fell silent. Austin had exhausted himself by a detailed description of the monument in the classic style he had personally designed for erection over their mother's grave. Garnet sighed; a gloom descended on him, less from melancholy regrets than from boredom, Ellen felt; or perhaps it was the prospect of a long visit by members of his family.

In any case he seemed to have grown oblivious of a sister-in-law he had shown no signs of taking seriously. Not that she would have welcomed his serious attentions. She thought she would dislike him even more than she had anticipated. He had about him something which she, the farmer's daughter and spurious lady, recognized as coarse and sensual. Perhaps this was what she resented, and that a Roxburgh should both embody and remind her of it. As he held the reins in his hands during what had become this monotonous drive, she noticed his thick wrists and the hairs visible on them in the space between glove and cuff. She turned away her head. She more than disliked, she was repelled, not only by the man, but by her own thoughts, which her husband and her late mother-in-law would not have suspected her of harbouring.

To escape from her inner self she looked out across the country, when her attention was caught by a party of men who could only have been some of the 'wretches' to whom Garnet Roxburgh had referred. The prisoners were divided into two squads, each engaged in pushing a hand-cart loaded with freshly quarried stone. Armed guards were shouting orders, unintelligible at that distance. The party had but recently emerged from a dip between two slopes. From dragging their carts to the crest of the second, the men were now proceeding to brake, those in front by digging their heels into the hillside, their bodies inclined back against the carts, those behind straining with their whole weight to resist a too-rapid descent. Every face was raised to the sun, teeth bared in sobbing mouths when the lips were not tightly clenched, skin streaming with light and sweat. In contrast to the tanned cheeks and furiously mobile faces, the closed eyes and white eyelids gave the prisoners that expression of unnatural serenity seen in the blind, and which makes them appear all but removed from the life around them.

Mrs Roxburgh was immediately glad of the lowered eyelids, and that the men most probably would not catch sight of her before the buggy rounded a shoulder of the hill ahead. She felt a pang of commiseration through the hardships and indignities suffered during girlhood, but was more intent on avoiding the prisoners' undoubted resentment of the physical ease and peace of mind they must imagine if they were to open their eyes.

So she clenched her gloved hands, and willed the horses to increase their speed. From brooding, and from biting on her lips, these felt thick and sullen. At least her companions had started a desultory conversation and were too engrossed in the past to notice the work-party of convicts before those unfortunate human beasts were lost to sight.

The landscape through which the travellers were driving was by turns cultivated and wild. An occasional stone cottage or hut built of wattle-and-daub looked the meaner for the tiered forests towering above them. The roads were consistently execrable. The two stout horses lumbered onward, darkened with sweat except where a lather had broken out from the friction of crupper and trace against their coats. Ruts frequently threw the passengers together with a violence which seemed almost personal in its intent.

However she held herself Mrs Roxburgh could not avoid unpleasant contact with her brother-in-law's nearside shoulder; when suddenly he turned to her. 'We shall arrive, God willing, for dinner. By which time,' he added, laughing, 'we should be fairly well acquainted with each other, whether we like it or not.' It was practically as though her husband his brother had not been there.

If she did not reply in words, she could not very well withhold the semblance of a smile from one in whose glance she recognized the provocative candour of the boy in the miniature. Not to have smiled would have made her appear sour, she thought, or offended by neglect.

Soon afterwards a drizzle started blowing in their faces. Her husband coughed and felt his coat. It was cold for the time of year. Trees in cottage gardens were heavy with unripened fruit.

Garnet Roxburgh apologized that their vehicle lacked a hood. 'Does the rain inconvenience you?' he asked her, instead of his obviously fretting brother.

'Not at all,' she replied. 'I am used to it.'

Again, in memory, she was Ellen Gluyas driving her cart to market at Penzance. Had they noticed her smile the Roxburghs might have found irony there.

But they remained unaware, and she was moved to take her husband's hand. She squeezed it and he looked surprised, wondering at the reason for her gesture.

They toiled on. The drizzle was blown past and behind them. Above an uneven crop of oats, through a gap in darkling trees, hung the faintest smudge of rainbow. She could feel her cheeks glowing, not only from the chill, but from the veiled surprises the country had to offer at every turn. Nor would she let a brother-in-law she must continue to dislike detract from her enjoyment.

'Here we are,' Mr Garnet Roxburgh was able at last to announce, 'at "Dulcet" – if not for dinner, then not long after.'

The horses were heading for feed and water down a lane to one side, but he pulled on their mouths and brought them to a standstill beside a white-painted wicket-gate set in a hedge and guarded by two cypresses. The hedge was of thickset clipped box; the cypresses had been trimmed too, as well as decapitated, which gave the precincts a military, if not a penal air. Faced with such rigid discipline almost any new arrival must have been deterred from judging the house itself at first glance, though it seemed pleasing enough, built for comfort rather than for show, even if drastically improved by those who had 'succeeded' in it. The general impression was of a low, widespreading structure behind a shallow veranda, the body of the house extended to considerable depth through subsidiary rooms and offices. Windows let into a shingle roof betrayed a cramped upper storey, probably for the use of servants.

Mrs Roxburgh felt she might have grown to love 'Dulcet', had fate planted her in it and her brother-in-law not been there.

Or perhaps she was being unjust. Perhaps he had a genuine love for the place, if for nothing and no one else; to have had them trim the hedge and the cypresses with such precision, and to have called for the painting of the wicket and the woodwork in general. For that matter, he may have loved the widow he married, who died in the unexplained accident.

'Aren't we coming down?' he was shouting to passengers deaf or numbed.

The light glinted on his teeth; his arms were open to receive his sister-in-law.

But Mrs Roxburgh waited for her husband to descend and turn in her direction, after which she accepted a hand she would have chafed, had she been given a less public opportunity.

Barking dogs were silenced by their interest as they started smelling her skirt between gulps of disapproval; while two men with disenchanted Irish faces and amorphous garments fumbled for the baggage stowed in the tray beneath the buggy seat.

On the veranda steps two women of nicer appearance than the pair of rustics attending to the luggage waited to greet the visitors.

'This is my housekeeper – Mrs Brennan,' Mr Garnet indicated the older of the women in a would-be jovial, though offhand manner.

In her middle age, the housekeeper seemingly suffered from nerves. Her lips trembled halfway towards a smile when guided by Mrs Roxburgh's example. The hair straggling from beneath a clean, though somewhat crushed cap, added to her air of distraction. Mrs Roxburgh had but a blurred impression of Mrs Brennan, much as though catching sight of the moon through tatters of grey-white, wind-wracked cloud.

'And Holly, her helper.' Garnet Roxburgh grew ever more offhand in his introductions.

While Mrs Brennan might have been handsome in her youth, the young girl was emphatically pretty at the present day, and in spite of a shapeless, grey dress and slovenly cap. Probably bold by nature, she was now intimidated almost to the point of tears by the arrival of strangers, perhaps also by her master's brusqueness, as well as the hubbub of dogs barking and wheels grating as the horses strained to be gone to their provender, the Irish cursing them to hold hard.

The visitors would have retired willingly to their own quarters and given way to their exhaustion, had it not been required of them to listen, admire, recount, and feast until well into the evening. They excused themselves from supper. At last they might have comforted each other, but Mr Roxburgh became convinced that the sheets on their great bed were damp. It was only the cold, she tried to persuade him. Damp was damp, he insisted; his sense of touch never deceived him. After wrapping himself in his coat and a couple of travelling rugs he announced that he would spend the night on the sofa. It was beyond her powers to reassure or comfort him, nor could she feel comforted herself, lying alone between the suspect sheets.

Not until morning was Mrs Roxburgh able to review her first impressions in tranquillity and what she believed to be detachment, and to record some of them in her journal after a late breakfast in their room. Settling herself in the loose muslin which sunlight and birdsong warranted, she prepared to indulge her blandest vice.

4 Nov 1835

Only now begin to feel revived after yesterday's journey and arrival. To catch sight of the bullock-wagon straining down the lane with our heavier trunks (and what our host described as a few of the 'unnecessary though indispensable luxuries' purchased by him in Hobart Town) has refreshed me more than anything. Mr R. will be the happier for laying hands on his books, myself simply from having my own belongings around me. To make my home in the wilderness!

There is no reason why I shld sound so ungrateful when Garnet R. is kindness itself. He is now gone about the business of the farm, and again I will sound ungrateful if I say I am just as glad. There is no reason for this. My dislike is quite *un*reasonable. I can tell that my Mr R. does not intend to take an active part in the life at 'Dulcet' (not through any lack of affection for his brother). He has already informed me in private that sheep and cows were all very well when he was courting the farmer's daughter, but in normal circumstances (outside of the pages of Virgil) they can only be counted among the bores. So it will be *my* duty to take an interest. There is no *reason* why I shld not. The country is both pretty and wild, the property evidently prosperous, the house spacious and filled with unexpected comforts, altogether unlike our own poor hugermuger farm at Z.

By all accounts the late Mrs Garnet Roxburgh's means was inherited from her first husband. In the dining-room hang portraits of Mrs Garnet and her Dormer spouse. After a glass or two of wine Mr R. remarked to his brother that he would have removed the likenesses instead of keeping them there as reminders. G. R. points out that they are valued as property in these parts – the frames alone. To be sure these are elaborately carved and heavy gilded, but what is within them does not please. Mrs (Dormer) Roxburgh has a long, an *ob*-long face, very pallid and shiny, not unlike lard. The lips are shown unnatural red, though perhaps the artist has attempted to give her a liveliness her flesh lacked. A dull but shrewd woman, I wld say, and attracted evidently to gentlemen of high complexion. If G. R. is ruddy-skinned, the late Dormer's cheeks were inflamed, and I recognize too well the look of his rather watery eye. Garnet too, enjoys his wine, from grapes grown on the place, the vines planted by Mr Dormer in the beginning. At dinner my usually abstemious husband was led on by his brother and caused me some embarrassment by proposing a toast which would have gladdened my heart in private, but not in the presence of G. R. I was too tired to more than pick at the fat goose they had killed by way of celebration, and cld not touch the pudding at all. I got away as soon as decency allowed and left the brothers to their childhood and youth.

Till Mr R. shld tear himself away I decided to make some effort at friendship with the housekeeper, who I found in the great stone kitchen scraping dishes, the girl helping. Mrs B. is a decent soul but suffers from a troubled mind I wld say. Several times I was told that she and her husband were 'free settlers'. When the husband (a glazier) died she was forced to look for a situation and came out from Hobart as cook to Mr and Mrs Dormer, who were good to her she says. She wld like to find good in everybody, unlike myself who more often sees the bad. Must take Mrs B. as an example, though it cld be with her as with so many others, more in her talk than in her thoughts. For instance I do not believe she sees all that good in her present master though she wld die rather than admit her secret view. While the girl Holly was gone outside to throw the scrapings to the dogs Mrs B. again informed me that she was a free settler, but that the girl had been deported from the Old Country for theft, and had done a term before being assigned. The twenty-odd men employed by my brother-in-law are all assigned servants. At dinner he referred to them as his 'miscreants', which I expect they are.

How much of the miscreant, I wonder, is in Garnet R.? Or in *myself* for that matter? I know that I have lied when necessary and am at times what the truly virtuous call 'hypocritical'. If I am not all good (only my dearest husband is that) I am not excessively bad. How far is it to the point where one oversteps the bounds? I wld like to talk to these miscreants, to satisfy myself, but do not expect I ever will.

While Holly was still absent in the yard I inquired of Mrs Brennan the nature of her mistress's accident. She became most disturbed, kept repeating that what is past is best forgot. Then it all came out as if she had only been waiting to tell – how the master while taking his wife for a drive along the mountain road had overturned the gig. Her neck was broke!

Later

I will concentrate on things other than the above – on the fine room in which we are installed, off it a little dressing-room where I am at present writing, while Mr R. is gone into the library, but only to read the books he has with him, some of which he has already unpacked (Virgil often makes me jealous!). The day is warm, if threatening. Outside my window an orchard: apricots and plums, as far as I can see, the crop only now colouring, and to one side a kitchen garden with raspberry canes as a separating hedge. Bees are on their way across the orchard to more rewarding pastures. Of all the birds I can hear, one (a goldfinch?) perched on a hawthorn outside my window reminds me with his thread of song that the line which divides contentment from melancholy is but a narrow one ...

When she had dressed herself, Mrs Roxburgh fancied taking a walk before dinner, but first went in search of her husband to ask whether he would consider keeping her company.

'Do you suppose I should be more profitably occupied?' He sounded and looked grumpy from behind his gold spectacles.

Then, when he had collected his outer wits, the skin gathered at the corners of his eyes, as he knew he must forgive her for her interruption. 'Thank you, no, dear Ellen,' he said, and they were re-united.

Leaving the library she passed through the house and realized too late that she had made for the kitchen offices (how her origins caught up with her!) where she found Holly in a store-room transferring, or rather, hurling potatoes from a sack into a wooden box. It was obvious the girl resented a task which had become unbearably tedious. Some of the potatoes fell wide of the box and bounced across the flags. A fine red dust from unwashed potatoes hung in the air.

The intruder sneezed, and the girl's nose was swollen, either from sneezing, or she could have been crying.

'What has made you unhappy, Holly?' Mrs Roxburgh ventured.

The girl snivelled, then broke into outright blubbering through swelling, plum-skin lips. 'Nothing!' she sobbed.

Realizing that Holly's nothing was equivalent to everything, the older woman regretted her misguided inquiry and tried to make amends. 'You must not upset yourself,' she advised; and unwiser still, 'Sooner or later you will find happiness in marriage with some honest man.'

'Marriage is not for me!' the girl positively howled, 'or if it is, it'll be old pertaters – or worse!' as she hurled a many-eyed monster across the floor.

Holly was in no mind to accept reason as the antidote to despair, so Mrs Roxburgh left her. Preparing to cross the yard, she stood an instant balanced on the edge of the step. The girl's fate might have been her own, that of a scullery-maid becoming a drudge-wife, had a rich man's caprice not saved her from it. Hardly caprice when Austin Roxburgh had loved her according to the rules of honour and reason. The years gave proof.

The sunlight which filled the yard, pandering to basking hens and a trio of white-frilled turkeys, should have dismissed any trace of an unreasonable sense of guilt. But sight of a pair of assigned men lazing on their axehandles instead of splitting a pile of logs caused her to move awkwardly. One touched his pudding-basin hat, the second ignored her. Their murmurs pursued her across the yard increasing her embarrassment. Yet their comments, if they were, remained unintelligible, and were overlaid besides, by a drooling of hens and the *pink-pink* of turkey poults. There was nothing to explain why she should feel ashamed; certainly not her clothes: a modest bonnet and her oldest walking-dress.

She was only at ease when received into the countryside. On the one hand lay fields divided by timber roughly piled to form barriers rather than fences and divide crops from herds and flocks; on the other, forest which neither invited nor repelled those who might feel tempted to investigate a passive mystery. She thought she might be tempted, but for the present yielded herself to the glare from emerald pastures and delight in the rounded flanks of grazing lambs.

Presently the road forked and she chose the lesser, its ribbon threaded through the trees fringing a mountainside. It was not long before she was enveloped by sombre forest; the road grew rougher, the light whiter, keener, at such moments when it succeeded in slashing its way through foliage. She became breathless in the course of her climb and undid her bonnet-strings, and shed the intolerable pelisse, and regretted that the soles of her boots offered so little protection from stones.

At one point a path, or more precisely, a tunnel, invited her to enter. She was walking for the most part over moss, breathing the air of another climate, amongst trees the butts of which were in some cases spongy as cork, in others hard as armour. Clumps of low-growing shrubs were draped with parasite flowers as white and lacy as bridal veils. Fronds of giant ferns caressed her, and she in turn caressed the brown fur which clothed their formal crooks.

She was so entranced she sat down in a small clearing intending to enjoy her surroundings while resting, in a dappled shade, on the compost of decaying leaves and bark, regardless of any possibility of damp and spiders. Removing the superfluous bonnet and loosening her matted hair, she felt only remotely related to Ellen Roxburgh, or even Ellen Gluyas; she was probably closer to the being her glass could not reveal, nor her powers of perception grasp, but whom she suspected must exist none the less.

The delicious cool, the only half-repellent smell of rotting vegetation, perhaps some deeper prepossession of her own, all were combining to drug her, at first with mild insidiousness, then with overwhelming insistence. She could have been drifting at the bottom of the sea, in the cove which had awaited the ship's prow, carved and festive. Then he was bending over her. She put up her hand to touch the incipient stubble on a ruddy cheek. Their plumskin mouths, perfectly matched, received each other, flowing, over-flowing, withdrawing. When she noticed a flaw: his lower lip had a dint in its too pronounced upholstery. Repulsion drowned the attraction she had felt. Tears were falling, warm and sticky, which she realized were not hers. The girl Holly was holding a knife in grief or anger. *You cannot frighten me Holly I am not the one you intend to kill.* The girl mumbling she will not serve another term it is the potato-eyes she is preparing to nick.

Mrs Roxburgh awoke all but choked by her dream, her boots protruding foolishly from under the hem of her skirt. The spangled net of sunlight had been raised from the clearing in which she lay, leaving her surrounded by a black and hostile undergrowth. Seizing her bonnet by the strings, and without thinking to brush herself clean of twigs and leaves, she hurried down the tunnel to regain the road. Here too, the sun had withdrawn. Uncontrolled impetus carried her downhill, her ankles twisting on the stones she dislodged, her breath sounding exasperated rather than distressed.

It was indeed exasperating now that she had reached the cultivated fields and grazing sheep not to be able to piece together a dream which was already becoming indistinct.

More than exasperating, it was something of a shock to hear the sound of hooves approaching at her back. She hurried on and hoped that the swollen rain-clouds overhead would convince the oncoming rider that there was good reason for her otherwise unnatural pace.

When the horse was only a few yards distant a man's voice called, 'If you would like to try, we could hoist you up, to ride pillion, or on the pommel, if you prefer.'

'Thank you, Mr Roxburgh,' she answered without turning her head. 'It would be far too awkward.'

At that moment the horse drew level, and Garnet Roxburgh bent down from the saddle and brushed from her back a few leaves which must have remained clinging there. She could only have looked a fright, her hair in disarray, her bonnet dangling by its strings from her fingers.

He made no comment apart from, 'I don't believe you trust me, Ellen,' in a tone of voice which only half-suggested he might be mocking.

'I can see no reason why I should not.' Speech was difficult in her state of breathlessness, and she blushed besides, for she had in fact been wondering whether the mountain road she had taken on her walk was that on which the gig had overturned and Mrs Garnet Roxburgh broke her neck.

'I enjoy walking,' she informed him, to add something to what was hardly a conversation.

'Do you ride as well?'

'I did. But Mr Roxburgh has forbidden it – since I took a fall.'

'Only one? A man can't claim to be a horseman till he's taken at least seven tumbles.'

She felt foolish in that she was unable to explain that her first had fatal consequences.

'If that old woman my brother would allow it, I have a little black mare which would suit you to perfection. Any lady who has tried her out sings her praises.'

Mrs Roxburgh blushed again, for her impulse was to ask whether many ladies had tried out the little black mare.

At this moment they were caught up in a preliminary squall of rain.

'You see,' he shouted as his horse went into a caracol, 'you should have accepted my offer!'

'Oh, but we are almost there!' she gasped, her cheeks slapped by the cold rain, her skirt ballooning as the wind got full possession of it.

She hurried to reach the shelter of the yard. There the two assigned men were attacking the wood-pile in a frenzy to demonstrate to the master their addiction for work, till such a deluge began, it was only sensible to take refuge with their axes in the barn.

Mr Austin Roxburgh was still comfortably seated in the library in front of a fire Mrs Brennan had lit against the cold.

'You are wet through,' he said to his wife with a resignation which suggested that he had expected nothing short of this.

'And you soon will be!' she rejoined.

It had not occurred to him to close a window through which the torrents were dashing.

She kissed his forehead and went to change.

In the morning Mrs Roxburgh lingered at writing in her journal, a luxury she appreciated increasingly since they had set out on their travels.

. . . anoyed with myself for not being able to remember this tantalizing dream. It has become no more than a blurred sensation. Did not mention it to Mr R. because he might find me ridiculous – or *irrational*.

While I was changing from my wet clothes Holly came to my door. Mrs B. has decided it will be one of the girl's duties to act as Lady's Maid. Holly had recovered from her black thoughts of the same morning. She was pretty and glossy as before. She wld like to enjoy some fun if I can cure her of her shyness. I gave her my figured poplin and the pair of ear-rings with bunches of garnets set in gilt leaves. H. was overcome, neeled and kissed my hands, I felt her tears on them. She said she had never owned anything so grand. I wld have felt more gratified had I not been sick of that old poplin and had I not thought the ear-rings made me look what Aunt Tite used to call 'trumpery'. Poor Holly has no means of knowing and looks like some pretty gypsy with bunches of glossy grapes in her ears.

At dinner Mr G. R. introduced the subject of the black mare. He is a man who will not be put off. My good husband yawned and said I might ride the mare if I felt inclined and she was not a mad-headed runaway. Garnet said he would ride her at the mountain a few times till she was recovered from a spell of unemployment and too much oats. Asked Mr R. as we prepared for bed was he no longer concerned that I might fall. He teased me and said I was less valuable for belonging to him these many years.

During the night heard sounds overhead as of heavy footsteps, muffled voices, occasional laughter. Mentioned it to Mr R. this morning, who claimed he had heard nothing. This surprised me as he complanes he is such a poor sleeper. I cld not resist reminding him. He said it is so, he does not get half the sleep he needs, but sometimes goes off into a doze, and whatever I *imagined* hearing must have occurred while he was in that condition.

When Mrs B. brought breakfast I returned to the noise I had heard and said I was at first afraid some escaped prisoner or 'bush-ranger' had broke in. The woman acted more than usually nervous – said she had been suffering from a toothache in the night and was looking for something to relieve the pain.

She did not return to collect the dishes but sent the girl who I also questioned. Asked whether the house was haunted, and had I perhaps heard a *ghost*. Holly's cheeks looked radiant, but her shyness returned. Said there was no ghost she had ever met. She had tried on her lovely gown on going upstairs, for Mrs Brennan to admire, and the two had been wondering what kind of husband she might get now that she can pass as a lady. A simple guessing-game such as I will never again enjoy!

After breakfast, after they were dressed, Mr Roxburgh said with an abruptness which startled his wife, 'How long, Ellen, do you suppose we ought to stay before we can decently escape from "Dulcet"?'

Mrs Roxburgh felt she had been ambushed. 'When we came

out for you to be with the brother you haven't seen in years? And Christmas not yet here!'

'Oh, well – yes – yes.' Mr Roxburgh wagged his head and shuffled.

Ellen Roxburgh was oppressed by her own glib words and a sensation as of her stays filling with an ampler form than the years she had actually lived with her respected husband could warrant. She recoiled at once from this premonition of a complacent, cosseted middle-age – by which time (if she reached it) the respected husband would more than likely have left her a widow.

Later in the morning as she sat with her sewing (a hated duty she sometimes prescribed for herself) she heard a thundering outside, and on looking out of the window, caught sight of Garnet Roxburgh on what she took to be her black mare. She was in a lather, nostrils distended pink, from being 'ridden at the mountain', Mrs Roxburgh presumed. Evidently the mare was to become one of her more unavoidable prescribed duties.

A few evenings later she was pouring tea for the gentlemen when her brother-in-law announced without preamble, 'Your mount is chastened, if you feel any inclination to try her.'

Austin Roxburgh, who had consented almost cynically to her riding the horse, at once grew anxious. 'Not alone, Ellen! I would not like you to ride alone. But there is no reason why you should not accompany Garnet when he rides out on whatever business calls him.' Anyone must have recognized 'that old woman' to whom his brother had laughingly referred.

Mrs Roxburgh gave no definite answer as she stirred the sugar in her tea.

In the morning, however, she sent the girl to the master to tell him that, if he would not be overly delayed, she thought she would ride out with him that morning.

That he must be delayed, she knew, for she lingered over dressing, hoping that she might change her mind, or Garnet Roxburgh leave without her.

Holly, hooking her into the habit, was again in the sulks. 'Ah,' she sighed when questioned, and answered as usual, ''tis nothing.'

Then she said, 'She's a pretty little horse, and gentle – if you don't lay whip or spur to her.'

'Oh? Do you know?'

'Mr Roxburgh allowed me to ride her. He taught me. He said I might use her sometimes – as a recreation – when she's not wanted by anybody else.'

Mrs Roxburgh was adjusting her hat. Her hand trembled at the prospect of finding herself in the saddle again.

'Is she so much in use?'

'Oh, no. Only by Mrs Aspinall – when she comes.'

'Mrs Aspinall?'

'The doctor's wife.'

'Is she here often?'

The girl replied, 'Not very,' and held the glass for her lady to see whether she looked trim.

Mrs Roxburgh might have looked handsome, in her hard hat, from behind the tightly gathered net veil, had she allowed herself to approve. But her thoughts were so far distracted that she even forgot to take leave of her husband.

In the yard the assigned man who acted as groom stood holding the mare beside a mounting-block. She flashed the white of an eye in the direction of her prospective mistress, but seemed docile enough. Mr Garnet Roxburgh was already mounted on a thickset strawberry roan. He sat with the glimmer of a smile on his face, whether in approval or mild censure it was impossible to tell.

Their setting forth was sedate enough. After curveting briefly, the mare responded to her rider's touch, perhaps sensing the hand of experience, for Ellen Gluyas had often bounced bareback for fun on their own hairy Cornish nag en route for serious labours in the fields, before she had ever ridden on more elegant and aimless expeditions on the slopes beyond Cheltenham.

Mr Garnet Roxburgh might have approved of his companion's seat. He glanced sideways once or twice, and down at the fall of her bottle-green skirt, without comment, however.

'What is her name?' Mrs Roxburgh asked, and her voice, she thought, sounded flat enough to match her insipid inquiry.

He considered it unnecessary to name horses, but some liked to call the mare 'Merle'. Mrs Roxburgh wondered which of Them it was.

When they had ridden a little way he suddenly raised his arm,

87

embracing the landscape as it were, with a sweeping, almost passionate gesture. 'Do you believe you would come across lusher pastures anywhere on earth?'

'I have not seen everywhere on earth.'

'Oh, come! As dry as my brother. That was a manner of speaking. Out of your experience, I meant.' He looked at her meaningly.

There was every reason why he should know that his brother had married her off a farm, so she did not hesitate in her reply. 'Ours was for the most part poor land – swept by winds from the sea. It could not compare with such luxuriance as this. But for all its poverty, I loved it,' she added.

To have humbled her seemed to have appeased him.

He said quite gently, 'I did not mean to hurt your feelings.'

She was not so sure.

A little farther on a flock of sturdy lambs stood grazing in a field of brilliant clover. She was about to express her delight when Garnet Roxburgh, who had not at first noticed the lambs, caught sight of them, and shouted at the top of his voice, 'God sod the bastard shepherds! But what can you expect of the scrapings from the streets of Dublin and London?'

There was no sign of any shepherd to prevent the flock pushing through a gap in a fence roughly built of logs. Garnet Roxburgh spurred forward, wheeled the lambs, and soon had them scampering back through the break. After which, he jumped down, and started to repair the collapsed fence by dragging three or four logs into place. Although not of the heaviest, they were awkward in shape and jagged where the branches had been lopped. As she rode up to rejoin him, she noticed the blood trickling from the back of one of his hands. His shirt was wet from his exertion and his face closed in anger.

She decided not to disturb what would have been silence except for his panting and a coughing from the now stationary lambs.

Still silent, Garnet Roxburgh re-mounted, and they made, purposefully it seemed, towards a patch of thinned-out scrub on a near-by rise. Here she saw a hut had been built out of its grey, natural surroundings from which it was all but indistinguishable.

The master started shouting again, and two slaves came tumbling out from under the thatch of leaves. 'By Ghost,' he cursed, 'if those lambs bloat you'll regret it! Do you suppose I employ you to grog yourselves stupid before the sun is properly up? If I wasn't such a soft-hearted noodle I'd set up my own private triangle and see my own justice done. Now, go to it!'

As the two shepherds, bleary from sleep and spirits, stumbled past in the direction of their flock, Mrs Roxburgh detected the authentic blast of rum. She might have been more distressed by memories if the present situation had disgusted her less. She could not sympathize with the neglectful and unsavoury 'miscreants', but was sickened by the uncontrolled passion of their master, who let fly at their shoulders with his whip before they were out of range.

His rage abating somewhat, they continued their ride, though without any definite aim, she felt. Garnet Roxburgh had withdrawn to brood amongst his thoughts.

In the circumstances she was relieved to notice flies gathering where the blood had oozed from the gash on the back of his hand. 'Have you a clean handkerchief?' she asked. 'I'll bind up the wound. My own handkerchief is too small to be of any use.'

He said no he had not, and proceeded to suck the wound with such concentration she thought she recognized more than a trace of his brother's hypochondria.

Until dropping his hand to the pommel of his saddle he remarked in what was intended as a lighter tone, 'You will not have a good opinion of me, Ellen.'

She was about to protest, against her true feelings, when he began afresh, 'You have never, I think, found me in the least congenial.' He laughed. 'You had decided against me long before we had so much as met.'

His charges were the more intolerable for being wholly true.

The black mare whinged and jumped on experiencing her rider's whip. 'You are making such false accusations,' Mrs Roxburgh lied unconvincingly.

'And are not prepared to take into account – unless they have taught you to disbelieve – all that I have gone through.'

'Oh, your wife! I know. And imagine how often you must relive the dreadful moment!'

'Which moment?'

'Why – if you ask – when the gig overturned.'

They rode in silence; then Garnet Roxburgh kicked out with his nearside boot in what must have been an involuntary spasm and struck her stirrup-iron through her skirt.

'It was not overturned,' he had decided to tell her. 'I took a corner too fast and the unfortunate woman was pitched out.'

Mrs Roxburgh could not decide whether she should sympathize more – or less. The fact that the subject had been raised at all, confused her.

'Either way,' she said, 'it was a tragedy'; and hoped it could be left at that.

They rode a little.

'You will not consider me sensitive enough to experience loneliness.'

She would have liked to believe, and guilt might have persuaded her had her glance not fallen on the wrist of the hand holding the reins; as on their drive from Hobart Town, she could feel repulsion rising in her.

'I am surprised,' she said, 'that at your age you did not remarry.' Although younger herself, she could enjoy the prerogative of the married woman to advise her widower brother-in-law.

He snorted somewhat bitterly, 'Marriage does not always cancel loneliness. And desirable partners have for the most part been whirled off in the dance by others more fortunate.'

Almost poetic, and coming from Garnet Roxburgh it did make her slightly sympathize.

She went so far as to say, 'Now it is your turn not to believe, but I am sorry for you.' At the same time she became aware that she had stiffened herself against the motion of her horse.

They must have returned by another way, for there, nestled in a hollow below them, she noticed the homestead, a picture of idyllic landed ease.

Garnet Roxburgh leaned down and stripped the head from a stalk of grass. 'In any case it will soon be Christmas, and then perhaps you will unbend, Ellen.'

'You are the one,' she cried, 'who holds unmerited opinions of others!'

He grinned and threw away the crushed grass-seed. 'I have invited friends to keep us company. Dear old Austin will love the opportunity of subjecting Dr Aspinall to interrogation on the moral, aesthetic, and scientific development of Van Diemen's Land, while you, I hope, will take to the doctor's wife. Maggie Aspinall is a lively and amusing young woman – not altogether appreciated by Hobart Town.'

Mrs Roxburgh confined herself to general murmurs of anticipated appreciation. 'Is that the river?' she asked, pointing with her riding-crop.

He looked at her sharply. 'Why, yes – that is the Derwent – beyond the house.' He had a certain expression for those he suspected of evading him, which she could not resist turning to catch before it left his face.

'It has been a lovely outing,' she said, 'but I am glad to be home – to describe for Mr Roxburgh all that I have seen.'

As they rode into the yard the same marionette of a servant was waiting to receive their horses.

That night she slept soundly, but awoke once to find tears on her cheeks and pillow, and realized that she had been dreaming of their misfortune, her second, consummate child, of whom they had never spoken again. She was glad to hear Mr Roxburgh snoring beside her; it would have been too painful had he asked her the reason for her tears, and soon, thanks to the fresh air and exercise that day, she was again soundly asleep.

Before long, Mrs Roxburgh was able to record in her journal:

Christmas Day, 1835

At 'Dulcet', Van Diemen's Land

. . . so little like what we know, I can scarcely take it seriously. Mild, but a sultriness could be preparing to descend upon us. No sign of rejoicing. After all, most of the poor wretches are 'prisoners' and what have they to rejoice about beyond the prospect of getting drunk in the course of the day? I would like to talk to them, but there is a gulf between us, and I have lost the art of common speech.

Mr R. gave me a nice kiss, saying he had forgot my present this year. Told him we have each other and need no presents, though I had embroidered him a book-mark.

Garnet R. has not come to life. I am not surprised since last night.

On the Eve the Aspinalls arrived from Hobart Town and we shall be subjected to them while the *festivities* last. Don't know why I shld seem to complane. They are in every way aimiable – at least Dr A. who is what one knows from Home as a reliable provinshul physician. I am less sure of his wife. She has a mole above her left eyebrow which I constantly find myself staring at. After we had left the gentlemen to finish their wine, she says 'I hope you will call me "Maggie". I am sure we will be great friends.' In replying I did not commit myself to words, but mumbled a few sounds which she cld interpret any way she chose. Mrs A. understood and was not put out, because this is the way she expects herself and others to behave. She began a great chatter about her friends in town, said I must pay her a *prolonged visit* and make the acquaintance of all these people, some of them 'charming', more of them 'ridiculous', while implying that this did not lower them in her esteem. I said I would pay her a visit only if my husband agreed, and again we understood each other. She asked whether I played or sang, and I replied, both a little, but so badly I never performed in public, and for myself only on wet days. She then sat down and went into a few runs at the Dormer piano, and tried out her voice in a rehearsal for her audience of gentlemen.

Mrs A. is what passes for pretty. Dark curls ajingle in her livelier moments which occur very frequently. Her cap all French lace and forget-me-nots, and her gown, in which I recognized the fashion of several years ago (not surprising in Van Diemen's Land) low-cut to show a handsome bust, the bodice trimmed with numerous little pink bows. Mrs A. informed me that the material of her dress was *gro de Naples* and she had paid a fortune for it.

What with the gentlemen lingering over their wine, the musician and I grew pale with yawns. Mrs A.'s colour returned as her audience arrived in the drawing-room. Mr R. would have liked to benefit from Dr Aspinall's medical advice, but the dr too far gone. Garnet R. leaned on the piano, all attention, and the lady was soon playing for him alone. I might have left them to it if 'Maggie' wld not have thought I was shirking a duty by not staying to pour tea.

I did go out to take the air and stroll a little. The moon was in its first quarter, the river a faint, silver coil in the distance. Often on such a night at Z., a country to which I *belonged* (more than I did to parents or family) I wld find myself wishing to be united with my surroundings, not as the dead, but fully alive. Here too, in spite of gratitude and love for a husband as dependent on me as I on him, I begin to feel closer to the country than to any human being. Reason, and the little I learned from the books I was given too late in life to more than fidget over, tells me I am wrong in thinking thus, but my instincts hanker after something deeper, which I may not experience this side of death.

So it seemed this Christmas Eve at 'Dulcet'. I might have grown disgusted with the inhuman side of my nature had I not realized that the music had stopped, and that the vastness was filled only with silence and the call of a single melancholy bird. As I returned in the direction of the house I began to hear voices, muffled at first, in opposition to my night-bird. By such a watery moonlight I cld not have distinguished the forms of those engaged in conversation, who in any case remained the other side of the box hedge. My heart bumped as I trod the uneven ground, and I almost fell by catching a foot in a cow-print which had set hard. Then I heard from across the hedge a hoarse female laughter which conveyed to me the picture of Mrs Aspinall's throat. Afterwards her words, 'Oh no, you will spoil my dress! Please, Garnet!' More laughter as he fumbled (I could not tell for sure, but sure I was). He mumbled 'Maggie!' over and over, as drunkenly as one of his despised shepherds. 'And tomorrow is Christmas Day.' 'Should we not go in?' Mrs A. asked. 'Your sister-in-law may realize we are gone too long, and disapprove. She seems to me lacking entirely in human warmth, and prickly with moral principles.' G. R. might have been retching. 'Ellen is morality itself!' 'Then let us – shall we? go in?' sighed Mrs A. There was the sound of what could have been a man's hard palm sliding exasperated down a stone surface as they disengaged.

I wld have liked to retire immediately had Holly not brought the tea things and I was forced to preside. When we were at last in our own room I cld not make up my mind how much to tell Mr R. So I told him nothing of what I had not seen, but experienced more or less, from the other side of the box hedge.

And now it is Christmas Day . . .

After he had risen and breakfasted, Garnet Roxburgh sent warning through Mrs Brennan that they would be driven to church in the carriage. Mrs Roxburgh relayed the information to her husband in what may have sounded an apathetic tone.

'Isn't it what we have done all our lives in accordance with what is expected of us?' Austin Roxburgh asked of his wife.

She replied, 'Yes.'

'Then I ask you – whatever you may feel – to prepare yourself as soon as possible – so that Garnet's friends may not take offence.'

Mrs Roxburgh obeyed.

The carriage, a large, open affair, not inelegant for the country, was drawn up beside the wicket-gate. Their host looked morose and livery, but did the honours by the ladies in handing them up to the middle seat. The two husbands sat facing their wives, backs to the coachman.

Mrs Aspinall was so busy accommodating her sleeves and expressing fears for her feather hat in an open carriage, she had no eyes for Garnet Roxburgh. His sister-in-law could not resist glancing his way, but once, whereupon he climbed up, and seated himself out of view of the ladies.

Those of the assigned men who were of the Protestant faith had been sent off in advance to walk the two or three miles to the church, while those who were beyond the pale she had noticed loitering in the yard with the barely concealed expression of anticipated carousal on their Irish mugs. On the other hand, the two women standing in the porch, watching the gentry depart, might have been remembering the last occasion they had received the wafer on their tongues: their faces were so altered in shape by melancholy sentiments.

Nothing happened on the journey except that Mrs Aspinall's hat almost blew off as they crossed the bridge.

Arrived at the church, Garnet Roxburgh, seemingly a warden, left them to attend to his duties. The congregation eyed his companions, particularly the relatives from Home. When they entered the commodious, though rather cold and forbidding church, the assigned population was already seated at the rear. Mr Garnet Roxburgh's party was ushered to the most prominent pews, an arrangement which Mrs Aspinall accepted with evident satisfaction, but this being Christmas Day, their company was unavoidably split, the doctor and his wife squeezed into the front row, immediately in front of the Austin Roxburghs, beside whom, between the aisle and Mrs Austin's right, a place was reserved presumably for Garnet. Mrs Aspinall made a considerable show of devotion, kneeling in rapt prayer, her plumed hat inclined above suppliant hands. So Mrs Roxburgh observed, who could not give herself to prayer this morning; her only thought was whether she dare suggest to her husband that they change places.

There was little in this austere temple to provoke those who look upon decoration as an incitement to sin and Popery, nor inspire others of shy sensibility who need signposts before they can venture along the paths of private mysticism. The only aesthetic stimulus to worship was provided by the lilies and roses bunched too tight and too upright in a pair of narrow-necked brass vases, one at each end of the communion table, and round the central arch a riband on which was inscribed in letters of gold, HOLY HOLY HOLY LORD GOD OF HOSTS.

While Mrs Roxburgh was pondering why the text should not be altogether to her taste, her brother-in-law came and took his place beside her. She thought he might have smiled at her, but was busy making more room for him by moving closer to her husband. Even so, Garnet Roxburgh tended to overflow against her. As he leaned forward in prayer, she could hear the cloth stretched to cracking across his shoulders, and when he eased himself back in his seat, she felt his thigh pressed inescapably into her skirt.

Mrs Roxburgh glanced at her husband, who sat staring straight ahead with characteristic gravity, waiting for the service to begin. Although hardly a man of implicit faith, respect for his mother and his dedication to *ipse Pater* had induced him to pay lip-service to the Christian religion. His wife was not to guess where faith ended and principle took over, but knowing her own limits and her husband's trusting nature, she would have liked to squeeze his hand, to demonstrate that they were the solid core in a largely incomprehensible world.

The service at All Saints was conducted with a fervour only convincing in that the season was Christmas. The 'prisoners' at the rear belted out the psalms and hymns as if they could not have done other than give of their best and heartiest. As the hosts swept onward against the foe, Mrs Roxburgh was again disturbed by her reluctance to accept the text on the riband garlanding the archway ahead. Yet there was no reason to complain when she belonged on the winning side.

It was in this frame of mind that she grew over-conscious of Garnet Roxburgh's voice, a not-unpleasing baritone. He might have been singing for her alone, whereas on Christmas Eve, she realized, he had not sung a note for the lively Maggie Aspinall. Mrs Roxburgh became distracted, vague, lost her place, which her brother-in-law found for her. His hand still had a scab on it from repairing the log fence the day they rode out together. Perhaps she would become indisposed, but it might not help; Garnet would surely carry her out.

In fact it was Mrs Aspinall who staged the indisposition during the last hymn but one, and that did not help either, because her

95

husband who was a doctor supported her as far as the porch. Mrs Roxburgh wondered whether she should follow, and lend her friend the moral support which only a woman can give another (at the same time it would remove her from the pressure of Garnet Roxburgh's thigh) but she failed unhappily to extricate herself.

At all events, it came to an end, not only the quavered sermon, but the turkey (one of the whites they had slaughtered for the occasion) and the martyrdom of Holly who all but dropped the dish on which she was bearing Mrs Brennan's fiery pudding ('it'll singe the last of me eyelashes off') and the roistering in the barn across the yard (somebody fell and the doctor was sent for). Her pale moon unusually flushed in its familiar wrack of grey-white cloud, Mrs Brennan made a brief appearance in a door-way, but must have thought better of her intention, for she drifted into obscurity.

Mrs Roxburgh wrote in her journal with what was only to some extent satisfaction and restored equanimity:

29 Dec 1835
The Aspinalls have been gone these two days. We are again plunged in monotony and peace. I do not complane, nor that the days are droning ones. If we are to continue in Van Diemen's Land, for what purpose even Mr R. can no longer see, I would not have it spring too many untoward surprises.

Mrs A. repeated that she wished I wld pay her a long visit, and I agreed that nothing wld please me better than to leave the brothers to recall their youth. Thus we parted on a note of 'friendliness' and no expectations of each other.

Mr R. and the doctor seem to have formed one of those friendships which fate and geography prevent maturing. They must content themselves with the wealth of useful facts they have exchanged in a short time.

As for Garnet R., I wld say he does not regret the Aspinalls' departure, if it was not for the scene on Christmas Eve which I overheard, and only yesterday a discovery I made through forgetfulness on the part of G. It was like this. Intending to write a line to Mrs Daintrey, I found I was short of letter-paper, nor could Mr R. help me out. My brother-in-law, who was present, joined in with, 'You will find paper, Ellen, in the box on my desk.' I went to avail myself of this offer. The box mentioned was a beautiful one I had already noticed, made from cedar, inlaid with panels of tortoiseshell, brass handles to the little drawers, the whole bound in a framework of the same metal. I opened the box and found a plentiful supply of paper and anything else I might have needed in the way of writing materials. Only on helping myself did I notice something which had no use in letter-writing: a small *bow* in pink ribbon such as might have trimmed a lady's dress! I found myself smelling this trumpery object, like I was a dog, but could not detect a distinct perfume, only a faint scent of the woman's body it had helped set off.

On my returning to the room where Mr R. was studying an account of the colonization of Van Diemen's Land, he looked up and asked, 'Did you not find letter-paper?' I replied yes, but felt I was in no mind after all to write a letter, because what was there to tell, and my head ached. I could only fidget and spin the globe and trace the possible routes of escape from this most hateful quarter . . .

Garnet Roxburgh remarked soon after, 'You no longer seem inclined to use the little mare I thought would win you over.' On several occasions he invited her to accompany him on expeditions which might have proved of interest.

Her husband encouraged her to accept. 'Go with him if you are disposed to, Ellen. You are not holding back on my account, I hope?'

She answered no, she was simply not disposed to ride round aimlessly.

'But there's purpose enough in Garnet's need to oversee those who are working on his property. You would not be riding aimlessly by accompanying him.'

She wondered how Mr R. would have reacted had she gone off into hysterics.

Instead she had a fit of remorse, and went and kissed him on a dry cheek. 'I wish I could oblige everybody – myself too.'

Mr Roxburgh hoped she was not becoming capricious.

Once as a girl Ellen Gluyas had set out walking to St Hya's Well, of which she had heard but never visited till then on account of its being several miles distant. She walked all morning in what was heat for those parts, and tore her stockings on brambles, as well as her flesh, till blood ran. Still she walked in the heat of the day, and came across scarce a human being, only cows staring at her as they chewed. She found the well (or pool, rather) in the dark copse where they told her it was, its waters pitch black, and

97

so cold she gasped as she plunged her arms. She was soon crying for some predicament which probably nobody, least of all Ellen Gluyas could have explained: no specific sin, only presentiment of an evil she would have to face sooner or later. Presently, after getting up courage, she let herself down into the pool, clothes and all, hanging by a bough. When she had become totally immersed, and the breath frightened out of her by icy water, together with any thought beyond that of escaping back to earth, she managed, still clinging to the bough, to hoist herself upon the bank. She sat awhile in a meadow, in the sun, no longer crying, perhaps smiling, for she could feel the skin divided on her cheeks as though into webs as she sorted out the tail of her hair.

For the first time in many years she remembered this incident, and how her presentiment of evil had oppressed her over months, and then come to nothing, or else she had exorcized the threat by immersion in the pool; whereas on this morning at 'Dulcet', foreboding became more explicit, almost as though she had heard a whip crack in her ear, or pistol shot. For years, or more precisely, since the training she received from her mother-in-law, she had taken it for granted that her Christian faith insured her against evil, until on Christmas Day doubts came faltering into her mind, even as the chariots of the hosts were charging through the stone arch towards assured victory. Nor could she look for assurance, here in a foreign country, in any of those darker myths of place which had dispersed her fears during her Cornish girlhood.

Instead she was faced with her own vulnerable image, swimming at her out of the mirrors in this ill-lit house, making her wonder whether those around her recognized what was happening to her.

But nobody had; they passed and smiled, or passed and ignored, out of familiarity. This morning there was the collision of pudding basins from the kitchen, and the sound of turkeys, like plucked instruments, from the yard, and lazy men clearing their throats, and Mr R. directing Mrs Brennan in brewing senna tea, which he hoped would cure the constipation he was suffering from.

As soon as she heard Garnet Roxburgh leave on his round of inspection, Mrs Roxburgh called Holly and said, 'Will you ask Tim to saddle the mare? The day is so fine I must take advantage of it.'

'But Mr Garnet, m'm, is already gone. Are you allowed to ride alone?'

Mrs Roxburgh refrained from answering a question which a lady born and bred would have considered impertinent, and the girl went to do as she was told.

By the time she returned her mistress was waiting to be hooked into her green habit, and to have the veil secured at the nape of her neck.

Although Holly appeared not to notice, the glass showed Mrs Roxburgh unnaturally drawn, her skin chalky, her lips thin; she moistened the lips inside the veil in which she was encaged.

But Holly, who had troubles of her own, remained unaware of anybody else's outward manifestations, and only remarked, 'I do hope the little mare is not too frisky, m'm, from too much oats all these days when you wasn't using her.'

Mrs Roxburgh's answer was not intelligible as she was making haste to pass through the house and reach the yard. She remembered also the day Dapple had thrown her and she lost her child. Now at least she was not with child and nobody could blame her for behaving irresponsibly.

As she reached the yard she could hear Mr R. in the kitchen still holding forth on the virtue of senna pods, and the pathos of the inadequate affection she and her husband had for each other worked rather painfully in her.

She swept past, leaving Holly on the step.

'Oh, m'm, take care of yourself!' the girl called, as though suddenly caught up into the scheme of things.

When Mrs Roxburgh reached the stable her mount was standing ready, while the groom put in time coaxing the ultimate reflection out of her glossy rump. The mare turned her head and whinnied. Tim smiled, but did not raise his eyelids, fringed almost invisibly with sandy lashes. He gave the impression that he felt he was taking part in a conspiracy.

After she had settled herself in the saddle Mrs Roxburgh lightly struck the mare's shoulder with her crop, and Merle started cavorting rocking-horse style, but only for a short space, before understanding was re-established between the two of them; the mare arched her neck, let the wind out of her belly, and resigned herself.

If Merle felt she was at her rider's disposal Mrs Roxburgh had still to decide whether to head for the strong-flowing river with the poplars rearing and flashing on its banks, or to choose the blander pasture-lands outspread at the foot of the mountain.

Her mind was only made up on hearing a voice calling from the direction of the river. She could not distinguish the words, but knew from their tone that they were part of some injunction issued by Garnet Roxburgh. Merle whinnied high, to encourage a prospective companion, and the other horse, today the blue, not the strawberry roan, answered deeper while coming at a trot.

At the same time Mrs Roxburgh put her mare almost straight into a canter. The fields were soon flickering and streaming. In her present frame of mind her civility might not have outlasted her brother-in-law's company. Had she been wearing spurs, which Mr R. had never permitted, she would have ploughed the horse's sides; instead she lashed her with the crop three or four times on shoulder and flank.

Exposed to emotions she had probably never encountered before, the innocent creature broke into a gallop, and from that, perhaps with freedom in mind, bolted up the rough mountain road on arriving at the fork. This was what Mrs Roxburgh herself might have chosen, but in calmer circumstances. She had never contended with a bolting horse. Exhilaration turned to dry, breathless anxiety. The mare's neck had grown rigid as she held her head close to the ground, or alternately, as high in the air as the martingale allowed; while the rider sawed, first tentatively, then in savage desperation at what she remembered as a velvet mouth. Stones were flying around them as the mare's shoes struck the loose surface of the road. Reverberations prevented her rider from hearing whether Garnet Roxburgh was still in pursuit on his cobby roan.

Then, on reaching the track, or tunnel, down which Mrs Roxburgh had turned on the second day of her visit, the mare scudded into the forest, the drumming of her hooves muffled by leaves and moss. Sometimes a fallen bough snapped so loud it chilled the heart, while low-hanging live branches forced the rider to lie hopefully along the horse's mane.

Mrs Roxburgh must have closed her eyes, when a sudden spattering of light beyond the lids made her open them. She saw they had entered the clearing where she had lain awhile on the previous occasion, and snoozed, and dreamed her obscure dream. As she was frightened then by the dream, something of a frightening nature was again prepared for her. An object to one side of the track caused the mare to whinge, shy, and half-rear as she leaped sideways.

The rider was not precisely thrown, but slithered free of saddle and stirrup, and landed somehow on one foot before falling spread-eagle on the miraculously soft leaf-mould.

A hedgehog was trundling in amongst the tree-ferns and other more amorphous vegetation. The mare in her panic had rampaged deeper into the bush, after which silence fell.

Ellen Roxburgh found herself sobbing as the cold sweat trickled down between her clothes and skin. Then she lay, occasionally renewing the handfuls of leaf-mould she clawed out of the ground. The ankle she must have twisted on landing, was throbbing, but not dangerously she felt. In between spasms, relief and silence plunged her into a state of invalid bliss.

She had scarcely time to enjoy it when again she heard muffled hoofbeats growing louder along the track her mare had brought her, and here was the chest of the blue roan, the rider's head held alongside his horse's neck to avoid the threat of overhanging branches.

The horseman had not yet caught sight of his quarry, but the horse snorted for what must have looked like some vast green bird trailing a disabled wing as it tried to flop its way to safety amongst the ferns.

'Thank God, Ellen! But have you broken something?' Garnet Roxburgh was so full of disbelief for their having finally met, his voice trembled.

At the same time a tremulous whinny came from the direction the mare had taken, and Merle appeared by little, furtive, almost repentant steps, and nuzzled first the bit, then the shoulder of the roan cob. The two horses stood squealing back at each other.

As soon as he had jumped down, it was obvious that Garnet Roxburgh could not make up his mind whether to secure the horses first or succour his brother's wife. He decided on the horses, seeing them tamed and exhausted by the chase. They were easily caught and tied to saplings a few yards apart; it was Ellen who offered difficulties.

Unable to hide or resist, she had turned, and was propped against a bank of immature tree-ferns. She was looking sullenly in a direction other than his.

'What possessed you,' he asked, 'to gallop off alone?'

'Nothing possessed me. I simply rode off on my own, to enjoy a freedom I've been denied since I was at "Dulcet"'; she might have added, 'if not always.'

'I'm sorry,' he replied, not altogether humbly, then became more practical. 'But have you hurt yourself in your fall?'

'It was not a fall. I jumped from the saddle when my horse took fright – and must have sprained my ankle – very slightly – I would say.'

He was advancing on her. Broken only by the horses easing the bits in their mouths, the silence was thickening round them. She would have continued to cultivate her intention of not looking at her 'rescuer', but from glancing along her own bosom, too exposed by the recent crisis, her glance was inevitably drawn to her brother-in-law's approach.

Garnet Roxburgh appeared both determined and stupefied, as though moves he might have contemplated making at his leisure had galloped instead to meet him; the resulting collision had perhaps unnerved him.

On reaching her he fell on his knees on the mattress of rotting compost. 'Dear Ellen – are you in pain?' Their relationship should have permitted the sympathy he was offering, but again she was repelled by the hands, lifting her habit, fumbling for her boot.

It was more than anything sight of her own openwork stocking which roused her to protest. 'Don't, please! I'm most obliged. It's nothing – Garnet.'

Her mention of his name seemed to loosen his self-control. 'Oh, Ellen – Ellen!' By now he would have been grovelling if passion had not more positively extended him.

What prevented her feeling afraid was to realize she was the one in control. She thought she heard herself snicker, before contempt (for both of them) made her suppress it.

She was again this great green, only partially disabled, obscene bird, on whose breast he was feeding, gross hands parting the

102

sweeping folds of her tormented and tormenting plumage; until in opening and closing, she might have been rather, the green, fathomless sea, tossing, threatening to swallow down the humanly manned ship which had ventured on her.

Destroying in a last moaning gurgle.

But whom? She could imagine the body of a murdered woman lying thus, a bundle of disarranged clothing, the flesh of a thigh half buried in leaves, the gaping corsage. But in this case the victim was a man, whose dead weight she was supporting, until he sighed, or moaned out of the depths to which he had been dragged. It was his choice, however. The real victim would have been Austin Roxburgh if conscious of the train of events. Of all three, she was the one who had suffered least – as yet; for when she freed her mouth from the mouth clamped to it, and lay contemplating the gently stirring fern-fronds above her, they sprinkled her surfeited skin with a fine moisture, and she closed her eyes again for an instant, to bask beneath the lashes in an experience of sensuality she must have awaited all her life, however inadmissible the circumstances in which she had encouraged it.

But this was only the briefest sensation.

Still covering her, his fingers-plaited into her hair, Garnet Roxburgh was ploughing her cheeks mechanically with his, but a changed tension in his body led her to expect accusations.

'Oh, Lord! What have you done to us, Ellen?'

She would have preferred to accuse herself and later. 'I was thrown from my horse, and while I wasn't in my right mind you took advantage of it.' Hearing her own defence, she knew it to be insufficient, as well as untruthful, but had to escape from what was becoming an increasingly loathsome situation.

Propped on an elbow at her side, he was staring at her, his eyes glazed with an insolent scepticism. 'If that was not your right mind, we shall never know it!' he declared and laughed.

While she had to perform, in front of his cynical stare, all the humdrum, the vulgar acts of re-arranging torn clothes, putting up her hair, retrieving by its veil the hat which had rolled amongst the ferns.

Only when she was again veiled could she feel to some extent protected – from Garnet Roxburgh's eyes, if not from judgement by herself upon herself.

However painful her ankle, and ungainly her movements, she must hobble as far as possible beyond physical contact with the one who was less her seducer than the instrument she had chosen for measuring depths she was tempted to explore.

She reached the sapling to which the now docile Merle was hitched, untied the reins, and succeeded in mounting by making use of a half-rotted log.

Garnet Roxburgh was sitting up, hands dangling in the space between his knees. 'We make such splendid lovers, Ellen. Won't you admit it?'

She could only have admitted to carrying away a cold, consummated lust.

'Wait at least,' he called, though not expecting her to follow his advice, 'and we'll ride home decently together – not slink in from different directions like a pair of sordid adulterers.'

Were he determined not to let her forget, she might have assured him how unnecessary it was to take such precautions; she did not think she would ever shed her loathing for either of them.

Merle needed no guidance: she ambled sweetly down the track, then the road; her gait, the set of her ears, seemed to condone the more uncontrollable passions; provided these are quite spent, there is no call for remorse.

But her rider was all remorse. She hated the shaggy, inscrutable mountain, the lush pastures with their self-engrossed flocks and herds, the name 'Dulcet', whatever had taken part in rousing inclinations she should never have allowed access to her consciousness.

On the flat road within sight of the house she might have given way to a dry rage, had it not turned to panic, for what she could not yet conceive.

Her rider's distress must have communicated itself to the mare; without pressure of any kind, she broke into a timid canter which carried them the short distance to the yard.

Mrs Brennan had come outside and was pacing with long, uncharacteristic steps, frowning at the sky as though expecting a storm or a revelation, then into the immediate distance, from which, hopefully, a human rescuer might emerge.

On seeing Mrs Roxburgh she looked terrified and cried, 'Oh

dear, what is it?' which were Mrs Roxburgh's own simultaneous words.

To extricate them from the impasse of a silence, the latter added, 'Is it my husband?'

'Oh, ma'am, yes!' It was all waiting for release and would now come tumbling out. 'Mr Roxburgh has taken a turn. But says you is not to worry when you come. Tim is ridden to town for Dr Aspinall. But we cannot expect them in quite a while – as you know. And must not worry, Mr Roxburgh was definite I should tell you.'

Dismounting at the block, his wife asked, 'Surely you haven't left him alone?'

The woman wrapped her hands in her apron. 'The girl is with him, while I come out 'ere to watch for you – and get meself a mouthful of air. My nerves will not stand a sickroom for any length of time.'

Mrs Roxburgh was forgetting to hobble, when the pain in her ankle returned.

'Ah, what 'as happened to yer, ma'am?' the housekeeper moaned.

'It is nothing. I twisted my ankle,' Mrs Roxburgh explained, and made as quick and as natural as she could across the yard and into the house.

The horse she had abandoned trailed her reins into the stables, whinnying and nosing for oats, whereupon the other occupants set up a commotion and almost kicked the shed to pieces.

Mrs Roxburgh swept on, and into the sickroom, with a show of authority and concern which impressed Holly, and was none the less genuine. Words of love and compassion had risen to the level at which they must overflow, if self-hatred did not dry them up.

At least her physical disability forced her to her knees at the bedside, where she soon had possession of the hand which remained a source of amazement: that it had been given to her to hold against her cheek such a parcel of fine bones and thinly veiled, meandering veins.

'It has passed, Ellen, and I feel very comfortable. From experience, we should have nothing more to fear – until next time, that is. Dr Aspinall will give us his opinion when he comes.'

'If only I had been with you!' Tears gushed out over the hand she was pressing.

'You went riding. Well, I expect it has done you good. We all need our diversions, according to our different tempers.'

The girl had left them on the mistress's arrival. Austin Roxburgh was lying raised against the pillows. The habitually tense or querulous lines in his face were relaxed in an imitation of serenity; his cheeks even made a show of colour. Had it not been for signs of fatigue he would have looked the picture of normal health.

Only when she withdrew her hand he began to look anxious, and complained, 'Why must you leave me, Ellen?'

'To change from my habit.'

Accepting the tiresome reason, he said, 'I look forward to the long, uninterrupted evening we shall spend together.'

It seemed as though his release from pain, and no doubt fear, had made him determined to invest their marriage of years with the tender glow of courtship.

She turned to disguise her unhappiness, if not her limp.

'What have you done to yourself?' Mr Roxburgh was quick to ask.

'My horse shied at a hedgehog. I twisted my ankle in falling.'

'Ah!' His breath was sharp, but he made no further comment beyond, 'Otherwise you are whole, I take it.'

She was relieved for the refuge of the dressing-room, and to change into a loose gown which declared her intention of not leaving their quarters that evening.

Mrs Roxburgh sat at the bedside, while her husband made disjointed conversation, or dozed, and she nursed her numbness, or provided such answers as would satisfy him. For the first time in her life she had reached that point where the guilt-ridden wish the past completely razed in consequence of a single lapse, so that they may start afresh somewhere in the mists of abstract, and possibly unattainable, bliss.

On Mr Roxburgh's announcing that he felt like taking a little soup provided there was nothing fat in it, Mrs Brennan brought him a plateful. The master presented his compliments, she said, and would pay his brother a visit after everyone had dined. 'I have laid a place in the dining-room, ma'am, if you care to prepare yourself for dinner.'

Mrs Roxburgh confessed she had no appetite, and did not wish

106

to leave her husband, but in the end was persuaded to toy with a breast of chicken on a tray. It would have suited her if she too, might have claimed to be an invalid, but could only enlist her insufficiently injured ankle.

When Garnet Roxburgh knocked on the door he must have heard the things rattle on the tray as she made her escape into the dressing-room beyond. Of the conversation between the brothers she heard not a word, what with the closed door and her deaf ears, but was attracted repeatedly to her own reflections in the looking-glass.

The long wait for Dr Aspinall after Garnet withdrew might have become intolerable had the invalid not been inspired by fits of unexpected gaiety.

When she had read to him awhile from Sir Thomas Browne, he stopped her by saying, 'An admirably modulated voice, Ellen. Who would have thought that a crude Cornish girl could be made over to become a beautiful and accomplished woman!'

Mrs Roxburgh was embarrassed more by the compliment than the slight. 'Crude I may have been, accomplished I am not.'

'When I used the word "crude" I did not mean to disparage you, my dear. It was to your advantage. The crude lends itself all the better to moulding.' He was caressing her cheek with the back of his hand. 'In a woman, at any rate. I do not think it applies to a man. Men are too rigid. There is more of wax in a woman. She is easily impressed!' He pinched her cheek, laughing for his own wit, and might have drawn her to him had they not heard voices approaching.

It was Dr Aspinall at last, bleary from the long drive and an aftermath of brandy supped before leaving, and perhaps also en route. After hearing details of Mr Roxburgh's attack and making a fairly disinterested examination, the doctor prescribed tincture of digitalis, which he had with him in his bag, and predicted that the patient had years of life ahead of him. Dr Aspinall was of that school of physicians which believes in making the patient happy by encouraging him to ignore his ailment and save his strength for payment of the fee.

Business concluded, the doctor accepted a further brandy and water (at which Mr Roxburgh joined him) and complimented Mrs Roxburgh on her looks.

'My wife, by the by, sends you her affectionate remembrances and continues hoping you will pay her the promised visit.'

'Perhaps sooner than she expects,' Mrs Roxburgh answered with a warmth she might not have expended on Mrs Aspinall previously.

In fact her mind was leaping with the hope which springs from a sudden idea, or inspiration.

Although it was understood that the doctor should spend the night with them to rest his horses, Mrs Roxburgh followed him out into the passage so as to waste no time in broaching her idea.

'When I said "sooner than she expects", doctor, it was because it is my opinion that we should leave "Dulcet" as soon as we can find lodgings at Hobart. I am afraid,' Mrs Roxburgh said, and did look most distracted and appealing, 'that my husband – in his delicate state of health – might suddenly be taken ill again – the next time perhaps fatally. In town he will have the benefit of your immediate attention. I would feel desperate if anything happened – and helpless – here at "Dulcet".'

Dr Aspinall squeezed her hand and smiled a benevolent, brandy smile.

'The simplest lodgings, provided they are clean,' she hurried on, 'where Mr Roxburgh can regain his strength before the voyage home.'

'You can depend on me, my dear Mrs Roxburgh,' the doctor promised, 'but Garnet will be keenly disappointed.'

'No doubt,' she admitted. 'But I'm sure he is fond enough of his brother not to wish to sacrifice him to his own pleasure.'

The doctor agreed.

After attending to the night-light and performing the ritual of kissing her husband on the brow (when, surprisingly, his lips were raised in search of hers) Mrs Roxburgh retired to the dressing-room, where Holly had made up a bed of sorts on the sofa. She was so weary she accepted thankfully this unyielding compromise, but not weary enough to neglect her duty to the one her mother-in-law had commended: the Divine Being, in old Mrs Roxburgh's parlance.

Young Mrs Roxburgh kneeled beside the improvised bed, but her knees were too pointed, it seemed, or the carpet might have been strewn with glass, or in worst moments, upholstered like a mattress of rotting leaves.

'Ellen?' Mr Roxburgh called from the bedroom. 'Are you praying?'

She replied yes, but so low he might not have heard.

She locked her hands faster, and screwed her eyes deeper into her skull. She longed to catch sight of old Mrs Roxburgh's Divine Being, if only as a blaze of departing glory. Perhaps it was her origins which made her believe more intently in the Devil than in the Deity. So tonight her prayers were but vaguely directed, and the shudders took possession of her limbs.

Again Mr Roxburgh called to her. 'I am in no mood for prayer. I am too tired – too fidgety. I could not succeed in concentrating.' His voice trailed off in a string of yawns.

Mrs Roxburgh arranged herself upon the sofa, but was unable to sleep. Although she was careful to close her mind to any image which might suggest her fall from grace, such thoughts as she had, trickled out as tears; the wet pillow heightened the fever of her sleeplessness.

Time must have passed, for the pillow-case had dried out, when Mr Roxburgh called, 'Are you awake, Ellen? I find it impossible to sleep. Come here, would you? I'd like to feel you lying beside me in this desert of a bed.'

She could only obey her sick husband's whim. 'But you will be less likely to sleep,' she warned. 'We shall disturb each other by our tossing and turning.'

'I would like to comfort you,' he said, 'for all you have had to put up with – married to such a creaking fellow.'

Her body ached, less than her spirit however, as Mr Roxburgh began to demonstrate his love. Perhaps the shock he had sustained that day had melted a tenderness inside him commensurate with the love he had known in theory he ought to feel, and only now saw his way to offering a semblance of it.

Mrs Roxburgh was racked: gratitude was the most she was able to conjure in exchange, and that can quickly turn to the gravel of remorse.

'Oh, no!' she protested. 'Please! I am afraid,' she moaned as she moved her head from side to side. 'You may have a relapse.'

But Mr Roxburgh remained gently obdurate: he could not

impress his love too deeply on her now that he had been prompted to do so.

Mrs Roxburgh, finally, could only lie, holding her husband's frail body to hers, and accept his miraculous gift.

After a night which, in retrospect, was less tormented than either of them had anticipated, she wondered whether to share with him the plan she had conceived for removing from 'Dulcet' to Hobart Town; when she found herself telling it.

Surprisingly, Mr Roxburgh replied, 'Yes. I am in full agreement. I expect Garnet's feelings will be hurt, but it cannot be helped. I've taken a dislike to this house. I swear it is still full of Dormers. I've heard them moving about overhead, as you claimed to hear, I remember, at the beginning.'

Mrs Roxburgh preferred not to embark on the subject of ghosts, and more practically suggested, 'Do you think you should tell your brother that we plan to leave?'

'I could – yes,' Mr Roxburgh pondered, 'unless you might do it more delicately. He could hold it against his brother for ever, whereas he can hardly blame a sensible wife for worrying about her husband's health.' His decision filled him with all the gravity of self-approval.

But Mrs Roxburgh grew hesitant. 'Let us at least wait,' she said, 'till the doctor has found us lodgings.'

While her husband kept to his bed it was easy enough to avoid her brother-in-law, but Austin Roxburgh at last tired of pampering; he took to rising in the morning and tentatively pottering about the house, but still retired in the afternoon; their dinner was brought to them, as usual since his illness, in their room.

Until Mr Roxburgh decided, 'You should go in, Ellen, and dine with him. Otherwise he may take offence, and find your dedication to a husband ostentatious.'

'If you wish it,' she said.

The leaves falling in the orchard made for melancholy. If the twitter of little questing birds provoked tremors of pleasure in her, the cold cawing of transient crows sank her spirits immediately. On the morning of the day when her husband gave his order she heard shots from across the paddock, and a desperate cry, whether from man or beast she was unable to decide. Her closing the window, she realized later, had been an ineffectual

110

response which shut out neither the echo nor her own disquiet.

The evening was cold for her return to the ritual of the dining-room. A white light was gathering above the decapitated cypresses and thick wall or hedge of box. In the fireplace two or three tree-roots snapped and crackled cheerfully enough. Even so, she was glad of her fringed shawl with the leaf-pattern; she drew it tight across her bosom, then thought better, and draped it loosely. As she waited for Garnet Roxburgh she could not determine whether the expression in Mrs Dormer-Roxburgh's eyes was that of male-volence or sympathy.

Her host arrived as she had expected, casually, disinterested, and cold. His features, his lips, seemed to have coarsened since last she saw him, but the transformation could have been oc-casioned by surliness.

'You have become a stranger, Ellen,' he said, and bore down to commandeer the hearth.

His voice sounded thick, as though he had drunk a glass of wine to fortify himself against their meeting.

'My husband,' she replied, 'is a demanding invalid.'

'Of course I would not begrudge my brother the attentions of a devoted wife.'

Then Holly produced the tureen, which should have dispelled any awkwardness. The girl went to stand it at the head of the table so that the master might serve from it.

'Mrs Roxburgh will serve the soup,' he decided.

Mrs Roxburgh did as she was told; the steam made her eyes water. Holly too, was red about the eyes and had lost something of her original gloss. Under the shapeless grey gown, Mrs Rox-burgh thought she could detect an ampler figure. The material ghosts of 'Dulcet' were running the gauntlet of Mrs Dormer's scorn. So Mrs Roxburgh lowered her eyes.

The circlets of fat on the surface of the soup would surely have displeased her husband. 'Is there ever,' she began, but gave up on scalding her palate and the back of her throat. 'Escaped pri-soners,' she tried it out afresh, 'do they ever survive to enjoy their freedom?'

'Not for long,' replied Garnet Roxburgh with evident appro-val. 'They are either shot in escaping, or brought back soon after for appropriate punishment and another term. A few of the bolters turn bushranger for a while, but are usually caught, and strung up beside the highroad as a warning.'

It was much as she had imagined while hoping to be told that freedom sometimes exchanges abstraction for reality.

Holly had removed the soup-tureen and brought an exceptionally fine fish, which Mr Roxburgh served as though not doing so.

His guest choked on a bone, but asked, 'What is it, Mr Roxburgh?'

'What? Oh, the fish. A trumpeter, I think. Yes, trumpeter.'

He sighed and ate, and ate and sighed. Holly fetched candles.

'This morning,' Mrs Roxburgh ventured, 'I heard gunfire – and such a cry, I can hear it still. Would it have been one of these wretches, delivered – whether mercifully or not – out of his misery?'

Garnet Roxburgh's jaws worked; his lips ejected a fragment of fish-skin. 'It was the mare – Merle – who staked herself so badly it would not have been practical to keep her. We can't afford to carry cripples.' His forehead seemed to swell as his jaws set motionless; his hands, which she so much loathed, and for one obsessed instant, had desired, threatened to send his knife and fork skittering across the plate.

Her own cutlery she laid together before extricating herself from her chair.

'Well?' he all but shouted. 'Who is to blame – but us all? Eh, Ellen?' He had jumped up after she had risen, and come round the table to thrust himself at her. 'I'm told you are planning to leave us to our festering!'

He was grasping, not so much at her hand, as for some immaterial support he had no hope of finding.

In refusing him her hand, she uttered, 'I can't make excuses for my own weakness – or ignorance. I still have not learnt enough to help myself, let alone others.'

She did not look at him again, but left the room.

Mr Austin Roxburgh was most disturbed on noticing his wife's pallor. 'It is you who are ill, Ellen!'

She was in fact a shambles of disgust, anger, and despair, both for the slaughter of the little horse, which she could only interpret as an act of deliberate cruelty, and for the human souls con-

112

demned to the torments of this island on which they too, had the misfortune to find themselves.

'These wretched creatures for whom there is so little hope!' She could not bring herself to mention the mare, for whose end she held herself responsible.

Austin Roxburgh might have moralized to console his wife had it not meant going against what he saw as retribution and justice.

Instead, in the morning, he devised an outing which he hoped would restore her spirits. The day was so clear and sunny he asked for a horse to be harnessed to the gig, and proposed that they should drive out together.

Austin Roxburgh drove like the upright man he was. It was unusual for him to take the reins, but he appeared to derive such pleasure from their innocent jaunt she could not demand that they change places.

They took the road along the riverside, where the grass was already strewn with the gold coin of poplar leaves. Fish leaped from time to time, or like thoughts rising, mouthed the surface of the stippled water.

'We must do this more often, Ellen,' Mr Roxburgh decided, 'when we are at home again – at Cheltenham.'

His desire to atone for the minor lapses, and ignorance of the major ones, made the morning glitter more perilously. She could only sit as upright as himself, when in less tenuous circumstances her body might have adopted some of the attitudes of self-indulgence.

Mrs Roxburgh was delivered to some extent from the nagging of her conscience on reaching the house and being handed a note which a messenger had brought from Dr Aspinall. Standing on the veranda steps the Roxburghs read the letter together; here at last was a guilt they could share.

A Mrs Impey, a widow in reduced circumstances, the doctor informed them, was prepared to put three of her rooms at his friends' disposal. Her establishment, a modest one he was careful to add, was situated nevertheless in a most respectable locality.

Mrs Roxburgh was overjoyed, though her husband at once showed signs of anxiety, if not downright alarm. 'Now we shall have to tell him,' he said. 'Will you?'

'No,' she replied. 'He knows!' She then began to laugh in a

manner which might have struck him as 'hysterical' in another woman.

'Who could have told him?'

'I have no inkling,' it was not entirely true, 'and since it is done, I shall make no inquiries.' Despite a disapproval she could sense mounting, she continued laughing; she took herself in hand only after they had gone inside.

Mrs Roxburgh, who had lost the inclination for writing in her journal, recovered it:

24 March   *Hobart Town*

. . . the house so small, the rooms so narrow, we might feel restricted had we not grown accustomed to ship-conditions on the voyage out. I shld also say, if it was not for *relief* at escaping from the *gloom* of '*Dulcet*'! So I am prepared to love our little house at Battery Point, and Mr R. is for similar reasons willing to overlook its limitations. We have the use of two front rooms. One is a dining-room, the other a parlour, or what our landlady likes to refer to as the *withdrawing*-room. Off this is our bedroom, most fortunately placed, because this will be my withdrawing-room in the event of unwanted callers. Mrs Impey is a small, bright person full of the best intentions. She is the widow of a former officer of the garrison at Port Arthur where she spent some years with her husband. When questioned about Port A. she held forth on its magnificent situation. As for the penal settlement, she says many of the stories are grossly exagerated by those who look for the sensational in life. Mrs Impey, I suggest, is too bright to admit any shadows into her scheme. Asked her whether she had not felt moved to return home after burying her husband. Here she did look a little downcast for one so bright, and said it was difficult for a woman to acquire the habit of making important decisions. Then she cheered up again, said that she enjoyed the society of Hobart Town, and so as not to lead a wholly frivolous life, gave lessons in needlework to selected young ladies of the better class.

26 Mar

Mr R.'s health improves daily. He already speaks of leaving if we can find a berth. We are told we can expect a ship at the end of the month or early next. Will be overjoyed if rumours become fact. Dr A. decided I was looking *peeky* and prescribed a tonic which I will take to humour him and my husband. I have to confess that my spirits are low, but at a level which no tonic can reach. A wind blows daily off the mountain along streets for the most part empty, in which approaching footsteps often alarm by sounding thunderous. Mercifully G. R. has until now left us in peace, except for the present of a dressed goose and 4 bottles of 'Dulcet' wine. Remembering how we ate goose our first night beneath his roof I could not bring myself to touch it. My excuse was that I felt bilious. Mr R. did justice by the goose, and ever since has been chiding himself for ingratitude towards his brother.

That forenoon, when Mrs Roxburgh returned from a fruitless expedition in search of matching buttons, a hooded vehicle with a livery-stable look was standing at the door of their lodging.

She was prepared to pass quickly down the hall and into her bed- withdrawing-room when the landlady darted out from the official withdrawing-room, and pounced.

'Ah, Mrs Roxburgh,' Mrs Impey tittered with more than her customary measure of brightness, 'our friend Mrs Aspinall has called to see you. In your absence I offered her a glass of Madeira and a dish of my little cornflour cakes. Now you will be able to join her. I feared your being delayed might deprive you of the pleasure of her company.'

There was no way out; the landlady's enthusiasm would have scotched the mere thought of one.

When Mrs Roxburgh entered, she found Mrs Aspinall seated by the window, from where she must have watched her friend's approach down the hill. It vexed Mrs Roxburgh to know that her unguarded thoughts had been exposed to Mrs Aspinall's stare; for choice she would have worn an iron mask in the presence of the doctor's wife.

Mrs Aspinall had adopted a languid air, or possibly the Madeira had imposed it on her, as she wiped from her lips a crumb or two of cornflour cake. 'I had almost given you up,' she said. 'It is not that I couldn't wait – Heaven knows there is little else to do – but my doctor has a fit if I run up a bill at the livery-stable. Yet it doesn't suit his pocket to invest in a carriage for his wife's use.'

Their own dependence on the doctor left Mrs Roxburgh at a loss for a reply. 'May I pour you a second glass of wine?' she suggested to bridge the gap.

Mrs Aspinall accepted, since her hostess could not know that it would be her third. 'Tippling in Hobart Town!' she said and sighed and giggled all in one. 'Ah, my dear, you cannot understand! You are of the other world, and pause here only long enough to dip your toe.'

'Here or there, my life is not so very different. To be sure, at home I have an establishment to run, orders to give, Mr Roxburgh's friends to entertain, but that is no great distraction. Not that I would care to exchange my quiet life for a more hectic one.'

Mrs Aspinall lowered her eyelids and sipped her wine. 'Blessed are the docile and easily contented!'

Mrs Roxburgh blushed. 'Is it so blameworthy?'

Mrs Aspinall flashed her eyes open, as though her purpose were to catch someone out. 'Have you received, perhaps, a visit from Garnet Roxburgh?'

'We've not seen him since leaving "Dulcet". He and my husband are in touch by messenger, and Mr Garnet Roxburgh contributes most generously to what would otherwise be a monotonous table.'

'I am surprised,' Mrs Aspinall said, 'considering the brothers are so fond of each other. And you, my dear, he praises to the skies!'

Mrs Roxburgh was aware that her hand shook, and what was worse, that a drop of Madeira lay trembling on her lap. 'I had the impression I was not at all to my brother-in-law's liking. We have scarcely one viewpoint in common. I am too quiet. He prefers a more dashing style in women.' She tried to disguise annoyance at her own ineptitude by diverting attention to the stain on her skirt, which she rubbed hard with her handkerchief.

'You are reserved, my dear, to say the least.' If Mrs Aspinall's smile were intended as her most agreeable, her look was purest verjuice. 'That is where your appeal may lie. Men of Garnet Roxburgh's temper have a craving for variety.'

Mrs Roxburgh was so embarrassed she could only offer a cornflour cake, which Mrs Aspinall refused.

Holding her head to one side, the latter tried out a wooing tone. 'Can't I tempt you to accompany us to a rout?'

'My husband does not care for large assemblies.'

'And his health, no doubt, would not allow it if he did. No, it is you, *Ellen*, I am enticing. Though with the promise of a doctor in attendance, it can hardly be called enticement. Even Mr Roxburgh should approve.'

'I thank you for the kind thought, Mrs Aspinall. But I am hardly equipped for a social life with the clothes Mr Roxburgh decided I should bring on this visit to the antipodes.'

'Oh, *clothes*!' Mrs Aspinall might have intended to make it sound as though she herself dispensed with them, but changed her tactics on seeing her error. 'At least you would have the satisfaction of seeing me in one of my familiar rags, while you, my dear, have I don't know what – the strength of character, I think it is called, which draws attention to itself even wearing a woollen shawl. That, in any case, is how Garnet Roxburgh sees it.'

The implications were so painful, Mrs Roxburgh frowned – painfully. 'If my brother-in-law is to be present at the gathering you offer, I am less than ever inclined to accept.'

But Mrs Aspinall leaned forward and lightly laid her fingers on a wrist (was she feeling for the patient's pulse?). 'You are too sensible, my dearest Ellen! At this rate you will not begin to live.'

The visitor rose, and fell to arranging her curls in their prescribed clusters. 'Then I shall go on my own – with my doctor – and in my rags – and regret your absence – though not to the extent that poor Garnet will.'

Needled by her friend's apparent mission of procuring her, Mrs Roxburgh said, 'Your pink dress is the one I will always remember.'

'Which pink?' Mrs Aspinall snapped.

'Which you wore at Christmas.'

'My old *pink*? That became indeed a rag, and I let the servant have it shortly after you saw it. Why on earth should you remember my pink?'

'You looked so charming in it. And the bodice so cunningly ornamented with all those little satin bows.'

'The Town knew that dress by heart. I grew to hate it.' Recollection had made Mrs Aspinall hoarse.

Almost at the same moment the voices of Mrs Impey and Mr Austin Roxburgh were heard in the hall. 'If she is, I will not go in,' Mr Roxburgh whispered loud. 'I shall lie down and rest till my wife has got it over.'

His wife finally had, and the same evening, after her emotions had subsided, wrote in her journal:

However unpleasant it is to detect hypocrisy in another, how much more despicable to discover it in oneself – worse still, to be driven to it by Mrs A. To be reflected in such a very trashy mirror! Yet this is what happened during a call I will try my best to forget. When here I am recording it!

Mrs Roxburgh glanced through what she had written to see whether it looked too explicit on paper, and decided it did not; but knew that she would be haunted by the facets of vice she shared with Mrs Aspinall. She tried to console herself with the explanation that if she had been drawn to a certain person, it was because some demoniac force had overcome her natural repulsion.

She was not consoled, however, and locked her hypocritically innocuous journal away.

On a day when she was at her lowest Mrs Roxburgh tied down her bonnet and ventured into the windy street. To her husband she had said she would take a walk, knowing how impossible it would have been to persuade him to accompany her. In roaming round the Point alone and unprotected, she had no aim, unless the vague one of escaping from her own thoughts. Not only vague but vain, she realized from experience. For it occurred to her that on the day she ordered them to saddle the mare so that she might escape from discontented thoughts and the general constriction of their life at 'Dulcet', she had ridden out to substantiate a thought she would have liked to think did not exist, from being buried so deeply in her mind.

In consequence, on this present chilly afternoon, she was strolling somewhat diffidently, buffeted by wind, threatened by a great cumulus of cloud, between the mountain which presided over man's presumptuous attempt at a town, and the shirred waters of the grey river rushing towards its fate, the sea.

As her landlady had remarked, it was 'difficult for a woman to acquire the habit of making important decisions'. Ellen Roxburgh wondered as she walked what important decision she had ever made, beyond that of accepting her husband's proposal, and on another occasion, giving way to her own unconfessed incontinence.

At the point where the street, which had become a lane, petered out in a stony path, Mrs Roxburgh was forced to pause, and grope for the support of a tree. Leaning against it, she held her arms around herself to contain what amounted to a nausea. The rough tree-trunk comforted her to some extent until she was fully returned to her senses, though still with traces of a melancholy which had its origins, it seemed to her, in her failed children; more, she was permeated by this sorrow her husband never allowed himself to mention.

Swept onward by the wind, her skirt blown in a tumult before her, she tried to persuade herself that her husband, like the tree which had offered sanctuary, supported a belief in her own free will. Yet she had been blown as passively against the one as against the other. The tree happened to be standing in her path, just as a crude, bewildered girl, alone and bereaved on a moor, could hardly have rejected Mr Roxburgh's offer.

So that she was dragged back into the forest clearing, the filtered light, the scents of fungus and rotting leaves, to the only instance when her will had asserted itself, and then with bared, ugly teeth.

Mrs Roxburgh opened her mouth in hollow despair, and the wind, tearing down her throat, all but choked and temporarily deafened her.

She stumbled farther, to what end she wondered, when she could have been seated beside the fire with a book, or occupying herself with sewing, in the speckless dolls' house at present their home.

Until, at a turn in the path, she noticed what might have been a bundle of cast-off clothes lying amongst the crabbed bushes: old, greenish garments, the sight of which suggested a smell of must and the body to which they had belonged. She would have hurried past this repulsive sight, when the bundle sat up, and showed that the clothes, far from being discarded, still helped partially disguise the nakedness of a living being.

Moreover, the man inside them had started directing at her a gap-toothed smile, out of a freckled, pocked complexion; the eyes, pale and lashless, in no way related to the invitation of the yellow smile, burned with cold hate as they inquired into every aspect of her figure; while a hand, its skin cured to a carapace, patted the form his body had moulded in the grass where he had been lying.

That he was addressing her, she saw, but could not distinguish the words as the wind immediately carried them away.

The man realized, and increased his efforts until some of what he was shouting reached her: '. . . where there's a hare's nest . . .' again the thread was lost, '. . . wouldn' be natural for puss to lie alone . . .' it was blown back.

She might have returned along the path had it not been a rambling one and the man already on his feet. To follow the path in the direction in which it led might have plunged her in a labyrinth of gorse, so she started up the slope of the hill beyond which she could see the roofs of aligned houses, and where she could hope to find the orderly streets she had abandoned.

Behind her she heard her pursuer progressing from his initial courtship, in which hares couched poetically enough, into the more obscene terms of his desperate human predicament, 'I url show . . . what you bitches of leddies . . . lead us on . . . all that most of us gets is from watchin' winders at night . . .'

Mrs Roxburgh ran or sprang. She felt fingers rake her back, a hand seize on one of her wrists. She was whirled round in her flight. Blackened nails were tearing at a brooch on her bosom. She was looking deep into the pocks and pores of a fiery skin as the blast of rum smote her in the face.

Then she had escaped, and was again running, clambering ungainly amongst and over rocks. If his obscenities had horrified her at least they were also memories of the past; the sound of his breathing frightened her worse.

'Well, then,' he suddenly shouted out of a silence, 'will yer be satisfied when you've killed a man? That is what it leads to from the moment we is born!'

For her part, she could not conceive what they were doing, the two of them, scrambling up this hill. It would have been more rational to fall and allow herself to be strangled by orange-callused hands, broken fingernails eating into her throat, had she not looked up, and there ahead was the vestige of a road, some kind of vehicle advancing along it, drawn by a pair of horses, their solid briskets and haunches at variance with the alarm betrayed by ears and nostrils.

As she stumbled, herself by now an animal flattening its exhausted body against the turf, somebody, a gentleman, sprang

120

down from the driver's seat, and charged towards them, whip-in-hand.

In her distress she did not recognize him until they were but a few yards apart.

With the whip-handle he began belting into her assailant, who needed little persuasion to retreat, frieze rags flying, hat lost, as he jumped rocks and tore through bushes.

Garnet Roxburgh recovered his breath, and straightened his coat, of a dark-green cloth with fur collar.

'You court disaster, Ellen. Remember this is Van Diemen's Land. An infernal situation won't be improved by your blowing on the coals.'

She was not yet able to speak, which absolved her from answering her brother-in-law. She followed him up the slope towards the buggy and its pair of disturbed horses.

She patted one of the cobs and let her hand lie briefly on his neck in gratitude.

Garnet Roxburgh explained that he had been to a sale at Bagdad, when it had occurred to him to pay his respects to his brother – and sister-in-law – on the way home.

He flipped at the horses' necks as he spoke, while she sat humbly, exhausted and related, beside him on the leather seat. The whip, she felt, must have less malice in it than his words, for the horses responded jauntily.

'Mr Roxburgh,' she slightly shifted her position, 'will be glad to see you after all this time.'

She noticed that they were re-entering the world of substance and respectability. Gentlemen were driving home, accompanied in some instances by wives. Mr Garnet Roxburgh of 'Dulcet' shook his whip once or twice as a salute to familiar faces. The ladies returned blank stares on perceiving his unidentified companion.

'I cannot thank you,' she attempted.

He winced, and shrugged his shoulders. 'I don't receive thanks, I only accept offers.'

They drove grating along the street.

'Most of us on this island are infected.' (She had heard it before, alas, and from her husband.) 'You, Ellen, though you are here only by chance, have symptoms of the same disease. I should hate my virtuous brother to know. But would love to educate you further in what you have shown yourself adept at learning – on one occasion at least.'

Because she would have preferred not to understand what she had been told, she sat looking at her meek hands; while the voice continued hammering at her.

'You and I would enter hell the glorious way if you could overcome your prudery.'

Then she said, 'I hope to redeem myself through my husband – an honourable man, as even you who love him must admit.' She paused before adding, 'I pray he will never have cause to regret our marriage.'

The horses were by now straining uphill towards the narrow house in which she and Austin Roxburgh temporarily lived. To avert the pressure of a contempt she could feel directed at her she inquired after her friend Holly.

'Holly has been returned to the factory, for reasons,' he said, 'which I shall not go into.'

Again she thought to hear the cry of that other victim of her brother-in-law's displeasure, the little mare who, conveniently, had staked herself. Anger and fear conflicted in Ellen Roxburgh, together with relief that herself, the least deserving of the three, was assured of a refuge.

They had reached the door. Garnet Roxburgh handed her down, but made no move to go inside and pay his respects to his brother.

Mrs Roxburgh did not urge him to hold to his original intention; nor did she reveal to her husband, as he carved the lamb, the peculiarly distressing circumstances in which she had recently found herself.

Instead she wrote:

6 April
Walked by myself round the Point. Magnificent views of mountain and river seen by an oppressive light – stormy to say the least. An unpleasant incident on which I do not propose to dwell. Only heartening to know that whatever bad I find in myself is of no account beside the positive evil I discover in others. I do not mean the instinctive brutality of the human beast, but the considered evil of a calculating mind. When I say 'others' I mean An Other (and no fiend imagined on the moor at dusk in my inexperienced girlhood).

How fortunate I am in my dear husband who is goodness itself!

At dinner Mr R. was anoyed at the lamb which he found tough. I said it cld be the knife. He agreed I cld be right as indeed I was. The evening we spent together continued uneventful. I was glad of it.

Would call in Dr A. Feel sick and ill. Nothing, alas, for which he would know a medicine.

Later

A *miracle*! As we were about to prepare for bed, dear Dr A. arrived with news that a brig (*Bristol Maid* I think she is called) had berthed that evening – out of England – and wld sail on the return voyage, in ballast as far as Singapore, thence via the Cape – Home! The good doctor is negotiating with the company's agent to secure us a passage, though their vessel he says, does not cater for passengers as a rule. Mr R. and I have finished our prayers and kissed each other. We cld of danced!

O Lord, my gratitude will know no bounds, nor will I cease to regret my shortcomings . . .

The day of days was a grey one splashed with blue, like many others experienced by them at Hobart Town. The Roxburghs were early aboard after hearing from the agent that the master was anxious to take advantage of a wind which augured well for their voyage to Sydney. Dr Aspinall, though not his lady, who was indisposed, accompanied them down to the ship.

Mrs Roxburgh was in something of a dither, counting and recounting their trunks, and visibly experiencing despair while that which contained Mr Roxburgh's books was temporarily lost. The cabin, although narrow, was nothing to complain about, as yet. There were sights and sounds, all the bustle of departure, to delight travellers who had been delayed against their will.

Captain Purdew, a decent, uncomplicated, seafaring man, had scarce introduced himself to those who were to be his passengers, when Mr Roxburgh broke away from their little group with a cry of what sounded like physical anguish.

'Here we are, my dear fellow! I was afraid we had offended you, and that in spite of my messages, you would not come. Now, thank God, we may depart in peace, our conscience at rest!'

Garnet Roxburgh's smile, as he reached the end of the gangboard and stepped on deck, suggested that he had little belief in the brand of sententiousness his brother went in for. He came on offering his hand here and there with the authority of o ie who considers himself a power in the community, but stopped short of his sister-in-law with such a slight, wooden bow that she alone could have recognized the ironical intent.

'If you must load yourself with conscience,' he replied half to his brother.

'Any plans and moves have been dictated entirely by my health. But I was afraid you might think us ungrateful after accepting your hospitality and kindness.'

Garnet sighed. 'Nothing is broken!' It was plain to his sister-in-law how much his brother bored him. 'Excepting a close relationship – and that, I imagine, rarely mends once fate and distance go to work on it.'

He was looking at Mrs Roxburgh, not so much expecting confirmation as to hold her responsible for the break.

For her the situation was becoming unbearable. Although she could scarcely bring herself to look him in the face, she had to; nor were Dr Aspinall, Captain Purdew, or her husband the slightest help, with their interjections, expostulations, and tenders of advice in the form of maxims and platitudes. The scene as it was written could only be played by Garnet Roxburgh and herself.

Such glimpses as she had of him on this morning of echoes and clinging cold showed him at his best and worst. Dressed in the close-fitting green coat with fur collar he had been wearing the day he came to her rescue, his figure showed an elegance of line which would have made him conspicuous anywhere in that primitive Colony. An intolerant, even insolent bearing, more pronounced today, made it clear that he was aware of this. As for the face, it glowed from an extra burnishing by the early morning drive. She had seldom allowed herself to examine his face for fear of being endangered by his looks. Now it almost literally stunned her to think that for a few instants those cheeks had rasped her own, and that the sensuality buried inside her had risen to the surface and wrestled with his more overt lust.

Mrs Roxburgh caught at a rope to steady herself under the weight of her immodest thoughts.

'Are you unwell?' he asked without evident concern.

'Thank you. My health was always excellent.'

Then she softened, in accordance with convention and circumstance. 'Isn't it a pretty scene? A watercolour!' she pronounced. 'In Van Diemen's Land, almost every landscape is a watercolour.'

He said that he had not noticed her taking advantage of it.

'I am without accomplishments,' she replied.

Now it was her husband coming to her rescue, or else to deliver the final blow. 'Garnet, dear boy,' Austin Roxburgh's voice began in the key it assumed for affectionate recollections of the past; it made him sound old-womanish, jealous old-womanish at that, 'I woke in the night, Garnet, and remembered the time your horse threw you – we were both still only boys in our teens – and they carried you home – you were white enough for me to think you dead. I went so cold. I couldn't imagine how I'd live without you.'

Garnet tried to break the mood by pummelling his brother roughly on the shoulder. 'And here we are – both alive – and living happily without each other!'

But Austin Roxburgh was not to be denied his ration of sentiment. 'You remember old Nurse Hayes? She was as alarmed as I. So much so, when you came to, she allowed us a drink of liquorice-water – and accepted a tot herself.'

Garnet Roxburgh was staring at the deck from under his eyelids; his mouth might have formed, and quickly sucked back, a bubble. 'I remember the liquorice-water. What poison!'

The brothers laughed immoderately as the sun showed from between the ribbons of watery cloud.

Captain Purdew announced that he would soon be forced to put their visitors ashore.

'And Nurse?'

'She died, of course. At a great age.'

'I remember she used to allow us to feel her goitre, as a treat.'

Seeing that it was a moment in which she could have no part, Mrs Roxburgh went below. The landscape which she thought she had begun to hate until on the point of leaving it, was breaking up into brilliant fragments under pressure from the suddenly dominant sun. On the companion-ladder her legs felt weak, her cheeks sticky, which she wiped with the back of a glove; while the voices of the brothers continued rising overhead, wreathing and intertwining as though in the last throes of a rememorative embrace.

Mr Roxburgh stood looking in at his wife. He was holding ajar the door of their crudely improvised cabin, his face paler than normal, for he had not found his sea legs on their first day out from Sydney.

'Are you not feeling well, Ellen?' Mr Roxburgh asked without intending it to sound peevish.

'It's nothing. The rolling of the ship. It will pass.'

She smiled, but shapelessly she could feel. She roused herself at once and prepared to leave her nest of rumpled sheets. She might have been rising from a greater depth, for the sinews of her throat grew visible and her mouth thin and strained. The awkwardness and effort of the whole operation was making her look ugly.

'Nothing,' she hastened to repeat. 'Now I am going to see to our beds so that Spurgeon will perhaps be less disgusted with me. Do you go back to your books and I'll join you shortly.'

Mr Roxburgh turned back into the saloon and she realized he had not been looking at her, but inward, into his own thoughts.

Later in the day they decided to take a stroll together since the swell appeared to have abated. Even so, it was difficult to keep up their dignity, and the action of the ship, together with the cluttered nature of the deck, soon forced her to let go of his arm. They were no worse for their independence. The clouds had thinned for a pale disc of sun to appear, fully exposed at its best moments, at others floating in a milky scud. Mrs Roxburgh pushed away the hair from in front of her eyes, and once, while recovering her balance, spat a flying strand out of her mouth. But no one was looking at that moment. Wrapped to the gills, Mr Roxburgh returned from a reconnaissance to lecture her on the virtues of studding sails, of which he had heard but recently.

'If the wind would veer slightly,' he said, and teetered, 'we could set our studsls. Then I should convince you. There is no prettier sight,' he added, 'than a vessel with its studsls set.' It rejoiced Mr Roxburgh to accumulate technical terms he would never be required to use in his own sphere of life.

The pale sun was making the sea look glassier. Its long furrows opened on coldly boiling depths into which the swaths of foam fell and were engulfed. Now that they were farther from the shore the gulls sounded less insistent. At a distance the land remained a lead- or slate-colour, when she would have wished to see it again looming in that blue haze of trees.

All the while the seamen were going about their duties, which enabled them to ignore a female: the bosun, his trousers rolled halfway up his calves, bristled with little hackles along the ridges of his great toes; a boy struggled to the side and emptied a kid of potato-peelings and grey fat to the more persistent of the gulls; while a replacement took over the helm from Mr Pilcher the second mate. A wiry fellow, of lined cheeks though not above his early thirties, Pilcher ducked his head in passing. They had not exchanged a word as yet, and perhaps an exchange would never come about. There are the souls who remain anonymous at sea in spite of the names one learns to attach to them.

Mrs Roxburgh staggered and clung alternately. She had adopted an ostentatious manner of breathing as though to demonstrate appreciation, and smiled, if only to herself. She loved listening to the sound of the sails.

She found her husband standing aft, staring at the wake, at the minute particles of foam streaming out behind them. The view of the wake was certainly more consoling than that of the great glassy graves opening to either side in the fields of ocean. Mr Roxburgh might have been trying to discern a design in the path they had made, or again, in his own thoughts.

He was growing noticeably restless, and shouted at her when he saw her watching, 'I'm going down. We'll be dining soon.' He looked bilious, but with an expression which suggested moral rather than physical distress.

'Aren't you feeling well?' it was her turn to ask; she was only too anxious to help: this was the basis on which their love was founded.

His answer was lost on the wind, his form in the companion-way, and she was alone until shy Mr Courtney barged past, large and healthy.

'Mr Roxburgh not of the best?' It seemed to give him courage to take advantage of someone else's infirmity.

'He has simply had enough of idleness. My husband is one whose mind must always be employed at something.'

It was all too mysterious for Mr Courtney, so he went away.

Shortly after, and uneventfully, the Roxburghs dined alone off more of the salt pork, which they were careful to shave close of fat.

In the evening they retired early.

Mrs Roxburgh let down her hair into a sea of silence where men's voices had ceased shouting. After they had said their prayers, a duty performed simultaneously and with the outward assurance which comes from habit, he embraced her, but absently it felt, which again was pretty usual. Listening to his snores Mrs Roxburgh was soon rolled into sleep in her upper berth.

4

It was the fifth day out and Austin Roxburgh had remained on deck longer than he would have expected of himself. Gulls hung in the clear air like bubbles in a glass. The sea billowed, a blander blue than at any stage of their course from Sydney. The breeze still favoured them. Veering slightly during the morning it began to blow from the south-east, which enabled Captain Purdew's crew to set the lower and topmast studding sails. To enjoy this prodigality of canvas was partly the reason why Austin Roxburgh had remained on deck. He could not give attention enough to this excessively beautiful crowd of sail, but stared and smiled with a proprietary expression at the rig he had appropriated as the mark of his initiation into nautical life. He was ignorant of more than the basic function of canvas, but the studding sails carried his hesitant spirit in the direction of poetry. So he strutted back and forth, his twilled overcoat blown open around him, or he would pause and stare, grinning at a blue, sun-blurred void, or alternately, at those who refused to see any connection between a superfluous gentleman and their own professional activities.

Mr Roxburgh was not immediately deterred. Sensitive to a point where he often became intolerable to those who knew him, he wore rhinoceros hide for strangers, particularly those deficient in education or of an inferior class. He would thwack his leg with his stick, baring his long, rather yellow teeth at the unfortunates of whom he disapproved, or who remained indifferent to his worth.

Thus he was tramping the deck, grimacing at the unmindful crew. Fascinated by so much of what he observed in life, whether beautiful or incongruous, he might have made use of it creatively had his perceptive apparatus not been clogged with waste knowledge and moral inhibitions. He would often isolate a form, or tremble with excitement for an idea, as though about to throw

129

upon it a light which would make it indisputably his. Then, instead, he grew resentful, or angry, sometimes even ashamed at his presumption. Once as he watched his wife descending the stairs in a topaz collar which had been his mother's, he was to such an extent illuminated that he resolved to commission Sir John to paint her portrait and had written away the following morning, but remained disappointed with the result, knowing that this was not the ultimate in revelation, which he himself had experienced as his wife shimmered on the stairs. None the less, everybody else found it a telling likeness, were awed by the gold frame, and paid respectful tribute to this materialization of the husband's wealth.

Where his wife was now, Mr Roxburgh had no idea. Without interrupting his own pursuits, he glanced around the deck from time to time, partly out of a sense of duty, partly because he was fond of her, but irritation left its heelmark imprinted in hard teak.

In the course of his revolutions he noticed Mr Courtney coming down from the forecastle, pausing briefly to inspect the cringle-making to which the boatswain had told off some of the younger crew members. From the lee of the pinnace Mr Roxburgh watched the first officer picking his way with expert ease through the animated forest in which he, by contrast, was lost. He was both expectant and apprehensive of Mr Courtney's arrival. He longed to join the mate in the kind of esoteric conversation the latter would know how to conduct amongst his fellow initiates, a free-masonry to which Mr Roxburgh could never be admitted it seemed, because he had not learnt the sign. In an even more despondent mood he would see himself locked in his solitary confinement cell, while those outside were able to communicate with the fluency, and according to the rights, of human beings.

As Mr Courtney came on, rubbing his hands together, it could have been as protection against rank and knowledge. 'With such a wind, we'll berth at Singapore, Mr Roxburgh, before you've even found your sea legs.' Intended to encourage the passenger, it probably consoled the mate.

Mr Roxburgh might have blushed, but a temporarily yellow complexion saved him from making a fool of himself. He remembered how, as boys, his younger and more active brother had learnt to tie a simple reef, and showed him how, and with what grateful pleasure he had received the demonstration. Now on

130

looking at the mate's perhaps deceptively candid eye he would have liked to ask him to demonstrate the tying of some immensely complicated knot.

Instead Mr Roxburgh asked, 'Have you the time on you, Mr Courtney?' and realized he had employed an idiom he would not have used in politer circles.

Without answering, the mate produced a battered silver watch, its face as open if not as large as its owner's. Mr Roxburgh could not thank him enough, but only after the watch had been returned to a serge pocket did he realize that he had failed to mark the hour.

It was too late to correct his mistake; the mate had removed himself with the exaggerated delicacy practised by men who are large but shy. Mr Roxburgh was relieved to think that his own ineptitude would remain his secret.

The ship was progressing as though born to an ease of motion, and the passenger, restored to solitude, recovered some of his self-importance. His mind glided marvellously when not threatened by the shoals of human intercourse or the bedevilled depths of his own nature.

Moods and any tendency to animal spirits had been discouraged from an early age by nurses, governesses and tutors on orders from the mother, who feared that too much of either might aggravate his delicate health. Books were countenanced if not morbid in sentiment. To surround her children with the solid architecture of life was the mother's object. 'You would not wish us to live amongst eccentric, needlessly ornamented furniture – spindly stuff which might collapse at a touch?' Thus she projected her own disdain to impress her elder boy, who visualized the horror of it. Following up, she pointed out that he must furnish his mind with what is indestructible. Yet she was far from being materialistic. While he was still a child she made him keenly aware of his moral responsibilities, with the result that he had awaited fatherhood with apprehension.

If failure to procreate living issue reduced him to silence on that subject, it shattered an unappeased grandmother: she began to recognize her years. She might have sat grizzling, 'One expects a different constitution in a Cornish hoyden,' but had grown to love a daughter-in-law she would not have accepted had it not been her habit to indulge the son she doted on. The elder Mrs Roxburgh was, besides, a good woman. In her old age an evangelical trait drove her to spend much of her time distributing bibles and patronizing orphans. Superfluously, she prayed for the gift of Charity twice a day, thrice on Sundays, excepting when she had a cold. Good works did not prevent her wearing a frisette till the night she died, the little, dangling curls from an exhausted fashion being the only sign of frivolity in her worthy life. She was much respected, but took it hard that certain acquaintances chose to remember how her father-in-law had been in trade.

It was unavoidable that family history should complicate to some extent the relationship between the lady and her son's wife. She had earmarked a clergyman's sister for Austin, thinking that something mature but mild would not 'aggravate', as she put it. She would not have spoken the word 'sensual', except in connection with abstract vice, and where her daughter-in-law was concerned, she translated 'sensuality' into 'health'. If only she had been able to consult with someone close, to lean upon her younger son, but he, alas, had defected earlier, to sensuality and worse, and been packed off as quickly and quietly as possible.

Because Austin was taught as a boy to suppress emotion, and soon preferred it thus, for fear that his preceptor might diagnose feeling as yet another 'symptom', none but his wife ever guessed that he must have reacted to his brother's forced departure as though he had suffered the amputation of a limb. His brother's skin, after a bath and a brisk towelling in front of the nursery fire, continued flickering on and off before Austin's eyes. He could remember an occasion when, seated beside the curiously woven brass fender, he had watched Garnet leap the rail, and stand crowing from amongst the coals, clothed in a suit of fiery feathers. He had awoken sweating from his dream; but Garnet had in him something of the quality of fire. Austin himself was not without it, if damped down, concealed by ash. He would not have had it otherwise – oh dear, no! but admired the free play of flames.

As he saw it, his mother and his brother were the opposite poles of his existence. He believed he found them united in his wife, whose sense of duty did not prevent her lips tasting of warm pears. He had never tasted his brother's lips, or not that he could remember. Garnet smelled of discharged guns and anointed harness, their mother of some dim melancholy, compound of lawyers' deeds and lemon verbena. She encouraged her elder son to cultivate the garden, which he did, if not literally: it was tended by too many gardeners. The art of horticulture was what attracted him, Latin names, dried specimens – not so far distant from his curtailed legal studies – rather than the flesh of living plants. But as token exercise and tribute to his mother, he would behead a few weeds, and fork at the moist earth, turning up bundles of flesh-coloured earth-worms. It sustained him too, against the wrench of his brother's departure. Their mother had come down the steps and laid a hand on her surviving boy's shoulder. They were standing under a medlar, treading a rich stench out of the fallen fruit. In this second bereavement Mrs Roxburgh would have liked to talk about her first, the father Austin could scarcely remember, and rarely attempted to.

Free of family responsibilities and ties, if not the ghosts they leave behind, Austin Roxburgh tried to feel exhilarated as he stood alone beneath this other tree on which his life now depended. Anonymous male voices drifted down at him from up there amongst the rope and canvas. He was unable to see the men themselves, but it did not bother him unduly; his wife excepted, he had more confidence in those with whom he was unacquainted. On and off he felt irritated thinking of his wife. Where could Ellen be? So dependable. She had soon learnt to pour tea of a strength soothing to his stomach and replenish the pot from the silver kettle slung above a little spirit-lamp.

The voices of the invisible sailors aloft were floating with the careless, designless ease of gulls' cries, gulls' frames.

'If one of them should fall!' Mr Roxburgh remarked aloud.

He was staring up. Anyone coming upon him would have caught him with his mouth and his thoughts open. He was not particularly thinking of the men, but instinctively touched his own ribs. His breath rattled in his throat as though he were emerging from out of a heavy blanket of sleep.

'There was a lad fell from the riggin' on the voyage out.' It was Pilcher, the second mate, with whom Mr Roxburgh had exchanged scarce a word all the way from Hobart Town; yet here they were, brought together fortuitously.

'Yes?' Mr Roxburgh would not be lured too far too soon.

They had gone across and were standing together at the bulwark. The wind was attempting to lift the passenger's cap, while the sea turned on its side as though preparing to reveal some hitherto hidden aspect of its realm.

'Yes?' Mr Roxburgh repeated so quickly it sounded unnatural.

'Poor Harry! Apart from his fall, d'you know what happened? Bosun forgot to weight 'is shroud.'

'He was buried at sea?'

'Where else? She's big enough.'

Mr Roxburgh and Mr Pilcher stood looking over the side.

Pilcher laughed. 'If the sharks don't get a man, it's the worms.'

Mr Roxburgh agreed; it seemed the only rational thing to do.

As they were placed, he could not have seen Pilcher without turning, but it would have been unnecessary to look: he knew his companion as that wiry individual of livid complexion and indeterminate age. He did not care for the mouth as he remembered it, thin-lipped, not unlike his own.

Mr Roxburgh shook himself to free his thoughts of a morbidity in which his mother and Nurse Hayes would not have permitted him to indulge. In search of a more wholesome image, he looked landward and saw that an opalescence had bloomed on the hitherto leaden slab of shore. An invisible sun struck at the land with swords of light, but only for a few moments, before the weapons were again sheathed, the target veiled in cloud and mist.

'What curious and beautiful tricks the light will play!' Mr Roxburgh at once regretted his remark, but needlessly; Pilcher appeared to consider it unworthy of his attention.

'Ever been any way in?' Austin Roxburgh thought to inquire.

'In where?'

'Into the interior.'

'Nao!'

The mate was of another element. He continued staring at the water, his contemptuous expression dissolving in what entranced him.

'Not if I was paid,' Mr Pilcher said. 'Nothing there.'

On the other hand, he seemed to imply, the sea was peopled with his like.

'Only dirty blacks,' he added, 'and a few poor beggars in

stripes who've bolted from one hell to another. The criminals they found out about! That's th'injustice of it. How many of us was never found out?'

Mr Pilcher spat into his element, but the wind carried the thread of spittle, stretching it into the shape of a transparent bow.

'That is certainly an argument,' Mr Roxburgh said.

'That is the truth!' the mate blurted passionately, and looked in the direction of the land. 'If I was sent out here in irons, for what I done – or what someone else had done, 'cause that can happen too, you know – I'd find a way to join the bolters. I'd learn the country by heart, like any of your books, Mr Roxburgh, and find more to it perhaps.'

The passenger was surprised that one whom he scarcely knew should be acquainted with his tastes.

'Experience, no doubt, leaves a deeper impression than words.'

''Specially when it's printed on yer back in blood.'

Mr Roxburgh winced, and sucked at his moustache.

'They wouldn't hold me, though,' Mr Pilcher continued. 'Not for long. No conger was ever slipp'rier,' he laughed, 'when his liberty was threatened. That's why I come away to sea. A man is free at sea. He can breathe. But I wouldn't suffocate there, neither – if I was put to it – in their blisterin' bush.'

Just then, the canvas tree above them shuddered and rattled to such an extent the mate appeared to remember his duties.

'Well?' He smiled, indulgently for him, and slipped away.

Mr Roxburgh was left with an impression of a vertical cut down either side of the man's mouth. Of course these were no more than lines with which the face had been weathered, but Austin Roxburgh could not avoid connecting them with their somewhat disturbing conversation. The conger was still twisting and glinting at a depth where he feared to follow, while in the element more natural to himself his hands had become unrecognizable as he tore a way through the blistering scrub, his nails as broken and packed with grime as the mate's own.

It was a relief when the arrival of a messenger rescued him from thoughts over which he had so little control.

'Mrs Roxburgh sent me, sir, to ask whether summat had detained 'ee.'

He recognized the boy who lent a hand in the galley, amongst his other duties, and helped Spurgeon carry the dishes down to the saloon. Usually blithe and elastic in all he did, his present mission had given him a primly formal, not to say ladylike air, perhaps in imitation of the one who had dispatched him.

'*Detain?*' the gentleman spluttered. 'How? What could detain one on board ship? Where time is of no account it isn't possible to be *detained*!' He appeared genuinely angry.

'She's worryin' that 'ee's gone so long,' the boy explained, gloomy now, as if this were one of the moments when lack of understanding in those who should possess it lowered his spirits.

Mr Roxburgh might have continued grumbling had the boy not disengaged himself from the unwelcome situation, skipped expertly beneath the mainsail, and made for the forecastle head.

Stranded thus, the passenger condescended to go between decks. On entering the saloon he found his wife busy with some sewing, an occupation he knew her to dislike. Such strength of mind in one he respected, and even loved, irritated him still further.

He frowned, and grumbled, 'I wish you wouldn't strain your eyes sewing by such a wretched light.'

She looked up, smiling too sweetly for his present fancy. 'Sewing isn't such a skill that one can't go along at it by instinct after a while.'

Each knew that in her case it was untrue.

Mr Roxburgh seated himself without taking off his overcoat. It made him look temporarily possessed by a sensation of impermanence. He proceeded to choose something to glare at, which happened to be the teasel-shaped flower, by now faded and wizened enough to justify throwing out.

'Did you enjoy yourself?' she asked.

'Enjoy myself at what?'

'How am I to know?'

'How, indeed! Or I!'

So they sat in silence awhile.

Then Mr Roxburgh so far relented as to reveal, 'I had some conversation with the second mate.'

'On what subject?'

'Difficult to say.' It made him glare at the dead flower.

Mrs Roxburgh sewed.

136

'That is,' he said, 'I can hardly remember, and if I could, it would be difficult to express in words.'

In fact, the mate's allusions had disturbed him so deeply he would have preferred to dismiss them from his mind.

Mrs Roxburgh continued sewing with an indifference born of obedience, which at last made itself felt.

'It was about the country beyond,' he was forced to admit, 'beyond the known settlements. Prisoners,' he positively drove himself, 'will sometimes escape. And wander for years in the interior. Supporting themselves off the land. Suffering terrible hardships. But as a life it is more bearable than the one they have bolted from.'

On passing a hand over his face he found he was perspiring for something he might have experienced himself. He realized, for that matter, he could have continued embroidering almost without end on the few words the mate had uttered.

Mrs Roxburgh's forehead had creased. She did sincerely sympathize with, and had suffered for, those who had been brought to her notice in Van Diemen's Land, but still had to bridge the gulf separating life from their own lives, whether stately rituals conducted behind the brocade curtains of their drawing-room at Cheltenham, or a makeshift, but none the less homely existence in a corner of this draughty little ship. Neither of them had felt the cat, only the silken cords of their own devising with which they tormented each other at intervals. Yet, she believed, she would have borne all, and more, were someone to require it of her.

How her mind was wandering! She felt ashamed and at the same time agitated. She got up and started an erratic tidying of their quarters as an excuse for moving about. Had she been her mother-in-law she might have prayed to their Lord Jesus for all those who must suffer the lash. But she herself was so constituted she could not pray with confidence; her prayers had seldom been more than words pitched without expectation into the surrounding dark.

Mrs Roxburgh glanced at her husband to decide whether he had guessed, but Austin Roxburgh was too engrossed in his own thoughts, and perhaps always had been.

Throwing off their mood they spent a pleasant, uneventful evening, dining by insufficient light until the captain called for the candles to be lit. There was not only Captain Purdew; Mr Courtney put in an appearance. Again, seemingly, it was Mr Pilcher's watch. It occurred to each of the Roxburghs that the second mate had not yet broken bread with them.

The ship's motion and the few mouthfuls of ale she had drunk made Mrs Roxburgh yawn; or it could have been the captain's story.

Towards the end of dinner Captain Purdew departed from the sea – for him, a rare occurrence – and was telling a land tale, of a carter and his horse. In celebration of the rare occurrence the worthy seaman heavily emphasized each detail, at times even striking the table with the flat of his hand. Mr Courtney, by contrast, had hunched his shoulders, and was sitting silent, looking at his place. He had spread his coarse, doggy hair with a liberal ration of pomade, perhaps knowing beforehand that, in the captain's presence, he would not contribute a word to the conversation, and might assert himself in this other way.

Nearing the end of a drive from Scole, Captain Purdew had encountered the subject of his story this side of Norwich, '... when the horse began to stagger. I'd been catching up on them for some distance in the trap, and suspected there was something unnatural in the animal's behaviour – till suddenly – he fell down!' The captain slapped the table so hard the glasses jumped and tinkled.

Hungry for further mysteries since his talk with Pilcher during the forenoon, Mr Roxburgh was merely frustrated by the plodding tale of the carter's horse.

'He fell down between the shafts,' Captain Purdew continued, 'and the carter began thrashing the poor beast with the reins.'

Mr Roxburgh might never have encountered a worse bore, while Mr Courtney hunched his shoulders higher and tighter for the superior he was unable to protect against the results of his tediousness.

'I don't mind saying I swore at him.' Captain Purdew turned to Mrs Roxburgh, who showed him the kind of smile which may be worn at any season. 'For I'd noticed that the dray was braking, and the man was far gone with drink.'

Mrs Roxburgh thought Captain Purdew was possibly in like condition, but held her head graciously when she could have let

138

loose a whole string of the yawns she was suppressing. From feeling them swell inside her throat, she saw them as the continuum of soft, unlaid eggs in the innards of a slaughtered hen.

She glanced at her husband. She would have liked to share with him her vision of soft eggs, but he was likely to disapprove of it as much as he would the sight of hen-dirt on her hands from plunging them into the bird's gizzard.

'"The brake, man!" I shouted'; and the captain demonstrated.

It seemed to Mrs Roxburgh that the whole of her uneventful life had been spent listening to men telling stories, and smiling to encourage them. It was a relief to catch sight of the boy, who entered bearing a dish with some of the apples they had taken on board at Sydney, and which were of a wrinkled, though hectic red. The boy's eyes were absorbed in a silent judgement she was unable to interpret, but this did not prevent her wishing to conspire with him in some innocent way. She wondered whether she would have been able to exchange confidences with her own son had she reared him. It was not then, unnatural, surely, that she should hanker after the trust of this crop-headed lad with the dish of feverish apples?

'I seated myself on the horse's head as he lay in the road,' the captain was explaining to Mr Roxburgh.

The latter nodded, but was looking in his wife's direction. Her head was the sole reality in this sea of words, or for that matter, life. It flickered at times, then burned steady, like any candle-flame, with the result that her husband was overcome with remorse for his irritable sallies earlier that day, and by a fear that he might not convey his love before one of them was extinguished.

In the circumstances, Mr Roxburgh was maddened by the captain's story. 'What *happened* to the deuced horse?'

'Why, the fellow unharnessed him. After which, I got up. And the horse heaved himself to his feet. He couldn't stop trembling.'

Mr Roxburgh too, had begun to tremble, with annoyance, and his ineffectual love.

As the ship lurched farther on its voyage, the diners seemed contained by a flickering of light rather than by timber.

Mr Courtney asked to be excused.

By the time the cloth was removed, and the captain as well, Mr

Roxburgh doubted he would ever learn to speak to his wife in simple words.

They continued sitting at the table which Spurgeon had concealed under a dull garnet-coloured plush. Mrs Roxburgh induced her husband to join her in a game of piquet. Neither cared for cards, but now they played.

At last Mrs Roxburgh pushed the game away from her. She began to laugh. Her elbows protruded sharply from the sleeves as she clasped her hands behind her head. 'Were you entertained by the captain?'

Mr Roxburgh grumbled in gathering up the disordered cards.

'Why,' she asked, 'do you suppose he told it?'

'Why do people speak? For the most part to fill in the silences.'

They fell silent after that. As her lips came together he would have devoured them contrary to his habit, but it might have given her too rude a surprise.

The ship was shaking with an odd, self-destructive motion while they prepared themselves for bed.

Mrs Roxburgh thought she would never fall asleep. Had *he* succumbed? She listened. She touched her face and could tell it had grown haggard. She would not sleep that night, but must have dropped off eventually, to be drifting through whichever element it was, hair blown or flowing behind her, while her face tried on credible expressions. Suddenly she was lashed. It was her hair turned to knotted cords. I will, I *must* endure it because this is my only purpose. She kissed his hands. And kissed. And looked down into his facelessness. Just as the beam, inexpertly fixed, perhaps deliberately, by the carpenter at Hobart Town, began slipping. It is piercing my husband's heart. It is lying embedded in the yellow waxen always unconvincing flesh. *Ohhhhh!* A mouth grows egg-shaped under the influence of despair.

Mrs Roxburgh awoke and looked down at the lower berth. Her husband was seated on the edge, head bowed, legs dangling. She recognized the whorl in the crown of dark hair which would have served as an identification mark in the most horrible circumstances.

'What is it, my dear?' Alarm made her voice sound raucous.

She was already climbing down, ungainly in her haste, her hair impeding a strained progress.

'It's the pain, Ellen! Oh God, the most awful pain yet!'

At once she rummaged for the little flask containing the tincture of digitalis and administered the drops in a finger of water. She kneeled at his feet, chafing his knees. At least she could now do something which would prevent anyone accusing her. She would infuse him with her own excessive health and powers of resistance. As she kneeled, she willed him to accept what she had to offer.

'I'll not have you suffer,' she was mouthing; 'you can depend on me, my dearest.'

'Oh, I'm not going to *die*!' Mr Roxburgh ground it out from between his teeth, and laughed without mirth, for the vise was still squeezing him.

Yet he was soothed by his wife's touch. He closed his eyes, and thought to hear his mother's voice, her commands for his welfare, as she proceeded to allay one of his coughing fits.

Now the world had shrunk to its core, or to the small circle of light in the middle of the ocean, in which two human souls were momentarily united, their joint fears fusing them into a force against evil.

As soon as she could safely leave her husband Mrs Roxburgh put on her mantle and resolved to see whether it were possible to procure some milk. She had eased him back upon the pillows, from where his expression and the regular rise and fall of his chest suggested that he might be dozing, or at least enjoying the relief which comes from exhaustion.

She herself was exhausted, she realized as she scrambled out upon the deck, but her condition added to the splendour of the night: the breathing of canvas overhead sounded the stronger and deeper for her almost drunken reeling through the forest of her hair, while short bursts of light from a recurring moon transformed the ship, despite its heaving, into solid sculpture.

Mrs Roxburgh made her way towards the galley, and was guided in her final steps by snores rasping in discord against the integrated sounds of sea and sail. It was Spurgeon the steward-cook, who had spread his blanket on the floor of his official sanctum.

'My husband,' she explained, 'is sick,' before begging a little of the milk they had taken on at Sydney.

Spurgeon was confused by the light he made after a fumbling with lucifers. 'You may be lucky,' he growled. 'If 'twas tomorrow evenin' I doubt there'd be enough to wet a baby's whistle. Milk will be off. If 'tisn't that already.' He stuck his nose inside a blackened can.

She waited patiently, determined there should be milk enough for her invalid, while Spurgeon, who seemed to have discarded the conventions to suit the hour and the circumstances, repeated mumbling, 'Sick, eh? With gentlefolk, I thought it was *mal de mur*.'

Too tired to compose an answer, Mrs Roxburgh pretended not to hear; while he warmed the milk on a reluctant fire in an atmosphere stuffy with sleep and charcoal.

When the milk was ready she was so grateful Spurgeon grew quite pleased with himself. He smiled along his nose at the favour he had done her, and glanced down at her wedding ring, or so it appeared.

'That's the lot,' he announced, '*ma'am*!' and laughed, and added, 'I wouldn' do the same for any other lady.'

Mrs Roxburgh was undecided whether she liked or disliked Spurgeon, but was free to hurry away. Slopping the milk slightly in her haste, warming her hands on the greasy vessel, she was panting with achievement; she would allow neither the steward's ambiguous behaviour nor the swaying of the night to confuse her.

When she returned to the cabin, the candle had burnt low, but Mr Roxburgh opened his eyes and looked as though prepared to check an inventory of her every feature.

'I've brought you some warm milk,' she said.

Tranquillity perhaps made him forget to remind her of his loathing for the skin of boiled milk.

She helped him into an upright position, and supported him in it with an arm, after first pouring into a cracked cup the greater part of the milk ration.

'There!' she coaxed.

As he sank his mouth she greedily watched, until she saw the string of milk hanging and swinging from his lower lip. Well, she thought, he has forgot about that at least. She recalled her father supping at a cup of hot milk in the kitchen after lambing. Pa

142

liked to soak his bread. He was greedy as herself for food, in the days when she had to make the most of a little.

But the beard of milk was trembling on Mr Roxburgh's lip. She almost wiped it for him, when she saw him suck the milk-skin into his mouth.

While the two of them rocked and swayed together on the bosom of the sea, and she explored with her eyes the cracks and knots in their roughly constructed berths, she thought how she would have loved to taste a door-step of fresh-baked bread, dripping with warm, sweetish milk such as he used to offer her when she was still a little girl, his hands in which the cracks never seemed to close, and the thumb with the horn-thing which always repelled, and sometimes frightened her.

She must have dozed, for she had allowed her husband to slip lower and the cup she was holding to tilt.

Austin Roxburgh appeared restored to an acceptable level of reality. He was gently sleeping. Once or twice he groaned, not in pain, rather for the dryness of an open mouth. Which he closed to moisten. Opening and closing, to suck at the air, and alternately, dredge for moisture. She was surprised to find how calmly she could contemplate his cheek fretting against one of her breasts. The breast had escaped from its covering, at its centre the teat on which his struggling mouth once or twice threatened to fasten.

She lay awhile longer, at peace. Then, ashamed of her opulence, she covered herself, and climbed to her own berth.

5

Since settling down to their life at sea, lulled by air and motion and the mystical permutations of canvas, there was little to convince the passengers that the days had not been created by men for their own convenience. Time, and its fellow conspirator space, subtler for its present watery guise, were never in more perfect accord, and when on the seventh day the ship nosed gently into fog, the impression of limitless unity was increased, if not for all the voyagers, for Mrs Roxburgh unquestionably.

Her husband had remained resting in his berth the whole of the day following his distressing attack, and the morning after that, still seemed indisposed to rise.

'There's a fog come up,' she announced as she looked in the glass and wrapped herself against the weather. 'Thick. Oh, thick!'

Her low, muffled voice made it sound the most desirable condition. Mr Roxburgh closed his eyes. He enjoyed being cosseted. In the absence of medical attention, Captain Purdew paid him frequent visits, sat on the edge of the bunk, and racked his memory for advice. But it was Ellen who knew. Her voice dulled anxieties, wrapped him in a fog of contentment where no equivocal shapes were likely to rise and endanger him.

Now as she stood looking in the glass at a blurred image which suggested that strands of mist had strayed down the companionway and through the hatches, its imperfection made her the more mysterious in his eyes.

'I shall go up on deck,' she announced, 'and take the air. But only for a little,' she added as a comfort.

Possibly she intended to embrace him, but on second thought, laid fingers briefly against his cheek. In his present state of mind the quickly withdrawn contact thrilled him more deeply than any overt demonstration. (Besides, he had once jokingly confessed, kisses tend to be glutinous.)

Mrs Roxburgh reached the deck. Her intention of returning shortly intensified her expectations. Had they not been cool, her fingers travelling over surfaces with that same hesitant tenderness with which she had touched her husband's cheek, might have seemed feverish. She emerged with an audible gasp for the swirl of fog, which rushed and entered, choking with fistfuls of white down, and parted, and united, on face or mast. She was not blinded by it, however; her eyes might have been jewels cutting such strands as offered themselves.

For a moment some more powerful influence acted upon the mass of fog. The blanket was torn open to reveal the distant land: hog-backed, of a louring, formal ugliness, it might have dispirited the observer had it not glittered like a chunk of sapphire. Long after the fog had closed on her momentary vision, Ellen Roxburgh continued watching, waiting for a sign, but it did not recur.

She went forward at last, past the helmsman, whom she decided to ignore from guessing at the expression on his face. On the forecastle head the fog was at its most obliterating. She could neither see, nor breathe, and might have retreated if her faculties had not been stimulated by a suggestion of danger.

So she continued weaving through the fog, while clinging to rope or timber for support (despite her daring, she was glad of their honest, reliable textures) and almost stumbled over a form, that of a boy she made out, seated in the shelter of a capstan, dripping moisture, although, it appeared, content enough.

'Ah,' she cried, 'it is you!' For it was the lad who sometimes served under Spurgeon at dinner.

Less at ease than before, the boy grunted. He was eating one of the wizened but sweet, Sydney apples, which were lasting bravely. For his moral support the boy tore out an extra large mouthful and sat chewing. It sounded more like the champing of a horse.

Mrs Roxburgh may have felt daunted, but ventured, 'I'm glad I have found you.'

He looked up, his eyes deepening with mistrust, if not horror, for until now he had only received orders from her, or silent glances as he carried out the used dishes.

'For company,' she tried to explain.

It made the boy more obviously suspicious.

'Why?' he mumbled through his mouthful. 'Are ye afraid?' She might have been asking for something he had never been taught to give.

'No,' she answered, touching with the toe of her boot a coop in which two wet hens sat huddled against each other. 'Everyone is occupied except myself. And the fog is so lovely I'd like to watch it with someone else who is unemployed.'

'Fog's no more'n fog.' The boy sniffed, or he must have sniffed, for immediately after, he wiped his nose with the back of the hand which held the apple.

For her part, she was reduced to childhood by the boy's logic, so that she knelt beside him at the very moment when his limbs were stirring with an instinct to get to his feet and assert his manhood by leaving her.

Lapsing spontaneously into her first language, she begged, 'Cusn't I stay with 'ee?'

It was too strange: a lady who could speak ordinary. The boy sank back against the capstan, cowering perhaps. He reached up with an arm, and twined it round one of the hickory bars, to maintain his balance, or protect himself.

'I'm not the master,' he said.

A certain innocence which life had not succeeded in exorcizing from her nature made her long for him to accept her. As a little girl, which she had become again, only briefly no doubt, she might have bribed him with some valued possession. But here she had nothing to offer.

'What's tha name?' she asked respectfully.

'Oswald Dignam,' the boy answered and brightened; to own a label seemed to lend him courage.

At the same time Ellen Roxburgh remembered her position and the wisdom and dignity she ought to possess. 'Why did you come to sea, Oswald?' she asked, not unkindly, but correctly.

'Food's regular.'

'That it is,' she agreed. 'But was there nothing else?'

'I dunno.' And then, ' 'Tis a life like any other that takes you up.'

The air had begun filling his hitherto cramped chest; a down of fog was stirring on his upper lip. The movement of the fog, the striving of the isolated ship, the sense of an expanding universe, began to bring them together at last.

Now that the boy had started, he confided, 'A man can save 'is money at sea.'

'What will you do with it?' she asked.

It was most important that she should know.

'Buy a ferret.'

'Aw? I dun't remember whether I ever seed a ferret. Praps once – to Zennor. Iss, some gipsies had 'n.'

She cocked her head. In the cordage above, beads of moisture danced, trembled, and sometimes fell.

The boy grew sullen again; he might have revealed too much of himself. 'A *animal* is company.' He was puffing out his lips in self-defence.

'Yes,' she agreed. 'I had a little pug.'

Hard bare feet squelching on the deck threatened to destroy their privacy, but passed.

'What happened to the pug?'

'She died.'

The melancholy sea air had at last drenched them. She could feel her hair putting out its saddest tendrils.

He said, 'I never had a dog.'

'I'll give you one when we come home. I'll buy you the ferret, Oswald.'

She spoke too fast, as though to prevent a doubt widening between herself and her protégé; promises, like prayer, can be an attempt at blackmail.

At the same time a fogbound voice began tolling, reaching deeper, always deeper into the void.

'What is that?' she asked.

'The lookout – conning.'

'Is there danger?'

'No more'n usual.' He threw away the sucked apple-core.

She did not try to measure a contempt she must have earned.

'It is time,' she decided, 'to return to my husband. If I stay too long, he suspects, I think, that I've been swept overboard. His fears make him irritable.'

'Ah?' It was only of faint interest to the boy.

Then, when she had got to her feet, he looked up at her, evidently trying to visualize a state which could remain for ever outside his experience.

As she left him, the boy's face was first blurred, then obliterated by the unconscionable fog. Sometimes toiling uphill, sometimes teetering sideways with little, drunken steps, she held tightly to the points of her elbows inside the pretty, fringed shawl. In this manner she preserved something of her physical self from the general amorphousness in which Oswald Dignam was lost and her own thoughts and hair floated as undirected as seaweeds. Yet, as she prepared to negotiate the companion-ladder, Mrs Roxburgh did make an effort to manage her hair, and wiped from her lips the last scum of drunkenness.

The afternoon passed soberly. The passengers took their customary nap and were prepared to dine when called.

'We shall grow liverish,' Mrs Roxburgh predicted.

Her husband did not answer because it was the kind of remark for which answers are not expected, at any rate in a well-regulated marriage. Sitting on the edge of the bunk preparatory to pulling on his boots, he was stuck by the superfluity of words with which the married state is littered.

When suddenly and brutally the sequence of events was wrenched out of his control. There was a ramming. And grinding.

At once a slow but inexorable turmoil of activity began taking place around them. A button hook and a chair fell upon them from a great height, for by this time Mrs Roxburgh, who had been standing before the glass, running the comb through her loosened hair, was thrown upon her husband's breast, against the cabin wall which formed with the bunk the trough where they found themselves. In their initial alarm they were struggling with each other as much as against a quirk of gravity. Half-fowl half-woman, Mrs Roxburgh was panting in her husband's ear. Her teeth must have gashed his cheek, he felt, but the shattering of several breakable vessels in the saloon beyond, dispersed any possible resentment he might have harboured against her.

Then there was the slither and trample of feet overhead.

'Mr Courtney, sir! Mr Court-*ney*?'

'Good God,' a second voice moaned obliquely through the fog, 'can't you see we've struck? A reef! Plain as your nose, man!'

'We're keel-ing!'

'. . . need to *tell* me . . .'

So the gull-voices of men called faintly in the outer air.

Mr Roxburgh observed his pins protruding from beneath his wife's skirts. His chest was protesting at her weight.

'Do you hear, Ellen?' asked his old man's voice. 'We've struck a reef!'

'Oh, my dear! I was thrown off my balance. Have I hurt you?'

He ignored that. 'We must stay calm and keep our wits about us.'

He was determined that they should not give way to emotion, but could not help being aware how ineffectual his voice sounded, as on all occasions when he gave orders. Yet others never appeared to notice.

'Yes,' she agreed, and succeeded in withdrawing her harsh breath from his ear, her disarrayed feathers from off his person, though they were still bundled together in the trough made by the bunk and the wall.

'We must make our way – somehow – on deck,' Mr Roxburgh decided.

'. . . that I haven't hurt you,' she persisted, and took his cold hand in her warmer ones.

He found it unnecessary. 'It's no time, Ellen, for delicacy of sentiment.'

It was she, however, who grew practical, initiating the series of grotesque movements necessary for their escape from the cabin.

'Ma'am? Mrs Roxburgh?'

She looked up, laboriously, and saw Oswald Dignam staring down at them from an unorthodox angle. His eyes were protruding slightly as he clung to the jamb of the swinging door.

'Captain Purdew, ma'am,' he called, then swallowed as the door caught his fingers. 'You must come up quick,' he recovered himself and shouted, 'on th' old man's orders.'

Though crisis and the pain from his jammed fingers had temporarily transformed him into a small, girlish boy, his sense of authority would not allow him to feel ashamed.

'We're stuck fast,' their messenger informed them, 'but will try to bring her off.'

Mrs Roxburgh herself was so dazed by the situation, as well as entranced by the sweet, milky face of what might have been a cherub on the ceiling of some great house, she answered only with an effort, 'Yes, Oswald. We shall get ourselves ready. And come on deck.'

She stretched out a hand to her husband. It felt surprisingly strong and capable despite the years in which she had been discouraged from using it. He was grateful for his wife's hand, and she for the opportunity to justify herself.

Oswald Dignam had disappeared under cover of their concentrated activity.

Mr Roxburgh began the climb towards the hook which held his overcoat, while his wife crawled in the direction of the carpet bag, to find she could not think what to pack. Instead she fumbled with the small leather dressing-case in which she locked her more valuable or intimate possessions such as jewels, journal, false hair, the prescribed smelling salts which she never used, and began stuffing in few random articles as though she were a thief.

'Wrap up as warm as possible,' she advised needlessly.

Already in his overcoat and cap, Mr Roxburgh was winding round his neck an interminable woollen muffler she had knitted to his specifications several autumns ago.

She tied her shawl tighter, the same green one admired by Mrs Merivale at Sydney, and made a grab for her mantle.

Her breath was coming in desperate grunts, as though she, not her husband, were the invalid.

'Take your time,' he appealed to her. 'All this is by way of precaution. I doubt the danger is as great as it appears, or if it is,' he cleared his throat, 'she's not likely to break up at once – not before they've launched the boats.' He would do his best till the end to impose some kind of logic on unreason.

She finished tying down her bonnet with what she liked to think firmer movements. 'Well, now?' Her smile was a wry one, but directed at him personally.

They began to scale the floor of the listing cabin, clinging with one hand to their sole article of luggage, with the second, clawing at any support offered by furniture or fitments, and after the same fashion, once through the doorway, navigated what had been the saloon. Neither would have admitted to the other that water had penetrated, when there it was lying before their eyes, oozing and lapping, an antithesis of ocean – a black, seeping treacle which the plush table cloth failed to stanch, while a teasel-shaped flower they had brought back on an afternoon at Sydney Cove was too light and withered to have been sucked under as yet.

Not until they arrived at the companion-ladder did the Roxburghs allow themselves to contemplate fully the dangers with which they might be faced. Up till now, they had been superficially irritated, he understandably more than she, by a rude break in their measured routine, and by having to adjust their physical bearing to the angle of a heeling ship, but now, suddenly, the cold air pouring down from above, was aimed at their defenceless bodies, and struck even deeper. Their souls shrank dreadfully under the onslaught, and would have wrapped themselves together in a soft, mutually protective ball had that been possible. As it was not, the man and woman were left flattening themselves against a wall, bones groaning, almost breaking it seemed, as they wrestled perhaps for the last – and was it also the first time? with a spiritual predicament.

Ellen Roxburgh then, was pinning her husband against the wall, grinding her cheek into his as she would never have dared. 'Tell me – this once,' she commanded, 'I have not made you unhappy?'

He fought back with a strength he had never thought he possessed. 'Ah, *Ellen*, it is no occasion for foolish questions!' His voice issued from its deepest source to expire at the surface amongst what sounded like dry reeds.

In the obscurity at the foot of the ladder he knew her eyes were staring at him, and he stared back: for the moment they were both contained in the same luminous bubble which circumstances threatened to explode.

It was she who broke. Her tears were streaming.

He would have started dragging her up the ladder, to protect her from that mortal danger, herself. 'You mustn't be afraid,' he ordered, 'or not till we know there's cause for it.'

'I'm not afraid for myself,' she cried. 'It's for you. And my child.'

'*Child?*'

'Oh, yes. I would not have added this to your cares, but it isn't possible – any longer – to avoid it.'

'My dearest dearest Ellen!' He fumbled for her face, to unite her tributary distress with the love he felt flowing out of him. 'Our child is our best reason for surviving.'

Only obtuseness and self-absorption could have prevented him seeking a reason for the frequent torpor, the growing softness and whiteness of the form which had supported him in sickness, and for the presence of which he found he craved increasingly. Now his contrition was the more intense and searing for the drought from which it sprang.

Again it was she who came to her senses, who began to protest, and assume her normal role of protector. 'We are wasting time! You go first, Mr Roxburgh, and I will follow with the bag. You must take care – more than ever – now that we have an ordeal to face – not to over-tax yourself.'

As they struggled upward, he issued a reprisal of warnings in lowest key. 'Ellen! Keep *calm*! As I told you. And especially since you have other responsibilities. Besides, they'll see that you've been crying if your manner is – noticeably – *agitated*.'

So they came out upon the sloping deck. Between them, though by no specific agreement, they were carrying the leather dressing-case. They stood bracing themselves against the list of the marooned vessel, which had brought upon them every distortion of grace, not to say abandon of propriety.

Never since boarding *Bristol Maid* had Mr and Mrs Roxburgh looked so awkward, foolish, and superfluous. It was not surprising that those who might be competent to deal with the present situation paid no attention to them as they stamped or slithered about their business. The passengers were made to feel they must pay for their ignorance. Humbly smiling, they prepared to accept their just deserts.

Mr Courtney, although very much the first officer coping with a crisis, took pity at one stage. His jacket unbuttoned, his mouth loose from shouting, he demonstrated with his large hands how their ship had brought up suddenly on a semi-circle of coral.

There it was, if they cared to look, a pale, greenish glimmer, on which the lovely lace of foam was being torn to further tatters.

Mr Courtney was of the opinion that nobody was to blame but the fog; they had been doing a bare five knots. He was so convinced he repeated himself several times over.

The fog was lifting, as though to expose the full irony of its work. The stranded ship had swung round and was lying broadside on to the sea.

'Close-hauling,' Mr Courtney bellowed at the passengers, 'could bring her off.'

The Roxburghs were appreciative if dazed. They intended to maintain hope, but in the face of the mate's practical knowledge they dared not contribute even the token of an amateur suggestion.

For his part, Mr Courtney, although a genia., kindly man, felt he had done his duty by the passengers, and was determined to dismiss them from sight at least. 'I advise you to take shelter, Mrs Roxburgh, in the charthouse or the galley.'

Presumably included in the invitation, the lady's husband was left to accompany her down the deck to whichever asylum she happened to choose. Mr Courtney, who had already limped away, might have stamped in level circumstances. Unusually sensitive to moral criticism from others, Austin Roxburgh wondered whether the mate had been concealing from the beginning a streak of that contempt which members of the lower classes often harbour against their betters, but shelved the theory for further examination at a more appropriate time. At the moment there was nothing for it but to follow his wife.

They proceeded, tittuping on their land legs, clinging to whatever was offered them by way of support. Over the side, the variable sea, now a milky, liquid jade, poured itself on the snoozing coral, the latter not so passive that it would not rise at times, to snap with a mouthful of teeth, or lash from under with swathed limbs.

Mrs Roxburgh came to the decision not to look seaward as she made her way forward. If asked to consider why she was choosing the galley in preference to the charthouse, her only reason could have been that she had visited the galley during their progress through a sea which had not yet grown hostile, in a gently breathing ship, which now lay stiff and stubborn beneath them, or grumbled, or shuddered. Aloft, a man was swinging, all sinews, tendons, muscular contortions, grinning at the wind as he fought the canvas. Herself straining along the deck beneath, Mrs Roxburgh felt relieved when this battered Punch was removed from sight, if not from thought; indeed, he might return in her dreams.

Remembering her husband, she glanced back once or twice to call and encourage. 'We are practically there,' she told him, whether her voice would carry or not.

She caught herself smiling, from habit, and was glad she could not see herself; at this point the only significance her smile could have had was that of an arbitrary, not to say perverse, decoration.

They reached the galley. Never much more than one of those protuberances with which the deck was capriciously furnished, it now resembled a tilted hutch. They blundered their way inside, into a consoling stuffiness, clean-swept of the utensils one would have expected. In a depression formed between the opposite wall and the steep floor, dented pots were lying, together with the shards of crocks, and the white shambles of what must have been the saloon dinner service. Over all hung the smell of cold ash and fat.

'Here I am going to stay,' Ellen Roxburgh announced, as though it might still be granted to her to exercise her will.

There was a fixed table behind which, on a similarly immovable bench, she succeeded in wedging herself, along with the leather dressing-case. (If she had sole control of this during the latter stages of their journey, it was what she considered natural, and would have wished.)

After perching uneasily beside her on the bench, Austin Roxburgh wondered aloud, '. . . whether I might give them some kind of assistance'.

Mrs Roxburgh did not answer, for the simple reason that she had withdrawn even out of reach of the husband whose protection was her chosen vocation. She would have liked to pray, but found the vocabulary and the necessary frame of mind for prayer, wrecked inside her. Mentally she was still too exhausted to sort out the wreckage, and recoiled moreover, from a possibility that she might never restore order to a spiritual cupboard which had not been kept as neat as it looked.

So she sat with her arms round that other responsibility, the child whose presence had been her secret burden over the last five months.

The sea raked the sides of *Bristol Maid* with increasing fury. As its spray lashed the deck, in collaboration with more vicious because more substantial whips in the form of snapped cordage, the galley walls strained and vibrated.

Those sheltering inside did not realize that the captain had appeared at the doorway, until he called. 'Are we in good heart?'

Captain Purdew followed it up with a curiously half-hearted laugh. These whom he was looking over through the doorway were officially his passengers, not pet animals to which he had taken a rash fancy and now regretted having acquired. Had they been pouter-pigeons or white mice – or easiest of all, silkworms, he might have disposed of them without a qualm.

Mr and Mrs Roxburgh assured Captain Purdew that they were in the best of spirits.

From their perch they sat looking back at the one who had them in his keeping, and who, they hoped, was possessed of benign wisdom and superhuman powers in spite of resembling an old, moulted member of the same species, Adam's apple wobbling above a dirty collar, blue-red flesh thinly stretched over such bones as were visible, and deposits of salt on drooping lids and in the corners of disillusioned eyes.

Captain Purdew braved their inspection. 'We have two stout boats which the men will lower at the first opportunity.' For more than the first time he glanced over a shoulder, and confirmed in a trailing voice, 'The sea is too high at present.'

Then he left them, not to direct further operations, but to avoid, one suspected, those of his subordinates who had automatically taken over. In fact, Captain Purdew was in much the same plight as the inferior beings, or unwanted pets, his passengers, though nobody might have admitted yet to the true state of affairs.

The Roxburghs languished on their perch, and to give each other courage, asserted from time to time that the storm was surely abating; when Mr Roxburgh made a most distressing discovery.

'My Elzevir! I don't remember – but could have left it – in the cabin – no, more likely the saloon.'

'Your *what*?'

'My Virgil.'

'Ohhh?' Her voice climbed to a point of disbelief which almost revealed an opinion of her own: that in spite of a respect for books instilled by her husband and mother-in-law, they were another kind of furniture, but unlike tables, chairs, and so forth, dispensable.

Fortunately Mr Roxburgh was too distracted to detect in his wife signs of possible apostasy. He had risen, apparently preparing, not so much to show his respect for books, as to demonstrate his adherence to a faith.

'You are not going back?' Her voice should have had more colour in it, but she was understandably debilitated.

'There is no danger as yet – from what they tell us.'

'Oh, no, no! There's no need to go back. Not for a book!' Whatever the eventual outcome, she had said it; in the present, however, the languid tones of female despair did not serve to restrain her husband; it made him, if anything, the more determined to carry out his intention.

When he had left her, and she had sighed out her formal disapproval, and tidied up some of the physical ravages, Mrs Roxburgh was secretly glad. It was the greatest luxury to be sitting alone, to give up the many-faceted role she had been playing, it now seemed, with mounting intensity in recent months – of loyal wife, tireless nurse, courageous woman, and more unreal than any of the superficial, taken-for-granted components of this character – expectant mother. Yet her body told her that this child was the truest part of her, of such an incontrovertible truth that she had not admitted it to the company of those 'formed' thoughts, affectations, and hypocrisies recorded in her journal, just as she had banned from its pages another, more painful truth – herself as compliant adulteress.

A reality accepted might have left her less detached had she not felt fulfilled, and had she not been reared besides, on the realities: she was still to some extent a lump of a country girl, chapped hands folded in her lap, seated on a rock amongst furze and hussocks in a failing light. In the ordinary sequence of events someone would have come courting the farmer's daughter, and got her with child and to church, in that order.

Mrs Roxburgh stirred on her bench. In her thoughts she was torn between reality and actuality. On breaking the sequence of events and spiriting her away, her preceptors had attempted in all good faith to foist what they recognized as a mind on the

156

farmer's daughter. Had she perhaps expressed herself too explicitly, Mrs Roxburgh wondered, if only by the tone of a phrase, the absence of a word, in her journal? The possibility began to rankle in her, along with her child, and a not entirely renounced lust.

She unlocked the dressing-case. There was the excuse of passing time, and incidentally, that of pacifying her conscience, while the light held. She searched through Mr Roxburgh's papers, letters, his journal, the fragment of a 'memoir' ('it is thought, not action, Ellen, which makes an eventful life, and for that reason – who knows – I may some day begin harvesting the fruits of thought.') These she could remember snatching up before she left the cabin. She fumbled with the velvet bag which held the few unimportant jewels she had brought on the voyage, and back through the individual documents without laying hand on the object of her search. As she rummaged, it became of increasing consequence to find, to read, to confirm that she had not written more of the truth than can bear looking at. Her breath rasped. In her mind's eye she saw the vellum-bound volume floating in the tipsy waters of the wrecked saloon, salvaged by her husband at danger to his balance, and finally her own complete equilibrium – if the prize had not already fallen to a member of the crew, or more likely, Mr Pilcher.

As the second mate emerged into the foreground of her imagining, it no longer occurred to her that a storm was raging round a shipwreck. It was clear that the elusive Pilcher, of reserved manner, and colourless eyes to conceal the depth of their vision, had shown by his behaviour and appearance that he was designed to be the instrument of her undoing. Armed with such hints and overt disclosures as the journal contained, he would break his silence, the lines on either side of his mouth opening like wounds healed but temporarily.

In the twilight of the galley she almost warded off an apparition as convincing as it was unreasonable; for there was no reason why her mind should turn to Pilcher, except through the contempt in which she suspected he held her, as well as the suspicion that had they met by a similar light on the Zennor road they might have hailed each other as two beings equally secretive and devious.

Mrs Roxburgh sat locking her hands, which had grown too

157

soft to resist her thoughts. The strength was drained out of her. She wished, and did not wish for the return of Mr Roxburgh, who might be floating, face down, in bilge water.

Her thoughts were inflating into monstrous waves. *My dearest husband* . . . In the absence of her own regrettable journal, should she open his and pass the time reading from it while there was light enough? She re-opened the dressing-case, which retained something of the original scent of expensive leather with which the English fortify themselves against their travels. Fossicking around inside the bag, her fingers, sliding between the sheets of grained paper, hesitated to advance farther. Would she find herself looking in a glass at a reflection which no amount of inherited cunning and cultivated self-deceit could help her dismiss?

Anticipation of her husband's portrait of her, whether it proved to be true or ideal, made her whimper softly. She did not think she could bring herself to unveil it – but might before Mr Roxburgh's return, because the fateful light, her uncomfortable posture, and skewed clothes, were encouraging her to know the worst.

Austin Roxburgh had set out on his journey back to the saloon aware of the foolishness of his desire to retrieve a book even though an Elzevir. It was not a matter of obstinacy, however; he had to prove himself, in the eyes of his wife, the officers, and crew. As he left the galley he saw that some of the latter were manning pumps, unsuccessfully he judged from the oaths. They blamed it on the listing of the ship, not on a situation so diabolically contrived that men were becoming as powerless as stone gargoyles.

Then something amazing occurred, the more improbable because, as always, Austin Roxburgh's vision was not that of a participant. The mizzen mast with all its attachments began to give way before his eyes. It fell, broken, bumping, lanyards torn out by the roots. The canvas leaves of the great tree were carried away, to boil like dirty washing in the surf.

Several of the crew pushed the passenger out of their way as they hurtled to repair what could not be repaired, or to hack off rubbish which might serve as a further hindrance.

Austin Roxburgh considered whether, on returning, he should report to his wife on the incident he had just witnessed. He decided against it, out of respect for her sensibility, and not because his secret already made him feel larger, braver, more important. Thus re-inforced, he continued on his dubious mission.

The day was darkening. Black clouds threatened to release a first volley of the pellets with which they were loaded. A deepening sea gargled hatred at its prospective victims. Somewhere land, that recurring promise, was doubtless hidden, awaiting re-discovery, but Mr Roxburgh did not glance once in the direction of what could only be several degrees less distasteful than vindictive ocean.

By the time he reached the companion-hatch he was crawling on all fours, not entirely out of cowardice; it was dictated also by sense: the waves which were breaking aft lashed him across mouth and eyes. When he had regurgitated most of what he had gulped, and was again looking out on a streaming world, he felt for a foothold on a ladder which was no longer familiar to him.

In the partial dark of what had been their stuffy but acceptable home, water had continued accumulating. All around, inside the fury of the storm, the sound of contained water could be heard, ominously slithery when more passive, or chopping and splattered as the little ship was swung grating on her stranded keel.

Mr Roxburgh peered through the gloom in his efforts to distinguish the object of his search amongst the general debris when suddenly '*My Virgil!*' floated into focus on the bilge undulating at his feet. He bent down, and with admirable stealth, as though tickling for an illicit fish, scooped up the book, then almost lost his slippery catch, but snatched it back out of the air, and finally secured it. The sodden book reminded him of another he had once examined, the victim of innocuous local flooding. Mr Roxburgh promised himself the luxury of heroic reminiscence beside a well-stoked fire when restored with his Virgil to the library at Cheltenham.

On deck after his return from the depths he again observed the wreckage of the mizzen mast, and was strengthened in his resolve not to mention the matter to his wife. His book he hid inside the bosom of his overcoat, away from the eyes of those who might not have appreciated the purpose of his exploit.

But nobody noticed Mr Roxburgh.

*

More conscious of her husband's existence in his absence than by his presence, Mrs Roxburgh sat with her fingers plunged like bookmarks between the pages of his journal, and wondered whether she could summon up the courage to open and read while she had the opportunity. She longed to be told of his love for her, but did not think she had the strength to face his doubts were she to come across any.

She was saved at last by seeing that the light would not have allowed her to discover the worst had she wanted to, so she stood up in groggy gratitude, inclining towards the slope as she had learnt. Desire to read of her husband's undamaged love was replaced by longing for the sight of land, and there it was, an iron horseshoe, not so far distant, but indifferent to human sentiments as well as the attentions of what appeared from the deck of the stricken ship an ingratiating, white tide.

Mrs Roxburgh struggled as far as the bulwark and clung to it, staring, open-mouthed, seemingly as insensitive and greedy as any gull scavenging offal from a ship's wake. She actually screeched once, and bowed her head, and retched into the black waves ramming at the sides of *Bristol Maid*.

She was at least delivered from a physical disgust and hopelessness, but the tears began to pour for the image of a husband to whose love she had renounced the right, if not to his knowledge, according to her own conscience. It was her conscience too, which heard his voice calling feebly above the lisp of bilge-water in the darkening, and by now probably submerged, saloon.

In spite of her inner predicament Mrs Roxburgh did notice, if vaguely, the demolished mizzen mast, and vaguely decided not to discuss it with her husband – should he return. As, indeed, he was now returning. He had not yet caught sight of her for the wreckage of mast and rigging. Relief brought with it anti-climax rather than stimulated guilt as she wedged herself into her place between the galley wall and the protective table. As he had left her, so he should find her, beside the closed dressing-case.

Mr Roxburgh was much elated by the recovery of his Elzevir Virgil. (More than anything he looked forward to a re-reading of the *Georgics* at the first opportunity which offered.) Perched on the knife-edged bench he held the book against his stomach for safety. This sodden, and to any other eyes, repulsive trophy had the feel of a familiar and beloved object which assured him of his own reality.

Seated beside him as he nursed his book Mrs Roxburgh was reminded of a doll she had been given. She had swaddled it in clean handkerchiefs. It was her child. She loved it, and cried bitterly when its head was ground to china splinters by a cartwheel.

So they prepared themselves uneasily for night and dreams, when shortly before the descent of darkness a horrendous cracking, a wooden thunder, the downward sweep of impetuous wings flung terror over the passengers' faces. They did not address each other, but rose simultaneously, and staggered out on deck, into an aftermath of silence. Through the rain which was stinging their eyelids the Roxburghs observed that the mainmast together with its press of canvas had been carried away over the larboard quarter. The crew were dealing after a fashion with a tangle of dangling yards and cordage. The jib-boom hung like a broken pencil.

Not knowing to what extent they were at the mercy of chaos the Roxburghs stood supporting each other, and accepted that the rain should drench them. Down it drove, through the last convulsions of twilight, while the ship, although stationary, appeared to be sucked into an inky mangrove estuary, if not the jaws of night.

Captain Purdew's figure looming at the moment of extinction might have made a darker impression had his voice and attitude not suggested he was putting in a purely gratuitous appearance.

'Well, she is gone,' he announced so softly that his statement might have been for himself rather than an audience.

He yawned and the tension left the sea-eroded skin; the once impressive frame gangled and creaked freely inside the clothes covering it. An experience he had half-expected all his life had just relinquished him it seemed, to his immense relief.

There remained, notwithstanding, a duty towards his passengers. 'Pilcher has made an attempt at launching the pinnace,' he told in words carefully chosen for polite ears, 'but the sea is too –' his voice was lost till he recovered it, '*heavy*', they heard.

The Roxburghs submitted to his opinion, after which Captain Purdew explained with extreme patience and a degree of natural courtliness, 'We're as high and dry on board as a nestful of gulls' eggs.' He gently pushed them back into the shelter of the galley, his enormous hands resigned to their own ineptitude. 'At dawn,' the last of his face soothed them with the information, 'we'll try again – and no doubt have better luck.'

Dawn, the palest concept, hung before their eyes during the hours of darkness. The Roxburghs could not sleep, but dozed, perhaps a little, against each other, on the sharp edge of the tilted bench. Their stomachs compressed by irregularity and fright had ceased to be part of their anatomy, so there was no question of their feeling hungry. They were hungrier for the dreams which eluded them soon after leaving their skulls.

Once Mrs Roxburgh all but succeeded in spelling out the evasive word, 'G–A–R–N–u–r–d?' Her lips were struggling with it, but failed at the cliff's edge.

At one stage he took her in his arms, and they lay along each other, lapping and folding, opening and closing with the ease of silk, fully enfolded if the coral teeth had not gnashed, they were sinking, sunk.

Mr Roxburgh awoke from some desirable unpleasantness to find his wife steadying him. He was on the verge of losing his balance.

'Are you well?' Mrs Roxburgh asked.

There was so little opportunity for being otherwise, her question sounded absurd.

So they dozed.

Captain Purdew's dawn entered the galley without their noticing. It smudged their faces with grubby shadow and drew from the corners of darkness the cold grey smell of ash parted from the original coals.

When the Roxburghs finally awoke it was to a splashing of voices and water outside. Expectation and sleep had renewed a physiognomy ravaged by dusk, and dismissed the more palpable fears. She sat biting her lips, pale eyes straining to make use of returning vision, while he had recovered something of the languor of his youth, eyelids hung too heavy, too dark, features refined by sickness to an unnatural perfection which almost precluded life. They jumped up, however, with gasps. Scrambling. Uttering.

In the small hours the gale had considerably abated, but the vicinity of the stranded ship remained lathered with a restless foam. Gulls were circling overhead, shrieking, but coldly.

Into this world of cold white light and water, beneath the blue-white of unearthly gulls, stepped Mrs Roxburgh, her skirt lifted to the level at which boot and ankle meet as she scaled the raised threshold of the galley doorway. Her husband followed. Despite an untended moustache and beard, he was still wearing that mask of youthful perfection which sleep had returned to him. If they had been vouchsafed an audience, its hoariest members might have trembled for what amounted, over and above the flaws, to the Roxburghs' spiritual innocence. But the attention of everybody, of whatever degree of understanding, was engaged elsewhere.

Launched at first light it seemed, the long-boat was bounding and thrashing on the water, still attached by its tackle to the parent ship.

Human voices could be heard shouting, one in particular rising above the others.

'You'll stave 'ur in,' Mr Pilcher accused whoever was responsible, 'and half of us 'ull be as good as sunk!'

The criticism was evidently aimed at the first mate, for at the heart of the general, though more subdued, vociferousness stood Mr Courtney, frozen into a frowning silence.

'If we're put to it, who will care to draw lots?' Disregarding his own subordinate rank, Mr Pilcher continued flaying the air as a substitute for his superior officer. 'I'll not be left behind, waving good-bye to them born with better luck!' Perhaps inspired by the motions of the long-boat dancing in frenzy at the end of its tether, Mr Pilcher blazed and twitched with passion.

Other advice was being offered in minor keys; normally muscular hands were united in knots which, this morning, did not hold.

When Captain Purdew was seen approaching from out of the wreckage of the charthouse, buttoning his jacket, hair flying, such of it as was left to him. If at nightfall the captain seemed to the Roxburghs to have relinquished his command, habit was driving him back to assume responsibility for a predicament which might prove fatal. So he shambled on, like a sleepwalker advancing into the heart of a nightmare, and arriving there, gave orders in a level, aged, but disciplinary voice, for the boat to be raised from the waters. As though that were possible. But it had to be. Himself lent a hand to perform the miracle expected of him.

The miracle almost occurred. The bows of the absurd cockle lifted, its whole length was raised into space, when it plopped back. The splash rose and hit them in their sweating faces. Then for an instant a lip curled on the greeny-white face of the sea and coral teeth snapped at the long-boat; whereupon human desperation helped raise her a second time. There she hung, dangling at the ends of the knotted arms, the blenched fingers, of convulsed bodies. They might have been prepared if necessary to secure the long boat with their own entrails.

But after an age of capricious resistance on the boat's part, and of muscles threatening to tear, and lungs to burst inside the racked ribs of her wooers, she allowed herself to be jerked higher than any of them would have hoped, then after a further pause, in which her dead weight seemed to condemn half the souls among them to hell, she was swayed in their direction, practically sailing through the air, clearing the bulwark with little more than a graze, before ploughing the shuddering deck.

When the operation was over, several of the men made no attempt to disguise the trembling of their limbs and faces as they chattered together, and one fellow of powerful build went and sat apart on the deck, holding his head in his hands, his feet splayed like great yellow talons supporting his weight against the list.

But the long-boat was reclaimed.

All that morning and into the forenoon, hands were busy repairing its fallible shell, while the work of victualling went ahead under supervision of the boatswain. Mr Roxburgh joined a chain of lads engaged in bringing up from below casks of salt beef and pork, loaves of bread already mouldering, and demijohns of water, to provision the pinnace and supplement the long-boat's stores, which the haste and enthusiasm of her premature launching had left somewhat skimpy; or rather, Mr Roxburgh went through the motions of helping as his mind ran with the tide. Below deck the perpetual lapping, only a tone above silence, recalled the many silent houses in which he had lain as a youth, by nightlight and sleepless, his feverish senses experiencing all the terrors of shipwreck long before he was confronted with them.

Mr Roxburgh appeared, and did in fact, feel calm enough,

since the unaccustomed physical activity had purged him of his more obsessive humours. By contrast, some of the brawniest seamen around him shivered for what they were about to encounter, while trying to laugh it off. He could see the gooseflesh prickling on those bull-necks.

Towards the middle of the day he rejoined his wife where she was half-standing half-leaning against the bulwark, shading her stare with a firm hand. She glanced up at him, and he was surprised to notice how little wrinkles of age and weather had seized upon the corners of her eyes and mouth.

'You must find a place and sit down,' he ordered. 'All this turmoil will wear you out.'

Was he trying to be rid of her?

But she looked at him, and both knew he would only leave her if forced.

She put out a hand and touched his sleeve in confessing, 'I no longer believe we are the ones who will decide.'

They had both, perhaps, weathered, or matured, and deeper than their skins. Their thoughts revealed themselves more obliquely under the salt which an uncertain sunlight had dried on their faces. A grime of salt and powdered ash encrusted Mrs Roxburgh's hands, most noticeably her rings, which she was wearing for their safety. They were not many (she had not set much store by precious stones after the first flush of her marriage) but now these few glittered most unnaturally.

'Should you be wearing them?' he asked.

'What else? Shall I throw them into the sea?'

Then at least they laughed together. They were temporarily possessed by an almost sensual indifference to their fate. Mrs Roxburgh's stance against the bulwark was not far removed from the slatternly; the scuttle of her bonnet had lost its symmetry, and the hem of her skirt several inches of its stitching, with the result that it hung in a dangerous loop. If Austin Roxburgh was more correct in appearance, he took advantage of their laughter to press himself briefly but deliciously against her side, as though they were alone, or in the dark.

She sighed at last, and petulantly. 'Do you think we shall ever get away?' Remissness on the part of a coachman might have delayed them in starting for the picnic she had organized.

'*They* will manage it!' Though cynicism and convention would have prevented him admitting it even now, Austin Roxburgh had the greatest faith in the working class.

Never more dismal than when handing food, Spurgeon came and offered them some, together with a word of warning. 'Here is something to chew on,' he muttered.

Mr Roxburgh remarked that he had scarcely any appetite, while accepting a hard biscuit and one or two shreds of beef fringed with beads of greyish fat.

Out of another convention, Mrs Roxburgh might have been preparing to charm Spurgeon into their saloon relationship of mistress and man, but the steward chose not to understand, and went away.

Some of the crew were stuffing their mouths with the haste which comes of sharpened hunger and fear that soon they must go short. Others choked and swallowed as they worked at repairing the long-boat. Even those who stood watching would offer a tool before the necessity arose, or take a turn at stirring with exaggerated care the pot of tar which played a major part in the caulking; while one or two, smiling and heavy-lidded, appeared drugged by the fumes they were inhaling or mesmerized by the rolling of a pitch-black eye into indifference towards the future.

As the Roxburghs looked on and waited they did as they had been told by Spurgeon. Although Mrs Roxburgh almost revolted in swallowing a lump of rancid fat, and splinters of lean stuck between their teeth, the wholly physical act of chewing began to pacify their squeamish souls. The biscuit was more austere than the meat, but responded to gnawing and sucking; reduced to a wholly insipid pap, it trickled down easily enough, and encouraged a sense of melancholy fulfilment in revived stomachs.

In the course of the afternoon the crew finished patching the damaged boat, with lead, leather, and scraps of blanket, their handiwork copiously daubed with pitch. It was past five by the time the boats were clear of the wreck. Mr Pilcher, in charge of the pinnace, had with him the boatswain, four seamen, and a lad, while Captain Purdew in the long-boat was accompanied by his first officer, the steward, a carpenter, five seamen, the boy Oswald Dignam – and the two passengers in addition. As the boats parted from *Bristol Maid* none of the survivors was able to believe that any of this had truly happened, so their dazed eyes seemed to express, their mouths either clenched, tight and resentful, or hanging slack with a look of watery injury.

Of all the company, Mrs Roxburgh was perhaps the most deeply moved: to be ejected thus from the cramped cabin and rather inhospitable saloon which her own moods, thoughts, and attempts at occupation had furnished as a dwelling place. Now she could not bear to visualize even the lumpy palliasse on which she had learnt to sleep, or the mirror in which her face had floated, often unconvincingly, amongst the frosting and the blemishes.

Here they were, however, in long-boat and pinnace. Mr Courtney was using his quadrant to make calculations, as the result of which, a course was set for the mainland, an estimated thirty miles to the west.

'Bye-bye, *Bristol Maid*!' a seaman aboard the long-boat shouted from the depths of his lungs.

He began at once to laugh and cough, exposing the ruins of some brown teeth set in expansive though bloodless gums, the tendons in his neck showing in relief like a protective bulwark.

Mrs Roxburgh decided not to turn her head, much as she was drawn to the hulk they were abandoning.

Despite the presence of gentry the crews of the rival boats started shouting ribaldries at one another. The burr and clash of their men's voices seemed to give them courage.

'See you in Wapping, Nat!' yelled a tiger from the pinnace.

'We'll wap in other parts afore we ever see bloody Wappin'!' answered a hitherto speechless youth.

'Ay,' a grizzled fellow beside him snuffled back the snot in his pug's nose, 'there'll be rocks aplenty with shag on 'en for those who fancies.'

The men fell into a gloom after that. Whether the object of their outburst was to disguise tender feelings in themselves, or to shock a lady they had at their mercy, they failed either way; for the lady, who showed no signs of being hard of hearing, continued taking a clear-eyed if somewhat exaggerated interest in the empty sea surrounding them.

If Ellen Gluyas resented their obscenities it was on account of Mr Roxburgh: that his sensibility might be offended, or that he should suspect her of countenancing 'men's talk'. But he gave no indication of having heard or understood, and soon they were all immersed in preoccupations of greater moment.

The sea which had appeared gentle enough as they drew away from the wrecked ship slapped at the boat's sides with increasing vigour, and a stately ice-pudding of a cloud evolved less passive forms and blacker intentions as it was moved towards them. The gold of a rampant sun and the threatening obscurity of storm and night offered an intolerable contrast to the more fearful among the castaways. Any of those who looked her way saw such a substantial *Bristol Maid* it pierced their conscience to know that they were abandoning her. Heeled over as she was on the reef, the little ship held firm, even when the sea raised a great white arm and brought it crashing down across her bows.

The restraint she had been taught to cultivate made it difficult for Mrs Roxburgh to cry, when Ellen Gluyas would probably have blubbered out loud, for witnessing something of the slow death of a ship. But Mrs Roxburgh did at last gently weep, hoping that none of the men, least of all Mr Roxburgh, would see.

'Ma'am, look! Yer shawl's trailin' over th' gunnel. 'Tis soaked!' It was Oswald Dignam's voice; he had wormed close, then closer she noticed, since boarding.

'Oh,' she sighed, 'the shawl,' and smiled at the boy like the benevolent patroness she was expected to be.

She had bundled the shawl over an arm, and forgotten about it. Now she hauled it in and wrung out the water from the drowned fringe.

'Thank you, Oswald. But will it, I wonder, matter?'

Because he did not altogether understand, and was afraid of damaging a delicate relationship, he did not answer.

The boats were blown on their reckless course.

Mrs Roxburgh realized that water had seeped beyond the soles into the uppers of her boots.

'Mr Roxburgh,' she asked, 'have you wrapped up?'

The crew sat staring at the passengers with a half-dreamy incredulity bordering on insolence.

'Yes,' he assured her, baring his teeth in the convention of a smile.

The sun was blinding in its last moments. It provided Austin

Roxburgh with an excuse for closing his eyes and shutting out at least the visible signs of his wife's solicitude for him. What he could not shut out was the sight of Captain Purdew. So he opened them again. Did this scarecrow of a man, under whose command they had placed themselves, still possess the wits and the self-respect required in an emergency? Involved in a personal disaster, the loss of his ship, the captain sat grinning at the horizon, until suddenly taking off his cap, and producing a comb, he started attacking his surviving strands of hair.

Something occurred so forcibly to Mrs Roxburgh that she elbowed her husband in the ribs, twisting and turning in the cramped space in which she was sitting. 'Mr Roxburgh,' she called, although he was beside her, 'where is the bag?' as she felt or kicked around with sodden feet for the dressing-case which should have been there.

He answered slowly, 'I've forgot it, I think. But what use, Ellen, would it be?' The fragment of a so-called 'memoir', the bilious journal! (His Elzevir Virgil was buttoned safely inside the bosom of his coat.)

Again Mr Roxburgh bared his teeth.

'Oh dear!' She began openly to cry, however he might deplore the show she was making of them. 'The bag! We have so little!'

Like a lover, the boy could not gaze at her enough.

'Ellen! Ellen!' Mr Roxburgh coaxed.

None of those who were listening understood, least of all Captain Purdew, his eyes trained on distance in the abstract, or the pinnace ploughing on ahead.

Mr Roxburgh had taken his wife's hand, plaiting his fingers together with hers, grinding the rings into them. It was a source of deep interest to the boy. He watched until darkness came down upon their heads.

6

It was becoming evident, not only to the sailors, but to the lands-
men in their midst, that the long-boat was barely seaworthy. Her
jury-rig was of little more use than a broken wing to a bird, and
in the absence of a rudder, a boat's oar had to be pressed into
service. By their first dawn, with the sleep still sticky on their
faces, the most optimistic of the company could not very well
ignore the fact that their vessel was leaky. So that bailing was included in the orders for the day. Those who were detailed for the
duty set to it, not so much with a will, as with the hope that
monotony would drug their minds. The Roxburghs were secretly
glad of a forced labour in which they might join. Mr Roxburgh
even discovered a method which he first demonstrated to his wife,
and later went so far as to explain to members of the crew. (Ellen
Gluyas simply bailed, head bowed almost to her knees; until the
random twinge of pain began darting through the disused
muscles of her back.)

Some of the men had taken to the Roxburghs, or else their contempt would not stand the strain of long keeping.

It was a fitful progress, by human as well as nautical standards.
From time to time intangible cats'-paws made a play for the improvised sail, which would start to fill, and falter, and subside,
along with unwarranted hopes. Manpower was Captain Purdew's
only recourse. The arms of those pulling on the oars bulged and
cracked, while teeth bit on oaths the rowers refrained from re-
leasing out of deference to a lady.

If an occasional expletive escaped from between the crew's
overworking lips, it was not that of a dead language, but one she
had forgotten on emigrating, as it were, from the country of her
birth. Mrs Roxburgh mused on the false impression it seemed her
fate in life to give, to rough sailors, refined acquaintances, even
her own dear husband – and one she preferred not to remember.

Trapped between the walls of a room she might have gone on to torment herself with speculation on the nature of the seed which had been planted in her body, whether it would grow to reveal her better or her worse side, and whose face it would wear. Here on the open sea she was more distressed to observe the superior performance given by the pinnace, and in her disheartenment, found herself resenting Captain Purdew's unwise choice of a boat for his command.

Towards the close of the morning, when condescension on the part of Mr Pilcher had allowed the distance between the vessels to decrease appreciably, Captain Purdew stood up, and with a hand on the improvised mast for support, signalled with the other to the captain of the pinnace. After much hailing, there took place a discussion laced with such professional detail the passengers could only take it on trust. Mr Roxburgh had his crypto-faith in those who perform feats of manual dexterity and technical miracles which might contribute to his personal welfare, while Ellen had the frivolous mind of which he accused her, and which she had ended by accepting. At least it allowed her to be less affected by the flow of arcane language. During the discussion she was drawn rather, to the boiling and bubbling of the sea, and re-called a glass door-stopper she had acquired with her rank of wife and lady, and which had become a source of innocent pleasure as it lay on the carpet of the morning room at 'Birdlip House'.

'You will have to take us in tow,' Captain Purdew was shouting at his second mate.

Although Mrs Roxburgh could sense that the mate's attitude to this decision was disrespectful, he was preparing to obey the captain's order, while she, so delighted by her vision of the green door-stopper, continued rounding it out, partly in her mind, partly in the sea water undulating beyond the gunwale. There was a girl called Matty Somerton, only briefly in her service, who had stumbled over the stopper while carrying a trayload of cordial. It had been something of a speciality with Matty to stumble and fall, tray in hand. She could not help it, she confessed, and on the stairs, always up, but never yet down.

Narrowing her eyes in the sunlight, in this seascape from which she remained detached, Ellen Gluyas knew that she should have felt more sympathy for her maid, from having brought suppers to

171

the lodger on a tin tray, and almost dropped it out of nervousness, in the refined atmosphere of books and medicine bottles. Sucked deeper still into the whorls of memory and water, she was less than a maid: her mother's drudge and her father's unpaid hand.

She was dragged back to the surface by seeing that the two boats had been manoeuvred to within a short distance of each other, and that Mr Pilcher himself was securing a hawser which one of the long-boat's crew flung across the gap.

Captain Purdew remained upright and unemployed, holding to the mast, grinning, and trying to suppress a moral anguish he was not yet prepared to admit. Since Pilcher's head was at an angle which allowed him to concentrate on the hawser, it was impossible to observe the lines, so deep as to be black, which fascinated Austin Roxburgh when he was in a position to examine the second officer's face. He felt peculiarly drawn to Pilcher, compelled by repulsion rather than inspired by the spark of positive attraction. He would have liked to find favour with this offensive individual, but could not feel that his aspiration would be recognized.

Having knotted the rope, the fellow suggested by the hang of his head and a thin-lipped shamefaced smile, that he was preparing to launch a joke. But humour could only have eluded Pilcher, and he turned to resume command of the pinnace.

They struggled on.

In the hands of others, and without compensating books or needlework, the Roxburghs were left pretty much with their thoughts. The solace of conversation was more or less denied them since both sensed that the foreign language they spoke might cause surprise, or worse, arouse resentment. So they confined themselves to such unexceptionable banalities as, 'Look, Mr Roxburgh, would you say that is an albatross?' or, 'It must be midday, Ellen, don't you think? by the position of the sun.'

Nobody could accuse them of not trying to comport themselves. It was during the silences that Mrs Roxburgh, to her own knowledge, got out of hand. In silence she was able to indulge, even flaunt, a difference she had been made to feel most forcibly as they helped her over the side, probing with a foot for the rope ladder, in her passage to the long-boat from the familiar deck of *Bristol Maid*. She was dangling, a bundle of incredible clothes,

172

cruel stays, and spasmodic breathing. She had been softened and made more defenceless, as was to be expected, by the precious child she was carrying, when in normal circumstances, she, if no one else, knew herself to be tough-fibred. So it was also frightening to be suspended in this airy limbo. The strong hands of rough, kindly men had held, only to relinquish her. Swinging and bumping on the rope ladder, she was at the mercy of her own initiative, and that of the wind filling her skirts, making of her a mute bell which would have emitted a pathetic tinkle had it attempted to chime. Other men stood goggling up at her ankles from below. One fellow blushed for her as he passed her on. She was quick to conceal the cause of his shame on feeling solid boards beneath her feet. Until now, she had been proud of her neat glacé button boots, bought a year or two before on a visit to London.

A day later, still set in one of the only two attitudes she found it possible to adopt in the space allotted to them, she only had to work her toes very slightly to feel the water squelching in her boots, a pastime not without its melancholy pleasure. When she was not taking her turn at bailing, a soporific so potent that sight of a trickle of blood from a cut in her hand did not detract from its effect, she sat and watched men exerting themselves, the certain rough elegance of even the thickest wrists alternately compelling and rejecting a boat's oar. As their movements fused and confused she saw above all her father's wrist flicking the whip with a movement of its own as they jogged side by side in the cart, or on feast days, the jingle. She stepped forward at last over the legs of the rowers and closed the scaly lids when the eyes were no longer looking at her and folded the hands on the wesket before hurrying up the road for help. Had she been left to mature naturally she had inherited that same chapped skin. Looking at her hands, Mrs Roxburgh noticed that she was returning, and not by slow degrees, to nature.

During the voyage, of circumnavigation as it seemed to have become, the shore so distant, if not mythical, the boy Oswald moved about the boat more freely than most, now taking his turn at bailing, now straining upon an oar, but always with an end in mind: to seat himself at the knees of one who was not so much the lady as a Divine Presence. Thus crouched, he would concentrate on the pair of hands lying in a lap.

He did not see them in their present shape, as scratched and filthy as a man's, but as he remembered them, like a pair of smooth, dazzling fish, only hidden to be re-discovered, while playing together in a white sea of fog. He had even experienced their touch, and shivered again at the approach of jewels, in particular the ring with a curious nest of stones which glittered like dark, clotting blood. The memory of this ring, rather than its counterfeit on a grimy finger, seared his already burning cheek.

'You are contributing as much, Oswald, as any of the men.' Mrs Roxburgh spoke with the dutiful kindness of the dull woman she felt herself to be.

So lethargic, she could scarcely raise a hand to remove a hair from her lips, or brush away the crumbs which tumbled down her front when she ate her ration of mouldy bread. If she glanced disinterestedly, it did not seem unnatural that the grey, and in some cases, green crumbs should be lying on the shelf her bosom provided. Agreeable enough in itself, her lassitude gave her a plausible excuse for neglecting her person, as well as an argument for not resisting, morally at least, the stares of the rowers and the boy at her feet.

It could have been lassitude again which was developing her faith, not in God, in whose service she had never been punctilious, nor in the more compelling gods of the countryside into which she had been born, but in the umbilical rope joining the long-boat to the pinnace. No, it was more than the ebb of her mental and physical powers, it was life itself dictating her faith in this insubstantial cord.

'You will bring us to land,' she said to the boy because he was so conveniently placed, 'and we shall find water – and limpets – winkles. Oh yes, I'm certain of it!'

She dismissed the painful probability of cutting her hands in the struggle to open shellfish, and could already feel the slither of fat oysters down her throat.

As they progressed, if they did, the smoother passages under sail, but more often jerked forward by manpower, she learned the least tic, the faintest convulsion, the essential ugliness of men's straining faces, if also their relaxed beauty while they rested sweaty and thoughtless after exertion.

Only at such moments, when she was most absorbed in her

174

lesson, did Oswald dare con her face. Then he would try to delve beneath the salt scales and ruins of the original skin, to reconstruct a beauty, true as well as legendary, which he had discovered for the first time on a foggy afternoon, and never again experienced a prefection he knew to exist, if only in a dream, or fog.

Mrs Roxburgh was driven to exclaim, 'How you love to ferret into a person's thoughts! What do you expect to find?' then regretted her indiscretion because the boy grew ashamed to the point of colouring up.

A seaman who had overheard increased his distress by invading what should have remained a private world. 'That lad 'ud stare out the clock's face, and not 'ave nothun to show for't.'

Full of good-natured insensitivity, the man kicked out at the boy, now thoroughly sullen from betrayal by the one he most respected. He sat clutching the canvas bag which held his possessions, unable to escape from his betrayer for the press of knees and hairy calves.

The afternoon dissolved into rain, which reduced every face, especially Mrs Roxburgh's, to the state of first innocence. What would she not have given for innocence enough to lean forward and stroke the rounded cheek of this boy who might otherwise remain closed against her.

Taking advantage of a burst of thunder which she hoped might prevent her remark carrying to other ears, she tried to re-instate herself. 'I was put in mind of the ferret, Oswald, we spoke of the other day. You remember?'

He did not appear to, or else would not let himself, and she was left with her image of small red eyes ferreting through Cornish furze and hussock after rabbits of ill-omen.

So she sat back and allowed the rain to drench her. It seemed a natural occurrence that the black rain should be rushing at them. She gave herself up to it inside her clothes.

Mr Roxburgh had been holding himself exceptionally erect ever since deciding that the inevitable could not be overcome. Seated on his wife's starboard side he was protecting her, whether necessary or not, with an arm numbed by duty. Mr Roxburgh's long thin fingers would have shown up blenched as they gripped the gunwale for support, had they not been blackened by sun and grime.

175

'Comfortable, Ellen?' he had formed the habit of inquiring, as though that too, were necessary.

For Austin Roxburgh the real necessity was the rather inconvenient volume buttoned inside his bosom. Its weight and angles had become his only solace. Would it be possible on a desert island to find sufficient shade in which to enjoy the pleasures of Virgil?

This was Mr Roxburgh's secret longing. Indifferent health, the irritability which comes of chronic constipation, even jealousy, no longer tormented him. He could not very well become jealous of a boy however secretive, so he told himself. For Austin Roxburgh had guessed the boy's secret after his wife had disappeared over the side, swinging and plunging on the rope ladder. Awaiting his turn, Oswald Dignam stood frowning away his emotions, nervously fiddling with the draw-neck of a glory-bag he was holding behind him. The most feminine member of the crew, he did not intend to be parted from whatever odds and ends he carried in the canvas bag with its sinnet-work in crimson twine, and did at last smuggle it past the boatswain's notice, to Mr Roxburgh's satisfaction. His own contraband made him approve of this bagful of secrets, and accept those less tangible which rose to the surface of the boy's face as his divinity sank.

Beneath the black sky, against the flap flap of a flagging sail and an increased grumbling of rowlocks, somebody spat over the side. It hit, and seemed to hiss before being swallowed. Their thoughts removed to an incalculable distance inside their skulls, the rowers' faces could have been turning in their sleep.

Austin Roxburgh had fallen to contemplating as far as he dared the mystery of virility as embodied in his brother Garnet. Risen from the hip-bath which Nurse Hayes had stood on the floor against the fender, the white flesh took on its worth in gold from firelight weaving out of the grate. If ever Austin were unwise enough in after life to let himself become intoxicated with strong drink, this same vision would materialize. At such moments he was all but choked by the ripple of his own throat. Now in an open boat Mr Roxburgh had perhaps grown a little drunk on rain, for he visibly gulped.

Of course he had always resisted any inclination to assess desire in more than aesthetic terms. So he made himself concentrate on the pins and needles in the arm protecting his wife, whose value had been increased by this child of theirs hidden inside her. He loved her, he felt, as he had never been capable of loving any other human being, excepting, perhaps, the imagined brother of his childhood. Plastered together in their drenched condition they were truly 'one flesh', an expression he had been inclined to reject as in bad taste, until the senseless caprices of nature invested it with a reality which had become his mainstay.

The Roxburghs gently rocked against each other, and she compiled a tender inventory of what their life together had been: instead of cabinets stuffed with Wedgwood (she positively hated the black) or Chippendale surfaces reflecting an arrangement of snuff boxes and vinaigrettes, or her own glossy portrait by Sir John, she listed flurries of pear blossom, and wasps burrowing in ripe pears, and a child's grave, and an invalid's narrow feet returning to life after she had slid the warming-pan between the sheets.

Sluiced by rain, Mrs Roxburgh would loll, and doze at intervals against her husband to an accompaniment of water on the move, but generally her protector remained upright, vigilant, watching the rowers in action or, when a cat's-paw caught at the sail, drawing in their oars, picking at the calluses on hard hands to allay inaction, occasionally spitting over the side an impoverished stream of tobacco juice.

That tedium was inevitable goes without saying. A sailor would suddenly lash an inactive leg over his other knee in far from characteristic pose, except that it was true to exasperation. Mrs Roxburgh yawned without bothering to put up a hand. Her husband no longer had reliable control of his wind. But each might have felt relieved that nothing was happening for the moment.

In his vigilance Austin Roxburgh seemed to remember all that he had never begun, or left unfinished: broken phrases dangling from his lips at moments when he had most needed to express himself, the resolution to follow an ascetic rule, to love all humankind, to give thanks to the Supreme Being, to round out his miserable fragment of a memoir, to undertake Sanskrit, Arabic, Hebrew, Russian, while there was yet time.

As for Mrs Roxburgh, she could not be certain that any of it had happened to her, but everything might still conspire to club her down and trample on her.

More than anybody, Captain Purdew had his preoccupation and appeared to have been considerably aged by them. 'The only time, ever,' he was heard to remark. 'It would 'uv been better had she gone down. Not to pull away and leave her sitting high and dry. Had she foundered first, no one need 'uv had it on their conscience.'

The vision of his stranded ship which so worked upon the captain's mind seemed also to affect those parts of his body most susceptible to suffering: his finger-joints, for instance, the knobs of which he was for ever testing, and a back which caused him to wince and mutter, and change position as far as that was possible.

'Ah dear,' he sighed, 'we got our boots mended at least'; and after running a furred tongue round lips encrusted with salt deposit, 'Along with its other purposes, a lead sinker in the mouth will keep thirst at bay – in-definitely.'

Since the wreck and his failing powers had reduced him to a dubious courtesy rank he had to content himself with making speeches of encouragement to the crew, who either ignored or humoured him as though they were saddled with a senile parent or simple child.

'I told ee not to fret thaself,' one of them advised. 'Frettin' only ever led to sour-crop.'

If somebody sniggered, it was out of abstract benevolence rather than ill-nature, and the captain either did not hear, or was buoyed up by instant prophecy, moral precept, and a flotsam of religious faith to which he would cling when all else failed.

'Mark what I've already predicted,' tribulation had increased his tendency to repeat himself, 'with wind in the jury-sail and Providence behind us, we can't but make landfall this evening.'

'It'ull take more'n wind, all right,' one fellow grumbled. 'Wind 'as left for other parts, like as it's gone from my empty belly.'

Captain Purdew frowned. 'There's a lady present,' he reminded.

If they had forgot it, it was because she had an equal share in their predicament.

The sailor's remark at least put the captain in mind of an important duty on which it was his habit to exercise the limping remains of his authority: he liked to attend to the rationing of victuals.

'Mrs Roxburgh,' he called, 'is ready for her share of mouldy bread and salt camel.' His decree was the less acceptable for his bleeding gums and staring eyes, and when he approached personally, creeping creaking between the rowers, almost toppling as his stiff legs negotiated planks on which the crew were seated, slopping through a bilge which defeated bailers, to lay his tribute in her jewelled hands.

'And a mouthful of water for Mrs Roxburgh. But swill it round well, my dear. Round and round. To satisfy the mouth. And hold it for a while. That way you'll make the stuff go further.'

Mr Courtney, now virtually commander of the long-boat, glowered and gloomed, and could not take his eyes off the master of the pinnace. Every man had, in fact, begun to find his neighbour to some degree odious. Without appetite, Mrs Roxburgh stuffed her mouth with mouldy bread for fear that she should find herself screaming into the face of a pitiable old man, and still might scream, in muted syllables of bread. The captain for his part suspected that he had always found women ugly; ships alone were for beauty and for solace; his own wife had never more than submitted to him with comparatively wooden gracelessness.

On the evening of the fourth day Mrs Roxburgh started out of a reverie thinking to have heard cries, which those of her companions within earshot soon translated into words. The pinnace without a doubt had sighted land. There it was, a fine-drawn thread of shore. Dusk was upon them, and only morning would reveal the extent of their fortune, but Captain Purdew called for a ration of rum from a small supply they carried with them in a demijohn.

At the sound of the tin pannikin striking against the stone lip Mrs Roxburgh resolved to refuse her tot if the rum should not give out before it reached her. As a gust of evening breeze wafted the stench her way, Pa's breath was too much for her; she was hard put to it not to vomit up the little she had in her queasy stomach. But every man was rejoiced by the fumes before consummation by taste; the mere theory of spirits was inspiration. Awaiting their turn some of them began humming, or muttering snatches of words, and one young fellow broke into whole verses of a song, in that high, yearning tone peculiar to his class when a prey to bitter-sweet thoughts in deserts and upon the high seas:

> Oh that I was gatherin' roses at Yeovil,
> Gatherin' the red red roses
> To put in-to my true love's hand.
> Oh that my girl would speak
> Or silent let me touch her cheek,
> Then I would gladly die,
> On beds of red red ro-ho-zez . . .

His passion was quenched at last in a spluttering of rum.

The plangent tone of the young man's voice, together with the potent sentiments expressed by his song, had combined with the scent of spirits to make Mrs Roxburgh drunk in advance, against her will. She was determined not to risk any further indiscretion, when instead of offering her the pannikin, her husband seized it for himself, and without hesitating, downed the contents.

'Haaah!' he ejaculated in half a laugh and half a cough. 'Overproof!' Some of it was seen to shoot out from under his moustache.

At that, most of the sailors laughed, not in malice, rather from kindred feelings. Instead it was the woman who had become the alien amongst them for not revealing whether she approved her husband's newly ratified alliance.

But Mr Roxburgh was off on another unexpected tack, telling of an evening as a young man at Douarnenez, '. . . when I fell flat on my face after an injudicious quantity of rum, to which a rowdy crew of Breton fishermen had introduced me for the first time.'

Several of the present company admitted to having warmed up on a drop from across the water, many a night at St Mary's, Polperro, Dawlish, or wherever.

Mr Roxburgh's eyes were shining with rum and reminiscence, the more intoxicating for being shared.

His wife had surprised a trait which she might have caused him to suppress by coddling him too assiduously in order to curry favour with his mother; while he, no doubt, saw his wife as the brittle work of art he was creating, the glaze of which might crack were she to become aware of her creator's flaws and transgressions.

The tears came into Mrs Roxburgh's eyes and she might have given way from seeing the strangers they had been to each other (and for that matter, might remain, till death overtook one of them) had she not realized that Captain Purdew had refilled the pannikin, and was holding the object, black and horrid, under her nose. One of the seamen closest to her had knelt in the bilge, hands raised as though preparing to assist in a ceremony. All were waiting for the lady to drink.

'Mrs Roxburgh,' the captain invited in a reverent whisper.

All were watching.

'No,' Mrs Roxburgh began, and made a movement to push the stinking vessel away. 'I hardly think – oh, *no*!' she snickered in disgust.

'Ellen,' her husband chirruped, 'you must take a sip at least, out of deference to the captain, and because,' he thought to add, 'the Almighty has brought us safely to land.'

For one blasphemous instant there arose in her mind the vision of a fish the Almighty was playing, the distended lip in which the hook was caught, her own; then she said, 'Oh dear! You are all against me,' and accepted the tin cup as though it had been a silver chalice, and despite her nausea, sank her face.

'This,' said Austin Roxburgh, winking at the congregation, 'is the original Cornishwoman!'

That her husband could have betrayed his own creation, granted it was under the influence of rum, made her blush and swallow, and what she experienced was not remission of sins, but a fire spreading. She was amazed and mortified to find she could swallow so much of the stuff – almost to the bottom of the cup.

As she gave back the pannikin she could feel the blood streaming through her veins, into fingertips, and sodden toes, though that most vital part of her, her belly, remained curiously cold and untouched.

Her companions sighed on witnessing their lady's demonstration of good faith, and were free to look about them again.

One of them asked, 'Where be our blessed land *now*?'

'Still where 'twere, I reckon.'

If not incontrovertible, it seemed to Mrs Roxburgh the only desirable conclusion as she sank back to loll against her husband's chest.

Night fell at least, and with it her blue-black hair she sensed escaping into sleep and water. We shall wake, she promised herself in leaving her body, and find we have arrived, and begin afresh.

It did happen more or less as she decided it would, with a few deviations from the foreseen.

Mr Pilcher was shouting through another milky dawn. ' 'Tis not the coast. It's a reef, or cay. Will we beach 'em, sir, if we find somewhere that'll suit?'

Flattered into thinking he had been consulted, Captain Purdew accepted the suggestion, while Mr Courtney scowled and sulked, and the master of the pinnace grinned back.

His derision, if it were, made Mrs Roxburgh touch her hair whereupon she discovered her bonnet gone, nor was it anywhere to be found however much she sidled and looked.

'What is it, Ellen?' her husband inquired anxiously.

'Nothing,' she replied.

She was relieved he did not appear to notice that her hair was hanging in dank disorder; he was still too sticky with sleep and stiff from the unorthodox position in which they were forced to spend their nights. Her impulse was to reach for the dressing-case, to avail herself of her comb and glass, until remembering that they had parted with the case some way back.

Almost every contingency had become by now acceptable. To find herself sitting in water up to her shins did not alarm Mrs Roxburgh. The sea-water inside the boat had risen by inches in recent hours. Bailing was intermittent, either because ineffectual, or because the thoughts of all those who performed the duty were directed at the land. Mrs Roxburgh too, had sat back at last, to feel and enjoy the milky warmth, the texture of tamed sea-water.

The surf by contrast was punishing the reef with such animal ferocity it did not seem as though any respite could be expected, when on rounding a coral neck, the pinnace and its insufficient relative the long-boat were vouchsafed the peace and protection of an elliptical recess rather than a bay, its curve as white as kaolin.

Always in the lead, Mr Pilcher was soon gesticulating from the shore after wading through milder, though to some eyes, still intimidating breakers. A sprinkling of sailors followed his example, leaping, pounding, racing one another when not battling through breast-high foam. Upon reaching land the men began hauling on the boats while cursing the coral which had torn their hitherto-impervious feet.

In emulation of the seamen, Mr Roxburgh jumped, and was junketed around, and nearly fell. She could have done nothing for this frail spillikin no longer her husband as he was whirled away. In any case, she too, no longer functioned by her own will, for that hairy man the boatswain was lifting her over the gunwale regardless of her wishes.

'Leave me – cusn't tha?' one of her selves expostulated as she flailed around in search of some solid object to help her in resisting an exit of which her mother-in-law would surely have disapproved.

She found nothing, and was dragged off, like any caterpillar from a twig.

'Ho-ya ho-ya! ho-*ya*!' the crews encouraged one another as they heaved the boats on to the beach.

Mrs Roxburgh succeeded briefly in escaping out of the boatswain's arms, to flounder a few steps before stubbing her boots on what must have been a coral hussock. Thereupon she sank, the boatswain resuming possession of her as she rose, more a wet hen than a woman, whose clucking cries remained mercifully unheard by any but her silent rescuer.

Long after the boats were beached, the sailors continued to curse the bleeding coral for lacerating their feet, while Mrs Roxburgh, deposited on land by the gallant efforts of the boatswain, saw that her pretty little boots (glacé leather with cloth uppers) were slashed beyond repair due to her own foolishness.

Still exhilarated by his tumultuous, and at the time alarming, experience in the surf, Mr Roxburgh glowed, and breathed deep. 'Who would have thought it possible!' until remembering his wife, he approached and put his arm round her, 'Ellen, you might have been injured!' with a sincerity she did not doubt.

'I am not,' she assured him, and formally added as she had been taught, 'thank you, Mr Roxburgh.'

It was at once evident that 'land' was too ambitious a word for the reef on which the castaways found themselves, though a beach of pulverized coral would make it possible to repair the long-boat at their leisure provided they could muster the materials. But of vegetation or shade there was little: nothing of that pastoral green Mr Roxburgh had hoped to find, in which to re-live the pleasures of the Georgics. Anything in the way of cover was of a grey, tough, sea-bitten variety: wiry bushes tortured by the wind, scurf of dead-green lichen, and fleshier shoots of a bitter weed which those of the men who were bred along the Bristol Channel and the Norfolk coast compared nostalgically with the samphire their women harvested at low tide from fields of mud.

For the most part level, the coral excrescence tended to rise towards the north-east, in which quarter alone, any who looked forward to solitude might hope to renew themselves. There the brush grew thicker, taller, but cowering before the strong winds to less than an average man's size, and nowhere concentrated enough to provide an adequate refuge for introspective souls.

Even so, there was an immediate dispersal, for physical as well as spiritual reasons, of those whom the two boats disgorged, everybody consoled, not to say dazed, by a freedom they had undervalued in the past. The men set out in opposite directions, on spidery, needled legs (there were cases where one leg might have been born shorter than the other, or else deformed by grappling the deck of a listing ship) their mouths thinned by desperation or thirst, the eyes of some closed on and off in an attempt to shut out an experience which still visibly flickered in their minds. But with all, the overruling impulse was to get away from one another.

They were brought to a halt by a revival of Captain Purdew's sense of his own authority. He proceeded to deliver something of an oration to emphasize that they had beached out of necessity, not for pleasure, and that once they were rested and refreshed, their prime concern was the repairing of the boats.

The seamen listened for the simple reason they could see no avenue of escape.

'And re-victualling – if foodstuff of any kind is offering,' the captain's voice persisted, high, dry, vibrating like sail with a wind in it. 'In that event,' he warned, 'remember we are a community, whose duty it is to pool our resources.'

Listening to this upright old man made Mrs Roxburgh melancholy. She suspected that those who are honourable must suffer and break more often than the others, which did not absolve the honourable from continuing to offer themselves for suffering and breakage. It started her looking for her husband, who must already have gone in search of the privacy his temperament craved.

After enjoying the luxury of a postponed, ungainly, and not unexpectedly, painful stool, Austin Roxburgh was wandering with little regard for purpose or direction, kicking at the solid though harsh ground for the simple pleasure of renewing acquaintance with primordial substance. Still walking, he unbuttoned his steaming overcoat to let in the sun and wind, then removed the garment and hung it on his arm. On or off, his overcoat seemed as incongruous as most human needs; human behaviour in its niceties must only excite derision on this desert island. Thus warned against acts of feckless self-assertion he resisted the urge to bare the leaves of his saturated Elzevir in the hope that the sun's blaze might dry them, and continued strolling through a park from which the statues had been removed.

At the island's southernmost tip, which had been whittled down to a narrow spine of razor-edged coral, opposing currents raised their hackles in what was probably a state of permanent collision. Much as he had grown to hate the sea, Austin Roxburgh felt drawn to this desolate promontory by something solitary and arid, akin to his own nature (if he would admit it, as he sometimes did). Overhead, the voices of invisible sea-birds sounded hollower, more ominous, in calling through infinity; the waves assumed ever more vicious shapes for their assaults on the coral; something – a sea-urchin must have died; and a white light threatened to expose the more protected corners of human personality. Mr Roxburgh was fully exposed. In advancing towards this land's end, he felt the trappings of wealth and station, the pride in ethical and intellectual aspirations, stripped from him with a ruthlessness reserved for those who accept their importance or who have remained unaware of their pretentiousness. Now he even suspected, not without a horrid qualm, that his devoted wife was dispensable, and their unborn child no more than a footnote on nonentity.

So the solitary explorer gritted his teeth, sucked on the boisterous air with caution, and visibly sweated. He might have been suffering from a toothache rather than the moment when self-esteem is confronted with what may be pure being – or nothingness.

Arrived at his destination, the dwindling headland on which he might have erected a moral altar for the final stages of his martyr-

185

dom, Mr Roxburgh discovered that he had taken too much for granted. Stretched on the ground as though consigning his meagre flesh to decomposition by the sea air, lay Spurgeon the steward. It could not have been an unpleasanter surprise.

'Ha, Spurgeon!' he managed to address the fellow. 'You have forestalled me!'

The steward did not attempt to move, but ejaculated, 'Eh?' from out of his emaciated, putty-coloured face and sparse tufts of beard.

'I mean,' the intruder continued, 'I hardly expected a human being here where the land has almost become sea again. Are you so attracted to what we have just escaped?'

'How about yourself?' Spurgeon answered.

It did seem to place them in the same category, but Mr Roxburgh rejected that.

'Ah, no!' Slowly Spurgeon rubbed his head against the crushed coral which for its next phase would be converted into sand. 'Not a "'uman being". No one can accuse me of that – where there isn't no more 'n skin an' bone, and a fart or two. I won't inconvenience you, sir, much longer.'

'Are you sick, then?' it was Mr Roxburgh's duty to ask.

Holding his precious book, he had seated himself on a stone beside this thoroughly repulsive object.

'Not sick,' the steward replied. 'The way I see it I'm simply fizzlin' out.'

He sat up, and proceeded slowly to turn his neck, which his companion quite expected to creak.

''Ere,' he said, parting the hair to exhibit a place above the nape, 'I'll be blowed if I'm not startin' a boil. And that's the worst sign of any. The sea-boils. See it?'

Mr Roxburgh would not let himself.

'Feel then,' Spurgeon invited.

Mr Roxburgh decided against it.

Spurgeon continued rubbing the nape of his neck. 'I knewed this mornin' early that I'll never come out of this. There's nothin' like the sea-boils for makin' a man fall apart quick.'

Faced with this human derelict, Austin Roxburgh realized afresh that his experience of life, like his attitude to death, had been of a predominantly literary nature; in spite of which, it was required of him to exert himself as a member of the ruling class, for so he must still appear to others in spite of his recent enlightenment.

'Cheer up, old chap!' he encouraged, and his voice echoed the accents of some forgotten tutor. 'Don't you feel – I mean – that you owe it to your wife?'

This initial piece of advice only made the steward glummer. 'If I 'ad one,' he mumbled.

'Never?' his companion asked.

'No,' said Spurgeon. 'Or not long enough to notice. But wot's the odds? A man sleeps the tighter without. There were never room for that many toe-nails in the same bed.'

The ridge of Mr Roxburgh's distinguished cheekbones coloured very lightly. 'Marriage,' he suggested, 'is not entirely physical. I should hate, at least, to think it was.'

'If it wasn't, a man could settle for a dawg. I did too,' Spurgeon remembered, 'after a while.'

'Of which breed?' Although by no means doggy himself, Mr Roxburgh welcomed an opportunity for leading their conversation down a safer path.

'Don't know as she was any partickler breed. A sort of dawg. That's about all. She'd sit an' look at me – and I'd look back. There was nothin' between us that wasn't above board.'

'The affection of a faithful animal is most gratifying,' Mr Roxburgh conceded; he found himself stuttering for what must have been the first time, 'but – mmmorally there is no comparison with the love of a devoted woman.'

'Don't know about that,' the steward replied. 'I weren't born into the moral classes.'

If Mr Roxburgh did not hear, it was on account of a sense of guilt he was nursing, for the many occasions on which he had abandoned someone else to drowning by clambering aboard the raft of his own negative abstractions. Her hair floated out behind her as though on the surface of actual water instead of in the depths of his thoughts.

He recovered himself and informed his friend, 'Salt water has medicinal properties. Or so they tell us.' He cleared his throat. 'Have you tried rubbing it with salt water?'

'Rubbin' what?'

187

'The boil, of course!' Elated by his own inspiration Mr Roxburgh resolved to overlook obtuseness in another.

'There's no way out if you're for it.' Spurgeon snorted so contemptuously he might have attained social status without his companion's realizing.

'But who's to know, my dear fellow, unless we try? The ability to correct wrong was vested in us for practical use.'

Mr Roxburgh would have been hard put to it to explain how he had come by a precept which was as reasonable as it sounded arcane; while Spurgeon looked the glummer for his own native ignorance.

The steward sat watching this ninny of a gentleman whose good intentions were driving him down the coral ramp towards the sea. After receiving a bash in the face from a mounting wave, Mr Roxburgh stooped to plunge his cupped hands.

There was little enough water in the cup by the time the physician reached the patient's side.

'Open up! Quick! The place!' Mr Roxburgh cried; faith, once lit, was blazing in him.

Of a damper humour, Spurgeon failed to kindle, but submitted his neck to the virtues of salt water.

Mr Roxburgh who originally had no intention of touching the boil was now faced with doing so, or the meagre drop of water would escape. So he set to, gingerly at first, grimacing with a disgust his patient was fortunately unable to see, and rubbed with stiffened, bony fingers, till the activity itself began to soothe, not the patient necessarily, but without a doubt the physician.

For the first time since landing on this desert island Austin Roxburgh was conscious that the blood was flowing through his veins. To an almost reprehensible extent, he throbbed and surged with gratitude. He was grateful not only to this unsavoury catalyst the steward, but to his absent wife, and the miracle of their unborn child.

He went so far as to take a good look at the inflamed lump which the steward had predicted would become a boil.

'Am I hurting, Spurgeon?'

'Yes.'

It was reason enough for discontinuing the treatment, after

which they rested awhile, side by side, when Mr Roxburgh became
for the second time inspired.

'Do you know what? Soap!'

'Soap? What?'

'If we could but lay our hands on some.'

'There's soap they brought along in case of caulkin' the bloody
long-boat.'

'But sugar as well.'

'I got a bit of sugar – if 'tisn't melted – for sweetin' up me rum
ration.'

'Soap and sugar, Simpson, have well-known drawing powers.'

The steward might have grown less inclined to humour an
eccentric gentleman's whims, but time hung half as heavy in a
mate's company, however undesirable the mate in the eyes of
ordinary men. Either anticipation of their disapproval, or friction
by salt water, or the prospect of a soap-and-sugar poultice, or the
tingling of an inadmissible affection, had brought the gooseflesh
out on Spurgeon.

While Austin Roxburgh tingled with his inspiration; in fact he
was indebted to old Nurse Hayes for a method she had used in
drawing the pus out of Garnet after his brother had scratched his
arm on a rusty nail.

When she had satisfied her own needs, and failed to set eyes on
her husband, Mrs Roxburgh went in search of him. At the same
time she could not have denied that she experienced a delicious
pleasure in being alone, even in her clinging, sodden garments,
her slashed boots, and hair by now too wild and too matted to
be dealt with by any means at her command. She must have
looked a slattern stalking through the scrub. Her elegant boots,
she suspected, might always have been what Aunt Triphena
would have called 'trumpery'. But the sun flattered her as she
strolled, and the wind, although gusty, was less vindictive than
while they were at sea. Each warmed and dried, and in performing
its act of charity, enclosed her in an envelope of evaporating
moisture, so that she might have been walking through one of
the balmy mornings she remembered on her native heath, except
that furze and hussock had been replaced by thickets which tore

more savagely, and starved creepers set gins for unwary ankles, and lizards were more closely related to stone.

She was content, however – and hopeful at last for her child: that he would survive, not only the physical rigours of what was no longer a doomed voyage, but also the moral judgement of those who might ferret over his features. She did pray that, whatever her shortcomings, the child would be theirs and no one else's.

A comparatively steep rise in the ground had reduced her gait to a dull and breathless plodding, when a change in the climate told her that she was emerging on the island's weather side. She was blasted by a gale. It took her hair and tossed it aloft, and filled her clothes, and spun her round amongst the quaking, but more inured bushes. She would have turned at once and made her way back had it not been for a bird's call becoming human voice. She looked down to where the land shelved towards the sea, and saw a figure, arms thrashing to attract attention. Again the cries were directed at her: it was Oswald Dignam's voice she heard. Holding herself stiffly and sideways in the vain hope of evading the gale, she began climbing down to meet him, her stumbling once or twice caused either by spasms of fear, or waves of pleasure at thought of a companionship so undemanding it could but add a benison to solitude.

The wind behind him, Oswald quickly reached her, together with a lash of driven spray, and opened a clenched hand to offer an amorphous mass of some kind of shellfish he must have battered from their anchorage.

'They's for you, Mrs Roxburgh,' his almost girlish voice gasped.

'Oh, but we must all share what we find, the captain tells us,' she replied sententiously.

'Who's to know?' the boy asked. 'If you 'adn't come I'd 'uv ate them meself – like anybody else.'

His natural, milky skin grown fiery on the voyage made him look the more indignant for what she had only half-intended as an accusation.

'Yes,' she sighed, 'we are all weak, I expect,' but did not add, 'and myself the weakest,' because he was only a boy.

Overcoming an initial nausea, she took the still quivering mess of mutilated shellfish from the palm on which it lay, and swallowed it at one gulp. To her consternation, some of the shell went

190

down with the flesh; other fragments she arrested with her tongue, and spat them out. She could feel that some of her saliva was dribbled on her chin.

It was Oswald Dignam's turn to smile his pleasure and approval.

He was again in love, she saw from the trembling and wincing of the face which observed her, and she would have gathered up his fiery head, as she had been tempted to caress its milder counterpart on a foggy afternoon at sea.

Instead she murmured with the kind of stiff formality he might have expected of her, 'Thank you, Oswald, you are indeed my friend, and I hope will always remain so.' As she spoke she felt the child inside her move as though in response to a relationship.

Oswald was deeper enslaved; beads of salt encrusting his eyebrows were visibly translated into drops of water; she watched them fall upon his cheeks.

'There's more, Mrs Roxburgh,' he managed despite a tongue which had swollen at its root. 'If you wait I'll fetch 'em for ye.'

He ran back towards the edge of the reef while she waited for this further tribute; probably no one, not even her husband, would have thought her worthy of it. So she could not help but smile, whether from appeased vanity or tender fulfilment it was not the moment to consider.

On reaching the water's edge, Oswald began bashing at the coral with a stone. The sight of his small, crouching figure made her clutch her own more tightly. Had he really been her child instead of a diminutive lover, she would have called him back. In the circumstances she continued watching, lips parted between pleasure and anxiety. When the sea rose, and with a logic which had only been suspended, it seemed to her now, swept him off the ledge on which he had been precariously perched.

Oswald Dignam was carried out, at best a human sacrifice, at worst an object for which there was no further use. Alternately sucked under and bobbing on the surface, he continued resisting his fate. His arms were raised several times, fists clenched, lips protesting against the mystery of divine prerogative, before the sea put a glassy stopper in his mouth. Although he was still being tossed and turned by surf boiling in and out of submerged potholes, she knew she would never see him again, unless as a wraith to be coerced out of her already over-haunted memory.

The victim of her clothes, her body, and the formless hazards, Ellen Gluyas ran down bellowing towards the water, where a rising wave warned her off. She stood an instant mewing ineffectually, before stuffing a knuckle in her mouth. More forcibly than ever, she was made to feel there was nothing she could do but submit.

But in accordance with the convention human beings are bound to obey even when their rational minds tell them the odds are against them, she was already starting back for help, running, scrambling by uncertain footholds and handfuls of grass, lumbering on, stumbling and falling, limping the last stretch, down to where the crew were methodically repairing the boats.

Her cries elicited only dazed attention from the men who were caulking the long-boat with a mixture of soap, fat, and grass. Three or four appeared to realize what had occurred, but of these only two followed Mr Courtney in response to Mrs Roxburgh's pleading. The others did not want to hear or know; Oswald Dignam the individual had slipped from the common consciousness as a result of what they had endured and what they might still have to undergo.

Arrived on the crest of the ridge above the scene of the boy's disappearance, the rescuers slouched back and forth, mumbling, as they searched the open sea with half-closed eyes. Only Mrs Roxburgh knew that it had happened, but could not convince these bemused, if not disbelieving, sailors, let alone spur them on to doing she knew not what.

She was desolated. She felt ill, and only too glad to spend the forenoon resting under a shelter some of the crew improvised for her out of a sail. The smell of crude canvas, of ants, and the attentions of flies made little impression on her. She must have dozed, in company with her swollen belly and the ghosts of her lost children, nor did she remember that she had not set eyes on her husband these several hours.

The caulking of the long-boat was proceeding parallel to, although not in accordance with the first officer's unsolicited directions, and more intermittently, Captain Purdew's trans-

192

cendental hopes, when Mr Roxburgh and Spurgeon came tittuping down towards the work-party. Sharing a secret gave them the expression of guilty drunkards arriving home under a transparent veil of bravado. They were ignored by those more importantly employed, nor did anyone think to inform them of Oswald Dignam's death, although he had been the steward's nipper and the cause of Mrs Roxburgh's inordinate distress. The sailors held their noses closer to their work, while Mr Courtney redoubled his efforts to impose his superfluous authority. As for Captain Purdew, his mind was wafted afresh in search of a salvation which might not be vouchsafed.

'Had I gone down with her at least. But the Lord won't overlook my record. Or will He?' The poor old man stood scanning the unresponsive seascape, his eyes those of a stale mullet.

Mr Roxburgh and Spurgeon continued smiling for their secret mission. Under cover of the general preoccupation it was easy enough to secure a handful of precious soap, while Spurgeon got possession of his hoard of sugar. They then retired to their own more esoteric rites at safe distance from the camp.

Moulding the amalgam of soap and sugar into a pliable ball, Austin Roxburgh grew so rapt he might have been casting a spell into the grubby, sweating mess.

Spurgeon was positively awed. ''Ow will we keep 'er in place on me neck?'

'Wait!'

When the medicament had been reduced to a sufficiently disgusting consistency the physician put it in the patient's hands, and fishing out the tail of his own good linen shirt, tore a resounding strip from it. The steward's disbelief in a gentleman's behaviour expressed itself in open-mouthed breathing which might have sounded like overt snores to anyone breaking in upon them. But nobody intruded on their privacy, and Mr Roxburgh applied the poultice to the inflamed swelling on the steward's neck, and bound it up, round and round, with the strip of shirt, sighing as he did so; he had come to love Spurgeon's boil for giving him occasion to discover in himself, if not an occult gift, at least a congratulable virtue.

They sat for a moment looking and not looking at each other, until the patient lowered his eyes to hide a gratitude which was threatening to spill over, and the physician roused himself from the trance in which his will had already induced a show of pus.

'Well, we shall see, old fellow!' he said in the brisk cheerful voice of one who had returned to his normal spiritual level and social station.

At the same time Mr Roxburgh realized how tired he was; he yawned like a horse, showing his gums and longish teeth. He felt he had all but dislocated a jaw. One might, he imagined, by too vigorous a yawn. It made him scramble to his feet and remember the wife who had been several hours' absent from his thoughts.

On reaching camp, Spurgeon a respectful distance behind him, he was directed to the improvised tent, where, he was told, Mrs Roxburgh was resting.

She was more, she was fast asleep it seemed when he lifted the loose canvas flap, prepared to share the tale of the boil and the part he had played – though not its deepest significance; gnostic delicacy would have prevented him revealing the secret of his occult powers. But she continued sleeping, and he lay down somewhat sulkily beside her.

When Mrs Roxburgh started up, and called out, ''Twas me! He wudn' a gone otherwise.' Eyes still closed, she struck her husband across the mouth with an outflung arm.

Mr Roxburgh winced for the numbing pain; he sneezed too, because his nose had shared the blow. 'Please, Ellen!' he protested. 'Obviously you have been through a nightmare, but I don't see why I should suffer for it.'

'No.' She sat trembling in her returning consciousness. 'I was not in control of myself.'

The loss of this cabin-boy, which the colours of her dream had transformed into a major bereavement, unloosed in her a need for affinity, a longing to be loved. She was prompted to pour out the tragic story on the one person close enough to respond to her distress; if the current sucked them under, they must rise from the depths revived and strengthened by their love for each other.

So she would have liked it had she not seen that Mr Roxburgh would not. Although recovered from the undignified blow she had dealt him, he had retired, it seemed, to the remotest corner of their relationship, where he lay just perceptibly smiling for what

194

she could not tell. At all events it was not the moment to break the news of Oswald's death.

Instead, she leaned over him, and drew her mouth across his parted lips, and breathed between them, 'You know I would not willingly hurt you,' and he put his arms round her, and she rocked him and cherished him, which appeared to be what he expected, and her distress at the boy's death was temporarily assuaged.

The light had almost wholly withdrawn from their suffocating canvas shelter. She must have slept, and Mr Roxburgh was still audibly asleep beside her. Outside, men's voices, Captain Purdew's, Mr Courtney's, and less frequently, Mr Pilcher's, were discussing a plan for the morning. The captain's intention was to head for the mainland, and after making landfall, to set course for Moreton Bay, always keeping inshore out of consideration for the scarcely seaworthy long-boat and the constant need of replenishing their limited water supply.

Mr Courtney promptly agreed; Mr Pilcher was more hesitant. When asked to declare his reservations, he answered, 'I agree – yes – to anythin' that be – reasonable, and water's as important as anythin'.' His reply was reasonable too, but for some reason, Mrs Roxburgh sensed, discouraging.

Although it was of the greatest importance that the men should plan the future, the exclusively male tenor of their conference began to bore her, especially since the talk of water had aggravated an intolerable thirst which was becoming her own pressing concern.

Forgetting the height of the tent, she rose to her feet, but was forced to her knees, and to crawling on all fours through the opening. Her hair, to which she no longer gave thought, hung round her face in ropes and mats, while her heavy skirt dragged behind her, ploughing a track through the sand such as the tail of some giant lizard might leave. Seated round the chart they were studying with such evident concentration, the men did not appear to find the figure of a woman on all fours in any way incongruous, if, in their present employment, they noticed her at all.

On getting to her feet Mrs Roxburgh walked discreetly past, under cover of her hair, in the direction of the boats. Here again, a group of sailors stretched on the sand paid no attention to her, but continued moodily pitching chunks of coral at the sea while talking in low voices, and by short bursts, of home and food.

Because her purpose in being there was the dubious one of looking for and appropriating the pannikin they had used in the long-boat, Mrs Roxburgh could not very well take exception to their lack of interest. She was only surprised that she could pass unnoticed, for the waning light had magnified the objects on which it was lingering, such as the great knob of porous coral with the tattered chart spread out upon it, and their normally loose-jointed, fragile boats. An illusion of light had changed the latter into a pair of louring hulks, just as the same tinkering process had moved the scrub significantly closer, emphasized the washed-out colours in the litter of broken shells, deepened the lines in Mr Pilcher's cheeks, and was drawing attention to the least hair in the tufts on a sailor's toes. As she slipped past in her unkempt condition she imagined she must have looked like some matted retriever or water-spaniel up to no good.

Particularly nosing round the boats, she felt herself guided by an instinct for cunning. If her design was not wholly dishonest, for not being altogether selfish (she did look forward to fetching water for the unpractical man who depended on her) it remained inadmissible according to Captain Purdew's code. So she was driven to slink, in her spoiled clothes roughed up like a retriever's coat, the lappets of her hair hanging and swinging like a spaniel's silly ears as she searched.

She came across what she needed amongst the tackle jettisoned from the long-boat before the caulking operation was begun. She hid the pannikin under her shawl, and had soon resumed her slinking, through a light which accused whatever it illuminated.

Here and there birds flew skirring out of bushes, or in one case, opened its beak and hissed at her from a grass nest in a hollow in the sand. Farther on, she found a nest unoccupied, and fell upon her knees beside it, and broke open one of the eggs, inside it a putrefying embryo, from which she tore herself near to retching, tripping on the hem of her skirt as she lumbered off.

Under divine guidance, she was prepared to believe, she was brought to a rock saucer in which water shone, sweet moreover when she tasted it. She dipped her shawl and wrung it into the tin cup, and only sucked the woollen fringes which had sopped the water out of the rock. Yet farther afield she came upon other pools, as well as mere hints of moisture, all of which she sopped up, wringing out the water into the pannikin.

She was standing thoughtfully sucking at the fringe of her shawl when she heard footsteps behind her, and a voice breaking the silence.

'What is Mrs Roxburgh up to?'

Without turning she knew it to be Mr Pilcher; no one else could have aimed such scorn at a target which met with his disapproval.

When she turned to face him she made no attempt to hide the half-filled pannikin; Mr Pilcher's instinct would surely have told him of its whereabouts.

'The gentry foragin' for 'emselves, eh?' he commented as soon as he saw.

'Surely it will harm no one if I take my husband – who is in poor health – half a cup of rainwater?'

'People like your old man, with all time on 'is ands, can afford to enjoy imaginitis.'

He reached out, took the pannikin from her, and drained it.

'That's what I think of the both of 'ee.' He returned the mug. 'Anybody's rights be as good as yours.'

'If that is how you feel,' she conceded, while her Cornish self struggled to restrain its temper, 'you must obey your principles. They are mine too, I expect, and rainwater is free for anyone to take – if they're so disposed.'

'Then you can fill me another mugful – disposed or not.'

'I am not your servant.'

'If we're not eaten by the maggots or the sharks, you may be yet. There's few servants didn't own to more 'n one master.'

'What in life has hurt you to leave you so embittered?'

'Not embittered – practical – for seein' what the likes of you persuade 'emselves don't exist.'

'You too, are given to imagining,' Mrs Roxburgh said. 'I am not all that you believe, for instance. I know and understand hardship – though I've grown away from it – and had it easy. I can remember winter nights when a teddy-cake was a luxury.'

'Am I right then, in imaginin' you was the servant who took 'is fancy?' Mr Pilcher had never looked so odiously vindictive.

'I was never anybody's servant. If Mr Roxburgh asked me to be his wife, it was – I believe – because he loved me. In a sense I am under obligation, but choose to serve someone I respect – and love,' she added.

While they were engaged in what could have been an 'imagined' conversation in so far as it was related to her humble, and consequently, unreal past, the shadows had been enshrouding them. Now a moon was rising, like a single medal of the honesty her mother-in-law liked to arrange in vases, because it was so reliable and needed no further attention. Against a drained sky, the present moon might have passed for transparent to those who had not made a study of its face and learnt its peculiarities.

Thinking she had worsted her opponent, Mrs Roxburgh was preparing to break away. 'My husband will be expecting me.'

But the mate's eyes were glittering, like her own hands she realized, as they held the empty pannikin.

He pointed to her rings. 'Will ye give me one?'

'Why ever should you want it?'

'As a memento!' He laughed, apparently embarrassed.

'Perhaps we'll never wake! And if we do, will you want to remember this bad dream?'

'I'm not one that can afford dreams, and might get meself out of some future hole if I have a little something to fall back on.' As he spoke he fell to fingering the nest of garnets.

'Take it!' she said. 'I no longer have any use for them. For that matter, I've never truthfully felt they were mine.'

She stretched out her hand, and he practically dragged the ring off, and fitted it on a little finger. Held to the light for him to look at, the garnets smouldered back at him.

'Now you too, can be counted among the capitalists,' she told him in making her escape.

She was glad of the accompaniment provided by her skirt, sweeping coral and brushing scrub, as she returned to the camp and a mouthful of rancid salt pork.

In the twilight before dawn the Roxburghs were awakened by voices and a sound of canvas, to find that their shelter was being dismantled. The men at work were not unkindly disposed towards them, and one went so far as to apologize to the tenants for the inconvenience they were causing them.

'Bosun'll bawl at us,' he explained, 'if we're not stowed afore the captain finishes 'is prayers.'

Mr Roxburgh laughed rather too heartily at the sailor's joke, then made a mental note to commend them all to their Maker when a more suitable moment offered itself. Since the greatest need for it arose, he had lost the habit of prayer, he was ashamed to realize, but his wife no doubt included him in her own petitions. Prayer, he had always suspected, came more easily to women through their cultivating a more intimate, emotional relationship with God. Or was that so? Could one be certain of anything?

His reflections ended by making him grumpy. 'If you don't get up, Ellen, you'll put them against us. They'll be in a bad enough temper as it is.'

'Ycs,' she murmured drowsily, but could not yet bestir herself in the delicious grey which stretches between sleep and waking, not even if her sloth caused the Lord God of Hosts to abandon them at full gallop. 'Yes,' she repeated sharper, and sat up too quick, wondering how she should dress for the day ahead, before realizing there was no choice.

She might at least have inquired after Mr Roxburgh's health had not her own heavy mind, and perhaps Mr Pilcher's scorn, been against it. More than anything her pregnancy outweighed her solicitude for others.

'Shall I give you a hand?' Mr Roxburgh offered magnanimously.

She was grateful to be pulled to her feet, and now that they were facing each other, she kissed him; it was still dark, though possibly not dark enough to satisfy Mr Roxburgh. Because she could feel a quivering in his rigid fingers she was careful to avoid the mouth.

After the launching of the boats, which developed into a turmoil of emotions, oaths, torn skin, bruised vanity, and barely suppressed hatred, they were able to set course for the mainland thanks to a wind the captain and his first officer had been hoping to catch. But still the long-boat limped. Mr Courtney was disconcerted to the extent that he decided on hailing the pinnace. An excess of shouting drew their attention, and when the distance between the two boats had sufficiently diminished, Mr Pilcher flung an unwilling hawser. Mr Courtney himself seized upon it with what appeared to Mr Roxburgh the air of a man taking up a gage. He made it fast. No doubt it would have gone against the grain to admit, even from between his clenched teeth, that the long-boat was once more dependent on the good graces of the pinnace.

Mr Roxburgh recalled his resolution to say prayers, but again the moment was not propitious; his heart was still padding irregularly he felt, as the result of his recent exertions, and someone had jobbed him in the eye with an elbow during the general mellay of clambering aboard in a stiff surf.

Remembering his wife's condition he deflected his thoughts ever so slightly in her direction, and was prompted to remark for her moral sustenance, 'We can thank God, my dear, for bringing us a few yards closer to civilization.'

He spoke at an instant when the wind veered, giving every indication of wanting to hustle them away from the coast and out to sea. As in so many of nature's manifestations, the squall seemed only to some degree capricious, beyond which it was driven by an almost personal rage or malice. Mrs Roxburgh dared wonder whether the Deity Himself were not taking revenge on them for their human shortcomings.

In the circumstances she was not sustained by her husband's untimely remark. Physically she was at her lowest. She had the greatest difficulty in preventing her head from being dragged by its unnatural weight down upon her slack breasts, above her swollen belly, and was only alerted by overhearing a colloquy hurled back and forth between the long-boat and the pinnace. Mr Courtney had resumed command of the former in the absence of the captain's faculties, and was upbraiding his subordinate Pilcher for making no move to adapt his rig to meet the sudden emergency.

Mrs Roxburgh's dull eyes and woman's ears did not adjust themselves to a situation as technical as it was masculine, until forced out of her apathy by the untoward emotion of the contestants and the sight of Pilcher taking an axe and hacking at the hawser on which they depended.

It was soon done: the long-boat was free to flounder on her

chosen course, to the best of her poor ability, and if Providence liked to favour her.

In the beginning, none of those aboard dared give expression to his thoughts. Glad of the occupation, some of the crew took of their own accord to bailing, for the water had started seeping through the martyred timbers in spite of the attentions received while beached on the cay. Mr Roxburgh joined them willingly. So did his wife when the tin abandoned by other hands floated towards her.

During a pause from his work it occurred to Mr Roxburgh to ask, 'What has become of the boy, Ellen? He didn't surely abscond to the pinnace?'

Because death promised to become an everyday occurrence in which tuberose sentiments and even sincere grief might sound superfluous, she answered in the flattest voice, 'No, he was drowned yesterday evening, gathering shellfish from the reef.'

Several steps behind in his acceptance of the situation, Mr Roxburgh was appalled by his wife's unexpected callousness. 'Why on earth didn't you tell me?'

'I forgot,' she answered. 'There were other things on my mind.'

It was not wholly true, but then, he would have recoiled from being told while horror at the death still possessed her, and later of course she had been shaken by the blows Pilcher dealt her in making his unjust accusations.

Just then Spurgeon, enjoying an invalid's privileges within earshot of his benefactor, was roused by what he overheard. 'What – the nipper *gone*? Oswald was a fine lad. But crikey, you can't blame the lady. Singin' out won't call back the dead.'

Although displeased that his wife should have found an ally in one he considered his personal conquest, Mr Roxburgh welcomed the double assurance that formal mourning was not expected.

A sigh or two, a click of the tongue, and he had done his duty. 'You are the one I'm sorry for, Ellen. The boy was so devoted to you.'

'I loved him,' she said simply, but again so dull of voice that Austin Roxburgh need not experience the slightest twinge, either of remorse or jealousy.

In any event, the distance which the recalcitrant pinnace had already put between herself and the long-boat increased the unreality of most human relationships. Faith in integrity persisted while the rope held, but with the severing of the hawser and gradual disappearance of the master boat, the horizon had become clouded with doubts.

Mr Roxburgh wished he was still in possession of his journal, to discuss his mood in rational terms, and thus restore a moral balance.

Now it was sea and wind holding the balance, or maliciously maintaining a lack of it as they were buffeted day and night, in which direction Mr Courtney, if questioned, professed to know.

'I'd say – by my calculations – we're a hundred and fifty mile to the east of Percy Island'; or 'At this rate we're headed back for the Cumberlands'; or again, 'With any luck, we might make landfall tomorrow evening at Bustard Bay.'

His clear but rather stupid eyes had never looked farther and seen less; his jaws beneath their doggy whiskers were cracking with responsibility.

While Captain Purdew, an old child huddled near his guardian's ankles, laughed low. 'Yarmouth, or Barnstaple, it's all the same – as God knows.'

It made sense to everyone: geography was anybody's guess; the chart might have been torn up and instruments tossed into the surf before they embarked on this erratic voyage.

Which in the days, or weeks, or months that followed, concerned Ellen Roxburgh more than anyone. On her the waters in the doomed boat reached higher, almost to her waist it seemed, clambering, lapping, sipping the blood out of her flaccid body.

That was the least part of her. Herself sank. The fringe of her green shawl trailed through depths in which it was often indistinguishable from beaded weed or the veils and streamers of fish drifting and catching on coral hummocks then dissolving free for the simple reason that the whole universe was watered down.

Somebody, a man, was holding a stinking vessel to her lips, 'Here Mrs Roxburgh is a drop of rum only a nip the dregs but will put new life into 'ee.'

She allowed it to happen, more than anything to pacify whoever it was that prescribed the cure, not because she feared life might be leaving her; everyone else, but not herself, she was so convinced, or egotistical.

And again was lowered into twilit depths where only a brown throbbing distinguished what she was experiencing now from anything she had experienced before. Grave schooners were sailing beside her brushing her ribs eyeing her through isinglass portholes. It must have been the rum causing the red-brown throbbing of her thoughts. As for the creature which had begun to persecute her in its increasingly remonstrative form undulating out of time with her own somewhere in the folds of her petticoats bunting nibbling at her numb legs this slippery fish was pushing in the direction of a freedom to which she had never yet attained.

Whether forced to it by mental anguish or physical stress, Mrs Roxburgh raised herself from the position in which her husband had been supporting her in the waterlogged boat.

'Ohhh!' she moaned, or lowed rather, through thick lips, her face offered flat to the sky. 'Aw, my Gore!'

It was a still evening, comparatively benign. In the circumstances, the sounds he had just heard uttered struck Mr Roxburgh as positively bestial. His sensibility would have shut them out had it been at all possible.

As it was not, he voiced the precept taught in youth, 'We must keep our heads, Ellen,' while going through the motions of soothing a delirious wife.

Who cried, 'There's no question – it's lost – however I tried – nobody can blame me, Austin – can they?'

Although startled by her unwonted use of his Christian name, he tried to assure her, 'Nobody intends to add to your sufferings by accusations,' and drew his fingers along the wet, blubbery cheek of one by whom he thought he had done his duty in every sense.

But she began clutching at his hand, whimpering and muttering childishly, in an attempt to draw him down to her level.

'Then what is it?' he hissed, as desperate as he was irritated.

On grasping the full enormity of the situation there was nothing he could do but accept. 'It is unfortunate, but neither of us will die of it,' he predicted.

All his life he might have been on equal terms with reality.

After delivering his wife of their stillborn child, and somebody had produced what must have been Oswald's glory-bag, he emptied the bag of its contents, the buttons, twine, a pencil-stub, a keepsake or two, a martyred prayerbook. In the absence of a conventional shroud the bag provided a substitute to accommodate this other, more portentous object.

Again Mr Roxburgh was satisfied he had done his duty; his hands only fumbled as he tightened the draw-string at the canvas neck, and out of his throat came a hideous sound as of tearing.

Weak from hunger and from marinating in brine, Captain Purdew dragged himself aft like an attenuated black cormorant. He seized upon Oswald Dignam's book, and began performing an office to which life at sea had accustomed him.

Mrs Roxburgh closed her eyes. The words she but half-overheard did not impress themselves on her mind; they seemed rather, to break upon her eyelids, to be turned away as a flickering of light.

'... man that is born ...

   ... forasmuch as it pleases ...

      ... thou knowest, Lord, the secrets of our hearts ...'

She stirred where she lay and ripples were sent through the water in the boat, to be answered by this faint plash beyond the gunwale.

'... our vile body ...

   ... His glorious body ...

      ... to subdue all things to Himself.

Amennn.'

Captain Purdew concluded with a twang, after which there was a re-settling of caps to an accompaniment of barely audible agreement or reservation.

If tears struggled out of the captain's eyes, it was because, as everybody knew, his wits were leaving him, and though some of the men were shaken by what had occurred, it was also for remembering wives and sweethearts, or even a favourite dog. By comparison the Roxburghs appeared untouched in the halcyon evening prepared for their child's burial. Beneath a peacock sky her face, reduced by suffering to a drained pudding-colour, wore an expression of assent bordering on tranquillity, while her husband, upright beside her, might have been enjoying congratulations for his performance in a classic role.

When Mrs Roxburgh remembered to ask, 'Did you perhaps notice a likeness to any of us? Children take after grandparents more often than a father or mother,' Mr Roxburgh laughed a high laugh, and uncharacteristically squeezed her.

'I shouldn't say . . . No! It was too soon, Ellen – and too brief a glimpse.' After that, he briefly sighed, for the pity of it, as it could not have been out of contentment. 'Since you've asked, however, I believe I did detect in him a touch of what might have developed into a likeness to myself.'

Then he kissed her on the mouth in full view of those who were watching, more in their dreams than through their eyes.

'I am so glad,' she replied, 'and that it was a boy, as you would have wanted.' The twitch of a smile, and she settled back into acceptance of wherever the future might float them.

Once in the days, weeks, years which followed, she did rouse herself sufficiently to ask, 'You are not going to leave me, are you?'

'How could I?' he answered. 'Even if I wanted to.'

Such an indisputable reason and barely modified rebuke might have hurt if strength were not returning to her sodden limbs, not through divine forbearance, as some might have seen it, but because, she realized, she was born a Gluyas. The rain had stopped; life is to be lived. She would have got to her feet like any other beast of nature, steadying herself in the mud and trampled grass, had it been a field and not a waterlogged boat.

In present circumstances, on a morning when the weather noticeably favoured them, she threw out the last of the thoughts which had been flickering all this time in her skull like phosphorescent fish. Her hands, she saw, were the same inherited extremities of rude but practical shape. If they had lost their native tan, it was not through a course in ladycraft, but by the action of sea-water. So she was still equipped for bailing, an occupation some of the strongest members of the crew by now tended to renounce.

Her work removed her, if not physically, from her husband Mr Austin Roxburgh, who remained huddled at her side. Although occasionally he gave a hand, it was but an apathetic gesture; he was not of course so hardened by monotony as she. Once on looking at him she surprised an expression, not quite despair and not quite disgust, but which might have been caused by the slow poison of apprehension. At all events she was wounded by it, and set about bridging the distance between them.

'What is it?' she asked. 'An attack is not coming on you again? Or are you grieving?' She put out her coarsened hand as though to shore him up with her recovered strength.

He appeared at first resentful of her kindness, like some pampered child preparing to take revenge for neglect.

'You know that my thoughts are always only for you, Mr Roxburgh,' she added without consideration for the truthfulness of what she was saying.

Thus his servant hoped to reassure him.

But he sank his chin against her shoulder. 'It is Spurgeon, Ellen. I think he must have died.'

For the moment only the Roxburghs were aware of what had happened; nor had the company noticed the tears shed by Mr Roxburgh for his recently acquired, unsavoury friend. Weakened morally as well as physically, he would not have attempted to conceal those tears, unless from his wife, and Ellen, he trusted, would mistake his grief for a natural process of crystallized moisture dissolving back into its original state of water.

Spurgeon the steward, already stiff, was pitched overboard by his crew-mates without benefit of canvas or lead. In this instance Captain Purdew did not read the burial service, perhaps because he did not realize anything had happened, or else he had mislaid Oswald Dignam's book. Spurgeon, some of those present suspected, is the corpse the sharks get. But who cares, finally?

That Mr Roxburgh cared, nobody but his wife guessed, and she must steel herself that her husband might survive.

As one who had hungered all his life after friendships which eluded him, Austin Roxburgh did luxuriate on losing a solitary allegiance. It stimulated his actual hunger until now dormant, and he fell to thinking how the steward, had he not been such an unappetizing morsel, might have contributed appreciably to an exhausted larder. At once Mr Roxburgh's self-disgust knew no bounds. He was glad that night had fallen and that everyone around him was sleeping. Yet his thoughts were only cut to a traditional pattern, as Captain Purdew must have recognized, who now came stepping between the heads of the sleepers, to bend and whisper, *This is the body of Spurgeon which I have reserved for thee, take eat, and give thanks for a boil which was spiritual matter* . . . Austin Roxburgh was not only ravenous for the living flesh, but found himself anxiously licking the corners of his mouth to prevent any overflow of precious blood.

Upon suddenly waking, Mr Roxburgh discovered his mouth wide open. He would have set about ejecting anything inside it, from his stomach too, had they not been equally empty. Emptiness, however, did not protect him from a fit of sweating shivers, which persisted after he had looked around him and seen that all, including Captain Purdew, were fast asleep.

So much for night and dreams. Glances exchanged by daylight promised worse, until in the course of the morning Mr Courtney stood up in the bows and drew attention to what first appeared a slate-pencil miraculously laid along the edge of the slate. Whether island or mainland, he personally was not prepared to speculate, but wind, sea, and general conditions being in the long-boat's favour, he ventured to affirm that they would make landfall before many hours.

The Roxburghs avoided looking at each other. Instead she clasped his hand, the rather delicate, attenuated bones and the boss made by his signet ring.

7

All trace of cloud was gone from the sky as they approached the shore. Faces bleared by rain and suffering offered themselves instead to an onslaught by ceremonial sunlight, which was grinding an already dazzling stretch of sand into an ever-intensifying white. Some of the castaways would not have been surprised had the Almighty ordered his trumpets to sound their arrival on the fringe of paradise itself.

They advanced lumbering through the turquoise-to-nacre of a still sea, which shaded into a ruffle of surf, scarce enough to wet the ankles. The long-boat practically beached herself, in the silence and amazement of those aboard. One or two jumped, but more of them tumbled out, to crawl like maimed crabs through the shallows.

Not unnaturally the passengers were again forgotten. It was Mrs Roxburgh who offered her husband a helping hand to clear the gunwale, as though he had returned to playing the role of dedicated invalid.

'Is it too much to hope, Ellen,' he whispered through bleeding lips, 'that we shall be left in peace awhile, to recover our strength – if not our normal, rational thoughts?'

'I expect so,' she murmured to comfort him.

The crew ahead of them were already either lying, elbows in the air, or cheek to the sand, while one soul more suspicious than the rest wandered in a circle, apparently attempting to sight the invisible insect, or malicious spirit, which was bound to start tormenting him.

Whether from extreme debility or devotion to duty, Captain Purdew was the last to leave the boat. Staggering ashore he fell on his knees where the sand still glistened with bubbles left by the retiring wave, and proceeded to give thanks to their Maker in what passed for an official voice, 'Almighty Lord, I pray that we may prove ourselves worthy of this unexpected blessing ... that we may be strengthened for the trials to come from having experienced your loving mercy ...' but went into a more private mumble, 'and fill our empty bellies, Lord ... and slake our unbearable thirst ... not with pebbles, nor lead sinkers. My dear, it wasn't me who would have abandoned *Bristol Maid*, if others hadn't been in favour ...'

At this point overcome by emotion, the old man fell on his face and united his bubbles with those of the receding tide.

As for Austin Roxburgh, he resolved to follow the captain's example, and give thanks, but privately, to God (more private still to his more convincing *ipse Pater*) at some later date. The present was not auspicious: he felt stunned by a silence of the earth as opposed to the thundering silence of the sea; his ears were left ticking and protesting.

Round them shimmered the light, the sand, and farther back, the darker, proprietary trees. Where the beach rose higher, to encroach on the forest, great mattresses of sand, far removed from the attentions of the tides, were quilted and buttoned down by vines, a variety of convolvulus, its furled trumpets of a pale mauve. Mrs Roxburgh might have thrown herself down on the vine-embroidered sand had it not burnt her so intensely, even through the soles of her dilapidated boots.

She was, besides, growing conscious of a smell, of more, an obscene stink, and saw that she was squelching her way towards the putrefying carcase of what she took to be a kangaroo.

'Phoo!' she cried; then her wits took over. 'Can it be used, though? There's plenty game that stinks as high on the best-kept tables.'

Hunger effected it quicker than it might have been. Mr Courtney succeeded in coaxing fire out of some dry twigs and vine with the help of flint and steel he had found in a shammy-leather bag strung round the late Spurgeon's neck. Roasting somewhat quenched the stink of putrefying flesh, and in those who waited, greed quickened into ecstasy.

There was not one who failed to claim his portion. The meat tasted gamey, as Mrs Roxburgh had foreseen, and was singed-raw rather than cooked. But Mr Roxburgh declared he had never tasted a more palatable dish, ignoring the frizzled maggot or two he scraped off with a burnt finger, and sat there when he was finished, sucking at a piece of hide as though he could not bear to part with it.

One of the men added to their comfort by discovering during a short reconnaissance of the adjacent forest several pools of only slightly brackish water, to which the party trudged, and scooped water by the handful, or lay with their faces in it, sucking up injudicious draughts. Mrs Roxburgh contemplated bathing her face and hands, for the stench of rotten kangaroo had been added to the smell of salt grime accumulated over weeks spent in an open boat, but on glancing round at her companions she suspected that such behaviour might appear ostentatious, and in any case, it could produce only superficial results. Since her return to land she had become aware of whiffs given off by wet clothes and the body inside them.

Seeing that evening was approaching it was decided to camp beside the water-holes, which in normal picnic circumstances would have provided an admirably restful setting, upon an up-holstery of moss, inside this vast green marquee, its sides just visibly in motion as a breeze stirred the creepers slung from some-where high above. The scene lacked only the coachman and a footman to produce the hampers.

Now at any rate Mr Roxburgh would have given thanks, in peace and quiet, after settling himself against a hummock, hand in hand with his dear wife, some little way apart from the others, had it not been for a curious noise, of animal gibbering, or human chatter, slight at first, then sawing louder into the silence.

Every head among them was raised as though functioning on sadly rusted springs, and there on a rise in the middle distance appeared one, three, half-a-dozen savages, not entirely naked, for each wore a kind of primitive cloth draped from a shoulder, across the body, and over his private parts. The natives were armed besides, with spears, and other warlike implements, all probably of wood; only their dark skins had the glint of ominous metal.

The two parties remained watching each other an uncon-scionable time before the blacks silently melted away among the shadows.

As soon as it was felt that the aboriginals had removed to a safe distance, the voice of speculation raised itself in the white camp: it was wondered what kind of dirty work the 'customers' would get up to.

Captain Purdew was of the opinion that 'Christian advances should meet with Christian results,' but sighed and added, 'unless our sins are so heavy they will weigh against us.' In any event, he sought to impress upon his command to refrain from opening fire on those who were no more than 'natural innocents'.

Despite the captain's injunctions, Mr Courtney and one of his men decided on their own account to overhaul the armoury of two muskets and a pistol, all probably unserviceable from exposure in the boat. They went so far as to load the weapons in case of an ambush during the night, and discouraged those who were in favour of kindling a fire to rouse their lowered spirits.

When he had exhausted his surprise at the black intrusion, and disposed of a dubious aesthetic pleasure in their muscular forms and luminous skins, Mr Roxburgh began to find the whole issue a tedious one. Reality had always come and gone in his presence with startling suddenness, and never more capriciously than since the wreck of *Bristol Maid*. So he could take but a fitful interest in the question of defence. His real, sustaining, and sustained life would only begin again on his return to the library at 'Birdlip House'.

Even Mrs Roxburgh was inclined to look upon the loading of firearms by Mr Courtney and his henchman as an example of the games men-as-boys see it their duty to play. She lowered her eyes at last, and with a blade of grass helped an ant struggle out of a depression in the moss.

Peace and drowsiness began to prevail; an idyll might have been reinstated but for the cold creeping on them through the trees, and if almost every member of the party had not been racked by diarrhoea. There was a continual tramping through the undergrowth and silence, in which a private condition was made distressingly audible.

'That infernal kangaroo!' Mr Roxburgh groaned at one stage. 'Why do you suppose you were spared, Ellen?'

'Who am I to explain? Unless I swilled less of that water than some of you others.'

Mr Roxburgh came to the conclusion that it was minerals dissolved in the water, and not the gamey kangaroo, which had caused their indisposition.

But he seemed to hold it against her that she had not suffered, and during the night when his spirits were at their lowest, confessed, 'I've often thought that I'd willingly die – there is not all that much to live for – but have wondered how you would manage without me.'

Mrs Roxburgh pretended she had fallen asleep.

In the morning the party, most of them considerably weakened, rose without encouragement before the light.

Captain Purdew – or was it Mr Courtney? decided they should return to the beach and there set course for Moreton Bay, which they must reach eventually on foot if indeed they had landed on the mainland and not an island.

Captain Purdew's wits took a turn for the worse when it came to abandoning the incapacitated long-boat. Like *Bristol Maid* it lodged in his conscience and would probably fester there for as long as he lived.

Whereas Mrs Roxburgh, who glanced back once as they trudged along the beach, resolved to put it out of her mind, together with the sufferings she had endured while confined to its wretched shell. Or had she the power to govern her thoughts? She must cultivate a strength of will to equal that of her sturdy body. The latter mercifully withstood every material imposition; for her clothes were weighing her down, and her husband dragged on the arm she had offered as a support in his debility.

So they struggled on, the men for the most part barefoot, and every one of them a shambles of appearance and behaviour.

'Halfway to Norwich the horse lay down . . .' Captain Purdew was heard to whimper.

The sun rose, to batter them about the head and shoulders. At one point the woman lowered her glance as though unable any longer to face the glare, and the rings she was wearing flashed back an ironic message. For a few steps she closed her eyes. Patterned with salt and sweat, her dark clothes might have been drawing her under, to depths from which she had but dreamt that she was delivered.

As for Mr Roxburgh, he had abandoned his overcoat and jacket (his boots had abandoned him) but was still wearing his waistcoat in the heat of the day to ensure safe carriage of the Elzevir Virgil buttoned inside.

Mrs Roxburgh could have cried for her husband's long narrow feet: pale and cold according to her memory, they were now ablaze.

From the sun's position it must have been the middle of the day, when the most torpid mind was compelled to take notice, by a hissing sound followed by a marked thud. A spear had planted itself obliquely in the sand a few feet ahead of Mr Courtney and the seaman who were leading the procession. The spear had scarcely ceased vibrating when a second grazed Captain Purdew's left shoulder, tearing the shirt and letting a trickle of blood.

Several of the crew started shouting, to assert their courage or disguise their fear, as Mr Courtney and his companion, who were in possession of the firearms, headed in the direction of some dunes to landward where fifteen to sixteen natives were seen to have congregated, their gibberish accompanied by overtly hostile gestures.

Above the pain and shock Captain Purdew must have been suffering from his wound, he was made frantic by the prospect of his subordinates committing violence. '*Ned! Frank!*' He shambled forward, emotion causing him to spit so inordinately that he sprayed Mrs Roxburgh's face in passing. 'We'll do no good by spilling blood!'

'Nor by palaverin', neether!' an anonymous voice rejoined.

The first officer and the promoted seaman were taking aim with a precision which fitted the sudden stillness.

A single report from one of the guns sounded horrendous to those who were listening for it; the second weapon played dead, to the fury of the seaman who had been counting upon his moment of glory.

The savages emitted horrid shrieks as one of their number fell, jerking and convulsed, and disappeared from sight amongst the dunes.

The captain was quite demented. 'We'll pay for it, I tell you!' he shouted.

He was, in fact, the one who did, for the next instant a spear was twangling in his ribs. It went in as though he were scarcely a man, or if he were, nobody they had ever known. As he toppled over he conspired with fate by driving the spear deeper in.

213

There were howls from the blacks, and the shouting of incensed, helpless sailors.

For the second time Mr Courtney took aim, but his gesture produced no more than silence.

Ellen Gluyas watched the bloodstain widening on the sand. There had not been so much blood since Pa and Will slaughtered the calf during their lodger's interminable stay.

Now she too, was interminable, transfixed by time as painfully and mercilessly as by any spear. She, the practical one, and a woman, should tear herself free and rush back into life – to *do something*.

But it was Mr Roxburgh who ran forward, to do what only God could know. Here he was, bestirring himself at least, in the manner expected of the male sex. Into action! He felt elated, as well as frightened, and full of disbelief in his undertaking. (It was not, however, an uncommon reaction to his own unlikelihood.)

He was several yards from the dying man when Mrs Roxburgh became aware of a terrible whooshing, like the beating of giant wings, infernal in that they were bearing down upon her more than any other being. Indeed, nothing more personal had happened to her in the whole of her life. For a spear, she saw, had struck her husband; it was hanging from his neck, long and black, giving him a lopsided look.

'Awwwh!' Ellen Gluyas cried out from what was again an ignorant and helpless girlhood.

Austin Roxburgh was keeling over. On reaching the sand his body would have re-asserted itself, but the attempt petered out in the parody of a landed shrimp.

'Oh, no! No, no!' It was the little skipping motion, of defeat in the attempt, which freed her; it was too piteous, as though all the children she had failed to rear were gesticulating for her help.

When she reached his side his eyes were closed, pulses could be seen palpitating beneath the skin, while the long black spear led a malignant life of its own.

At least there was no sign of blood.

'Oh, my husband – my darling!' She was blubbering, bellowing, herself the calf with the knife at its throat.

He opened his eyes. 'Ellen, you are different. The light . . . or the brim of that . . . huge . . . country . . . *hat*. Raise it, please . . . so that I can see . . .'

In her desperation she seized the spear and dragged at it, and it came away through the gristle in his neck. At once blood gushed out of the wound, as well as from the nostrils and mouth.

She fell on her knees.

'I forgot,' he said, rising for a moment above the tide in which he was drowning. 'Pray for me, Ellen.'

She could not, would never pray again. 'Oh, no, Lord! Why are we born, then?'

The blood was running warm and sticky over her hands. Round the mouth, and on one smeared temple, more transparent than she had ever seen it, flies were crowding in black clots, greedy for the least speck of crimson before the sun dried the virtue out of it.

*

Huddled on the sand beside a husband with whom the surviving link was his dried blood, Mrs Roxburgh had taken refuge inside the tent of matted hair which, hanging down, could be used to protect her face from the flies, as well as screen her to some extent from what might provoke a further wrench of anguish.

Had she been a free agent she would have chosen just then to succumb to the heat, the weight of her clothes, and numbness of mind, but heard a shot followed by an outburst of laughter, and raised the curtain enough to discover the reason why the second incongruous explosion should follow so closely upon the first.

The men, it appeared, had begun digging a trench in the sand in which to bury their late captain, scratching with their hands alone in a frenzy of application to create the illusion that they were occupied positively, while hoping that the officer who had joined them at their work might come up with some plan to reduce their plight. During it all, a youth named Bob Adams who had a record as a sawney, started digging with the butt of one of the impotent muskets. Which went off. Mr Courtney's ally, Frank Runcie, cursed fearfully, and the officer himself used every word of a vocabulary to which his blunted authority entitled him.

It was a relief for the others to laugh. 'At any rate, nobody stopped it!' one fellow guffawed, and some of the others persisted in labouring the joke.

When Mrs Roxburgh glanced again, the sailors and officer had finished their game of sandcastles: Captain Purdew was decently disposed of, his tomb decorated with a pattern of the hand-prints of those who had shared his last trials. It did, however, face them with the problem of how to deal with the passenger whose wife sat mourning over him. Not one of them would have cared to intrude on the lady's grief, least of all Mr Courtney, whose duty it was to take the lead and offer some form of condolence.

Mrs Roxburgh made no attempt to help, simply because she could not have been helped.

A solution was provided by the blacks' return, the more dignified among them striding directly towards their objective, others capering and play-acting. The party of ineffectual whites was soon surrounded by the troop of blacks, all sinew, stench, and exultant in their mastery. One of them ripped the shirt off Mr Courtney, another the belt from Runcie's waist.

Mrs Roxburgh might have felt more alarmed had any of their play concerned herself, but the natives seemed intent on ignoring a mere woman seated by her husband's corpse. In the circumstances, she no longer felt constrained to turn her head or hide behind her hair. To the spectator, what was happening now was far less incredible or terrifying than the events leading up to it.

The blacks had begun stripping their captives garment by garment. One fellow's skin was such a glaring white, the tuft of hair below his belly flared up like a burning bush. Mr Courtney's testicles were long, slender, pathetic in their defencelessness. Because she had never been faced with a naked man, Mrs Roxburgh at this point looked away, and instead caught sight of her husband's naked feet.

She hung her head, and wept for the one she had failed in the end to protect.

After much laughter and caracoling as they bore away their spoils into the scrub, the blacks returned and started driving their white herd, by thwacks and prodding, into the dense hinterland.

Watching her companions disappearing from sight, Mrs Roxburgh wondered what she could expect – probably very little, at best the luxury of lying down to putrefy beside her dead husband.

While the sun sank lower the landscape was subjected to a tyrannical beauty of deeper blue, slashed green, and flamingo feathers. She who had been reared among watercolours whimpered at this sudden opulence, the saliva running down her chin.

There was almost nothing she might risk looking at, least of all her husband's feet, austerely pointed at the luxuriant sky.

When again she heard voices and saw that some black women were approaching. A high chatter interspersed with laughter suggested a kind of game: the words tossed by the women into the cooling air could have been substitutes for a ball. This, Ellen Roxburgh sensed, was the beginning of her martyrdom.

The females advanced, six or seven of them, from hags to nubile girls. On arriving within a few yards of the stranger, one of the girls bent down, picked up a handful of sand, and flung it in the white woman's face.

Mrs Roxburgh barely flinched, not because sustained by strength of will, but because the spirit had gone out of her. She was perhaps fortunate, in that a passive object can endure more than a human being.

Her tormentors were convulsed by their companion's inspiration, and several others followed suit throwing sand, until one more audacious member of their set darted forward and dragged the prisoner to her feet.

Ellen Gluyas had not encountered a more unlikely situation since forced as a bride to face the drawing-rooms of Cheltenham. The difference in the present was that she had grown numb to hurt, and that those she had loved and wished to please could no longer be offended by her lapses in behaviour or her scarecrow person.

The party of women strolled round her in amazement at the spectacle; one or two were moved to pull her hair, unlike their own which had been hacked off within a few inches of the roots; the large woman with heavy jowls who had yanked her to her feet, caught sight of and started fingering her rings, their stones not entirely dulled by grime.

'Take them if you want,' Mrs Roxburgh insisted, and with no thought for whether she might be understood. 'They no longer have any value for me. Do, please, take them. Only leave me my wedding ring.'

The natives glowered and cowered on hearing for the first time the voice of one who might have been a supernatural creature, so that the prisoner herself worked the rings off her swollen fingers and offered them on the palm of an outstretched hand.

The monkey-women snatched. An almost suppressed murmuring arose as they examined the jewels they had been given, but their possessive lust was quickly appeased, or else their minds had flitted on in search of further stimulus.

A young girl came up behind her and was tearing at her bedraggled gown. It required no special effort to remove the tatters. Petticoats provoked greater joy in the despoilers, but short-lived: the stuff was whipped off as lightly as a swirl of sea drift, leaving the captive standing in the next and more substantial layer, her stays.

Glancing down her front Ellen Gluyas recalled a certain vase on the mantelpiece of the room where old Mrs Roxburgh spent her days after her son's bride was installed. Now that she was stranded under the most barbarous conditions on a glaring beach, the image of the slender-waisted vase, its opaque ribs alternating with transparent depressions, brought the tears to her eyes, if it was, indeed, the vase, and not its gentle owner, her hands of softest, whitest kid upholstered beneath with pads of crumpled pink.

So the daughter-in-law indulged herself to the extent of weeping a little; the little might have turned to more had not the black women whirled her about as they tore at her corset. She came to their assistance at last, to escape the quicker from nails lacerating her flesh.

She was finally unhooked.

Then the shift, and she was entirely liberated.

They ran from her trailing the ultimate shreds of her modesty, as well as the clattering armature, their laughter gurgling till lost in their throats or the undergrowth to which they had retreated.

Thus isolated and naked, Mrs Roxburgh considered what to do next. While still undecided, she stepped or tottered a pace or two backward and trod upon something both brittle and resistant. She glanced down the length of her white calf and noticed the hand with signet ring, of the one for whom she could do nothing more. She was propelled, logically it seemed, in the opposite direction, up the slope, and found herself amongst those burning mattresses of dry sand laced with runners of convolvulus such as she had noticed farther back along the beach.

She bent down and began tearing at the vines, in her present state less from reason than by instinct, and wound the strands

218

about her waist, until the consequent fringe hanging from the vine allowed her to feel to some extent clothed.

Her only other immediate concern was how to preserve her wedding ring. Not by any lucid flash, but working her way towards a solution, she strung the ring on one of the runners straggling from her convolvulus girdle, and looped the cord, and knotted it, hoping the gold would not give itself away by glistening from behind the fringe of leaves.

It was her first positive achievement since the event of which she must never allow herself to think. She might have felt consoled had she not caught sight of the aboriginal women returning.

They bore down, less mirthful, of firmer purpose than before. Their captive went with them willingly enough (what else could reason have suggested?) into the forest, which was at least dark and cool. If she sustained physical wounds from swooping branches, and half-rotted stumps or broken roots concealed in the humus underfoot, she neither whinged nor limped: the self which had withdrawn was scarcely conscious of them. What she did feel was the wedding ring bumping against her as she walked, a continual source of modest reassurance.

After but a short march the party of women reached an open space in which the other members of the tribe were encamped. Children left off skipping and playing at ball to examine what at first appeared to them a fearful apparition, until one by one they found the courage to touch, to pinch, some of them to jab with vicious sticks. The men on the other hand paid little attention to what they must have decided on the beach was no more than a woman of an unprepossessing colour. As males they lounged about the camp, conversing, mending weapons, and scratching themselves.

Nowhere was there any sign of the long-boat crew or their officer. Mrs Roxburgh felt she could not hope to see them again. As for her own future, she was not so much afraid as resigned to whatever might be in store for her. What could she fear when already she was as good as destroyed? So she awaited her captors' pleasure.

Those who had brought her to the camp led her to a hut built of bark and leaves, at the door of which a woman, seemingly of greater importance than the others, was seated on the ground with a child of three or four years in her lap. Not anticipating favours, the prisoner passively resigned herself to inspection, but thought she detected a sympathetic tremor, as though the personage recognized one who had suffered a tragedy.

Whether it was no more than what Mrs Roxburgh would have wished, or whether harmony was in fact established, it but lasted until she noticed the child's snouted face and tumid body covered with pustular sores. From time to time the little girl moaned fretfully, wriggling, and showing the whites of her eyes.

The women held a conference, as an outcome of which the oldest and skinniest among them approached Mrs Roxburgh and without ceremony squeezed her breasts. These were hanging slack, shapeless, fuller than was normal in preparation for her own child, which she should by rights have been feeding. Relieved of the necessity for making milk by the dead baby's premature birth, she was pretty sure her breasts were dry; nor was the hag satisfied by her investigations.

The assembly of women, and more than anyone the mother, were none the less determined to transfer the sick child to the captive's arms. The child herself left Mrs Roxburgh in no doubt that she was to become the nurse, for a mouth was plunged upon her right nipple, and the yawed hands straightway began working on her breast. Compassion inspired by the memory of her own attempts at motherhood was flickering to life, when her foster-child doused it beyond re-kindling. On discovering that she had been deceived, the little girl bit the unresponsive teat, and spat it out, and screamed and writhed in the nurse's arms. Pain alone would have driven Mrs Roxburgh to drop its cause, but the mother's looks dared her to, and the blows she received on her head and shoulders from the attendant women, persuaded her to keep hold of the wretch.

Presently, when she had quieted it, she seated herself on the ground beside a fire burning near the entrance to the hut, and hoped she might be, if not forgotten, at least ignored. She sat mechanically stroking the diseased arms, the greasy hair. An automaton was what she must become in order to survive.

Round her the blacks were proceeding with their various duties, beneath a splendid sky, beside a lake the colour of raw cobalt shot with bronze. Despite her misery and the child in her arms, Mrs

Roxburgh could not remain unmoved by the natural beauty surrounding her. Evening light coaxed nobler forms out of black bodies and introduced a visual design into what had been a dusty hugger-mugger camp. What she longed to sense in the behaviour of these human beings was evidence of a spiritual design, but that she could not, any more than she could believe in a merciful power shaping her own destiny.

For lack of a better occupation, and to keep her dangerous thoughts at bay, she continued rocking her disgusting charge. Once she caught herself saying aloud, 'Sleep, sleep,' and by grace of some mechanism, 'sleep – my darling,' more for her own comfort than the child's; the sound of her voice, she realized, was a consolation.

She could feel quickening in her, not only that abstract hunger for absent faces and familiar voices, but desire for food to fill the hole which actual hunger had gnawed in her belly. The air was alive with distracting scents as the women tended the embers where they had laid fish, varieties of root or tuber, and a brace of small furred animals, their muzzles and almost human hands still testifying to the agony in which they had died.

Mrs Roxburgh could have fallen upon these agonized creatures, torn them apart, stuffed her mouth, even before the fur was singed, the flesh seared, before the blood had ceased bubbling in them. But when the feast was ready she was not invited. As superior beings the men set about gorging themselves with appropriate solemnity. Without a doubt the physical splendour, both of the mature males and more slender youths, was worthy of celebration. Occasional morsels were thrown to the wretched females, who grovelled in keeping with their humble station, and scooped up the scraps, and shook off the dust before devouring them.

The captive was free to listen to the noise of sucking, bones being cracked, and to watch the contortions of black throats. Food had at least sent her charge scuttling back to the mother, but this left the nurse with nothing to distract her from her own hunger.

Towards the end of the meal, somebody (it could have been the child's mother) flung her a fish-tail and a dorsal fin. She snatched them up from out of the dirt and started sucking at the glutinous membrane, risked her mouth on the barbed fin for the sake of a shred of flesh she imagined she saw adhering to the base, ran her tongue round her lips and teeth, licked her deliciously rank fingers – and whimpered once or twice to herself.

(Could she perhaps crawl out after dark and scavenge for the bones of those small furred animals? But dogs carried off any remains their masters had failed to swallow. One partially bald cur bit her as she tried to seduce him into sharing his booty.)

While dusk crept amongst them, and shadows became increasingly entwined with tree and smoke, an elder rose and led the tribe in a kind of lament. The prisoner concluded that the natives were at their prayers, for their wails sounded formal rather than spontaneously emotional. She considered adding at least an unspoken prayer of her own, but found she lacked the impulse; her soul was as dry as her hanging breasts. If she had ever worshipped a supreme being, it was by rote, and the Roxburghs' Lord God of Hosts, to whom her mother also had paid no more than lip service. Her father was of a different persuasion: as a young man he had belted out the hymns, but fell silent later on. A silent girl, she had inherited his brooding temper. As she now recognized, rocks had been her altars and spring-water her sacrament, a realization which did but increase heartache in a country designed for human torment, where even beauty flaunted a hostile radiance, and the spirits of place were not hers to conjure up.

Under the pressure of darkness and common desires her captors were sorting themselves into families and the huts allotted to them. Darkness might have encouraged her to disappear had she known which direction to take. An aching body and numb mind persuaded her instead to crawl inside the hut to which the mother of her charge had retired, together with other women and children and the elder who had led their prayers. By good fortune the mother elected to keep her child for the night, allowing the nurse to enjoy the freedom of her own dreams.

She had lain down on the edge of a somnolent fire which increased the airlessness of the hut and added to the warmth given off by the bodies crowded there. As cold encroached from out of the forest and off the lake, she edged closer to the buried coals, and turned to roast her other side. What she might be suffering physically she barely felt, for she was soon absorbed into tribal dreams broken by soft cries of children together with other more mature grunts and moans.

During the night she returned to her body from being the human wheelbarrow one of the muscular male blacks was pushing against the dark. There was no evidence that her dream had been inspired by any such experience, but she fell back upon the dust, amongst intimations of the nightmare which threatened to re-shape itself around her. Her trembling only gradually subsided as she lay fingering the ring threaded into her fringe of leaves and she became once more part of the suffocating airlessness and moans of sleeping blacks, her own sleep so deep and dreamless she might have died.

She awoke by a colourless light in which human forms were already moving, fanning half-dead fires to life, airing their grumbles, urinating. By the time the surrounding trees had risen through a mist, the tribe appeared to have re-assembled, and the lamentations of the evening before were repeated in a cold dawn. Whether the wailing was intended to exorcize malign spirits, the captive felt that some of her more persistent ghosts might have been laid by this now familiar rite. She was, moreover, comforted to find herself still in possession of her body, even though aching, and frozen where it had not been seared; the life was flickering back inside her like the first hesitant tongues of fire the blacks were coaxing out of buried embers.

Such scraps as had been left over from the evening meal were brought out from net bags and soon consumed. The prisoner would have gone hungry had she not salvaged a charred fern-root let fall by one of the privileged. Inside the layers of dust and ash the root had a bitter flavour of its own. She was grateful for it. Afterwards she went down to the lake as nobody attempted to restrain her, and would have drunk from it had not a little girl approached through the mist and brought her to a hole in which furze of a kind had been stuffed. After removing this bush the child motioned to her to drink. Mrs Roxburgh was surprised at the sweetness of the water.

'You are my only friend,' she said when she had finished.

The little girl laughed and dimpled. She rubbed her thighs with her hands, and may have been blushing under her skin. She would not speak, but accepted to hold a proffered hand, and even pressed it, though cautiously.

'I'd give 'ee a kiss if tha wudn' take fright,' Ellen told her. 'Or wud 'ee?'

To share her unhoped-for happiness, she might have risked it. But the child looked so grave she left it at that, and they returned to the camp hand-in-hand.

With the exception of this little girl, she had been so ignored by her captors she hoped her day might continue undisturbed. The men were gathering up their spears, clubs, nets, and ropes with the solemnity of the superior sex preparing for an expedition. The men did look superior. Contrasting with the women's irregular stubble, curly manes of well-greased hair hung to their shoulders. Where the women slouched, grown slommacky from bearing children and carrying loads, the males were for the most part still personable in old age, disfigured only by the welts from incisions deliberately inflicted in patterns on their chests, backs, and often handsome faces.

As the men departed with an arrogance proper to a mission of importance, Mrs Roxburgh was ready to throw in her lot with the depressed women, when they suddenly descended upon her for some calculated purpose. Three of them seized her by the hair, stretching it to full length, even yanking at it for extra measure, while one beefier female began hacking at the roots with a shell.

The unexpectedness of the operation and the pain it caused made the victim cry out. 'Leave off, can't 'ee?' Ellen Gluyas shrieked, and then, as Mrs Roxburgh took control, 'Why must you torture me so? Isn't it enough to have killed my husband, my friends?' She was about to add, 'Kill me too, rather than hurt me,' but knew at once that she did not want to die.

After forcing her down on her knees her tormentors continued hacking and sawing. Between the shell and the efforts of those who were assisting, and who leaned back fit to tear out the hair by the roots, they got it off. Recovered enough from her pain and fright (at one stage she thought she might faint) the victim put up a hand and found she had become a stubbled fright such as those around her, or even worse. From the bloodied hand returned to her lap she knew she could only look horrifying.

But the women had not finished their work. They dragged her to her feet. Next the hide of some animal was brought, filled with a rancid fat with which they smeared their passive slave; she could but submit to her anointing, followed by an application of charcoal rubbed with evident disgust, if not spite, into the shamefully white skin.

Although nauseated by the stench, her sunburn smarting from the friction of the charcoal, she was beginning to feel after a fashion clothed, when again she was forced down upon her haunches. A young girl fetched a woven bag containing what could have been beeswax, with which they plastered her bleeding scalp. From a second, similar reticule, an old woman produced down by the handful and bundles of feathers. She could feel the old, tremulous fingers patting the down, planting the feathers in her wax helmet. An almost tender sigh of admiration rose in the air as the women achieved their work of art.

Laughter broke out, a stamping of grey-black feet, a clapping of hands. Only the work of art sat listless and disaffected amongst a residue of black down and sulphur feathers shaped like question marks.

If they had made her the object of ritual attentions, they had not forgotten her practical uses. Again pulled to her feet, the slave was loaded with paraphernalia, and last of all, the loathsome child, heavier it seemed than the evening before.

Their setting out was less ostentatious than that of their men. From the first moment they plodded, but no less purposeful for being flat-footed. Instead of spears they carried long, pointed sticks. They chattered unceasingly and with apparent cheerfulness. Now and then somebody thought to prod the slave; in more usual circumstances it might have hurt, here it served to punctuate the monotony. She looked down once and saw the pus from her charge's sores uniting with the sweat on her own charcoal-dusted arms.

Disgust might have soured her had it not been for a delicious smell of dew rising from the grass their feet trampled and the bushes they brushed against in passing. The sky was still benign. Were she presently to die, her last sight, her last thought, would be of watered blue.

But she would not, must not die – why, she could not imagine, when she had been deprived of all that she most loved and valued.

Arrived at their destination, the women threw off their loads and started jabbing the ground with the sticks they had brought. She too, was encouraged to join in the search for what proved to be a kind of tuberous root. Any they unearthed were popped inside the net carry-alls. Although unskilled, aching, and still shocked by the operation to which she had been subjected earlier that morning, she was relieved to be rid of the child while digging, and free to indulge in the luxury of her own thoughts: a potato-cake she remembered frying on a bitter night of her impoverished youth; an aigrette with a diamond mount she had worn in her hair to a ball; Oswald Dignam's milky skin seen through the weft of fog at sea. She encouraged random images rather than consecutive thought, which might have driven her to search for a cause or reason for her presence in a clueless maze.

Something of the maze was indeed suggested by the natives' movements, meandering over the hard earth, crossing and re-crossing one another's tracks in their interminable search. Yet the black women's fate was not so far determined by invisible walls that science and experience could not guide them; their probing was almost invariably attended by success, while the benighted slave stabbed the ground more often than not fruitlessly.

The sun's weight upon her shoulders replacing the weight of the child in her arms, she grew to hate the hard grey earth with its tufts of wiry, dead-seeming grass, although in the course of wandering from patch to patch, she realized she was beginning to develop a skill in 'potato'-sticking, and when one of her companions looked in her direction, she laughed with pleasure for her discovery. Overcoming her instinctive suspicions the black woman laughed back. Both fell silent after this exchange, partly since their shared emotion had been but imperfectly conveyed, more because pleasure had to succumb to the demands of drudgery.

During the heat of the day the company rested in the shade beside one of the several lakes watering their country. Two inexhaustible girls shed the fibre shawls they wore and started diving for lily-roots. The prisoner narrowed her eyes, lulled by the contrast of shade and glare and her vision of the two swimmers, their slender arms and still shapely breasts regularly rising above an undulating sheet of water-lilies.

She may have dozed, but only briefly. She awoke to find the child was being restored to her arms, where it immediately resumed its grizzling.

The whole of life by now revolved round the search for food, which her own aggravated hunger made seem the only rational behaviour. It was in any case what she had accepted as the answer to the hard facts of existence before she had been taught the habits and advantages of refinement. Consequently when some of the hunters returned to the camp that evening with the carcase of a kangaroo slung from a green pole, and a detachment appeared from the direction of the shore, several glistening monsters dangling by the gills from the hooks of their fingers, she would have joined the other women, childlike in their shrieking and hand-clapping, had it not been for the child in her arms.

As for this actual child, its snouted face had a dead look. Or was it what she hoped to see? Were she to be honest, she did wish the creature dead, even though its owners might accuse her of casting a spell.

She looked about her. Everybody was too engrossed in preparing for the evening's feast to intercept their slave's evil thoughts.

The child stirred, jerked awake, and stuck a finger in her nurse's eye.

Tonight again, the prisoner was offered no more than scraps: a bone to gnaw, a fragment of the beast's scorched hide to chew or suck, acts which she performed while aware of her own ugly greed and the filth which had become an accepted part of her blistered hands. She was comforted, however, by the smells she snuffed, the fat she licked, and her saliva trickling down her throat into a wizened stomach.

Had her stomach been less shrunken she might have been made unhappier by unassuaged hunger when, later that night, lying in the hut, in the ashes from the fire, alongside the family to whom she was assigned, she was forced to listen to three women taking their turn to satisfy (or so it sounded) a man's demands. Her own prospects would have given her greater cause for alarm had she not felt that the spiteful nature of her mistress must resist any move on her husband's part to add to his seraglio.

Surrounded by the stench of rancid fat and sweat, the blanket of wood-smoke, the grunts and cries of animal pleasure, she dared for the first time resurrect her own husband, the image at least of what she remembered: the fastidious hands and glossy whiskers, the eyes too deeply concentrated on an inner self she had never been privileged to meet. Whatever his deficiencies or hers (in retrospect she thought that perhaps she had loved him most for the ailments and the crankiness which called for her sympathy or forbearing) she willed herself to experience that greater reality which dreams can bring; and fell asleep in Mr Roxburgh's embrace.

She was disconcerted however to find herself subjected, then submitting, to coarser treatment. Ohhh she detested what she was physically incapable of resisting, most of all the hairy wrists and swollen veins. Exhausted by the ensuing struggle she could only lie like the spent fish she was, gills subsiding as emotions expired.

She awoke stiff and cold except where the embers touched her, still surrounded by the sighs, the breathing and dreaming of others, while her own dream faded into ash-colours, and she realized that it was not Austin but Garnet Roxburgh who had possessed her.

His continued immanence and her own disgust forced her to her feet at such speed that she was almost stunned by a blow from one of the saplings supporting the thatch of leaves. She fell upon her knees, and crawled instead on all fours towards the entrance, like any sow shaking off the night and lumbering out of a foetid sty. Without having seen them she knew that her breasts must be swinging lean and russet as she lurched into a pearly light. Dew raining down along her spine and rump cleansed her to some extent of her dream. It was her locked joints which were making her groan in her efforts to stand erect.

But the hour before dawn offered compensations. Her ghost drifted with the wraiths of mist, among the ghosts of trees, and found itself again haunting the shore, a bland, unobstructed verge which presented no sure way of escape to a lost soul, a woman, or a rational being. If one of them accepted to be seduced by its beauty, and a second fainted at the prospect of a footsore journey, the third, a sceptic, feared that this ribbon of sand might

228

not lead to Moreton Bay, but could double back upon itself to create a prison in an island.

Reason might have made Mrs Roxburgh more disconsolate and lost had it not been for the sound of a receding tide. She stood awhile in the shallows, letting the wavelets play round her ankles, rubbing one sandy shin against the other, listening to the clatter of shells and pebbles as the current dragged them back and forth. She found herself smiling for these lesser pleasures which appealed to what Austin Roxburgh deplored as 'the sensual side of Ellen's nature'.

The cold broke in upon her at last. She recoiled shivering from the expanse of colourless water, and sky as colourless except for the hint of an apocalypse, to stumble back in what she hoped was the direction from which she had come. She positively panted after the tribe to which she now belonged. What if she never found it, and spent the rest of her days on earth (if not in hell) circling through the scrub till her bones gave up? She longed for even the most resentful company of whatever colour. She might have bartered her body, she thought, to one of the scornful male blacks in return for his protection.

To indulge in such an unlikely fancy could not be regarded in any degree as a betrayal, but while she walked, her already withered fringe of leaves began deriding her shrunken thighs, and daylight struck an ironic glint out of the concealed wedding-ring.

So her lunging and plunging through the forest was as much an attempt to elude her thoughts as to find the camp she had unwisely deserted. She was made quite feverish by her search, in the course of which she came to a hollow where she was halted, indefinitely it seemed, by the horror which paralysed her.

Directly in her path a fire had but lately burnt itself out Amongst charred branches and the white flock of ash gone cold, lay a man's body set in a final anguished curve, the roasted skin noticeably crackled down one side from shoulder to thigh. One of the legs had been hacked away from where the thigh is joined to the hip. If the skull, bared to the bone in places by wilful gashes, grimaced at the intruder through singed whisker and a crust of blood, grime, and burning, the mouth atoned for all that is fiendish by its resignation to suffering.

Mrs Roxburgh only gradually realized that she was faced with the first officer's remains. She was left gasping and sobbing, not so much for decent stolid Ned Courtney, her relationship with whom had never been more than rudimentary, as for the death of her husband and her own insoluble predicament. She might have forgotten her intention of finding her way back to the vindictive but necessary blacks, and lost herself deeper in the forest, if two children had not appeared, full of admonishment and anger which could only have been inspired by their elders. Although she took it for granted that these children had been sent to spy on her and lead her back to captivity, she was ready to surrender herself. They first beat her about the shoulders with switches, which in the circumstances she felt, then of their own free will offered her their moist, childish hands, a gesture she accepted gratefully.

During the journey back the children found a crop of berries, some of which they forced into her mouth. The berries were watery, insipid, but not unpleasant. Shortly after, halfway down a slope, she caught her foot in a vine which had escaped her notice, and tumbled like a sack off a cart. Imitating her fall, the children rolled downhill and landed in the same heap. They all lay laughing awhile. The young children might have been hers. She was so extraordinarily content she wished it could have lasted for ever, the two black little bodies united in the sun with her own blackened skin-and-bones.

Not surprisingly, her wish remained ungranted. The children cleared their faces of smiles, and they marched on.

At the camp they found the men had already departed on the day's errand, while the women were at work dismantling the huts for setting up, it eventuated, at no great distance from their former site. The women had little but scowls and pouts for the recalcitrant slave, whom they loaded with the heaviest sheets of bark and thickest swatches of leafy thatching. However capricious the present manoeuvre she carried her loads willingly enough, grateful for her reinstatement in the community to which she belonged. (Only at evening she discovered the reason for their arbitrary move: fleas are less predatory on virgin ground.)

Later in the day a troupe of females and middle children proceeded by instinct or pre-arrangement to the beach, where fishermen had been casting their nets. A hush had fallen upon the men, some of them immersed up to their heads, others but waist-deep in water, like stanchions to which the nets were attached. The women, if incapable of silence, chattered in subdued monotone like birds at roosting. Less controlled, the children scampered around and about flinging handfuls of wet sand which the sun transformed into arcs of light.

Suddenly even the children were stilled as they noticed a shuddering of the water some distance offshore. This barely visible disturbance of a calm sea, like the very slight agitation of a sheet by innumerable hidden bodies, was moving ever closer to the mouth, then into the belly of the net, the outline of which could be traced from the black blob of one motionless head to the next, and closer inshore, the more exposed human stanchions. When a distinct collision took place underwater. Single fish, mercurial enough to appear as liquid as their element, leaped briefly above the surface. There began a frenzied shouting, and hauling on the net. Women shrieked, children squealed, as all dashed into the mild surf to join in dragging the net to land, when they were not dabbling their hands after an individual catch of slippery and, in most cases, elusive fish.

Not until the beach could the extent of their haul be estimated, as the men, all ribs, lungs, and teeth, stalked glistening around their slackened net with its silver swag. As for the ecstatic women, they were already stuffing their holdalls. Children playing with escaped fish squeezed them to make the milk shoot out of soft roes.

The slave had no part in any of this, unless when a fishy opalescence clashing with a transparency of light induced in her a certain drunken tranquillity. No doubt hunger, revived by the scent of roasting flesh, would overcome revulsion from the sight of fish twitching and dying round her on the beach.

She was in fact already brought halfway back to her senses by the full 'dillis' with which her masters were loading her. She was soon staggering under the weight – of food which is, after all, life, as she had forgot while sipping chocolate and without appetite nibbling macaroons at Birdlip House Cheltenham.

Arrived at the camp, she dumped her load, and was immediately sent back for more. It occurred to her that she had been free all day of her loathsome charge, the pustular child, and that the mother had not come to the fishing. On their return from the beach, the expression on the woman's face had been one of puzzled grieving, while the child lay inert outside the hut, like a stricken animal for which little can be done beyond dispatching it, as Ellen Gluyas knew.

In this case, approaching death actually quickened life in the living. Mrs Roxburgh knew that she had wished for the child to die. Perhaps for once her wish was being granted. Yet from looking at the unknowing mother, she was not able to rejoice in what amounted to her own evil powers, and wondered whether she could expect for herself some form of appropriate retribution.

While she was returning to the beach her mother-in-law came into her thoughts, and she was pleased to have her company. Old Mrs Roxburgh had always hoped that the clothes she possessed would see her out. As might have been expected, she was dressed in her brown kerseymere of several winters, over it the black bombazine spencer she had worn in mourning for her husband. It was hardly the hour, and the wrong season, for a parasol, but thus she might have held its great pagoda of lace and muslin tilted against the antipodean sun to protect a complexion which was still her pride.

'I shall not delay – or embarrass, I hope – if I walk with you. I should like to see my son.'

'I haven't seen 'n sence several days.'

'You haven't – *what*?' Shock made the old thing forget herself. 'You haven't forgotten all you have been taught?'

'The words,' Ellen could only mumble, 'seem to be falling away.' This was what she truly feared in the event of long association with the blacks.

'But are you not keeping up the journal? I only suggested it to help you learn to express yourself.'

'Oh, the journal – it's lost!' Now she was crying. 'We both lost them before – before Mr Roxburgh died.'

'It was not Austin who died, but his brother. You forget they buried Garnet in Van Diemen's Land.'

The old woman was looking at her so keenly out of her white-kid face, where Ellen noticed for the first time a little patch of rouge, dry and peeling, on each cheek. The expression of the eyes and the two patches of dry rouge made her wonder whether her mother-in-law were less innocent than she had appeared hitherto.

'And where is your garnet ring, Ellen?' the old creature persisted.

Although her glance was directed at the blackened hand to which the ring belonged, she showed no interest in the more noticeable tatters of flesh or the wedding-ring which its owner felt the fringe of leaves no longer concealed adequately.

'I gave the garnets to a person who claimed to be in greater need of them than I.' Mrs Roxburgh constructed her sentence along lines which she felt might appease her mother-in-law.

But in any case, the next instant she dismissed from her mind an inquisitor she had so unwisely introduced, and thrust her way through the grey scrub upon the same expanse of sand and light where the blacks were still sorting fish.

Again she became their beast of burden. As they loaded her back and sides, she took it they were not unkindly disposed, by their ingratiating show of teeth, rumbustious laughter, and possibly, jokes.

One of them went so far as to smack her rather hard on the bottom.

'Aw, my life!' she shouted in the tongue they might have understood. 'As if I dun't have enough to put up with!' She could not give over what were by no means counterfeit giggles.

(Although she would not have admitted it to her mother-in-law or any lady of her acquaintance, or confessed it to Mr Roxburgh, leave alone Garnet R., she had always preferred the company of men.)

Back at the camp, the women were busy scaling fish, using the sharp blades of shells. They took no notice of the arrival of the laden donkey, herself smelling by now as rank and fishy as the commodity she had been carrying.

At the entrance to the hut of the family to whom she was assigned, a ceremony was taking place. A wrinkled, elderly man of evident importance was squatted beside the sick child, weaving signs, making passes in the air above the prostrate body. The family expressed their gratification when at last the physician–conjurer drew a small brown stone, or unpolished crystal, out of the patient's mouth. There were cries, there was hand-clapping. Only the slave could not bring herself to join in their celebrations, for her own encounters with death showed her that the child was beyond cure.

Instead she broke in with the announcement, 'Can't 'ee see she is gone? She's dead!' It sounded the more terrifying for being unintelligible to her audience, just as her emotion, her bursting into tears, must have seemed disproportionate to those who had not shared her sufferings.

While Ellen Roxburgh wept for her own experience of life, the pseudo-physician, to judge by his excited jabber, appeared to be holding her responsible for his failure. He did not succeed, however, in rousing an opposition. For the first time since the meeting on the beach, the captive and her masters, especially the women, were united in a common humanity.

They allowed her to accompany the funeral procession, trapesing into the forest until they found a hollow log in which to shove the body. At once their grief evaporated, except in the mother's case, who was prepared to keep up her snivels, but only awhile, for they were returning to the fish feast.

On this occasion the captive was first allowed a head, even a half-raw liver, but as the company grew sated, nobody thought to prevent her reaching out of her own accord to snatch a whole fish from off the coals, burning her fingers and lips in her haste to devour.

Finally she too was satisfied, not to say gorged, bloated, stupefied. She scarce heard the blacks wailing at dusk to appease whatever spirits lurked in the surrounding air. She would surely have been free to join in their prayers if so moved, but her soul had grown too dull and brutish to concern itself with spiritual matters.

A couple of days after the fish orgy, the blacks struck camp. There was good reason for doing so: the stink of rotting fish-remains was becoming intolerable, and the fleas had grown so aggressive that human beings could be seen scratching themselves with the vigour of their similarly afflicted dogs.

As the huts were dismantled, the sheets of bark were loaded on the women when the slave looked incapable of carrying more. They started out, the men as vanguard, the female sumpter-beasts and children trailing behind. A clear morning, laughter, and songs, made the migration less insufferable than it might have been. Glancing up from under her load Mrs Roxburgh was inspirited by glimpses of blue haze, the aromatic smoke from the firesticks they carried along with them, and the dark forest alternating with stretches of open country, this latter a dead green illumined in places by the light off reflective lake-water.

Later in the morning a halt had evidently been made, for those at the rear of the file were suddenly squeezed concertina-fashion against those in front. In consequence the slave dropped most of her load, but was rewarded by improved vision. What she saw was a group of men standing round a vast grey tree, at an elbow of which a flock of pied birds repeatedly swooped, squawking in anger.

One of the blacks procured a length of vine, and by looping this round the trunk and pressing on the latter with the soles of his feet, was soon hauling himself in an aerial squatting position towards the bough at which the birds were directing their displeasure. Upon arrival he thrust his arm inside a hollow, and pulled out a small furred animal, and dashed it from high to his companions on the ground; where the beast was clubbed to instantaneous quivering death.

From engravings in the library at 'Dulcet' Mrs Roxburgh believed the little creature to have been what is called an 'opossum'. Exhausted as she was by the journey, and chafed raw by her load of bark, she felt no more than a slight tremor of sympathy, brushing it aside with her filthy hands as though it had been the folds of an actual, and as proved by experience, superfluous veil or fichu, before returning to the state of detached assent with which she received almost every occurrence in this present life. The opossum, moreover, was food, to be stored in one of the netted 'dillis', though whether she herself would benefit by it was doubtful.

The women again loaded themselves. Not long after the march had been resumed, there was a repetition of the foregoing scene, with incensed birds revealing the whereabouts of an intruder in their elective tree. But the men were conferring longer than before, and with exaggerated laughter in which the women and capering children finally joined. Until the slave realized she had become the object of their attention and mirth. She was dragged forward, the vine was produced, and a grinning giant of a man indicated that

235

they expected her to climb the tree in the manner already demonstrated.

Mrs Roxburgh immediately became faint with terror. If she could have but conjured up her hardy girlhood; instead it was as though her spirit had taken refuge in stays, petticoats, a straitening bodice, the great velvet bell of a skirt, in fact all the impedimenta of refinement bequeathed to her by her mother-in-law. Her actual blackened skin, her nakedness beyond the fringe of leaves, were of no help to her; she was again white and useless, a civilized lady standing surrounded by this tribe of scornful blacks.

When one fellow more scornful than the rest, and more vindictive, thrust a firestick into her buttocks, and again, and yet again, she cried out in pain and fright, 'No, no! I expect I'll do it. Only don't hurt me.'

In imitation of the man she had watched climb the tree farther back, she looped the vine and felt for a hold with the soles of her feet, and began this fearful climb. If her strength or courage threatened to desert her, a firestick was held beneath her person, and the fear of burning drove her higher – or else it was the spirit of Ellen Gluyas coming to Mrs Roxburgh's rescue.

Indeed, she found herself close enough to the bough to thrust her arm inside the hollow and feel around for animal fur, which was there, warm and springy, on the tightly curled, slightly shivering muscular body. Compunction made her falter, but only for an instant. She dug in her own desperate claws, and hauled, and brought the creature well outside its nest before the pink little snout opened and the teeth were sunk in the back of her hand. Then she did scream with pain, and the blacks below roared and cheered, and clubbed to death the animal she let fall.

Somehow slithering she began her worse descent. As she was tossed from branch to branch, her greatest fear was for her precious girdle. If she clutched, it was at air, by handfuls, fistfuls of perfumed leaves, everything either evasive, or stubborn like the tree itself, but after a last long agonizing embrace with the abrasive trunk, she landed on earth in a state of pins and needles, torn skin, broken nails, and a throbbing hand.

She was scarcely more alive than the dead opossum, but her girdle had held and she was comforted to see amongst the leaves, her ring.

When she had adjusted her dress the other women did her the kindness of helping her load, and the file moved on.

The site chosen by the elders of the tribe for their next camp was a stretch of flat sandy ground separated from a sound or river estuary by a mangrove thicket. The grey, deformed trees, the grey water and sandy soil depressed the captive, shaken and exhausted besides by her experience earlier that day. Her companions had immediately set to work re-erecting the bark huts. She too, was expected to work, digging with a flat pearl-shell and her hands the shallow trenches she had noticed surrounding the huts at their previous camps. She imagined them to be a practical device for draining off the water in the event of a tropical downpour, but in her present frame of mind would not have cared had she and all of them been inundated and drowned like ants.

Needing to relieve herself, she went a little way apart from the others, into the mangroves, and when she had finished squatting, took the opportunity to stray farther and investigate the lie of the land. By the view she had from the water's edge she was persuaded that they were living on an island, separated from the mainland only by this narrow strip of water. In her dispiritment and acceptance of her fate, she was glad that her discovery absolved her from making an attempt to escape by following the coast to Moreton Bay. She was immured, not only in the blacks' island stronghold, but in that female passivity wished upon her at birth and reinforced by marriage with her poor dear Mr Roxburgh.

She was standing stubbing her toes on the moist grey sand and reconsidering whether Mr Roxburgh had in truth been poor or dear (of course he was! her dead husband of glossy whiskers and exquisite hands) when two children appointed as spies arrived full of frowns caught from their elders, to lead her back to camp, and she went as was expected of her.

This present camp differed in no way from the last; except that it was free (at first) of fleas, she was not plagued by the ailing child, and food became less plentiful. As the blacks grew emaciated they were more inclined to glower and sulk, and to beat or pinch their servant, whom they may have blamed for the dearth which had been visited upon them. There was the occasional opossum, snake or lizard, and once or twice the huntsmen

237

brought in a species of small kangaroo. Otherwise the tribe subsisted on fern-roots and yams. Fish, it seemed, had migrated to other waters. On a memorable evening Mrs Roxburgh snapped up from under her masters' noses a segment of roasted snake, which produced in her an ecstasy such as she had never experienced before.

There had been occasions in the past of course when a happy conjunction of light with nature had roused tender sentiments in her, or even more deeply felt emotions, although to be honest, they were more than likely the response her husband and his mother would have expected of any individual with pretensions to sensibility. By the same code, she listened to Mr Roxburgh reading Latin verses, in hopes of his esteem rather than her own distraction. If she attempted to convey that his exercise had given her pleasure, her drooping shoulders and hands dutifully folded in her lap must have told him more, had he observed them; perhaps the poor man had. The ecstasy of physical passion she had experienced with her husband scarcely ever, and with her one regrettable lover it had been not so much passion as a wrestling match against lust. Now reduced to an animal condition she could at least truthfully confess that ecstasy had flickered up from the pit of her stomach provoked by a fragment of snakeflesh.

She bowed her head, humbly as well as gratefully, for what she had been vouchsafed, and whatever God might have in store for her.

As she developed an aptitude for climbing trees she was sent in search of birds' nests in addition to opossum. Not only fresh eggs, but the addled and fertilized were relished by the blacks. Sometimes she found honey-combs; the empty ones were in themselves a prize for the maggots and other insects in their disused cells, but a full comb was a major source of ecstasy, in which the blacks generously allowed her to share. When they had devoured the best of the honey, her masters would eke out their enjoyment by sopping up the dregs with bark rags. They would give their slave the honey-rag to suck when everyone else was satisfied and only a faint sweetness remained in the dirty fibre object. None the less, as she dwelt on memories of more delicate pleasures evoked by sucking the honey-rag, she might have swallowed it down had its owner not snatched it back.

She was submitted to worse humiliation when the women were

238

searching their own and their children's heads for vermin. They urged her to join them in their hygienic pastime. Nothing was wasted, and as her nails grew more skilful at crushing fleas and lice, she found her fingers straying to her mouth, then guiltily away, as they had if ever she was caught out picking her nose and disposing of the spoils when a little child.

Surely she could not sink any lower? A vision kept recurring of her friend Mrs Daintrey's tea table, the Worcester service, the sandwiches filled with crushed walnut and cinnamon butter, and a tea-cake on its doily in the silver dish. At least it would never enter the heads of any of her acquaintance, not even Maggie Aspinall slopping her Madeira, that Mrs Roxburgh could sink to the level of bestiality at which she had arrived.

Sometimes seated cross-legged beside the coals she would snigger with imbecile lack of control at a situation as wretched as it was unalterable, and her long leathery breasts, not unlike brown, wizening pears, bumped against the hollowness inside her. As a result of which, she might fall to snivelling and whimpering, before attaining to the state of apathy she was resolved to cultivate. She must.

To add to her mental and moral confusion, a subtly different performance was expected of her in the role she had been assigned in the beginning. Whereas the women of the tribe continued to scratch and beat the slave, to relieve their feelings and spur her on to perform her duties, they submitted her also to ceremonies, and when released from their worldly preoccupations, treated her with almost pious respect. They anointed her body regularly with grease and charcoal, and plastered her cropped head with bees-wax, and stuck it with tufts of down and feather as on the occasion when she was received into the tribe. They enthroned her on an opossum skin rug after smoothing it with their flattened hands, and sat in a semi-circle staring at her. Their faces were her glass, in which she and they were temporarily united, either in mooning fantasy or a mystical relationship. What the blacks could not endure it seemed, was the ghost of a woman they had found haunting the beach. They may have felt that, were the ghost exorcized, they might contemplate with equanimity the super-natural come amongst them in their own flesh. Yet they lowered their eyes at last; could it have been for recognizing their own shortcomings? Ellen Roxburgh accepted the possibility, and in her turn, looked away.

Members of other tribes, several of which must have shared the island, called on their neighbours at intervals to examine the phenomenon, their faces expressing incredulity, fear, envy, as well as worshipful respect for this demi-goddess temporarily raised from a drudgery which the blacks' practical nature and their poverty-stricken lives normally prescribed. She played up to them. As she had conciliated Austin Roxburgh and his mother by allowing herself to be prinked and produced, she accepted when some elderly lady of her own tribe advanced to adjust a sulphur topknot; it might have been old Mrs Roxburgh adding or subtracting some jewel or feather in preparation for a dinner or ball.

What might have toppled the whole formal structure was a fever which frequently glittered in the divine as well as the human eye, stimulated less by the craving for food than by the forthright stench of male bodies, their hard forms prowling up and down, engaged in no discernible pursuit beyond that of stalking shadows.

God forbid! Not wholly bereft of her rational mind, Mrs Roxburgh would have expected disgust to protect her, yet knew too well that loathing can feed a fever; and now the skies, the goddess's natural habitat, translated from watchet into peacock, and from peacock to flamingo, were what she had also to resist, along with the darkness in which human weakness plunges mortals.

During this time of tribal famine and individual fever, Mrs Roxburgh noticed that a play was being enacted round her, by the large, jowled woman, her chief tormentor among those who had discovered her alone on the beach, the big fellow who had driven the slave to shin up a tree and drag an opossum out of its nest, and the prettier of the two girls who had gone diving for lily-roots in the heat of the day. There was a night in particular when Mrs Roxburgh hoped she had no part in the play, the three evident protagonists of which were coming and going, prowling round the hummock on which she was sitting. Seated or lying, most of the others were too exhausted by hunger to notice. But herself became particularly aware of the flumping and stamping of pale soles beneath black feet, the smell of crushed ants and of armpits, the crackle of breaking sticks, and ejaculations of the roving actors.

She was forced at last to contribute to the action when the great warrior squatted beside her, placed the top of an index finger on one of her shoulders and drew the finger downward and across her body until it all but arrived at the nipple, to which it was obviously attracted.

At once the two aspirants for the fellow's sinewy favours started a hissing and a chattering. Each of the women was armed, the girl with a club, her rival with one of the pointed sticks used for digging. Mrs Roxburgh might have experienced greater alarm had she provided more than the spark from which their emotional tinder took fire; she was but the indirect cause of the pandemonium which ensued.

Carried away by their jealous fury the two women were abusing each other. The man leaned against a tree and watched as though warming himself at the passions he had roused. When the more agile girl leaped at her rival and bashed her on the head so savagely that it was laid open. Bellowing with pain and rage the woman retaliated with such a jab that the yam-stick pierced the girl's side below the breast. She fell without a sound, and the man saw wisdom in making off before anyone held him responsible.

There arose a frenzy of ear-splitting speculation as relatives of the contentious women rushed from different corners of the camp. The wounded victim was sat propped against a tree, from which position they could better examine the bloody mess her assailant had made of her scalp. Somebody brought a handful of charcoal and rubbed it in. Nobody finally seemed of the opinion that the deep gash was more than a superficial cut, though the woman moaned fearfully, and her complexion was drained of its black, leaving a sediment of dirty yellow. Eyes shut, she did not leave off grinding her head back and forth against the tree.

Dreadful shrieks from those in support of the young girl left Mrs Roxburgh in no doubt that she was dead. Yet she lay so naturally, her wound practically bloodless when the murderous stick was withdrawn from her side, her breasts so youthful and shapely, that she presented the same picture of grace and beauty as on the day when she rose laughing and spangled from beneath the quilt of water-lily pads.

Affected by her renewed acquaintance with death in the midst of continuing life Mrs Roxburgh's pangs were revived, and she added her grief to that of the mourners, and took her place without second thought in the procession forming to carry the body into the forest.

But where they had allowed her to attend the funeral of the child she had nursed, now they waved her back, uttering what sounded like warnings; and a hitherto respectful, elderly man went so far as to punch her in the chest.

So she stayed behind, curled up on the edge of the fire, in the hut which was hers as much as anything she might lay claim to – excepting of course her wedding ring. As she fell asleep she felt inside the fringe of leaves which she had but recently renewed, and without detaching the ring, slipped it on as far as the first joint of her ring-finger. She hoped it might lead her to dream of her husband. But the night remained confused, her dreams filled with hostile and unrecognizable shapes.

By the first light of morning she saw that the child members of her 'family' had returned without their elders, and she fell to wondering how the mourners were conducting their vigil in the depths of the forest.

She crawled outside about dawn, and after first recoiling at the shock of cold, went shivering amongst the trees, somewhat aimlessly it would have seemed had she not invested her action with purpose by remembering how her mother-in-law advocated a 'healthy morning constitutional'.

She was rewarded at last when the scrub through which she had been struggling was transformed into a mesh of startling if chilly beauty. Where she had been slapped and scratched at first, she was now stroked by the softest of fronds. Shafts of light admitted between the pinnacles and arches of the trees were directed at her path, if the hummocks and hollows had been in any way designed to assist human progress. But she felt accepted, rejuvenated. She was the 'Ellen' of her youth, a name they had attached to her visible person at the font, but which had never rightfully belonged to her, any more than the greater part of what she had experienced in life. Now this label of a name was flapping and skirring ahead of her among the trunks of great moss-bound trees, as its less substantial echo unfurled from out of the past, from amongst fuchsia and geum and candy-tuft, then across the muck-spattered

242

yard, the moor with its fuzz of golden furze and russet bracken, to expire in some gull's throat by isolated syllables.

She might have continued on her blissful journey and ended lost had other voices not broken in and a most delectable smell mingled with the scent of drifting smoke. She altered course in the direction of the voices, and eventually came upon a party of blacks whom she recognized as members of her tribe. All appeared and sounded languid as a result of their night's activities; their faces when turned towards the intruder wore expressions which were resentful and at the same time curiously mystical. She realized she had blundered upon the performance of rites she was not intended to witness. There was no immediate indication of what these were; most likely the ceremony was over, for she sensed something akin to the atmosphere surrounding communicants coming out of church looking bland and forgiven after the early service.

The morning air, the moisture dripping from frond and leaf disposed Ellen Roxburgh, naked and battered though she was, to share with these innocent savages an unexpectedly spiritual experience, when she caught sight, to one side of the dying fire, of an object not unlike a leather mat spread upon the grass. She might have remained puzzled had she not identified fingernails attached to what she had mistaken for fringes, and at one end, much as a tiger's head lies propped on the floor at one end of a skin rug, what could only be the head of the girl she remembered in life laughing and playing amongst waterlilies.

After swallowing their surprise at the intrusion on their privacy, the initiates regurgitated; it came spluttering back as rude and guttural sounds of anger. Women rolled up the dark skin, as well as gathering the head and what she saw to be a heap of bones. It was easy to guess from the greasy smears on lips and cheeks how the flesh had disappeared. The revolting remains of the feast were stuffed inside the dillis which accompanied the women on their outings. Mrs Roxburgh might have felt sickened had the stamping and threats of some of the men not frightened her instead. The elderly man who had punched her the evening before to deter her from following the funeral procession, ran at her now, but stumbled over a tree-root, and no longer being at the height of his powers, fell prostrate before arrival.

243

The party moved off, driving the offender before them. As it seemed their urgent aim to leave the scene of their rites as quickly and as far behind them as possible, they hurried past the culprit after a while, and soon forgot, or did not bother to look back, to insult and remonstrate.

Mrs Roxburgh followed, not so far behind that she would be likely to lose her way. As she went, she tried to disentangle her emotions, fear from amazement, disgust from a certain pity she felt for these starving and ignorant savages, her masters, when she looked down and caught sight of a thigh-bone which must have fallen from one of the overflowing dillis. Renewed disgust prepared her to kick the bone out of sight. Then, instead, she found herself stooping, to pick it up. There were one or two shreds of half-cooked flesh and gobbets of burnt fat still adhering to this monstrous object. Her stiffened body and almost audibly twangling nerves were warning her against what she was about to do, what she was, in fact, already doing. She had raised the bone, and was tearing at it with her teeth, spasmodically chewing, swallowing by great gulps which her throat threatened to return. But did not. She flung the bone away only after it was cleaned, and followed slowly in the wake of her cannibal mentors. She was less disgusted in retrospect by what she had done, than awed by the fact that she had been moved to do it. The exquisite innocence of this forest morning, its quiet broken by a single flute-note endlessly repeated, tempted her to believe that she had partaken of a sacrament. But there remained what amounted to an abomination of human behaviour, a headache, and the first signs of indigestion. In the light of Christian morality she must never think of the incident again.

*

During the days following the rites in which, she had to admit, she had participated after a fashion, shoals of fish appeared in the straits separating the island from the mainland. This in itself would have given cause for joy, although nothing to compare with the netting of a sea-monster on the ocean side.

The fishermen were beaching the creature helplessly parcelled in the net as the rest of the tribe broke through the trees fringing the shore shouting, 'Dugong, dugong!' and raced down over the dunes, breasts flipping, arms thrashing the obstructive air. One little boy who turned a violent somersault paused but an instant to decide whether he had broken his neck.

Almost before the beast was dispatched by spears, individual butchers began hacking at the flesh. Fires were kindled in the evening light, while anticipation brought out a glow in dark skins long before the feast itself was ready. In the rush to satisfy their own hunger the blacks were less conscious than usual of their slave, who succeeded in raking from the coals a lump of the rather blubbery flesh. Her eyes were bulging as she strained to chew, her lips running with fishy fat, and she all but growled a warning at one of the dogs, who kept a prudent distance, trailing his plume of a tail as he watched her for scraps.

He did not receive any, however. Mrs Roxburgh's only thought was to fill the hollow of her own insides, and regardless of whether she might burst, to grab another slice out of the ashes if she were lucky and remained unnoticed.

This evening her every stratagem succeeded. Uncomfortably gorged, she rubbed her greasy hands with sand to appease a convention she faintly remembered through the veil of exhaustion hanging between herself and it. She was tolerably happy, happier in fact than the principal source of her unhappiness should have allowed. In 'not remembering' she continually recalled the incident of incalculable days ago. It seemed less unnatural, more admissible, if only to herself. Just as she would never have admitted to others how she had immersed herself in the saint's pool, or that its black waters had cleansed her of morbid thoughts and sensual longings, so she could not have explained how tasting flesh from the human thigh-bone in the stillness of a forest morning had nourished not only her animal body but some darker need of the hungry spirit.

Her lips had not closed from brooding when the blacks started wrapping any scraps of dugong in wads of grass, gathered together their possessions, and departed in some haste for their camp on the other side. So she had to follow or be left behind in darkness. The blacks themselves she suspected of being afraid of the dark, and for that reason had taken the precaution of renewing the fire-sticks they were carrying with them on the journey. As they climbed the ridge separating the ocean from the straits, night was

245

poised in readiness to close in upon them. Several times the travellers' chatter broke, and was mended but diffidently. Silent consent seemed to call a halt beside a small lake, on the surface of which torch-light and the ghosts of their fleshly forms underwent a series of fearsome fluctuations. Their customary wailing, either of supplication or lament, which broke from the wayfarers at this juncture had never been more appropriate.

In Mrs Roxburgh's case, appeased hunger had increased her daring, and she joined in with what began as a parody. If the desire to mock left her it was not through the failure of courage, but because the spirit of the place, the evanescent lake, the faint whisper of stirring trees, took possession of her. When the blacks resumed their flickering march almost in silence, she could smell their fear. If she too, flickered intermittently, it was less in fear than because she might have come to terms with darkness.

They reached the camp, and she stubbed a toe, and somebody pushed her with such force and complete disregard for decency that she bumped her head against a tree; and saw stars. Everybody recovered their irritability and their tongues on returning from the shades into what was safe and familiar. Little children left in the charge of the aged and the halt were running hither and thither, bleating like black lambs, before becoming re-united with their mothers. The family of the child they had buried continued to regard themselves as her official owners, an arrangement which indifference and lack of choice on her part gave her no reason to deplore. The hut filled with smoke and body-smells, and fleas, had never provided a more desirable home or the ground a more accommodating bed.

The camp fleas' greed for human flesh might have dictated another move had there not appeared more significant reasons for removal. She could sense a restlessness in the air, actually visible at times in fingers of smoke tapering in the sky above the mainland trees. Not only this, but ambassadors from neighbouring tribes arrived with intelligence which elated those who received it and involved them in unusual preparations.

Men ordinarily engaged in sharpening and repairing their tools and weapons when not out hunting or fishing began building a flotilla of canoes out of bark sheets slit with stone knives from the trunks of certain trees. The observer became more engrossed than any of those engaged in the operation. She was both fired and fearful. If canoes implied a voyage to the mainland, she would be faced with coming to a decision more positive than any she had hitherto made in a life largely determined by other human beings or God: she must resolve whether to set out on the arduous, and what could be fatal, journey to the settlement at Moreton Bay.

For the time being, preparations for the sea-crossing and for the functions her adoptive tribe expected upon arrival were enough to blunten her forebodings. She was in any case well schooled in warding off her worst thoughts, and was made less vulnerable by the various and exacting labours her owners now demanded of her, such as carrying loads of bark upon her back, gathering firewood, minding babies, digging for a white clay in particular demand at this season. All of which she performed with what might have seemed to others who did not share the blacks' preoccupations, the manner of one engaged in a secret mission. But there was nobody present sufficiently detached, or capable of interpreting what amounted to nervous excitement. She got the hiccups on one occasion from swallowing too fast a lump of glutinous possum flesh with the fur still attached to it. The black children laughed to hear her. They were growing to love their nurse, and initiated her into their games, one in particular which resembled cat's-cradle, with a string spun from hair or fibre. Skill at cat's-cradle was a talent she had never suspected in herself, but she won her children's admiration by her ability to disentangle them. She indulged their every caprice, and received their hugs and their tantrums with an equanimity which approaching departure made it easier to maintain. She was at her blandest in searching for and mining the whitish substance which reminded her of Cornish china-clay. The gloves of fat and charcoal and accumulated filth which had become an habitual part of her dress were now streaked with white in addition. If her hands trembled as she grubbed the clay surrounded by peace and a chastened sunlight, her exertions could not have accounted for it.

The morning the tribe assembled for the crossing to the mainland was of a whitish blue intensifying as the fog lifted. It would have been a leaden soul indeed who failed to respond to the dash and glitter, the shouts and laughter of those who were embarking, the runaway wavelets feathering the straits, and a scent distilled by the wind out of smoke and rampant eucalyptus leaves. It was Mrs Roxburgh's chief concern not to appear over-responsive.

They had seated the slave-nurse amidships, in a nest of children, between the two paddles of one of the larger bark canoes. Anticipation and the chill of morning had brought out the gooseflesh on her arms and shoulders and a blue glint in the whites of her eyes. That she did not feel colder was due to the warm bodies of the children heaped around her, their skins still smooth and bright, unblemished by the life which was preparing for them. From time to time she touched a head or stroked a cheek to allay the apprehension which had rendered her charges unusually silent. She could have eaten them on such a morning, but only when they were safe inside her allowed them to share her joy. Instead she pinched back the snot she saw oozing from a button nose, and the little boy started a caterwauling for an attention he had not experienced before. She laughed, and reassured him, 'Dun't tha knaw, love, I wudn' harm ee?' He understood her words even less than her offending behaviour, but quieted down in the absence of any alternative.

As they were propelled, plunging and rocking, over the water, the spray from the forward paddle was dashed repeatedly in their faces. Ellen sought to comfort her children with an example of spurious calm, because any display of her true feelings, her exultation and straining hopes, might have thrówn them into a panic. Without apparent reason, she remembered how in other days she had been tormented by a dream both waking and sleeping, of a ship's prow entering the cove (she had never yet while in her senses seen Tintagel) and how later still she had scratched the name upon an attic window, not out of affection she thought, rather from frustrated desire. Now she had no desire beyond the simple wish for a 'tay-drinking' at the end of a fearful, still only theoretical, march.

The navigators paddled, first to one side, then the other. Smoke from the coals they carried to renew their fires on the farther shore stung Mrs Roxburgh's eyes. Habit made her reach for a great orange-mouthed shell and start bailing the water they had shipped, in such insignificant quantities her action was hardly justified, and in any case they would soon be there. The green tinge invading bronze cheeks was arrested by a bark keel grating and bumping over sand.

The children jumped out and scampered off, the nurse accepting that they had no further need for her. She had done her duty by them, and would soon be faced with a graver duty towards herself.

In the meantime she was too busily employed helping carry tackle from the boats, and soon dazed besides by the glare from the mounting sun, the sultry pall of stationary air, and the press of strangers from the mainland tribes already foregathered. The foreign blacks were as importunate as the ants crawling up her legs, but where the ants stung, their human counterparts pinched, poked, and breathed upon the phenomenon from the island, who was spun about by her owners in their determination to display a rare possession. In fact, while the camp was not more than half pitched, some of the women interrupted her labours and took her aside, to plaster her head afresh with beeswax and decorate her hair with tufts of down and yellow topknots so that she might appear at her best. She was again brought forward and put on show. The blacks were for the most part lost in open-mouthed wonder as they examined the exhibit from every angle, but a flock of big white parrots alighted on a neighbouring tree, shrieking and discoursing, their sulphur crests raised in disapproval of a monster such as might have roused the derision of country folk at a fair.

Mrs Roxburgh was relieved when allowed to resume her menial duties of digging ditches and gathering firewood.

In the course of the day, incoming tribes joined those already encamped, who greeted the new arrivals with bursts of wailing, to signify joy it would seem, whereas she had only ever sensed in the chorus at morning and evening the doubts and forebodings of a troubled spirit.

She kept to herself as much as she could throughout the day, but was grateful when her children expected her to pick up the pieces after a quarrel or take part in their sporadic games.

Many of the mainland blacks were endowed with a physical grandeur which made the islanders look runtish, but every one of them was hideously scarred by incisions which could only have been deliberately inflicted, in patterns which distinguished one tribe from another. The women, unless adolescent girls, were all either plodders, or innately dejected souls who disguised their true nature under a contralto cheerfulness. These latter were the most inclined to pinch or pull.

Mrs Roxburgh longed for night, except that she would then be forced to consider an escape which terrified her.

As night approached she saw that the blacks were planning celebrations of some kind. There was a continual weaving and interweaving of their paths while the air fizzed and crackled as though with invisible sparks of anticipation. Some of the men already danced and postured, struck one another, recoiled, and laughed. They roamed, or squatted together in chattering circles, and resumed their stalking, their sinews as tense as their eyes looked feverish.

One giant of a fellow, a natural clown by any standards, would twirl, and leap in the air slapping his heels, and entertain those within earshot of his patter. She could tell that he was respected and envied. What most distinguished him from his companions was an axe, or hatchet, which he wore in his woven belt. She wondered now he had come by his hatchet. It was much coveted by the other blacks, who would stroke it, and some of them attempt to prise it away from the owner.

But the giant was equal to their cunning. He would slap down pilfering hands, and leap expertly out of reach, keeping up the gibberish which made others laugh.

She admired him for his agility and enjoyed the jokes she could not understand. When he disappeared from sight the axe-head continued glinting in her mind. It was plunder such as might have fallen to any black from any wreck – that of her own unhappy experience included. But she would have liked to know where he got the hatchet.

Then, during one of his leaping turns, she found herself so close to the clown she realized that what she had taken for conventional scars were unlike those left by tribal incisions. The expanse of the man's back was covered with what appeared to be a patternless welter of healed wounds.

She had been digging a drain round one of the freshly erected huts. She hung her head above the earth she was heaping at the

250

base of a bark wall. She knew that she was breathless, and not from physical exertion.

When she looked again, the man leaped, and was lost in the crowd. He did not return, perhaps having finished his display, and she was left with her vision of a 'miscreant' according to the doctrine of her brother-in-law Garnet Roxburgh.

As the light was gathered in, the trampling increased, the coming and going, the stench of ants and bruised leaves and human bodies. The women had begun lighting fires, not to cook a meal, but rather to illuminate a ritual of some kind. The slave was expected to contribute fuel. Carrying her bundles of sticks she had resumed her habitual state of mind, of dull indifference. The darkening scrub was alive with male figures, prinked with feathers, streaked with clay of various colours. She now understood why she had been put to grubbing clay on the days preceding their departure from the island; her own tribesmen were white-streaked. Some of the men, when she came across them face to face, were wearing slender bones stuck through the cartilage separating the nostrils. The bones made them look especially fierce, but there was no reason why their fierceness or splendour should impress her. They were none the less superb, as their women did not fail to recognize, while humbly building, then kindling, and stoking the fires.

In a pause from her labours Mrs Roxburgh had gone into deeper scrub for the simple purpose of urinating. She had barely finished squatting when, to the embarrassment of each, she saw the great pseudo-black approaching. In the dusk the axe-head resting on his belt was more than ever a focus point. It convinced her that the man was some escaped prisoner who had taken up with a black tribe and probably acquired their more horrid ways to add to his natural propensities.

At the same time the longing to speak again with someone of her own kind (if such he could be called) produced in her throat and side a felted chuffing almost as distressing as more dangerous symptoms.

The man came straight towards her, and when they were but a few yards apart, was brought to a halt. She saw that, in spite of his size and strength, his shanks, his dangling hands, were trembling.

To help him out of his difficulty she said to him in her native tongue, 'Where's tha from, eh?' then, on remembering who she was supposed to be, she sternly asked, 'Are you a Christian?'

The man stood mouthing sounds, like an idiot, or one in whom time or shock had destroyed his connection with the past.

Her hopes shrank. Where she had glimpsed for an instant the possibility of rescue, it now seemed as though it was she who must become the saviour, not of a rational being, but a lost soul.

'If you can't tell me who you are,' she babbled breathlessly, 'perhaps you will still be able to help me'; and stepping forward, she took him by the hand.

The man might have been struck. His formless mumbling loudened, in the course of which saliva flew out from between his lips, almost as though he were taken by a fit. But she had reached a stage where she could not have felt frightened, nor disappointed, only detached from everything that had ever happened or might still be in store for her. She had been rendered as impervious as lead, and would sink, if necessary, without a qualm.

When she thought she could detect in the man's gibberish the first semblance of an intelligible word. 'Gee–a–jur–juk–juk–tch–ar–tcack!'

'Your name is Jack?' She all but wrung his hand from him.

'Jack – CHANCE!' He pronounced it 'Chaunce', and there followed a smile which the effort and a battered face could not prevent looking misshapen.

Gratitude and relief threatened to spill out of her eyes and mouth, but she managed instead, 'My name is Ellen.'

He had withdrawn inside his leather mask, through the slits in which, eyes of a pale, drained blue were looking at her suspiciously.

'We shall have to trust each other,' she persisted. 'Only bring me to Moreton Bay and I promise they'll give you your pardon.'

The mask in wrinkled leather immediately set into a rusted-iron visor. 'No – *ppardons* – for the likes a' me. A stripe for every day since I bolted!' He produced a noise which may have been intended as a laugh.

She realized she was still holding his hand and how cold and hard it felt in hers. He *must* be hard; the life he had been forced to

252

lead could only have made a brute of him, if he were not one by birth.

Then the brute began shivering, and she dropped the hand lest his anguish should prove contagious.

'They can't refuse you a pardon – Jack – if you bring me to them. It would be unjust and unnatural.'

'Men is unnatural and unjust.'

She was so desperate she cried out in anger. 'They won't dare! I am Mrs Roxburgh!' Had she not temporarily lost her detachment she might have heard herself and disbelieved.

The convict evidently had. He looked her over quickly in the manner of a professional who could have made his first mistake, and disappeared through the trees in the direction of the hubbub and fires.

She had scarce time enough to indulge in self-pity, for two of the women came in search of her and dragged her with them, back to the scene of the festivities.

It was by now fairly dark, so that the fires, behind which the female blacks were seated in rows, burned more brilliantly. Somewhere about the middle of the dark assemblage the captive recognized the women of her own tribe. Here her companions led her, after considerable trampling between the rows of seated figures, and vocal protests and outright blows from those who were trampled over. The errant three were squeezed at last into the conglomerate, sweating mass.

From where Mrs Roxburgh found herself she saw there would be no opportunity for escape, either alone, or accompanied by the convict were he to experience a change of heart. If anything, she felt relieved. To have started screaming in a drawing-room would not have been worse than to return by the way she had come, between the rows of correctly seated black women.

As yet, there was not a man in sight, although from the surrounding dark, voices could be heard whenever women's chatter and the roar and crackle of the fires allowed. As the fires heaved and resettled the sparks shot upward towards a sky pricked with their counterpart in early stars.

The women were growing impatient: they sighed, groaned, some of them shouted; the rows of seated figures swayed with what looked like an early stage in drunkenness.

Ellen Gluyas swayed with them as a matter of course. Pressed in amongst the black women, her body had begun, not disagreeably, to sweat.

The darkness erupted at last, hurling itself in distinguishable waves into the firelit foreground. White-ribbed men were stamping and howling the other side of the fiery hedge as they performed prodigious feats related to hunting and warfare.

The rows of women swayed in time with darkness, slapping their thighs, or in the case of the older, croaking grannies, the possum-skin rugs covering their string-and-paper thews.

Ellen Gluyas was swayed with them, although she would rather have joined the men, the better to celebrate what she was reliving. She was again dancing as they carried in 'the neck! the neck!' at harvest, and as she danced she twitched the corner of her starched apron. (It was, in fact, her recently renewed fringe of leaves.)

One of her neighbours looked at her askance, but only for an instant. They were all swaying seated melted together in runnels of light and sweat.

The dance performed by each successive tribe made its own comment. Now there was a great snake uncoiling, at first slowly, then in involuted frenzy. Arms worked so hard their elbows threatened to pierce the ochre-stippled chests behind them; black thighs in motion were all but liquid with reflected light.

The women swayed in time, and bowed, and swung their too-heavy heads, and righted themselves, and clapped or slapped, either with a smart sting of flesh or the muffled thump of opossum fur.

Dust rising made the captive sneeze. But she bowed her head and swayed in time. She slapped and moaned, and was carried away. She might have been carried further still had it not been for the sudden vision of Mr Roxburgh: his beard failed to conceal the wound in his throat through which the blood continued welling. (Or had they burnt him? In her drunkenness she could not be sure.)

She clapped and thumped and moaned, and bowed her head until it hung between her thighs. It inspired her neighbours to increased frenzy.

Her vision was making her cry out: one of his legs had been torn off at the hip; she could smell the smell of crackled skin.

Now when the great luminous ochre-scaled dripping snake had almost driven itself into the dust by its exertions, she saw upon raising her head that the tail's hindmost vertebra was becoming detached.

There it was, wriggling and contorting of its own free will.

The women's voices climbed, 'Ulappi! Ulappi!' to acclaim the dancer of everybody's choice.

The captive woman bowed her head upon her splayed thighs, buried her face in her fringe of leaves, from which she might never recover herself.

When at last she sat up, her eyes were closed, her lips parted to receive – the burnt sacrifice? the bread and wine?

She knew that the man, this Ulappi, was dancing for her the other side of her clenched lids.

Possum tails attached by strings to his belt flumped and cavorted against his buttocks; even at a distance they stroked her skin with such delicacy she could barely distinguish fur from the wind in which it danced. There was less doubt about the hard chest she bumped against ('what is "paps", Mamma?') the pig's-bristles got by singeing, the channel down which the sweat poured, as far as the bronze cauldron where it was seethed and evaporated. As they whirled.

When she opened her eyes she saw her wishful partner submerged by a rushing wave of fresh dancers.

She lost interest, unless in the gristly neck of one seated in the row ahead, an old woman made conspicuous by red markings. Mrs Roxburgh thought to recognize the grandmother of the girl who had been killed for love. The day following the girl's death, after the secret ceremony in the forest, the woman had blossomed red in mourning for her grand-daughter. Mrs Roxburgh might have felt more resentful, that her widowhood had not been formalized in red ochre, if widowhood, as she saw it embodied in Aunt Tite and old Mrs Roxburgh, were not a formality in itself. (Well, wasn't it but another figure in the formal dance?)

Ellen sat picking at her fringe of leaves. The corroboree was over, except for the embers, the ashes, and the continued exchange of hoarsened voices. As the tribes detached themselves from one another she knew that her hoped-for rescuer would not re-appear.

Thus she was again saved from undertaking the hazardous

journey to Moreton Bay. As her owners claimed her and led her away, she was persuading herself it was reason for relief rather than dejection to remain their chattel, when they came face to face with a second group advancing upon them as though by arrangement. She recognized by his topknot and the dilli containing the magic stone carried under one armpit, the physician, or wise man, or conjurer, who had failed to resurrect the dead child.

The two parties halted. Had she not been so closely confined by those surrounding her, the chill which swept over Mrs Roxburgh might have betrayed itself after some grotesquely physical fashion; for she could tell that her keepers and the physician–conjurer were entering upon a contract of which she was the principal, perhaps even the sole clause.

The outcome was that this 'Turrwan', as the others constantly referred to the magician, took charge of her, and she could but presume that she had become his property.

The new owner behaved respectfully towards her, less from thoughtfulness she felt, than because he was an elderly man. The hut he occupied was in almost every respect similar to the one from which she had been given away. The eyes of two other women dozing beside a fire were kindled by the newcomer's entry. No doubt resigned to custom they gave no indication of active resentment.

As the slave prepared herself for the night by easing a hip into the ground not too far distant from the fire, a child started crying, and she thought how she might console herself eventually by caressing and consoling this child. But for the time being it was Turrwan who distracted her attention in that she was the object of his. Although of an advanced age he was wiry enough to be reckoned with and had an eager eye which she must quell by a coldness in her own.

Mrs Roxburgh would not have believed that she could act so cold.

Turrwan seated himself at last on the opposite side of the hut, and after taking out his magic crystal from the dilli, and polishing it awhile to impress, he lay down, if not to sleep, to watch.

She composed herself, but did not sleep, or perhaps she did; for how else can Ulappi have entered? to be standing over her. She has nothing to fear. He is a tinner from near Truro, deported for taking a donkey from Hicks's field, at Michaelmas.

Herself was the donkey. She must have slept in spite of her intention not to lose consciousness. She lay and listened to her 'husband' the magician having a nightmare or pleasuring one of his true wives the other side of the dead fire. Ellen ground her cheek against the twigs with which the floor was littered, and wished for morning.

The following day was a drowsy one filled with haze. Her improved station relieved her of some of the drudgery. She was kept company by a handful of older ladies who would have taught her how to spin a thread out of hair or stitch together an opossum rug had she shown any inclination. Instead she could now afford to feel bored, or within reason, give way to anger. She lay beneath a tree, her back towards them, idle to the elbows and the ankles. Had she known the language she might have commanded somebody to fan her or tell her a tale.

Incidentally she realized that most of her life at Cheltenham had been a bore, and that she might only have experienced happiness while scraping carrots, scouring pails, or lifting the clout to see whether the loaves were proved.

It was in consequence a relief as evening approached to join her inferiors in the preparation of fern-root. All around them was the sound of chopping. It soothed her somewhat, until she cut her finger on the sharp edge of the shell she was using. She sucked the wound, before remembering to rub it with charcoal.

Some expectancy, evening smoke, or the men's return from hunting, made the women restless.

A kangaroo was put to roast.

Turrwan appeared and squatted but too visibly beside his acquisition. She did not so much as avert her eyes since the film of coldness she was learning to assume made this unnecessary.

Whatever entertainment might have been devised for the evening, she soon realized it would not take place according to plan. A discordancy was arising, nothing audible in the beginning, nor were there visible signs of dissent. She was aware of it, however, in puffs of smoke, through currents of air, in the sound of sticks breaking underfoot.

Suddenly the surrounding scrub exploded. A fight was on. She had no means of discovering what had caused it. As dusk fell, warriors came and went in the clearing where the women continued at work. Blows were exchanged, to the meaty sound of thwacked flesh and the stubborner thud of wood upon bone. A spear whirring and hissing through leaves was arrested in flight by the trunk of a great, shaggy tree.

A second spear met with what must have been its intended target: a man fell headlong into a fire, from which the women dragged him not to safety, but to a less-agonizing death. The black buttocks quivered an instant, twitched, and contracted.

The fact that this was in earnest did not make the occasion more real than the corroboree of the night before. The rites of each were equally inebriating, or so it seemed to one spectator, as the men who had danced their way through the maze of dreaming now made the more direct approach to death, which in her own experience was but another figure in the dance.

Some of the women had started screaming; they were pulling one another by their short hair.

In what was becoming a darkness, of night, dust, heaving branches, and a soft, sticky rain of what she did not have time to discover, she might have made some contribution of her own, and went so far as to indulge in an initial twirl when she was stopped short by running against a human being.

Before she could evade the consequences of this too-precipitate encounter, she was seized by the hand, and whether she liked it or not, forced to depend on her abductor for any further step she might take in the savage dance. For the moment there was nothing for it but to mark time amongst the milling bodies involved in this orgy of bashing and blood, until he saw an opportunity for making his intentions clear by extricating himself and his prize from the scrimmage. She was dragged behind him like some inanimate object, away at least, until she collided with a sapling, when both of them, because joined, were unavoidably halted. Had it been daylight still, she would most probably have been temporarily blinded by the blow. In the circumstances she was only deafened by the drumming in her ears.

She might have continued rooted like the sapling, had he not dragged her away. It was the only outcome for hands which were welded together.

He was as steel to her more passive lead, but when she was not a painful lump condemned to bumping behind, and at intervals, against him, she thought to hear an insubstantial tinkling as she flitted over the uneven ground.

Always joined: it was ordained thus by the abductor become her rescuer.

That he had chosen to play the latter role was doubtless the subject of an unintelligible mumbling such as she remembered from their first meeting. On this present occasion she felt too dazed to help him out, but he succeeded at last in breaking into speech of a kind through his own efforts.

'The crick,' she heard. '. . . leave no tracks i' the crick –'

Shortly after, she stumbled, and felt water round her ankles, at times up to her knees as she floundered in unsuspected potholes; sand, soothing to the feet, gave place to more deceptive mud, with the occasional rock or log against which she stubbed herself. She imagined the rosy veils the water must be weaving from her blood.

'Do you know the way?' she asked in the course of their silence, and thought he mumbled back, 'I oughter know unless I forgot.'

If allowed, she would have been happy to subside anywhere in this dark world, since exhaustion was making their journey, finally her life, pointless. But he forced her on, and by degrees, sensing that it was neither will nor physical strength, but a superior mechanism which drove him, her mind and clockwork limbs learned to cooperate with his.

At last when light began to thin out the solid but no longer painful darkness (she had grown too numb to react humanly to the most vicious blows and scratches) she heard him say, 'I reckon we'll camp here for a bit in the gully,' and felt at liberty to fall down where she was. She lay there as grey and indeterminate as the early light surrounding them.

She did not doubt but that her companion would know what to do next. In the circumstances she could not afford to be distrustful. Beyond her numbed physical condition, her blurred vision, and mere tatters of thought, he was chopping at branches with the hatchet he carried in his belt, driving stakes into the ground, building a shelter of sorts, low and shapeless, scarcely distinguishable from the living bushes. She saw that the bark cloth he had worn across one shoulder and through the belt, had been torn off during their flight through the scrub. That he was stark naked apart from the belt and a few remnants of feathers in his hair, did not, or rather, must not, disturb her. In her own case she had the satisfaction of knowing that the swathes of vine about her waist were to some extent intact, and her wedding-ring still where she had knotted it.

She awoke only under compulsion. He was prodding at her with horny toes. '. . . if you want to get inside. We'll be safer, anyways, for not showin' ourselves.'

She should have thanked or smiled at him, but her face and voice had lost the power to do so. Yet she must summon up the strength to reach the hut since he made no attempt at assisting her. Mrs Roxburgh might have felt put out by evidence of what she knew to be uncouthness, but Ellen Gluyas crawled gratefully enough into the luxurious privacy offered by this shelter.

She lay aching, smiling after a directionless fashion, even when the entrance was darkened by her companion's figure stooping and following her in.

Without any further communication, he lay down, turned his back, and was still.

She slept, and woke, and slept, and woke. The sun must have climbed high. She was conscious of a criss-cross of bird-song imposed on light and silence. Fingers of sunlight intruding through the green thatch stroked her body and that of the man stretched beside her. The incongruous had no part in the world of limitless peace to which her senses had been admitted, perhaps by divine compunction, until some invisible bird derided human simplicity with an outburst of ribald mockery.

Returned to a rational state of mind she was at once aware of her companion's snores. The hut, moreover, was filled with a stench which might have become intolerable had she not remembered kneeling in her pinafore beside a fox's earth. She too, would be smelling pretty foxy were she able to smell herself. She sighed, and snorted, and thought how foolish she must look, naked and filthy, beside the naked filthy man.

When he started a broken yelping, his body twitching, his free shoulder warding off whichever the danger pursuing him.

He sounded in such obvious distress she put out a hand and touched his back to break the nightmare.

'It's a dream,' she tried to persuade him. 'Jack!' she raised her voice in a command.

But neither her voice nor her hand was able to restrain his desperate twitching, and she realized she was touching the scars she had noticed on his first appearing at the blacks' camp, when their apparently motiveless welter distinguished them from the formal incisions in native backs.

He let out a single yelp more bloodcurdling than any of those preceding it, and she snatched back her hand and put it for safety between her breasts. She felt perturbed for having touched on an area of suffering he might have wished to keep from her.

Nor was she reassured by his calling out soon after, '... lay off, can't yer? – 'Twasn't me! – I only give 'er what she asked for –' He fell to drivelling and sobbing; anything further was meaningless.

Then he wrenched himself round. He lay on his back, waking, she could see from the lashes risen on the lids, before the face turned and he was staring at her out of pale eyes, as remote as those of the dead.

'It was a nightmare, Jack,' she explained feebly, 'which I tried to free you from.'

'It was no dream. I could feel it. They'd strung me up to the triangle, and started layin' inter me. I was in for a good 'undred stripes. Treadmill after.'

She began counting on herself as he spoke, but only got as far as two: it was her nipples.

'Are you afraid,' she asked, 'that I'll not keep my word if you take me to Moreton Bay?'

His answer to that was but a snuffling as he ground his head back and forth against the earth floor of their refuge.

He is an animal, she decided, but for all that, tractable.

She put out her hand and touched him on the wrist. 'You must trust me,' she said.

He neither stirred nor answered.

Thought of her own husband's not wholly justified trust made

261

her avert her face so that her rescuer might not see it swelling.

'If you have a wife,' she found herself exploring, 'you will
surely understand.'

'She was not what you would call my wife, but as good as one,
in the Old Country.'

'How she must have suffered losing you!' He showed no sign
of being moved; it was she who suffered for the woman separated
from her convict lover.

Had it not been for his detachment, she might have re-lived
against her will the last moments of what represented her real life.
As it was, she only re-enacted them, brightly lit as for a troupe of
actors on a stage seen from the depths of a darkened theatre, a
woman stepping forward to drag a spear from out of the throat of
a man lying wounded upon the sand.

Was she becoming callous? Surely not, when the moment before she could have cried for the woman who lost her convict
lover.

She heard a renewed cackle from the bird of ribald voice.

She felt anger creeping on her. She was angry at the behaviour
of this unmoved and unmoving, this crude man, whom she should,
she knew, accept and understand for what he was, considering her
own crude origins.

She hoped he had not been aware of her anger; she needed his
sympathy and understanding. 'Did you know, Jack, that I lost
my husband – that he was cruelly murdered – along with the
members of the crew?'

'I heard tell,' he said, 'among the blacks. They was provoked
though, by whites.'

So she did not know where she stood.

'No one is ever,' she heard herself managing the words as
though they had been pebbles, 'is ever wholly to blame.' She
added as an afterthought, 'Except Mr Roxburgh – he was
innocent.'

In the long, expiring, golden afternoon, she drowsed again, and
sank. When she returned to the surface, rudely pulled, or so it
seemed, she realized that nothing more violent than a breaking of
sticks was responsible for disturbing her rest.

She dragged her bones outside the hut. Jack Chance was coax-
262

ing a fire. A heap of bronze feathers was glinting in a spangled evening. As Ellen Gluyas she would have busied herself plucking and gutting a brace of pigeons, but Mrs Roxburgh had her aches to cosset, nor could she resist the luxury of being waited on.

She might have rewarded her servant with a smile had he shown himself conscious of her presence. He carried the dangling birds to the creek, and returned with them encased in mud coffins which he buried in the depths of the fire.

She heard her languid, tutored voice. 'It was clever of you, Jack, to catch the birds. You learned it from the blacks, I suppose.'

The voice from the past made her wonder whether her friend Mrs Daintrey would find cause to reproach her for neglecting to write.

'It was my business,' he said, 'long before I would of guessed that blacks could know about it.'

'Oh?' She would have liked her assigned slave to entertain her, but he had fallen silent, and would not be lured out she saw, so she went to the creek and washed herself; she cleaned her teeth with a finger: it was the first time she had attended to them since – when? she could not remember.

As the evening drew together, a shimmer as of pigeons' feathers was transferred to it. She frowned, however, recalling the dangling heads, the broken necks.

She squatted beside the fire and waited, as he was squatting on the opposite side, thus far respectful of formalities.

'You must tell me how you trap the birds,' Mrs Roxburgh encouraged.

She almost expected candles to illuminate her ignorance in the mahogany surface of an endless dinner.

But it was the moment when he reached out to take the coffins out of the fire. Broken open, they revealed neat pigeon-mummies, for the feathers had come away with the casing of baked mud.

The diners wasted no time before tearing into the flesh. Mrs Roxburgh burned her lips, her fingers; a drizzle of precious gravy was scalding her chin, not to say her breasts. Practice, and hunger more regularly satisfied, had made the convict comparatively adept at dealing with such a situation; they had taught him table-manners, moreover: he ate almost finically, holding his head on one side, and crooking a finger.

Mrs Roxburgh had to forget about him before devouring the more pungent innards, left in the bird by the cook for reasons of practical economy. She was only halted by the skeleton, and a pair of legs and crimped claws from which the coral had departed.

A melancholy descended upon her, increased by the contracting light and a dying fire.

'What was her name – this woman?' She ran her tongue between her lips and her teeth to extract the last fragments of pigeon, and knew she would be looking her ugliest.

He laughed. 'Why would you be interested, I wonder?' He spat a pigeon bone into the fire. 'She was called "Mab", if you wanter know.'

She had hunched herself since the untended fire and night at her back made her conscious of the cold. 'That is a name I never heard, not in the country I come from. Nor, for that matter, in England, where I lived after I crossed the river – after I was married.' This latest gap in her knowledge which old Mrs Roxburgh and Mrs Daintrey had omitted to fill might have depressed her further. 'Mab.' She spoke it flat, as though testing it for its flavour and texture.

Her companion, for all his attempts at refinement during their meal, did not attempt to restrain the wind escaping from him.

'It was her name.' He belched softer than before. 'I never thought about it.'

'Tell me,' she ordered, yawning, 'about the birds.'

By now he appeared only too ready. 'Well, you see, I was in the trade. There was always a market for cage-birds – linnets, finches, thrushes, but none as popular as the linnet. 'E's the most cheerfullest songster, longer-lived – tough, you might say – 'e'll adapt 'isself to neglect. Most birds and animals – plants too – is neglected – once the whim to own 'em dies in the owner.'

'Then why did you carry on, Jack, at what amounts to an immoral trade?'

'If we considered only what's moral we'd go 'ungry, wouldn't we? an' curl up an' die. There's too much thinkin' – an' not enough. Would men go with women, or women with men, if they started thinkin' of the trouble – the deceit and treachery they might run into?'

'Not all men and women are treacherous or deceitful.' But she scowled at the fire, and dug into the ground with a stick her hand found lying beside it.

'I'm not saying as you – a lady – is treacherous and deceitful – or would know about any of that. *I* know, because I'm one who's 'ad the hard experience.'

Was he innocent enough not to have recognized her true station in spite of the clues she had dropped for him? She might have enlightened him there and then, in plain terms, had it not occurred to her that he could have been subjecting her to cynicism, in which case he would expect the worst of her at any level.

So she confined herself to saying, 'Whether I am a lady or not, I was deceitful – I believe – but once.'

She was annoyed by what she heard as reply.

'Why do you laugh?' she was quick to ask.

'Oh, no! I'm not accusin' nobody!'

'But laughed.'

'Praps none of us thinks 'ard enough to remember what we done or was.'

Their surroundings had all but disappeared. The black was relieved only by the remnants of their fire. This, and what did amount to accusation, made her feel most desolate.

'Why dun't tha stoke 'n op, Jack?'

He said it could give them away if aborigines happened to be camped in the vicinity. Shortly after, he went so far as to tear off a branch and beat any life out of the embers.

She had no choice but to crawl inside the hut. In doing so she wished he might not follow; she had grown to dislike him; she would have preferred to lie alone and think how she would employ her freedom were she ever to reach Moreton Bay.

But he followed her inside, bringing with him, together with the now familiar stench, a warmth which combined with her own as a comfort against the hostile night.

A night-bird whirred over and past, and was wound up. There was only the silence to listen to, and moisture falling to the ground outside, and the sound of her own eyelashes, and Jack Chance clearing his throat.

It alarmed her when he spoke, although in a voice lowered out of respect for the past, 'When I was in the cage-bird trade as I was tellin' you, Ellen, I took to goin' farther afield to meet the demand. I 'ad a little place on the river at Putney, on the north bank, and did well enough at 'Ighget at first, but begun to find it more profitable to go into 'Arfordsher, and even as far as Suffolk. Suffolk for linnet. I'd drive there with a 'orse an' cart. I'd sometimes spend several days, sleepin' under the cart, and makin' my catch early an' late. I kept my birds in the cottage at Putney. I'd drive out daily around the streets, sellin' to whoever was in need of a songbird, among who was a good few genuine fanciers.'

'And Mab, I suppose, stayed to mind the birds at Putney?'

'Birds was not in Mab's line. An' she couldn't abide the country – bad enough Putney, let alone Suffolk. She come up there with me once. I fixed a bivouac inside a field, in the shelter of a 'edge, an' cooked 'er a nice supper of larks. It was no go all the way. She 'ad it against the blessed grass for wettin' 'er feet.'

'What was Mab's line?'

'She were a cress-seller. She lodged with folk in a court off 'Oborn, to be in good time for Farringdon Market, where she bought 'er cresses off the dealers, early. Then she'd go hawk it door to door, damaged stuff mostly, a girl like 'er in business on 'er own.'

Since recovering his tongue he was anxious to use it, and inclined to prattle. It detracted from his stature, she felt, what she remembered of Ulappi the dancer and Jack Chance the escaped convict. She might not have entrusted herself to a babbler. She came of silent stock; and Mr Roxburgh ever judicious.

Listening to this light-coloured voice telling about his girl, she asked, 'How did she look? Was she tall? And of what colour? Was Mab pretty?'

Well, it was only right to take an interest in this poor cress-seller, rising early in the court off Holborn (she knew how the girl's hands must have looked) to hawk her inferior wares from door to door.

'She was black – like you,' he began reconstructing carefully. 'Dark lips. On frosty mornin's I'd tell 'er she looked like she'd had a feed of cherries – the juicy black uns. She was big-built, too. You're not more than two parts of Mab, Ellen.'

'I was never thought small. I'm above medium, wouldn't you say?'

He might not have been giving it thought, when suddenly he surprised her. 'Big enough. And pretty.'

From what she had been taught she should have resented his licence, but in the circumstances, was more displeased with herself.

They had lost their inclination to talk. She listened to the cart grinding its way in and out of ruts, and the squeak of a wheel which needed greasing. It was a lopsided vehicle, though gay-painted, the little horse a sturdy bay with hairy fetlocks. She could smell the dew from the fields beyond the hedgerows. She loved to rise early, and go outside their bivouac without her shoes, and feel the dew on the soles of her feet.

She did not think she could stomach the dish of larks. (If pigeon, why not lark?) Nor birds moping and dying in captivity. Some of them huddled tragically from the moment they were snared, and in the jolting cart, pressed together, their plumage filthy with their own dirt.

'I can imagine,' she said, 'Mab's feelings – when you was sentenced.'

He did not answer. It sounded as though he was breaking a stick into little pieces.

'Is your term a long one?'

'Life.'

He spoke so flat and matter-of-fact, sympathy was not called for. It shocked her none the less.

'Her term is no shorter than yours.' She knew it was herself of whom she was thinking. 'I can understand her suffering.'

'Nobody 'as suffered without they bit the dust at Moreton Bay – least of all Mab. Mab, anyways, is dead.'

She lay crying as soft as she could so that her 'rescuer' might not hear. Beyond the thatching of twigs and leaves, stars were reeling and melting, to mingle with her tears and blind her. A person, she supposed, might choke on grief if she did not take care.

She was prevented from dwelling on this morbid and precipitate possibility. Jack Chance was touching her arm; he was stroking her wrist, she realized. If she did not withdraw, it was because her body for the moment seemed the least part of her, or because it might never have been touched, not even by her husband Mr Austin Roxburgh, dead these many years.

He continued stroking.

'Why do you cry, Ellen, when it isn't no concern of yours?'

'Oh, it is! But it is! Mine as well as yours and hers.'

When he kissed her thigh through the loops and trailers of vine-leaves she twitched so violently that she rammed her knee against what must have been his face.

He cursed, not necessarily Mrs Roxburgh, or not as she heard it; it was a curse against mankind in general.

'Oh,' she cried, 'did I hurt you?'

'I reckon nothin' could hurt me but another taste of the bloody cat.'

Her hand went out to make amends. 'That will never happen, because I'll not allow it,' Mrs Roxburgh said. 'You can rest assured, Jack.'

Was she so sure of herself? He must have felt her hand trembling on his forearm in a gesture which was meant to comfort him.

For his part, he no longer wavered. He began to handle her as though she had been a wheelbarrow, or black woman, for she had seen the head of her adoptive family take possession of his wives after such a fashion, in silhouette against the entrance to the hut. The breathing, moreover, had grown familiar.

'No!' she whinged; was she not after all Mrs Roxburgh?

He dropped her and lay beside her.

After a while he breathed in her ear, 'If I am to trust you, Ellen, you should trust me. Two bodies that trust can't do hurt to each other.'

She was not entirely won because, according to her knowledge of herself, she was not entirely trustworthy.

At the same time she longed for a tenderness his hand had begun again to offer as she lay moaning for her own shortcomings.

She allowed him to free her of the girdle of vines, her fringe of shed or withered leaves, which had been until now the only disguise for her nakedness.

'What's this?' he asked her.

'What?' Although she knew.

'This ring.'

'It's my wedding-ring.'

He made no comment. He was, as she had always suspected, a decent man at heart.

But suddenly she was taken by a panic. 'If I lose it I am lost!' Whereas she knew it was this man on whom she depended to save her.

She began such a lashing and thrashing, her broken nails must be tearing open the wounds which had healed in his back. It was this, doubtless, which decided him to return her aggression.

He could not press her deep enough into the dust. Yet with aroused hunger rather than anger or contempt. It became a shared hunger. She would have swallowed him had she been capable of it.

Then lay weeping, 'Tchack! Tchack!' Now it was herself had to find her way back inside a language.

While he asked too blatantly, 'Can you love me, Ellen?'

They had to protect each other at last from demands with which neither might have been able to comply, encircling, caressing with a feathered tenderness. They must have reached that point where each is equally exalted and equally condemned.

She had lain an instant or an age when she experienced a twinge. 'Aw, my life! I ricked my neck! Rub on it a little, cusn't tha?' But he had dropped off, and where she had been stroked with feathers she was now encased in a sheath of rough, unfeeling bark.

In the course of this encircled night she thought to hear, '. . . both of 'em dabsters . . . truss th' pigeon 'sthe pigeon – trussed . . . never let on . . . not a word . . . I wouldn' of ef she hadn' . . . is Ellen who'll . . . maybe . . . shave us Lord . . .'

She was too tired. She was not for saving not even herself only for slipping deeper down let them sentence her for it.

She awoke to a steely light scribbled on the dust and shadow of the hut.

He was kneading her arms. 'Wake up! Hey! Ellen? It's later than I reckoned for. If we don't look sharp they'll catch us up. There's not that much distance between us.' Louder since she had last heard it, his voice was again level, cold, that of a man with a contract to fulfil.

She turned her face, preferring memory to appearances. 'Yes,' she answered, 'we must start.' But made no move.

'I've warned yer,' he said. 'You're the one with most to lose.

269

If I shycock round the bush for the rest of me life, that's what I've come to expect.'

After that he crawled outside.

In the mood in which she found herself she would have liked to drowse. The alchemy of morning was changing steel into gold. It slid along her skin bringing the flesh back to life. She glanced sleepily along her as far as the armpit. All that she saw belonged to an age of gold in no way connected with a body scarred, withered, and blackened by privation; nor yet the form which luxury had polished and adorned; not even her clumsy, protuberant girlhood. She lay stropping a cheek against an arm, hoping to arrive at layers of experience deeper still, which he alone knew how to induce.

She shuddered for the goose walking over her grave. She sat up. She must dress herself.

The defoliated vine was lying of a heap in the dust beside her, the ring still attached to one of its thongs. Slipping the ring on the finger to which it belonged, she crawled outside as she was. Not yet ready to be seen, she walked some way into the bush before discovering what she needed: she tore at and twisted free several lengths from a vine smothering a shrub, and wound the vine about her waist so that she was once more clothed. The vine was tougher, the leaves furnishing it more leathery than those which had served her thus far. It occurred to her that she might continue wearing her ring since there were no blacks to hide it from; but she ended by threading it again on a runner, and knotting it as before. If asked for a reason, she might not have been able to find one unless – yes, she would have answered, 'My finger is now so thin and shrunk, a ring would slip off and be lost.'

She felt elated by this explanation, as well as physically relieved after squatting to defecate.

On returning to camp she found that he had demolished their hut. He had raked the ashes and strewn them with brush. He was ready waiting for her.

Noticing his sullen glance at her renewed girdle she said as nicely as she knew how, 'You must not be angry. I had to make some preparations. And did not keep you waiting long.'

'I'll not be the loser,' he mumbled, and they moved off.

It was a glum start to a journey, she thought as she followed, springy at first, though she soon found that her ankles ached and that her feet had not recovered from the first stage of their flight.

He was carrying the spear and waddy, and the cumbrous net retained from his life with the aborigines, which it would have been improvident to abandon. He had made no attempt to cover his nakedness in any way since losing the strip of bark cloth. His sole article of clothing was the belt from which hung that relic of a white past, the salvaged hatchet.

This morning she was not disturbed by the scars in the convict's back, not even by those which her nails must have re-opened and where flies were scavenging for dried blood.

He strode, yet primly, his buttocks spare and austere. It surprised her at first that she should be looking at the buttocks at all, and in such detachment. Or perhaps it was not surprising. Their nakedness notwithstanding he might have been leading her on a polite, if over-brisk walk through a wild garden.

When compassion stirred in her again, it was for the buttocks rather than the scarified back: that the naked buttocks of a grudging, powerful man should make him look so peculiarly dependent on her mercy. She felt moved to stroke them, to make amends, if this would not have lowered a noble creature to the station of a horse or dog. But she did genuinely pity the convict, and would have liked to heal those innermost wounds of which she had received glimpses. Could she love him? She believed she could; she had never fully realized how much she had desired to love without reserve and for her love to be unconditionally accepted. But would this man of lean, disdainful buttocks, love her in return?

By daylight she could hardly think what manner of pact they had made during the hours of darkness. Had love been offered truthfully by either party? Or were they but clinging to a raft in the sea of their common misery? She could remember her panic, a sensual joy (not lust as Garnet Roxburgh had aroused) as well as gratitude for her fellow survivor's presence, kindness, and strength. She also remembered, if she dared admit, that which was engraved upon her mind in illuminated letters: *Can you love me Ellen?* Did he truly wish for love? Or had he made use of her body as part payment of a debt?

She was shocked by her own thoughts, as well as physically

271

shocked when Jack Chance stopped without warning, and she, in her thoughtfulness, collided with him.

'What,' she panted, 'is it, Jack?'

He did not answer, perhaps considering her too foolish by half. No doubt his stopping short signified an enemy, or the alternative, an animal to eat. So she did not press for an answer to her question, while withdrawing from their forced contact, not so far that they did not remain united by the warmth of their interrupted exertions.

While she waited she picked a flower not unlike a jasmine, white, but scentless. Smelling the flower made her feel trivial and superfluous. Drops of her sweat fell upon the immaculate petals.

Presently he moved on and she followed. Neither spoke. Perhaps he hated as well as despised one who was little more to him than a doxy met by accident.

On her side, the expedition had become something of a plodding match. As the sun rose it beat them about the head and shoulders with weapons of bronze. She bowed her head; the convict did not appear to turn a hair.

They climbed, or alternately, descended, ridges of quartz and granite which tore feet already torn, past obtrusive branches which whipped and slashed, felted drumsticks which thumped upon her breasts, and more ignominiously, buttocks protected only by her fringe of leaves, while more vindictive low-growing bushes harrowed and pricked arms, thighs, the entire human façade.

At one point she could have sat down and started crying, but looked ahead and saw the convict laid open and bleeding from hacking a path for them. On catching up, she noticed that some of the thorns had remained embedded, and that the blood they had drawn still oozed to the extent that it hung tear-shaped from the wounds.

Thinking she was some way back, he shouted, 'I reckon ye must be tired, eh?'

She answered with a colourless, 'No,' and snuffled back the mucus threatening to fall.

She was so grateful for his inquiry she seriously wondered whether she dared ask him if he loved her, then controlled this foolishness. He might have told her what he believed she would wish to hear, or not have answered. In any case, there would be occasion enough to ascertain during the years spent together in this expedition to Moreton Bay.

Farther on he began laughing, and called back, 'Do you sing, Ellen?'

'I was never musically inclined.'

Even so, she tried to remember, again out of gratitude, some song which might entertain him, and did come across the words of a ballad she and her mother-in-law had practised on a wet and empty afternoon. (Old Mrs Roxburgh enjoyed dabbling her fingers in the keyboard, and derived an almost unbridled pleasure from crossing her wrists.)

Ellen Roxburgh sang for her deliverer,

> When first I met thee, warm and young,
> There shone such truth about thee,
> And on thy lips such promise hung,
> I did not dare to doubt thee.
> I saw thee change, yet still relied,
> Still clung with hope the fonder,
> And thought, though false to all beside,
> From me thou couldst not wander.
>
> But go, deceiver! go –
> The heart, whose hopes could make it
> Trust one so false, so low,
> Deserves that thou shouldst break it . . .

Her guide showed no sign of appreciating her attempt at amusing him. He went so far as to spit into a bush they were passing. (Mother Roxburgh had a particular aversion for those of the lower orders who spat.)

When Ellen remembered from farther back,

> Wee Willie Winkie
> Run through the town,
> Opstairs and downstairs
> In 'is nightgown;
> Tappin' at the window,
> Peepin' through the lock,
> 'Time all children's in the bed,
> Past eight o'clock . . .'

She had sung it in a low, shamed, because unmusical voice, but it must have pleased him, for he shouted back, 'Go on! Wotcher stop for?'

She giggled. 'I dun't remember no more – if there was ever more to it.'

They trudged.

To break the monotony and silence, she called, 'It's your turn, Jack.'

He grunted. 'Can't remember. Nothun fit for a lady's ears.'

Again she might have reminded him that she was a lady only by adoption but was either too breathless from the present climb, or perhaps her companion had influenced her in favour of caution.

At the conclusion of their next descent they were received into a straggle of trees which proved to be the outskirts of a thick forest. By contrast with the sun's fire, the dark cool felt downright liquid; moist leaves soothed flesh suffering from martyrdom by thorns as a plaister might have; feet gratefully sank into carpets of humus and hussocks of moss.

It prompted the convict to confess, over the shoulder which carried the net, 'Mab had a sweet voice, but songs was never much in my line.' After a pause of a few yards in the name of delicacy, he brought himself to the point of admitting, 'I could always imitate the bird-calls. That's what led me to take up catchin' as a profession.'

Nothing would have induced her to behave so unprofessionally as to break the silence with a comment. If her mere physical presence might disturb him, the leaf-mould would surely help make it less obtrusive.

Presently he began to demonstrate his talent. From out of the trills, the suspended notes, the lush warbling when bird-vanity seemed to disguise itself as innocent rejoicing, she thought to recognize the thrush.

'I 'ad a little bird-organ I'd carry with me, but didn't use it over-much. I'd say me voice served me better.'

A while farther, in darkest forest, he launched into a prolonged jugging: the sound spilled and glowed around them and would have illuminated worse shades than those through which they were passing. In spite of her exhausted blood and torn feet, everything in fact which might have disposed her to melancholy, she

274

was throbbing with a silent cheerfulness; until, from somewhere
in the distant sunlight, an actual bird announced his presence in a
dry, cynical crackle such as she associated with the country to
which she and the convict were condemned.

Soon after, they came out into the blaze she had learnt to accept
as their normal condition in life.

They marched, and she never dared ask to be informed on the
progress they were making, but assumed that her guide was possessed of knowledge he did not wish to share. Seduced by the
mystery of timelessness, she might have chosen to prolong the
journey rather than face those who would quiz them upon their
unorthodox arrival.

That, she preferred not to think about, since the settlement at
Moreton Bay had begun to exist for her in brick and stone, in dust
and glare, in iron and torment, as though she too, had escaped
from it only yesterday.

He told her one night as they sat warming themselves at the
fire after a dinner of roasted goanna, 'I was never out of hobbles
the years I spent at the settlement. They kept all us lifers in chains.
I forgot what it was to move like a free man, but I noticed more
for bein' slowed up. I reckon I got to know every stone, every
stump, on the tracks round Moreton Bay – the hairs in another
ganger's nose, the corns on the next feet at the treadmill. That
heavy light you been floggin' against all of summer. None of it
you can forget, Ellen.'

She would not.

He said, 'We didn't go without our little luxuries and pleasures.
Some of the coves at the lumber yard – that is where the "better
class", mostly short-sentence men – is put to work at makin'
various articles – nails and bolts like, boots, soap and so on –
some of these beggars might bake a pumpkin and pertater loaf,
and smuggle a lump to our mob if we was in good with 'em. It was
lovely, I can tell yer. And terbaccer. There was one elderly cus-
tomer whose sentence was just on finishin', who they put to shoo
away the cows from the corn down around the point. This codger
– a gentleman by all accounts – used to grow a fair crop of the
weed. 'E'd hide a wad of it under a stone for we gangers to come
across. We'd pass round a pipe and enjoy a coupla puffs while the
overseer was away.'

His usually lifeless eyes shone. 'By Ghost, I could do with a pipe of terbaccer! Or cud to chew.' Deprived of it, he spat in the fire, and ran his tongue over craving lips.

She had noticed before how the more perfect among his teeth were stained brown, as though still influenced by tobacco; the worst of them were rotted stumps.

Now he put his hand on her knee. 'What we've got, Ellen, is often better than what we haven't.'

She did not exactly shudder.

'What is it?' he asked.

'It's cold by this time of evening.' She hoped to have hidden the truth of the matter.

He appeared convinced to the extent of drawing her close; when for days he had not touched her, seeming to have taken a dislike to physical contact, or perhaps remembering his dead mistress.

So she must make amends to him for her passing revulsion. 'Shan't we go inside? We'll find it warmer.'

He said, 'If that is what you want,' and laughed, but gently.

Because it was what she most desired, again she shuddered, and hoped he would interpret it as shivering.

She wanted to be loved. She longed for the vast emptiness of darkness to be filled as she encouraged him to enter her body and pressed her mouth into his, against what she only momentarily remembered as a grille of broken, stained teeth.

What she offered was in some measure, surely, a requital of all he had suffered, as well as remission of her own sins? Of deceit, and lust, and faithlessness. She hoped that if they could prolong their journey to Moreton Bay, if not lose themselves in it for ever, she might, for all her shortcomings, persuade him to believe in true love.

So she cried out, and he redoubled what might have been demonstrations of love. Or was it desperation? After they had fallen apart, exhausted, they continued soothing each other with the hands of hardened criminals.

Again she remembered the teeth, and was driven to kissing his throat, a cheek, a shoulder, one of his nipples, disguising her remorse as tender frenzy.

Because he no longer responded, she asked, 'After Mab – was there no one, Jack, you could bring yourself to love?'

She lay listening for his reply. A wind was ruffling the roof of the hut. There were moments when the thatching failed to protect those inside against a cold interrogation by starlight.

'Nobody at Moreton Bay,' she suggested, 'you was able to form a relationship with?'

Nobody could sound as crude and awkward as Ellen Gluyas.

'There was the women,' he said, 'at the female factory. But who in chains could ever take up with a woman? with the iron eatin' into 'is legs! An' the women – they wasn't chained, but as good as. The poor sluts was never 'ardly let draw breath. They was put to pickin' oakum, an' other occupations. They did the laundry for we men, so far as it was done.'

Her interest was to some degree requited; more when he rolled over and submitted her again to the length and weight of his body.

He grunted, and said, 'I'll tell yer,' when ready to resume the topic they had dropped, 'there was one – an Irishwoman – we'd look at each other. I never got to know 'er bloody name, not even after we was in a position to speak to each other. Some fight shy of askin' or tellin' names – like there are those who'll not tell why they was sentenced or 'ow long they're in for. Oh, some are only too ready to boast – make it sound bigger than it is – like you'll find inderviduals in real life. An' some are all for jemmyin' a cove's secrets out of 'im. But speakin' for meself, I respect delicacy if I reckernize it in others.'

She had never felt more indelicate, but waited, and he continued after moving his hand until it rested in the moist hair between her thighs.

'This woman I see'd often enough. She was one of a party they used to march down early from the female factory to the 'orspital – as we in our gang was trailin' out to hoe along the point, or hull maize, or break stones for road-makin'. These women were nurses, see? though I'd lay a bet none of 'em was in any way experienced before they come to the Colony. They was that rough. Whores among 'em. But here it's a case of a pig in a poke. Anyways, this Irish never missed lookin' in our direction – in mine I was persuaded of course, though the others were shoutin' at 'er. She'd those eyelashes you see on some of the Irish, so thick they look like they're gummed together, or loaded with flies.'

She tried flickering her own lashes in the dark, but could barely persuade herself she still had them; they might have been singed off by the sun, or the rims of her eyelids eroded by privation.

She asked, 'Well?' because his silence was a protracted one.

'That's the way we pass our lives – a mouthful o' pumpkin loaf, a quick draw or chew at the crow-minder's bacca, a try at catchin' sight of what's inside the shifts of a gang of Dublin and Cockney molls. In between the 'ard labour. Or 'arder still when they strip us naked and string us up at the triangles – for the good of our moral 'ealth.'

She flinched.

'I fell down once. I reckon I must of fainted, but I'm still not sure. The surgeon that was standin' by – this was for our general physical well-bein' – kicked me to see if I wasn't dead. I oughter been. When they pulled me to me feet I could 'ardly stagger. This was the worstest experience I ever 'ad of a bastin'. I would of said the bones was showin' through me hide, whether or not. Anyways, the flies got to work on the cuts. I was turned septic. Yairs, I was a brake on the chain-gang, whether at the mill or the stone-bustin'. So this same surgeon – great-'earted, considerin' – ordered me to 'orspital.'

She was clinging to him in horror and disgust: the smell alone, of putrefying flesh (or rotten teeth). But either from abstraction or from conjuring this Irishwoman, he showed no sign of appreciating her sympathy.

'I was deleerious at first. I would not of knowed nobody. The chaplain prayin' – very thoughtful – was about the first thing I saw. One Sunday, as a special treat, the Commandant visits the 'orspital. By now I can take notice – and hate. I can see 'im lookin' at me, out of the corner of an eye like. 'E's brought 'is missus, a pretty little piece with pink roses inside of 'er bonnet. You can see she's off colour, like the patients from their own stench – some of 'em layin' on the boards in their shit, that the nurses is none too willin' ter dispose of. "It's pitiful! What – oh, what can we do for them?" the lady squeaks from be'ind 'er 'ankercher. I felt downright sorry for 'er. Well, you did! She's whisked away pretty smart though, soon as ever she give tongue.'

He remained mumbling awhile on the situation.

'This Irishwoman would wipe my arse. She'd a rough hand.

278

But the eyelashes. "When me strength returns," I tell 'er, "you'll help me, wontcher? Sooner if you 'ear 'em talk of dischargin' me." She made no promise, but I could tell by 'er stance she was dependable. An' that is 'ow I bolted for the last and most successful time from Moreton Bay.'

Her throat had grown bitter from thirst. She would have gone outside to quench it, regardless of whether he had finished his story. Were her promises equal in his mind to the Irishwoman's silence? It tormented her.

'One evenin' she distracted the guard afore they was due to be changed. It'd been a hollycaust of a day. They was leanin' sweaty on their muskets, only thinkin' to be marched off to the barracks to their grub. I climbed the wall with the 'elp of a barrel I'd 'ad me eye on. Even the spikes was of assistance. Though I've a scar or two ter show for it.'

From his tone of voice she thought this must be all, when presently he all but crushed her in what she knew to be gratitude: she was acting as proxy for this Irishwoman of gummed-up lashes; she must not, she did not, feel resentful; she returned his embraces as though she personally deserved them.

It was the woman herself who might have resented, and hearing this Mrs Roxburgh when the fever was abated, 'Well, now you are free Jack, and will remain so if I have anything to do with it.'

He did not answer, perhaps did not hear for the silence which had built up around them.

It did not prevent her hearing the feet approaching from two directions at once. Converging on her, so it seemed. She was lying stretched on the scrolled couch. The striped cerise silk blazed in a sunlight such as Cheltenham had never seen, the gilding of the scrollwork bronzed and blistered by unnatural heat (the gold leaf was in fact peeling like sunburnt skin). She shaded her eyes and rearranged her neck on the bolster as though expecting an assignation. She had shed, she noticed, the fringe of leaves which was her normal dress, and the hair in her thighs appeared to have been formally curled in the same style as the scrolls of the daybed on which she was waiting, on cushions melting into a dark cerise sea.

All around, dust was proliferating amongst the stones. To one side, where the gutter would have lain had this been a street, an evaporated creek had left behind wrinkles of curdled mud. A pair of heifers in milk too early for their years meandered past her, snuffing at the dust for the odd blade of grass until goaded into a lurching run by the flies stinging their rumps.

All this while the feet, she realized, had been approaching.

It was the contingent of women marching under guard from their quarters to the hospital. Their frocks of a coarse, grey-green cloth fitted them shamefully about the breasts and buttocks; their boots were designed only for plodding.

She lay smoothing her nakedness, it could only have been waiting for her lover, under her neck the bolster in sweating cerise. Soon after, he did approach with an assurance which her promises must have stimulated.

But she thought it as well to remind, 'I am the one on whom you depend,' before taking possession of him.

He affirmed, by word as well as physical ardour, that it had not been any but herself, never Mab, and least of all this Irish moll.

As she covered him with her breasts and thighs, lapping him in a passion discovered only in a country of thorns, whips, murderers, thieves, shipwreck, and adulteresses, the gilded day-bed refused to yield, nor yet when one of its legs screamed.

And as the party of women reached them, the gang of male felons, she noticed from round the corners of her kisses, came shambling from the opposite side with an almost sensuous rustle of chains. The women began murmuring. One hostile voice suggested that a poor whore could open her legs as wide as any wealthy harlot. She would listen to no more. And smother her lover rather than allow him to be drawn back into the ritual of chains and licence. But he wrenched his head free just as the fly-ridden Irish lashes paid flickering tribute, not to himself, but to his double in the chain-gang. She was so incensed she started banging against the suddenly petrified bolster the head she had been cosseting.

'Mab!' he screamed in agony.

The light was increasing around them, putting on the iron greys she most dreaded in that they made her more aware of her rags of flesh and physical exhaustion. His grey face was turned towards her, supported in the absence of a pillow by the wishbone of an arm.

'What is it?' he asked.

280

It took her by surprise, because she had thought him still asleep.

'You must have been dreaming,' she replied uneasily.

'I would of said you was the one.'

'Both of us then. Mine was a dream I shall try to forget. Do you also forget yours,' she advised in what sounded like an echo of Mr Austin Roxburgh at his most cranky and most rational.

She lay a little longer in hopes of being allowed to doze, but knew that he would rise at any moment and announce that they must prepare themselves for the day's march.

Whether today's or tomorrow's or yesterday's it was all one by now, a continuous seamless tapestry, its details recurrent and interchangeable. Giant, wooden birds stalked the earth, or paused to consider the similar movements of the apparitions confronting them, or flumped towards safety if some more than usually grotesque gesture destroyed their sense of security.

There was an occasion when she fell down, scattering skywards a cloud of ashen parrots. She would have continued lying on the ground and perhaps become her true self: once the flesh melts, and the skeleton inside it is blessed with its final articulate white, amongst the stones, beneath the hard sky, in this country to which it can at last belong.

But he had got down, and was beating on her skull with his fists. 'Come on, fuck yez!' he was shouting. 'Wotcherthinkwereeerefor? Ter *die*?'

She could not summon breath enough to answer before he had dragged her up and along. They had returned into the timeless frieze, of burning earth, and ghosts, and ghostlier living figures.

That evening he made no attempt to build a shelter or hunt for food. It was he who lay as though dead.

'My love? My darling?' She gathered in her arms this detached object, or rare fruit, his head. 'Jack?' For the moment she was their only strength.

Then they lay apart, as brittle as any other sticks. Had anybody trodden on them, their bones must have snapped, at once and audibly.

The sun was well launched in the sky by the time they awoke. For once neither of them nagged that they ought to press on. Each could have been grateful. There was little positive movement on either side, except when she stretched out the arm nearest him, and he shoved his fingers between hers, but inert and stiff as the cold toast in a rack.

They lay thus, in passive communion, and snoozed, and throbbed, and groaned, and tossed (he yelped once) under a sifting of trees, and ants crawling over their all-but-unfeeling flesh.

The bird-calls must have roused him in the end by playing on submerged memory. The birds themselves rarely became visible, or if they did, were more shadow than creature, their wings a flirt of what might have been leaves instead of feathers. But their voices could not deny their presence, and might even have been celebrating a joy in living.

About noon, after however many days, he sat up, listening awhile, hands hung between gaunt knees, then took the spear on which they depended, and left the place which she supposed they regarded as their camp, roofless and fireless though it was. She noticed him stagger once before she lost sight of him, and experienced a qualm: what if she lost him altogether? If that were possible of one whose will must be stronger than his body. Just as her own will had been so finely tempered by adversity, adversity itself must capitulate in any physical encounter. Or so she was persuaded.

She passed the time coaxing a fire, as she remembered seeing the black women, using sticks and fibre; and waited for him. As she sat beside her fire, and he had not come, the tears ran trickling over her sharp knee-caps and down her filthy shanks. In some degree, the tears were solace for his absence, as well as an expression of the tenderness she felt for him: his wasted arms, cratered cheeks – more than any part of him, the broken teeth which had roused her disgust.

When he reappeared he was carrying what she saw at first as an armful of speckled feathers, until a neck dangling as far as his shins, like the broken spring of a jack-in-the-box, and a pair of claws curled in death, showed her that he had speared one of the giant birds of wooden gait and human demeanour. So a feast was promised.

Preparing for it they did not speak, but communicated by grunts and sniffs; if their hands touched, it was doubtless only accidental. She thought she could detect moral censure directed by the convict at himself for having murdered the human bird, and incidental disapproval of the manner in which she was laying out the corpse. Hunger, she knew, was making her slapdash. While plucking the bird she did more than once tear away strips of bluish skin, the feathers still rooted in them.

Once she was unable to resist draping such a strip around her neck. 'Look, Jack! My feather boa!'

Her own whim made her laugh, then on seeing his mystification she was at once glad that he could not grasp the extent of her frivolity.

Again, while chewing at the tough, though fortunately glutinous, half-roasted meat, she began asking without thought for the consequences, 'When you were with the blacks, did you ever taste –?' but stopped before she had compromised herself.

'Did I ever what?'

'Once,' she mumbled, 'they killed a dugong. It tasted of hog.'

'Nothing unusual about dugong.'

She threw away the bone she had been cleaning. She feared she might be boring him. It was a relief at least to have averted the dangers surrounding her experience of tasting human flesh on a morning the stillness and pearliness of which seemed to set it apart. But with the passing of time she would not have known how to exculpate herself, or convey to the convict the sacramental aspect of what could only appear a repellent and inhuman act. He would not have understood, any more than he had recognized the semblance of a feather boa she had hung frivolously around her neck.

Strengthened by food, he set to work hacking off branches, and built them a shelter according to routine, and they lay inside it as on every night of their life together. But tonight he neither spoke nor touched, and she wondered, if only in a brief, melancholy flash, whether she could sense disgust, either at her behaviour, or even her unspoken thoughts.

The morning which followed was so gently perfect, compounded of birdsong, shifting leaves, and speckled light, she hoped he would not in any way attempt to destroy it; in fact she went so far as to pray that the next stage of the journey to which they were committed might be postponed.

She looked at him to see whether he had intercepted her prayer as sometimes he happened upon her thoughts.

Far from meddling with her thoughts and prayers, he was looking so remote that she more than likely did not exist in the world to which he had withdrawn. It was a state of affairs which her present limpid frame of mind found altogether agreeable. She liked to believe that rest and their feast of emu meat had restored to him what she remembered as authority and strength, and was even persuaded that she saw a nobility transcending the convict's origins and fall from grace, to contradict Garnet Roxburgh's opinion of 'these miscreants, the sweepings of the London streets'. She realized with resentment that in the eyes of her brother-in-law she must stand equally condemned, since unrestricted association with the convict made her his accomplice.

Oh, but the injustice, Mrs Roxburgh might have pleaded in her own defence, in such brutal circumstances.

And she had loved this man, even if she also pitied and needed him. She did still love him.

'Love', the old thing reminded in a more than usually tremulous voice, 'love' is selfless, never sensual. Ellen was unable to contribute to a conversation the subject of which was so vast that it could not be understood except by the instincts.

She raised her arms. It was love, whether selfless or sensual, which had restored the youthful skin to her breasts, the hollow in a smooth, leaf-patterned flank; the tendrils of hair singed off ritually by her black mentors were again stirring in the armpits.

Her face she was unable to see, unless when she turned it towards him, and it became reflected in his.

Illusions of beauty and suspended time increased as the day declined. Birds balanced on trapezes slung between trees grew accustomed to the presence of intruders and descended seemingly by ropes of light. Still in mid-air, some of them were catapulted skywards by anxiety, others landed, flitting and flickering, themselves like brown leaves as they foraged over mould and in the crevices of shed bark.

Growing restless in the later afternoon, she got up and wandered off on her own, without any explicit aim, and burst through the thicket upon a sheet of water strewn with lilies. In this instance the beauty of the flowers conflicted with knowledge acquired during her enslavement by the blacks, but without giving further thought to it, she plunged in, and began diving, groping for the roots as she had seen the native women. However clumsy and inexpert, she was determined to make a contribution by bringing him a meal of lily-roots.

This was how he found her, breathless, goggle-eyed, and half-blinded as she surfaced, hair plastered, shoulders gleaming and rustling with water.

He squatted at the water's edge beside her heap of lily-roots. 'When I rescued a lady,' he shouted, 'I didn't bargain for a *lubra*.'

'Wouldn't go hungry, would ee?' she called. 'Even if tha was a gentleman.'

After which he slipped in, and was wading towards her as she retreated. It was sad they should destroy such a sheet of lilies, but so it must be if they were to become re-united, and this after all was the purpose of the lake: that they might grasp or reject each other at last, bumping, laughing, falling and rising, swallowing mouthfuls of the muddy water.

In the gaps between mangled lily-flesh he made the water fly in her face by cutting at it with the flat of his hand. She could not imitate his boy's trick, but followed suit after a fashion by thumping the surface and throwing clumsy handfuls at him.

He caught her by the slippery wrists, and they kissed, and clung, and released each other, and stumbled out. Their aches were perhaps returning. He stooped and stripped a leech off her.

While they were lying on the bank resting, happily she would have said, her restlessness took her again as her eyes started roving over the branches of a tree a short distance from this sheet of provident water. She remembered how the blacks had fired her to climb a tree, to drag a possum out of a hole, and how, as she grew hardened, she swarmed up trees regularly in search of birds' nests and wild honey. Much of this experience had been difficult and abrasive, when here was a tree furnished with branches almost as a ladder with rungs.

She could not resist it.

Jack the convict, her saviour-lover, must have been dozing. His hand gave like a weakened lock to allow her her freedom. She moved carefully, remembering, when she did not care to remember, that other hand on which she had trodden unintentionally. She did not wish to hurt this sleeping man who depended on her, and whom she truthfully loved.

285

She was soon climbing, breathing deep, planting her spongy, splayed feet on sooty rungs. She was rejoiced by the solitary nature of her undertaking at the same time as it released tremors of guilt from her. She continued climbing, and as she rose the sun struck at her through the foliage furbishing her with the same gold.

'Hey! Ellen!'

Jack Chance too, was climbing, but she hardly dared look back in the direction of the ground. She was afraid of falling. (Or was it the broken hands? the rotted teeth?)

The branches immediately affected by her climb were vibrating and undulating round her like tasselled fans. Together with light and air, they were the allies of her recklessness. She was only half-aware when torn by the spikes with which the black trunk was armed. Once or twice she felt for her girdle of vines to assure herself that it held. At one point she dared glance down, and there was the ring jiggling on its cord, and not so far below her the crown of the convict's head, darkened by water except where a whorl at the centre exposed the tanned scalp beneath.

Her throat contracted, was it from pity alone? The fact that she ' could outclimb the man made her less dependent on him. She experienced a second spasm which she could not pause to interpret; she was far too close to the tree's crest. She had stuck her head out between the branches, and was clinging reeling and breathless before an expanse of haze.

Had she been alone she might have hung there indefinitely, swayed by the tree and her exultancy, but in the circumstances felt bound to warn, 'Better climb no higher, Jack. Between us we may snap something.' The common sense of it made her sound irritable.

He did not accept her advice, but seemed to become more stubbornly determined to stand beside her, or else to bring them down in a simultaneous descent, in a blaze of light and cataract of green, to be driven deep into the earth, still together.

'Jack!' Mrs Roxburgh shouted; it was becoming an order. 'I forbid you! Such foolishness!'

Even so, he would not stop, and in her anger she descended to meet him. She must have stubbed part of his face with a toe, but she did not regret it. She would not have cared had she put out one of the brute's eyes. She had no wish to die – not if her beloved, lawful husband were to expect it of her.

Upon arrival at the convict's level, she panted, 'Do you want to kill us?' At that height the mast between them was still pliant enough to sway, though less alarmingly.

Exertion had dulled his eyes: they had never looked paler, nor more extinct. 'Why – if you love me,' she breathed, 'will you not believe in my gratitude – and love?'

But she could not restore lustre to his eyes; perhaps it was the mention of gratitude. Though running sweat, his skin felt cold, which she now tried to warm, after sidling round the mast, by pressing against him as far as she could, by chafing, moulding with her free hand a flank, a shoulder, the sinews of his neck.

'Jack?' His lips were cold, and at their thinnest.

So Mrs Roxburgh frowned and sighed, and in her distraction looked out through the foliage.

'Why,' she cried, 'that is surely a barn! Or a house, is it? Not that many miles off. Isn't it a ploughed field? Oh, God be praised! It's over!'

Before the tears rushed out of her eyes she had identified the cocoons or maggots which become sheep on consideration by one who has lived amongst them.

'Aw, Gore!' Ellen Gluyas bellowed; and blubbered softer, 'Dear *life*!' She had scarce undone the withy hurdle before they came pushing, scuffling past, their fuzz of wool teazing memory.

He was looking where she had directed his attention. 'That's a farm all right – at several hours walk, I'd say. That's Oakes's, I reckon. And beyond, in the distance, you can see the river. There was never such a vicious snake as Brisbane River.'

His voice might have sounded too flat, too evenly measured, had she given thought to it, but she could not wait to feel the ground under her feet. She slithered down. She was distressed thinking of her hair, still short enough to suggest it had been cropped as punishment for some crime she had committed.

'Do you suppose they'll take us for human beings?' Mrs Roxburgh asked when he had rejoined her.

She could not stop touching her hair, her arms, her lashless eyelids, while he withheld from her the reassurance for which she was hoping. They reached the camp in silence.

Although evening was approaching, it was darker than it should have been; the light, the air foreshowed a storm.

'At least we have food left over,' Mrs Roxburgh pointed out. 'We shall need all our strength for the last lap. Shouldn't we eat before starting?'

'Can't you see there's a storm'll break at any moment?'

'I'm not afraid of storms. There's been too many.' She had begun tearing at the left-over emu. 'Eat!' she commanded. 'There's plenty.'

'I'm not hungry,' he mumbled back.

Although tonight she first adopted a finical attitude towards her food, Mrs Roxburgh was soon gobbling the sinewy meat after wiping off a swarm of ants and any maggots. 'All our strength,' she repeated between mouthfuls.

He sat neither eating nor watching.

'Oh, Jack,' she called from a full mouth, 'you are not – sulking, are you? Or is it the storm? Surely a man cannot be afraid of thunder and lightning?'

He did not trouble to answer.

Remorse pricked her for taunting him when she was pretty sure of the reason for his silence. She could never match his delicacy. *Gluyas's Ellen a regular gobble-gut – and otherways greedy slut.* Self-knowledge caused her first to gulp, then to hiccup unmercifully.

The hiccups became downright violent when she noticed an aged aborigine standing at no great distance. He must have discovered them by accident. Too old and too frightened to effect an immediate retreat he was now fearfully observing them.

Jack Chance lost no time, but tried to make the stranger feel at home by talking with him. The old man replied only by desultory murmurs.

'What does he want?' she rasped between her hiccups.

The convict did not interrupt his attempts at conversation. If the aborigine kept his silence, he appeared gravely entranced by his vision of food.

Presently the convict hacked off part of the carcase with his axe. The old man silently accepted the meat, hid it under his bark shift, and left them by walking backwards.

In her nervous state Mrs Roxburgh was exasperated. 'What did he *say*?'

'We couldn' understand each other good. His tribe is camped farther to the west. So it seems.'

'But we should have held him!' Nobody could accuse her of thinking 'killed' because they could not read her thoughts, or if they were to, she had grown, most understandably, agitated. 'Now he will go back, and they will come and murder us unless we make a start at once.'

He reminded her that the blacks feared to travel by night, and that the storm would make them even less inclined.

She might have been convinced and pacified if her opinion of herself had not sunk so low. It was the hiccups too, which continued to rack her, and the swags of cloud billowing black almost upon the crests of the trees, and the wind which had risen, threatening to snap any but the stoutest trunks. She wished she was still the girl who understood the moods of nature through close association with them, or the lady she had studied to become, acquiring along with manners and a cultivated mind a faith in rational man (whether a condemned felon, or even that fragile gentleman her late husband answered this description, she was not sure). In the circumstances Mrs Roxburgh could only crawl inside a bush shelter and hope that Divine Providence would respect her predicament. She might also have wished to remain alone, but could hear Jack Chance the convict crawling in behind her.

Soon afterwards the wind fell. The rain which took over from it lashed at the dry earth and at the twigs and ineffectual leaves overhead. It was not long before the nakedness of the creatures huddled together inside the hut was completely sluiced.

During a pause in the watery onslaught Mrs Roxburgh ventured, 'We shall never sleep, Jack. We'll be too soaked and wretched for that. It would be more reasonable to push on and reach the farm.'

Curled on his side, he ignored her.

'If there is a moon.' She could not remember how much of a moon they might expect.

What she did see was the lamp standing on a farmhouse sill;

she heard the people getting out of bed, running to the door, welcoming one of their own kind.

She chewed at a thumb-nail until she found herself biting on the quick.

'You're no company,' she complained, 'when we've every reason for celebrating.'

At least the rain had poured itself out; the storm was passing; a steely glimmer instead of total obscurity should have heartened the survivors in the hut.

Mrs Roxburgh had survived so much, she yawned and said, 'I believe I look forward more than anything to my first mouthful of tea – from a porcelain cup.' Then, to jolly her servant, she asked, 'Do you enjoy your tay, Jack?'

He could only bring himself to mump, 'It's too long since I tasted what you'd call tea. At the settlement, 'twas no more 'n green stuff – sticks – if the crowminder ever smuggled us a pinch.'

'What else, then,' she tried again, 'that you can remember? that you will ask for?'

She might have been coaxing her child, and at last, it seemed, she had roused him into taking an interest. 'A dish o' boiled beef. With the wegetables to it. And praps a 'ot dish o' peas in addition.'

He was a simple man, and she could never help but feel fond of him.

She was smiling to herself for her own munificence as much as for the hearty meal her companion conjured up, when he cut her down. 'Askin' is all very well, but receivin',' he reminded, 'is a different matter.'

Whereupon, he broke.

She was alarmed to hear him sobbing like this in the dark and wet. 'But my dear – my darling,' she was pawing at the little child he had become, 'you know I'll make it up to you for all you've suffered. Nobody would do more for you,' she herself was by now crying into the nape of his sopping neck, 'not even Mab.'

She succeeded in forcing him round until he faced her. She was holding him close, against the wet flaps of her withered breasts: her little boy whom she so much pitied in his hopeless distress.

He did in fact nuzzle a moment at a breast, not like an actual child sucking, more as a lamb bunting at the ewe, but recovered himself to expostulate, 'Mab is the reason why I'm 'ere in the Colony.'

'Mab? How?'

'I killed 'er. I slit 'er throat.'

They were shivering, shuddering, in each other's arms.

'That's why I'm doin' me life term.'

'Perhaps there's a reason,' she chattered, 'why you're not to blame.' If there were not, they would have to find one, that no one should accuse her of complicity, in coupling with this murderer.

'There's often reason why the condemned is not to blame, but the law don't always reckernize it – not what it don't see written down.'

His arms tightening around her as though to impress an injustice on her, implicated her more closely with his crime.

'Was she not – true to you?' Mrs Roxburgh not only gasped, she had good reason to hesitate.

'No. She was not. Mab, I found, had took up with a young feller, a sword-swallower – and fire-eater. The night I caught 'em at it, 'e got away. Mab was the one 'oo was outfaced. Praps she thought she could remind me of what she was worth by simply throwin' back the sheet and showin' me 'er wares. She didn't persuade me, as it 'appened. 'Er fancy boy 'ad left behind the tools of 'is trade when 'e made 'imself scarce, and that's 'ow Mab – 'ow both of us struck unlucky.'

The night had quietened, except for a solitary floating bird and sudden freshets from an aftermath of rain.

'Do yer believe I was guilty? Eh?' Her monstrous child was prodding and pummelling at her to hear her pronounce his innocence.

His demands became more peremptory, the wet hands more positively determined on remission.

She thought, and said, 'I believe many have murdered those they love – for less reason.'

At once he removed his hand from her throat, and began plastering her with kisses, wet from rain as well as slobbery with relief.

'There, Ellen! There! I knew we'd understand each other.'

But did they? Now that they were again lovers he might suspect her of faithlessness, and kill her in the night with his little axe.

She wished she might die painlessly, then again knew that death was her last wish. As he grappled her to him in the wet dark she only hoped she might live up to his expectations.

When he had taken his pleasure, he said abruptly, 'Your heart isn't in it, Ellen. It's like as if you'd went dead on me.'

'Oh,' she moaned, 'my bones are aching!'

'Not more, I would of said, than at other times.'

'You mustn't expect too much of me. You know it's Mab you love still.' There was no longer any reason why she should speak with bitterness.

He continued stroking her, but absently.

'The night I finished Mab I didn' know what I was doin' at first. It didn't strike me that the young feller might warn the family where she lodged, of the scot I was in. Or the people might hear of 'emselves and come to look. Not that they did. I reckon the sword-swallower must have scuttled quick an' quiet, glad to be out of a nasty mess. Mab, I dunno. She accepted what was comin' to 'er. She made no sound or move, even when she must of knowed it was the real thing.'

He spoke with a warmth and intensity she had not heard in his voice before, and what he told her, she suspected, he was telling for the first time.

'I stayed on in 'er room, regardless. I couldn't think, only of Mab. It was a poor sort of lodging by most standards. Little enough furnitures. A big dresser, which the family what let the place didn't know what to do with. Mab kept 'er things in the dresser. Apart from that, there wasn't much – a wash-basin, on the floor, for want of a stand – a piss-pot she'd empty out the winder – a chair with its bottom all but gone. I knowed the 'ardness of the bed, but 'adn't always noticed it. That night I learnt every corner of the room by 'eart. And Mab, Ellen. I was never worse in love and she never give 'erself so trustful as on the last night I spent with 'er.'

But it was Ellen's throat he was kissing with renewed passion, and for all the fear, horror, cunning, which had been fluctuating in her since dark, she found herself responding to it. She must keep in mind that tomorrow she would again become Mr Austin Roxburgh's widow, and must plead, not for a murderer, but a man to whom she owed her life.

'That is more of my record, Ellen, than anybody knows. And no doubt you'll hold it against me.'

Mrs Roxburgh could not altogether lie, nor altogether speak the truth. 'I shall remember,' she told him, 'only those parts you wish me to'; since her own hunger for love had returned.

Some while later she heard, 'I come to me senses at last. I knewed I mustn't stay till mornun.'

She had been startled out of a doze, and did not realize at first that the morning to which he referred was none of hers.

'I remembered 'ow a friend of Mab's would come afore daybreak and the two girls start for the market to stock up their baskets with the cresses they sold. I got away easy enough from the 'ouse, and began makin' me way to Putney, till I thought better on it. I bought meself a hoe an' a bull's-eye lantern, and joined the longshoremen. I lost meself in the sewers. Picked up a pretty decent livin' too, from retrievin' articles of value. It's wonderful what goes down the sewers. It's a good life once you get accustomed to the air. An' rats. Rats is worst. They'll set on a man if 'e don't watch out. Their bite goes deeper, and is dirtier, than the bloody cat at Moreton Bay.'

He laughed, and by now she too was able to see it as something of a sombre joke. She was committed to following him through whatever subterranean darkness he led, however foul the unchanging air, however daunting the rustle and splashing of rats. She could not have borne to be bitten, though. She could accustom herself to slime, and would grope through it up to the elbow in search of 'valuable articles', hopefully a sovereign, at least a silver spoon. She only prayed that she might be preserved from ever touching a drowned cat.

'I used to take me haul to a Jew at Stepney who'd give me not above 'alf its worth. But I was in no position to complain. The important thing was to fill me belly and lay low – and keep a little ready cash for greasin' a palm that might turn nasty. There's ale 'ouses at Stepney an' Wappin' where I'd 'ang around – never too long – there was allus the odd face to put you in mind of a peeler on the loose. I'd down me plate of 'ot meat – dumplin's if I was real 'ungry – and shoot the moon. I used to doss in one of the 'ouses along the river which was all that was open to the likes o' me. A regular free for all inside when everyone was laid end to end. Nobody was choosy, least of all the bugs. I'll not mention the women.'

He would not have had to. He could not guess at the extent to which she was taking part. Out of shame, or in hopes of forgiveness, she pressed closer against her innocent protector.

'My downfall,' he said, 'was this cottage at Putney – the prettiest little place you could imagine. And those birds of mine. 'Course I knew it must of been all up with the birds. But was proud of me place. I wanted to take a look at it again. So I walked down one evenin' after dark, and moved in quiet like, with me bull's-eye lantern. The place smelled – well, it smelled dead – of birdshit, and dead birds. They was no more 'n feathered skeletons lyin' on the floors of the cages. All my linnets and finches. I 'ad a pair o' nightingales. Well – in spite of my quiet movements and the bull's-eye lantern, a woman 'oo lives at the corner come an' said she done what she could for the birds till the outlay got too much for 'er. I think she was honest. It was 'er old man I reckon, 'oo blew the gaff. Never liked the look of 'is physog. One o' the long yeller ones. Anyway, the peelers come for me first thing next mornun. Found me settin' in the arbor beside the river. I couldn't get that stink of birds' corpses outer me nostrils. And the river allus appealed to me – right from when I was a boy down from 'Arfordsheer. There's times when the river gets to be the colour of pigeons – both sky an' water. I love that river. Well, they come. It was time, I reckon. What else could I of done?'

He yawned, it sounded with relief for having told it, and must have fallen asleep soon after.

Her vision would not be shaken off. There was the husk of a bird still lying on its back, its claws crisped, amongst the scattered seed, the grit and droppings. The incised eyelids were the last detail to fade. They had detached themselves and were floating, mauve-grey, beneath the arbor, above the pigeon-coloured water.

As she lay batting her eyelids, the magic slide of her dream was replaced by the interior of this leaf hut. It must have been very early, for the light was at its steeliest. During the night the damp had been to some extent dried out by the heat of their bodies. There remained the familiar, if anything stronger, stench of foxes.

Mrs Roxburgh rose as far as the low-pitched roof allowed. She was hunched and aching, but would have felt no less cramped and crippled in more luxurious surroundings. She might have expected to awake to a sense of joy on such a day, or to be carried away by a tumult of excitement, but overall she knew that she was angry with someone, about something.

She began kicking his thigh. 'Wake up!' she shouted. 'At this rate the sun will be up before we're started.'

Anybody must have agreed that the situation called for sternness on Mrs Roxburgh's part, so she kicked again, and hurt a toe. 'Jack? Aw, my Gore!' She could have cried, less for the pain than her failed attempt at dignity and authority. 'The blacks are sure to come,' she persisted at her loudest, 'after being warned by that old man. It will be all up with *me* – if not you, perhaps.'

She administered a last, moderating kick before withdrawing outside.

Still hunched and aching, as though the roof had not left off pressing her head into her shoulders, she knew that her anger was directed at herself. Her greatest strengths were perhaps her cunning and her stubbornness, one of which was possibly provoked only by a man's presence, the other also dependent on him: although she had the will to survive, doubtless she would have succumbed had the convict not dragged her along. Of course he had the strength, the physical strength, until at this late stage in their journey he seemed to be making demands on her for that moral strength she had rashly promised in the beginning.

Now while she stood in the grey morning, chafing her arms and shoulders, it was not the convict she despised; it was her wobbling, moral self, upon which he so much depended. Alarm mingled with exhilaration to cause the shivers, as she contemplated the landscape and the power given to an individual soul to exercise over another.

She could hear him inside the hut, sighing, yawning, hawking, returning unwillingly to life. She regretted kicking him and wondered how she might make amends. He would hardly believe that her anger had not been intended for him when, at the time, herself had not understood.

He joined her at last in the shiversome morning, and she simply said, 'I am sorry.'

'For what?' Such simplicity on his part made it more difficult for her; yet he was not simple, as his life and his survival showed.

'Let's start at once,' she said, 'on this important day.'

At the same time she took his hand and they walked thus for quite a distance. He did not exactly hang back, but today it was she who was leading him, and the hand she held was unresponsive.

'Why sorry?'

He had returned to what she had decided to ignore, hopeful that his simpler side, which did at times predominate, would persuade him to drop the matter. Instead it appeared that his cunning would prevail.

'You was not tryin', Ellen, was you? to excuse yerself for what we been to each other?'

'How can you ask such a thing? Sometimes you're hardly delicate, Jack!' Her neck might have showed the blushes she could feel, had it not been for the accumulation of dirt and a skin become almost as rough as bark; worse than her physical condition was the knowledge that her blushes had been whipped up by a recurrence of anger against herself.

'Oh, I'm no gentleman. I don't allus use the right word. And act as I feel. I would of thought you knowed that by now.'

'Yes indeed, I do!' she answered tight and dry, and with an added effort, or extra tightening, 'I should have thought *you* must know that my affection for you will always make me overlook your faults.'

Because in the course of her embarrassment she had dropped the hand she had been carrying she was now able to force the pace.

And what would others know? she wondered when the distance between them allowed her to indulge in more private thoughts. Even if the pardoned convict respected the laws of decency, would society think to see her reflected in his eyes, or worse still, the convict in hers?

She was marching, or stumbling, into the sun, blinded by it. She could hear him following heavily, more like an animal than a man.

Once she panted over her shoulder, 'Are you sure we are going in the right direction?'

'If we aren't, we're not far out,' he mumbled seemingly at the ground.

She was pretty certain her instincts and her desperation would have taken her in a straight line to the farm they had sighted the evening before, but the strain had begun telling on her.

So she paused and waited for him. 'Are you tired?' she asked, her solicitude mingled with expectancy.

'I'm not by no means fresh.'

The rims were sagging under the bloodshot eyes. How would those who had not known him as a man, leave alone returned his embraces, receive this shambling human scarecrow?

Constant preoccupation with the inevitable made her twitter. 'Do I look a fright, Jack? My awful hair!' It worried her more than her nakedness, for hair is a curtain one may hide behind in an emergency.

'I reckon there'd be those who wouldn' know you.'

He wiped her mouth, and kissed her on it. It would have seemed no more unnatural than on the other occasions had she not been about to re-enter what is commonly referred to as civilization almost as naked as a newborn child.

It was here that Mrs Roxburgh looked down and saw that she had lost the vine she had been wearing as a gesture to propricty; worse by far was the loss of the wedding-ring threaded upon her fringe of leaves.

She began to cry and teeter. 'We must go back! D'you suppawse I left 'n at the waterhole? Or hut?' She could not remember. 'Could only be one place or t'other. My ring!' she moaned.

'You are carryin' on like a imbecile,' he told her.

If she were, she was also too tired, battered, ugly before her time, frivolous even at her best moments, or perhaps but the one against whom circumstance bears a grudge.

So she said, 'You ent ever goin' to understand. My wedding-ring!' and started turning in her tracks.

'What's in a ring that'll bring back yer husband?'

She was already walking away from him; she hated this convicted murderer.

'And ringless didn't prevent you an' me becomin' what we are to each other.'

The truth in his insolence did not make her admit defeat; he had to run after her and start hitting her about the head with his open hand. 'If you wanter be taken by the blacks, then go, and good luck an' riddance to yer!'

She fell down, and he sat beside her, waiting for her to recover her wits.

'You're very often right, Jack. I wish I could always appreciate it.'

He was looking at her with an exhausted helplessness in which she shared.

But roused herself.

'It can't be much farther on,' she said, although the distance they had covered since escaping might prove to be the least part of the journey; she almost hoped it would.

When they were again on their feet she limped forward, taking the lead, as she sensed he expected of her. She must have looked a sight: her lacerated feet were causing her the greatest pain; the damp and cold of the night before were at work in her bones; the sun, as always towards the middle of the day, was becoming their chief torturer. The fluctuations of the landscape before her suggested that she might be launched upon the early stages of a fever.

Soon after, she slowed up, and when he came level, grinned at him with what must have looked ferocious insistence. 'We must help each other, mustn't we? whatever the outcome.'

He answered, 'Yes' with a detachment which hardly recipro-cated the sentiments she had intended; nor did his stare, from behind the curtain of sweat, suggest that she was part of his vision.

Yet a little distance farther they put their arms round each other, as of one accord, hobbling, staggering, on.

She told him, 'Even in mid-summer you could draw a bucket of water from the well under the sycamore that would take the breath out of you. Pa found the well. He had diviner's hands. The twig would bend for me too, but not regular.' She sighed. 'It was the coldest water.'

When here they were, walking over these blazing stones. The bird laughing.

'Did I ever tell you, Jack, how I walked all the way to St Hya's and let meself down into the pool? In they days people went to the saint for all kind of sickness. What I went there for I dun't remember not at this distance. Or if I were cured. I dun't believe a person is ever really cured of what they was born with. Anyway, that is what I think today.'

In fact she was thinking of the engraving in the book she had found in Mr Roxburgh's library, in which the inhabitants were shown escaping from the Cities of the Plain. Whatever had happened the couples were holding to each other as desperately as she and the convict, and every bit as naked. Because of the nakedness she had not asked her husband to explain the situation.

Now, as they escaped from one hell into what might prove a worse, however fulsome their reception at Moreton Bay, this man was leaning on her so heavily she hoped she was not a similar drag. She no longer believed in physical strength; it was the will that counted.

'Do you think you will undertake the voyage Home after we have reached civilization?' Her teeth were clicking like pebbles inside her mouth. 'Or perhaps you would find the associations too painful.' If her grip loosened, her arms slithered papery up and down his ribs. 'Sydney, we are told, is going ahead. I am inclined to advise Sydney. Set yourself up in some safe business with the reward they'll give you. My husband will contribute to it handsomely – of that you may be sure.'

What she was thinking, doing, saying, she did not know – perhaps dying on her feet, had a breath of cool not come at them through a gap in the scrub ahead.

When they emerged from the trees, there was a field with rows of methodically hilled plants, and but a short distance beyond, the house, and the more imposing barn, each built of roughly hewn timber slabs.

'There, you see? Just as we planned!'

In speaking, she turned towards him, but did not recognize Jack Chance the convict: some demon had taken possession of him.

'Ah, Ellen, I can hear 'em settin' up the triangles – in the gateway to the barracks! They'll be waitin' for me!'

Immediately after, he turned, and went loping back into the bush, the strength restored to his skeleton.

Her torn hands were left clawing at the air. 'JACK! Don't leave me! I'd never survive! I'll not cross this field – let alone face the faces.'

But she did. She plodded gravely across the rows of tended

299

plants as though they had been put there, cool and sappy, for the comfort of her feet.

'They are – teddies ?' She sighed unnatural loud before reaching a track which wound down along a hillside towards the barn. Ruts and hoof-prints had set like iron. She fell among the cow-pats and crawled farther, a lopsided action dictated by the ruts, until halted by the barn and a pair of man's boots, the latter serviceable in the extreme, as grey and wrinkled as the earth in which they were planted.

Mrs Roxburgh could not have explained the reason for her being there, or whether she had served a purpose, ever.

8

'*Naked?*' The voice was just discernible; it was a woman's, and of a tone she had not thought to hear again.

She heard shoes approaching, spattering over bare boards, then retreating as soon as a door squealed.

She lay with her head in the dirt because she could not raise it; the flies were busy settling, partly on blood, partly on the moist cow dung with which her arms were smeared.

Then the shoes were returning, the door squealed a second time, and she was enveloped in what could have been a cloak, or simply a coarse blanket.

Mrs Roxburgh was most grateful for whatever it was, even more for the woman's voice. 'There, dear! You are here. Nobody will want to know what 'appened till you're ready to tell.'

Swaddled in the voluminous garment or harsh blanket, as well as what sounded like the woman's genuine concern, she thought she might never want to 'tell' (you cannot tell about fortitude, or death, or love, still less about your own inconstancy).

Mrs Roxburgh said, when she had sufficient control over teeth jaws, limbs, to be able to risk her voice, 'I will only want to sleep and forget,' when she knew from experience that she was aspiring to the impossible.

'That you shall,' the vast woman answered, gathering up her new child.

After which the child was dragged, if solicitously (the owner of the wrinkled boots might have been adding his support; she could not be sure) on this latest stage of her journey.

'We must all help one another,' Mrs Roxburgh giggled as her toes came in agonizing contact with a splintered step, 'mustn't we?' Then she was hoisted over the threshold.

'Yairs, yairs,' the woman agreed; heat and hardship may have flattened the voice but without destroying conviction and kindness.

Mrs Roxburgh bowed her head beneath a weight; in all memory a house had never seemed so stuffy or so dark. With the remote hope of catching a glimpse of sky between twigs she would have glanced upward, but the operation defeated her. Perhaps she would remain for ever downcast, and those who like to think the best might mistake an affliction for humility.

This woman would, who remained all around at the same time as she was giving orders in the distance. 'No, no, Ted! I can bring the tub meself – but not carry the full kettle – and not the bucket of cold neither. We mustn't *scald* the poor soul.'

They had sat her to wait upon what her fingers slowly discovered in the dark to be a leather throne, its woodwork carved, but very roughly, with a leaf-pattern. Was she worthy of her throne? Horsehair pricking through her coarse robe suggested she might never be.

Mortified, she hung her head lower still.

The tub had been dragged towards her, or so it sounded, across the boards. Water hissed furiously on being poured into tin. Over and above her heavy woollen robe, the pains she was suffering, her shame, the love and gratitude she had never adequately expressed to anybody, she was now enveloped in a cloud of steam.

'I do not – think I can – *bear it*!' she cried.

The male boots were retreating as though in fright.

'I'll water it down,' the woman promised. 'You've nothing to fear now, love.'

She would have liked to think so; she would have liked to find the woman's hand and kiss it for a promise made in the face of human experience.

Only the woman, since they were alone together, was too busy disrobing her patient. However silent her nurse's unbelief in what she saw, Mrs Roxburgh heard it.

There began a great soaping, she could smell it, and then a flannelling, which made her suddenly leap, and withdraw unsociably into a corner of her pricking throne.

'There, there! Gently!' said the woman, and modified her actions in accordance. 'What is your name, love?' she asked.

'Ellen.'

'Ellen what?'

There was the slip-slop of dreamy water, the passage of a sweating, soaped flannel.

The woman did not press for an answer. 'I am Mrs Oakes,' she informed instead. 'And my husband – Ted Oakes – was a sergeant in his day. We come here with the first contingent. We was Wilshur folk. Ted received a grant for 'is services, and that is 'ow we is farmin' beyond Brisbane River.

'It's a good life,' she added, in case her patient might not believe.

Ellen Gluyas was only too ready. She sat whimpering in the dark house, moved by all that her senses recalled, through creaking boards and warm flannel, somewhere the smells of milk and smoked bacon, and was it – yes, it was raw wool. Outside, cows' hooves were thudding homeward down a hard path. She thought that she might not be able to endure this onslaught by the present on accumulated memory.

'Will we sit you right in the bath, Ellen?' Mrs Oakes inquired.

Ellen shook her head. She was afraid that, if she spoke, a bubble might shoot out of her mouth instead of words.

'Well, not yet perhaps,' Mrs Oakes agreed. 'Everythin' gradual like.'

She would have been at a loss after that had her patient not informed her, 'I lost my wedding-ring, which I brought almost here, threaded on a vine, carrying it all the way from the wreck.'

Mrs Oakes was at once suspended. 'You're a survivor,' she asked, 'from the wreck we've 'eard tell about? From the *Bristol Maid*?'

It had become too terrible to answer.

'Are you Mrs Roxburgh?' the woman asked.

The patient shook her head. 'You won't persecute me? And string me up to the triangles? No one will believe, but a person is not always guilty of the crimes they's committed.'

'Come, love, you mustn't work yourself into a state. Nobody's goin' to persecute you.'

'Not when I'm guilty? Not wholly – but part.'

In the silence which followed, except for the stirring of water and the squeezing of a flannel, she ventured to add, 'I am not Mrs Roxburgh, whatever you may think. I am Mab, but can't tell you her other name.'

Mrs Oakes must have stolen away, for Ellen overheard soon after, 'When the boys come in, John must take a fresh horse, Ted, and ride to the settlement, and tell as we have a survivor, and ask what we should do. 'Tis the one they call Mrs Roxburgh, an' the poor thing deleerious.'

From the grumbles and the shuffles, Ted Oakes must have wished they had not been saddled with any of this. It was his wife who appeared the sergeant.

'It's our duty,' she reminded, 'and now come and give me a 'and to lift 'er on the bed.'

They hoisted Mab to higher than she had been accustomed. She lay squirming amongst the wool and feathers.

'Do tha want to suffocate me?' she cried.

But settled after a pat or two.

The boys must have returned home. She heard male bodies fling themselves down on benches, questioning, then groaning and protesting, as they slurped at some kind of pottage. She heard fists slammed against a table, and after an interval, the angry hoof beats of a horse urged too abruptly from a walk into a canter.

Mrs Oakes brought a yellow candle, then another, which did not so much illuminate the darkness as obscure any part of the room which lay beyond their vicinity.

'What would you like to your supper?' she asked, as though she might produce any manner of delicacy.

'I don't know,' Mrs Roxburgh replied, fretting her head against the feather pillow. 'If I can remember, my maid will bring me it on a tray.'

Mrs Oakes did not wait, but went and fetched a bowl of something.

'There!'

She spooned a mess, soft, sweet, and bland, into the patient's mouth. It made Ellen cry, even as she masticated and swallowed: she was not equal to the memories it evoked. For that reason she was soon fed, and clamped her jaws together whatever ideas her nurse had.

'This way we'll never get you better.' Mrs Oakes sighed.

She left the room with the tepid bread-and-milk barely touched.

Now that her eyes were more accustomed to the light Mrs Roxburgh took advantage of her nurse's absence to explore the room from where she lay. It was of an altogether gaunt appearance, its walls of unadorned grey slab. As far as she could distinguish, the few sticks of furniture could never have possessed any but the humblest virtues. What might have passed for embellishment was of such a rudimentary nature it must have been done to occupy the craftsman rather than to beautify a chair or cupboard. Because her own furniture came crowding round her, the whole rout of barley-sugar or fluted legs, explosive silks, chiming crystal, under the brooding swags of cynical brocade, she closed her eyes. (In any event, none of it was hers, less than ever since she had elected to go dredging the sewers.)

When her eyes were again opened she noticed between shutters left ajar a face darker than the night around it.

She might have shrieked had not her nurse been standing by the bed.

'Have they come for me?'

'Who?'

'The blacks!'

Mrs Oakes said, 'That is Jemmy. I would trust 'im – and all of our natives – if Ted and the boys were gone a month.'

It was innocence on Mrs Oakes's part. Mrs Roxburgh did not believe she would trust anybody, whatever their colour. She would not trust herself, she thought.

Suddenly she began to shiver. 'Do you suppose they'll be gone a month?'

'Why – no!'

Mrs Oakes latched the shutters after slamming them to.

She felt her patient's brow and went and brought some bitter-tasting stuff.

When she had extricated herself from the relentless and evil-smelling spoon, Mrs Roxburgh gasped, 'My husband was an invalid.'

'Your husband?'

'Yes.'

Mrs Oakes laid the spoon in a saucer.

'Delicate though he was, Mr Roxburgh would have made every effort to save me – had not those blacks murdered him.'

'Tt! Tt!'

'Poor Jack! My dearest husband!'

'Don't fret yourself, pet. I'll stay 'ere beside you. No one will harm you – unless it be a dream. I can't prevent dreams, can I? only break up the attack when I see it takin' place.'

Mrs Oakes was arranging herself on the leather-and-horsehair throne.

Mrs Roxburgh raised herself amongst the feather pillows. 'They've murdered Mr Roxburgh, but will the whites – kill Jack?'

Mrs Oakes decided to doze.

The same limping, waterlogged boat brought them to the shores of morning, Mrs Oakes's large face misshapen from resting on the leather gunwale, Mrs Roxburgh's limbs probably for ever rusted, her lips so tightly gummed she could not masticate the air.

Mrs Roxburgh informed her fellow survivor, 'On most of these islands there's shellfish aplenty, but see that you don't tear your hands. And water – can we but sop up the dew with our handkerchiefs.'

Mrs Oakes was putting up her hair by instinct. 'What I'll bring you will put more heart into you than any rotten whelks – unless you don't *fancy* a fresh egg, an' cup of milk warm from the cow.'

Mrs Roxburgh did not refuse what she felt she should have denied herself, considering.

By the time Mrs Oakes brought her offerings Mrs Roxburgh had persuaded herself that she was justified in accepting them. 'With his spear and net, he need never *starve*, I'm thankful to say. Otherwise, how should I swallow this egg?'

'I don't rightly know, dear,' Mrs Oakes replied; she would have liked to, none the less.

A mouthful of egg revolved on Mrs Roxburgh's tongue as she ruminated on the sounds which reached her: hens drooling at their morning work, hornets vibrant inside a wall, a calf which must have been deprived of the teat. After the nurse withdrew, the patient dozed, while the hours twittered away. If she opened her eyes, nothing was so insignificant that it failed to amaze. She would stare at the whorl in a worn floor-board, the necklace of wax on an extinct candle, a pool of light lying thick and yellow as the egg-yolk of earlier, until drowsiness possessed her afresh.

From the heaviness surrounding her she judged that it must

have been towards noon when she heard the sound of hooves in the yard, and first one, then a second dismounted rider, who proceeded to exchange indistinct remarks.

Whatever was in store for her she hoped she might acquit herself convincingly.

Spurs were soon ajingle in the passage, which shuddered at the same time with what she had come to recognize as her nurse's approach.

Mrs Oakes's honest cheeks were glowing with heat and pleasure, as well as relief. 'This is Lieutenant Cunningham, dear, surgeon to the garrison. Now we can be sure that you will get the best attention this side of Sydney.'

'Mrs Roxburgh?' The young lieutenant's voice rang out in a determined effort to assert his rank and sex.

The gong sounding in her head so bemused her she could not have denied the worst accusation.

The surgeon picked up her wrist which, by that shuttered light, might have been a scroll of sloughed bark. She could feel him slightly trembling. His practical profession's abstract side allowed him, while taking her pulse, to display a certain mystical detachment and avoid looking at the patient's face.

For the moment she was free to investigate her visitor. Where her nurse was red, the doctor was pink, not yet cured by the climate she supposed. There was an edging of white where his neck joined the collar of his tunic. From its glimmering in the darkened room, she took this white band to be skin. It added something unprotected and tender to the young man's general appearance, and this, together with the deferential, slightly tremulous hold on her wrist, led her to suspect that the lieutenant had never yet experienced passion.

At once she grew ashamed of her thought and looked to see whether her nurse had intercepted it, but the room was too dark, and of course, both her attendants too innocent.

It only now occurred to Mrs Roxburgh that self-knowledge might remain a source of embarrassment, even danger.

'More light, please, Mrs Oakes.' It was evident that Lieutenant Cunningham was more at ease with older women and in giving orders to subordinates.

As Mrs Oakes pushed back a shutter the patient winced for the shaft of light which was aimed at her. She might have felt more exposed had she not realized that she must remain a mystery to them: her body, for which they were concerned, was the least part of her.

She lay passive, though one corner of her mouth twitched in the direction of a smile as the surgeon, assisted by Mrs Oakes, carried out his examination.

'Ticklish, are we?' The nurse laughed indulgently.

The doctor frowned. 'Captain Lovell sends his compliments,' Lieutenant Cunningham delivered the message with a formal earnestness not unmixed with personal goodwill, 'and is looking forward to hearing your own account of your adventures as soon as your health is fully restored. I shall see to that,' he assured her, knocking once or twice on her ribs to emphasize his authority, 'and Mrs Oakes,' he was polite enough to add. 'We shall have you on your feet in no time, and bring you down to Moreton Bay.'

Mrs Roxburgh could not envisage it; she cowered. 'My feet would not stand another journey. They are ruins.'

'We shall send a carriage. Well, it's not *sprung*! But the best we can provide.'

'Surely we might be attacked by blacks – or worse, escaped prisoners?'

The lieutenant was amused. 'Don't worry. You'll have a military escort.'

Mrs Roxburgh's distress was not relieved. 'Shall I have to listen to the prisoners' screams as they receive the lash?'

Now it was the surgeon's turn to feel distressed; he had never dealt with a similar situation. 'You'll find the Commandant's a humanitarian, unlike his predecessor, of whom I can see you must have heard.'

'What became of the predecessor?'

The young man had broken out in a sweat; his golden whiskers could not disguise it. 'He met with an accident.'

'Was he murdered? Or simply killed?'

'Better if you don't inquire into painful matters which don't concern you.'

A pulse had begun fluttering in her throat. 'It does concern me – why the good and the bad are in the same boat – and the difference between killing and murder. Until we know, we shan't have justice – only God's mutton for Sunday dinner – those of us who are lucky enough.'

Seeing that she was beside herself, he turned away.

'Do you play at cat's-cradle?' she asked.

Instead of answering, the surgeon produced a selection of medicaments out of a valise he must have unstrapped from his saddle, and after taking the nurse aside, gave his instructions in a low voice.

Then again, in the louder, jollier tones intended to reach the ears of the sick, 'It's chiefly a matter of rest, Mrs Oakes, and nourishment. Mrs Roxburgh is lucky in having a very remarkable constitution. She'll live to a ripe old age, I'd say.'

But Mrs Roxburgh whimpered back, 'What shall I do with a ripe old age? Without my husband?'

Mrs Oakes sucked her teeth, and clucked, 'Dear Lord, how pitiful! But it's only to be expected,' and the amiable young surgeon joined in, 'You'll change your mind, you will see, Mrs Roxburgh. Mrs Lovell herself is organizing a wardrobe. All the ladies are contributing. It will be that much easier now that we know your size and shape.' He checked himself, again embarrassed, but hurried on towards his departure. 'You can rest assured, ma'am, of a warm welcome. We had heard of the wreck of *Bristol Maid* and were shocked to think of what we imagined the loss of everybody else on board.'

'How did you hear?' Mrs Roxburgh asked.

In the end, she could not trust (oh, she should have known!) this hitherto amiable, but too glossy, too fulsome young man.

'We heard from the only known survivor. Of course there may be others still to be discovered, as you have been. I hope there are.'

She looked at him out of eyes which he afterwards failed to describe for the Commandant. 'All dead. Some of them probably eaten. Only the condemned survive.'

At that the surgeon took his leave, but heard the voice muffled by the door which Mrs Oakes had closed behind them. 'I ask nothing for myself. Only a pardon for my poor husband. I am the one who has committed the crime. I think he could not believe in me. For that reason, he ran back.'

It was something at least that stout Mrs Oakes was shaking the house in conducting him away from the sick-room, but the voice of darkness continued faintly pursuing the surgeon. 'Even if Jack is not – destroyed – if he simply lies down and dies – I must give myself up as his murderess.'

That evening the nurse felt so ravaged and exhausted after her duty the night before, as well as the necessary attentions she had lavished on the patient during the day now past, she said to her husband when she had fed him, together with their three voracious sons, 'I'd take it kindly, Ted, if you'd sit up with Mrs Roxburgh tonight. I do believe I'm at the end of me tether – temporary like,' she hastened to assure him.

Ted Oakes, a large man, looked so alarmed his wife might have felt justified in congratulating herself had she been harbouring a grudge against him.

But Mrs Oakes was without malice even when he muttered, 'I dursn't, Emily. What would I do if she wet 'erself?'

'You probberly wouldn't know,' she answered, 'or if she was to tell you, well you'd only have to rouse me i' the room beyond.'

Ted Oakes continued heaving and shaking his enormous form to signify his unwillingness. 'And,' he said, 'if she was to start quizzin' me? I never 'ad no practice at conversin' with a lady.'

'Between ourselves, the poor soul may not be all that of a lady.'

Mrs Oakes did not elaborate, but after she had washed the dishes, and scoured the pan, and he had smoked his second pipe, and she had dosed the patient, and doused the candles, excepting one which she hid behind a little, hitherto useless screen embroidered by Emily herself during a slow courtship, she manoeuvred her victim in the direction of the leather-and-horsehair throne. 'There!' she did not actually command. ''Tis no more than the edge of the battlefield, beside the doorway, hid behind this blessed screen, and call out to me if need be. She, poor thing, wouldn' notice if Jemmy was in your place, she's too heavy with the laudanum prescribed by Mr Cunningham.'

Without waiting for outright refusal Mrs Oakes left her husband to it.

It was an occurrence more alarming than any in Sergeant Oakes's experience, worse even than mutiny at the prisoners' barracks, or when some bolter or other ambushed the captain and they brought his body down from the mountain, the head all bloody where the eyes had been, the cock and ballocks cut off of him. Yet now it was but a still night, in which his son's snores in the adjoining room competed with the stranger's breathing the other side of the flimsy screen.

Were she to wake! Sergeant Oakes was running cold between his flannel and his skin. But might have dozed.

He was roused by a wind which had risen, and which was rustling round the eaves and under any shingles which happened to be loose; or no, it was this woman's voice.

'Is it you, Mr Roxburgh – Austin?'

The sergeant was too terrified to answer.

'Then I know it isn't. Mr Roxburgh had nothing against me. Or has he?' she sighed. 'It is hard to tell what human beings may have done to one another.'

The watcher's flesh would have prickled without benefit of the horsehair with which his chair was stuffed.

'I know who it is,' the woman assured him. 'It's Jack. There's no need to be afraid. Give me your hand at least, my darling. I'll show you. I'll put it where it will warm quickest.'

The watcher writhed to such an extent the flame leaped on the candle the screen was shielding, then subsided almost to extinction before recovering itself.

'Jack?'

Sergeant Oakes cleared his throat. ''Tis not Jack. 'Tis nobody.'

'Don't tell me!' She did not laugh; it must have been the sheet slithering.

When inspiration clapped the sergeant on the shoulder, and he lowered his voice into a whisper more determined than desperate. ''Tis not nobody, neether. 'Tis Mrs Oakes – your nurse.'

The patient seemed satisfied awhile, except she was for ever turning and fretting, and at last went into a lengthy, scarcely sensible rigmarole. 'Poor Pa! I'd knaw your breathin' anywheres. You always was more silence than words. You never knawed me like I knawed me father. Had time to, all they winters, all they sheep 'n teddy-hoen'. We should 'uv drove the few mile on to Tintagel, day we fetched th' 'eifer to Borlase. So I never did see – Tintagel. It was Mr Austin Roxburgh who come. The gentlefolk! I was overlaid with pool de swa. I was plaised as puss for a season.

Not the swansdown. That were black. An' later. They nights were so cold we could 'ear our teeth chatterin' to one another when we kissed. Poor Pa! I loved you too. If you knawed, you wouldn' be skulkin' behind th' old screen.'

Forced to make water at this point, the watcher stole away, but when he returned to his post she was still at it, though less personal, so to say.

'Gee op, Tiger! If you place. We're not op the hill to Zennor.'

And again, 'My ewes idn't penned, and rain comin' as big as cannon-balls by the looks. Shoo! For life's sake, run!'

He shivered to feel it rushing past, the rain, the wool; there was one fleece had thorns in it.

'Oh,' she sighed, 'you have not filled the scuttle, Mattie, or built me a fire which will warm my thoughts.'

His head was near to busting with confusion and sleep.

'Oh, Mrs Daintrey, do you fancy chocolate? Or will it make us liverish?'

She would not let him be.

'Mrs Oakes, your husb'n . . . My husband, Mrs Oakes, had a mole . . .'

Dang me, what will she come at next!

'Ellen can tell a token when she sees one. This one is blacker than any face I ever see'd. The whole world will perish by it. Shut the window, won't you? Oh, please . . . Sergeant . . . fetch your . . . pis-tol . . .'

*

It was Emily leaning over him. He knew her by the scent of her hair. The candle had fizzled out in the socket leaving a smell of cold wax.

'Did she pass the night peaceful?'

He could not tear himself quick enough out of the tormented leather. 'I couldn' say. She slept, I reckon. We both did. But it was a sort of madness, Emily.'

He made straight into the morning he knew, and was soon wiping his hands on the rather greasy rag he used when he rinsed the cows' teats before milking.

Mrs Oakes sent messages to Moreton Bay by one or other of

312

her three sons: Mrs Roxburgh showed every sign of regaining health and strength, though still in no condition to travel. In any event, Mrs Oakes would have been loth to discharge her patient: they had developed a fondness for each other. Mrs Oakes could not think how she would spend her days if the object of her cosseting were taken from her and herself left with the company of men preoccupied with beasts and weather. She would dearly have loved a girl-child, but since she had not been so fortunate, here was this ailing stranger, not without her childish ways.

They were happiest sipping mint tea while looking at mementoes of the Old Country. The yellowed letters and locks of wan hair infused the farmer's wife with a delectable melancholy. 'Sad, isn't they?' She smiled and at the same time wiped an eye.

'Do you regret your life?' Mrs Roxburgh asked.

'No. Why should I? This is where I belong now. It's different for a man, perhaps. A woman, as I see, is more like moss or lichen, that takes to some rock or tree as she takes to her husband. An' that is where we belong.'

'I have no husband – no children. I'm in every respect free.'

Mrs Oakes made haste to encourage her friend. 'But that needn't be the end of the matter!'

Their discourse might have taken an awkward turn had Tim not arrived at the very moment from the settlement with a parcel of clothes sent by Mrs Lovell: 'to try like, for size.'

'Why, they's lovely! Isn't they, Mrs Roxburgh?' Mrs Oakes could not give over rummaging amongst the garments. 'You 'ave to admit people is good.'

There was everything from stays to petticoats, and two dresses, one in black Paramatta out of respect for widowhood, and one less sombre, in garnet silk.

'Now I don't want to go against your feelin's, Mrs Roxburgh, but this is the one which will suit your style of beauty.' Mrs Oakes held up the garnet silk. 'It's real lovely, won't you admit?'

Mrs Roxburgh laughed low. 'I don't know about my "style of beauty", or what will suit it, except to be clothed, I suppose, now that I am returning to the world.'

For the present, she made no special effort to return; the clothes she had been sent she accepted out of necessity rather than with enthusiasm. Since finding her feet, she preferred the old

313

homespun shift provided by the farmer's wife. Clothed in its shapeless drab, she slip-slopped into most corners of this honest house, and was frequently lost in contemplation of a pan of milk or batch of bread, or feeling her way as far as the yard, took stock of whatever it had to offer, a hen for instance, her brood stowed away amongst her feathers, the silly faces of the poddy lambs. Over all, the sun, which she no longer knew whether she should love as the source of life, or hate as the cause and witness of so much suffering and ugliness.

Her own ugliness, physical at least, had begun receding, so she learned by touch and from the images in a distorting mirror, the only looking glass the Oakes possessed. Its depths reflected fluctuating shapes in which she was at first reluctant, then grateful to admit that she detected traces, scarcely of beauty, but of what is known as 'looks'.

On an evening when the light and sounds of life in house and yard were irresistibly benign, Mrs Roxburgh went so far as to drop the old woollen shift and stand fully revealed before the glass. She was at first too amazed to move, but then began to caress herself while uttering little, barely audible, cries of joy and sorrow, not for her own sinuous body, but for those whose embraces had been a shared and loving delight.

When Mrs Oakes came to call her patient to the evening meal she found Mrs Roxburgh standing dressed in the garnet silk.

'There! You see? What did I tell you?' The good woman blushed for her own perspicacity.

Mrs Roxburgh was indeed smouldering and glowing inside the panels of her dress, but at once grew agitated. 'Leave me, please! It was foolishness on my part.'

'But love, I doan' un'erstand! Perfect is perfect, as I see it.'

'I should not have done it. Please, go! I am not ready to be stared at.'

Mrs Oakes could only withdraw, and when Mrs Roxburgh finally appeared she was every bit the widow. The black gave her skin a yellow tinge, and her hair, which had grown long enough by now, she had screwed into an austere knob and fastened at the back of her head.

'Isn't it cold for the time of year?' She had locked her hands together, and was carrying them, thus controlled, in front of her.

314

'If anythin', I'd say it's steamy,' Mrs Oakes replied absently.

The farmer and his three lads subdued their exchange of information out of respect for the widow's dignity and feelings, as she sat amongst them on one of the same hard benches, tasting her soup, and frowning either for some thought of her own or an over-large lump of potato.

She was seated in the shade of a tree, dressed in this same widow's black, brushing biscuit-crumbs from her front, and finishing the last of a glassful of lime cordial, when Lieutenant Cunningham surprised her. The tree of shiny, dark, all but black foliage and spreading habit, was native by appearance, hence belonging to the catalogue of items the surgeon felt bound to dismiss out of loyalty to his origins, yet the rudiments of aesthetic instinct made him pause, if not to enjoy, to wonder at this picture of black competing with black. What made it oddly satisfying was perhaps the air of tranquillity emanating from tree and woman and the light which spangled both.

The patient looked startled on becoming aware of her doctor's presence, as though realizing that a precious convalescence was ended and that the intruder had come only to sentence her to life.

'I was not expecting you,' she said (when in truth she had been expecting him daily) and put up a hand to add to the protection already afforded by the shady tree. '. . . so long since your last visit I took it for granted you had no intention of renewing our relationship.'

The tone of voice was flat and practical enough to contain no trace of grievance or of coquetry.

'Precisely,' the young man replied. 'Since you are fully recovered, there has been no need for my services.'

She moistened her rather thin lips.

'I've come today,' he continued, 'simply to convey the Commandant's regards and tell you what he is arranging for you.'

'I wonder whether I am prepared.' She averted her face behind the no longer protective hand, which was held so stiff he could not help but notice how it trembled.

'Then you must prepare yourself,' he advised as gently as his youth and inexperience conceded.

315

She looked beyond him to a landscape already blurred by heat for a reassurance she did not expect would be forthcoming.

'You would not understand the wrench of parting from my friends the Oakes.' She knew as she spoke that she was offering an untenable excuse.

'But you can't impose on them for ever!' It had not been his purpose to sound so brutal.

That she must agree was obvious; to remain silent would suggest a lapse into childishness, but silent she remained.

It encouraged Lieutenant Cunningham to deliver the message entrusted to him and be done with responsibility. 'Mrs Lovell, I assure you, will see that you want for nothing during your stay at the settlement.'

'I don't believe I can bear to face the prisoners.' Mrs Roxburgh was almost choking on her words.

'As the Commandant's guest you will hardly need to.' Out of necessity and his own embarrassment the lieutenant might have lied.

But it had become increasingly his aim to carry out instructions and escape without delay from this deluded widow and her possibly contagious obsessions; his experience hitherto was of placid wives and fizzing girls.

'On Friday next the Commandant will send a conveyance (I've warned you, ma'am, not to expect a sprung carriage) with military escort as promised, and a lady to keep you company.'

So it would take place, Mrs Roxburgh saw. 'I shall do my best to behave as I am expected to.'

The young lieutenant thought it strange, but only momentarily; it was no longer his affair.

He hurried on. 'I should have thought, Mrs Roxburgh, you would welcome all these plans for your comfort.' The surgeon had spurred himself into an excess of cheerfulness. 'I must also tell you that His Excellency the Governor is looking forward to making your acquaintance and hearing your own account of your adventures when you reach Sydney.'

'His Excellency? At Sydney!' Mrs Roxburgh's ineffectual hand fell to her lap; she might not have felt capable of facing this ultimate in trials.

'I understand the Government revenue cutter,' the lieutenant

316

concluded, 'will be sent for you as soon as it completes another mission.' It was some consolation to him to be sailing under official colours, for he was again troubled by this woman's eyes.

'I must try,' she uttered, low and dry. 'Yes, you are right. If only on account of my petition. I must not forget I am responsible to someone – to all those who have been rejected.'

Lieutenant Cunningham's sang-froid was only restored as he urged his horse along the homeward track regardless of branches whipping and tearing. On rubbing his cheek he realized it must be bleeding from a cut. He laughed with relief and exhilaration, and thrashed his horse to further effort with a switch stripped from a bush in passing.

On Friday next the farmer's wife roused her friend earlier than necessary. So little of what is portentous occurred in Mrs Oakes's life that an event in any way out of the common became something of an emotional disruption. The men would not have admitted to it, but made themselves scarce at daybreak in order to avoid farewells. Sergeant Oakes would never wholly forgive Mrs Roxburgh for the night he had kept watch by her sickbed. As for the sons, language did not convey, except when they grunted, private like, at one another. Still, they would remember her as a phenomenon which had appeared after lambing, in between sowing and reaping, before courtship and marriage. She would remain their glimpse of a never quite ponderable mystery, something more than a woman who had crawled naked out of the scrub into their regular, real lives: Mrs Roxburgh of *Bristol Maid*, the myth their children, sniggering and incredulous, would finally dismiss for being too familiar, yet incomplete.

'There you are, Mrs Roxburgh, dear,' Mrs Oakes announced on the Friday morning, 'I have put up your things.'

They had been made into a clumsy parcel, not that they were her belongings any more than anything ever had been.

The two women sat together awhile on the veranda. They were so attached to each other, and trusting, it was natural that they should hold hands, Mrs Oakes's dry, spongy palm, and Mrs Roxburgh's, which fate had worked upon to the extent that the original plan was long since lost and the future become indecipherable.

317

It did not occur to the farmer's wife to speculate over any of this; to her the hand was simply precious; so she squeezed it, and in some degree to avoid the unavoidable, confided, 'I do declare I forgot to boil up the chickens' mash.'

'Then let us go together,' suggested Mrs Roxburgh, equally unpurposed, 'to do what you forgot.'

But they remained sitting. The morning had become too drowsy. For two pins, this daughter would have laid her head upon the mother's bosomy apron, drawn by its smell of laundering and flour. Mamma had never smelt thus, but of lavender water and violet cachous, and the chalk she continued puffing into the fingers of gloves she did not use after leaving Lady Ottering's service.

Such fragile excuses and delicately scented delusions could hardly hope to survive: the women were startled out of their thoughts by the sudden jingle and champing of metal, grinding of wheels, and soon after, piecemeal voices.

Mrs Oakes grew raucous. ''Tis the carriage, Ellen!' as though it could have been other than what they both feared.

The good woman pounded at such a bat towards the yard the veranda threatened to become disjointed.

Mrs Roxburgh sat forward, hunched against whatever was prepared for her. For the moment this was wrapped in silence and the stench of leather and horses' sweat. Mrs Oakes seemed to have withdrawn from her life; there was nobody to offer guidance to one whom Mrs Roxburgh herself had long accepted as a lost soul.

Somebody was at last approaching, by way of a frail bridge it sounded, suspended over the chasm of silence. The footsteps were not those of her friend. Truly Mrs Oakes had been persuaded to abandon her. Mrs Roxburgh folded her hands in her lap, in one of those attitudes she had learnt and then forgot. If she could but remember her lessons, together with some of the more helpful tags of common prayer.

The stranger's feet were treating the boards not so much with actual disdain as an amused, gliding irony. It was the step of one who might always express disbelief at finding herself where she happened to be.

A not unpleasing, genteel contralto was aimed at the target. 'Mrs Roxburgh? I've come to keep you company on the drive

318

down to the settlement. You may not remember,' the woman, or rather, the indisputable lady reminded, 'we have met before – which makes the occasion – for me at least – a most agreeable coincidence.'

So Mrs Roxburgh could no longer postpone investigating this individual, acquaintance as well as harbinger, and was faced with a figure dressed in brown, finical from the toes of her boots to the bridge of her noticeably cutting nose.

'Do you not recall,' she asked more gently, abashed perhaps by tales she had heard as well as her reception at this humble farm, 'how we met, the day our mutual friends the Merivales paid you the visit, on board ship? Surely you must?' She was reduced to begging.

Out of the turmoil of emotions, of storm and shipwreck, of death and despair, of trust and betrayal, Mrs Roxburgh did begin to recollect the brown woman's accusing nose.

'Yes,' she sighed. 'I do, of course – Miss . . .?' The lady could hardly have lost her maidenhead for frightening off the men or tearing out the entrails of those unwise enough to approach.

'Scrimshaw,' the beak slightly squawked to fill the gap in a deficient memory.

The eyes, dark enough to daunt the casual opponent, were piercing as deep as Mrs Roxburgh's own. Finally the women seemed to understand each other.

Miss Scrimshaw extended a hand firmly encased in brown kid. 'Mrs Roxburgh,' she advised, 'I do not wish to push you unduly, but suggest that for practical reasons we start without delay, to arrive before nightfall. In these parts, as I know from several months residence, one cannot leave too much to chance.'

'I leave it to you,' Mrs Roxburgh murmured, who had spent her whole life in other people's hands.

Miss Scrimshaw hurried on. 'Look!' she exclaimed with such vehemence that the spray flew out of her mouth. 'Mrs Lovell, who is kindness itself, has sent you this.' The emissary began disentangling the string from a cardboard box she carried suspended from her second hand. 'She realized that you were not provided with a bonnet, and did not wish you to travel bareheaded.'

With a conjurer's flourish Miss Scrimshaw whisked out of the box what must have been a woman's last fling at girlhood, a gauzy, but somewhat squashed affair from which the nodding pansies, daisies, or whatever, had been thoughtfully stripped, and replaced by a broad band of crape, the pretty ribbons by crape streamers, and over all a veil, likewise crape.

Miss Scrimshaw bared her teeth to guide the novice towards an enthusiasm she seemed to lack.

Then Mrs Roxburgh agreed, 'Yes, Mrs Lovell is kind, she is most thoughtful,' and settled the bonnet on her head, and drew the veil to disguise her face.

While Miss Scrimshaw was organizing their departure Mrs Roxburgh searched without success for Mrs Oakes. In the end it seemed like almost everything, immaterial.

'Such good people, I understand,' Miss Scrimshaw remarked as they took their places in the unsprung carriage.

Mrs Roxburgh could not answer. The escorts spurred their mounts, and the latter sidled and dropped their dung. Only as they wound their way downhill did she raise her widow's veil to glance back, and there was her friend standing like a crudely modelled statue at one corner of the primitive barn. It struck Mrs Roxburgh that everything which one most respects, and loves, is rapt away too soon and too capriciously. Then the scents of laundering and baking, not to say the smell of boiled mash, rushed back, and she started sneezing.

She lowered her veil, thankfully.

Miss Scrimshaw said, 'There is something in the air. I do so sympathize. I am affected by it regularly. Oh dear yes, what we suffer! But must, I suppose, put up with it.'

So they ground on, and were rolled at dusk along the tracks linking the scattered buildings which composed the settlement at Moreton Bay.

'You see, Mrs Roxburgh, I was correct in my calculations,' Miss Scrimshaw announced and laughed.

Mrs Roxburgh was more than ever glad of the veil falling from the brim of her bonnet. It dimmed lights and concealed thoughts. But would she hear the sounds she most dreaded? For the moment she did not.

The Commandant's house was set in what appeared by twilight a spacious and well-planted garden from which heady, dusk-induced perfumes were wafted through the windows of their bone-breaker of a vehicle. The residence itself, at this hour less a house than a series of illuminations, was revealed as an amorphous sprawl behind jutting verandas, the whole effect suggestive of practical comfort rather than official presumption.

Mrs Roxburgh felt drawn to the house. She would have liked to burrow in without being received, and to remain there unnoticed. But this was not to be. The Commandant himself had been waiting for them, and had come out, and was standing on the steps, a fine figure of an officer, obviously enjoying the power and benefits which the command of a remote but unimportant outpost brings.

Captain Lovell's hand guided his guest out of the carriage and compelled her up the veranda steps. 'You are almost as punctual as Miss Scrimshaw would have wished.' He glanced back in ironic approval at his subaltern, who came as close to a giggle as an Awful Presence might allow herself.

'Come!' he commanded the prisoner. 'Everybody has been waiting to see you.'

'Oh, please!' Mrs Roxburgh protested.

Miss Scrimshaw came to her charge's defence. 'Poor Mrs Roxburgh is fatigued to say the least.'

In the light from the doorway the Commandant's eyes were an enamelled blue; he had the cast of face which might flush and swell, a mouth which might brood whenever thwarted; all of which would have amounted to flaws in another, but added to Captain Lovell's looks.

The looks or flaws were on the verge of displaying themselves when the one who was presumably his wife appeared, surrounded by a clutch of little children, fair-haired, blue-eyed, all of them agog. The mother too, was on the fair side. She made a rather crumpled impression, not unlike the gauzy bonnet which must surely have been hers before handed over to the object of her charity.

'Everybody will want to see her, but not before she has put her feet up.' Mrs Lovell decided with a firmness unexpected in one so frail and evidently harassed. 'Mrs Roxburgh is not on parade, Tom.'

Although he made some show of grumbling and snuffling, the Commandant accepted his rebuke amiably enough. 'To hear your

mother, anybody would think me a tyrant. Wouldn't they, Kate?'
he appealed to the eldest little girl, who considered his question
too foolish to answer.

At the head of her platoon of children, and seconded by the
inevitable Miss Scrimshaw, Mrs Lovell marched their guest to the
room she was to occupy.

'After all you have endured I can imagine that you will appreciate being left alone. Not that you haven't been alone enough,'
Mrs Lovell added, and blushed, 'lost in the bush for months on
end – except for the company of blacks, of course, as we have
heard – and the man who rescued you.' Mrs Lovell blushed
deeper still. 'I mean,' she said, 'a room of your own, with the
comforts civilization can offer, will have its appeal.'

Mrs Roxburgh realized that she was standing stripped before
Mrs Lovell, as she must remain in the eyes of all those who would
review her, worse than stripped, sharing a bark-and-leaf humpy
with a 'miscreant'. To the children, she was of even greater interest: they saw her squatting to defecate on the fringe of a blacks'
encampment. Only the children might visualize her ultimate in
nakedness as she gnawed at a human thighbone in the depths of
the forest. Finally these children might, by their innocence and
candour, help her transcend her self-disgust.

Meanwhile the mother, with renewed tact and kindness, had
produced a jug of barley-water, and a dish of fruit 'from our own
garden'. If Mrs Roxburgh preferred to retire, a servant would
bring a collation to her room. 'Do not think, Mrs Roxburgh, that
my husband, or anybody, expects of you anything you would not
wish. We are so happy to see you alive.'

After which, Mrs Lovell sailed off in her swell of children.

'You should know, my dear,' Miss Scrimshaw reminded, 'that
you are something of a heroine, and must pay the price accordingly.'

'I cannot claim to be what I am not.'

Miss Scrimshaw was too well-bred or too wise to persist.

Mrs Roxburgh was relieved that, thanks to crape, she had been
able to hide her rising distraction until after the spinster had removed herself, when on raising the veil she saw that she had bitten
into her lips, and that the blood was running. Soon after, she
threw herself upon the bed, a bundle of falsehood and charitable

322

clothes, to give way to what was partly guilt, and partly frustrated passion.

She resumed control of herself to admit the servant bearing the cold collation on a tray. She was ravenous, and fell to stuffing herself with ham and mutton alternately, until she got the hiccups. It was the all-too-fat meat, together with her own greed and sensuality.

When at last she slept, she dreamed of a transcendent love which in its bodily form walked just ahead and might ever elude her, at Putney or anywhere else in the actual world.

She awoke early, refreshed to the extent that she imagined herself on a visit to a friend: Mrs Daintrey perhaps, in Gloucestershire? or could it be the visit, much discussed but never paid, to Mrs Aspinall at Hobart Town? She was relieved to dismiss the latter possibility by seeing where she really was.

She rose and, after exploring her room, decided she must wash herself at the wash-stand put there for that purpose. Soap crude by standards other than colonial made her laugh at least as she lathered herself happily. Yes, she was happy. She would have enjoyed dressing her hair in style had there been enough of it.

During the night somebody had removed her weeds and laid out in their place a muslin gown patterned with knots of pansies, or heart's-ease she had heard them called. When she had put on the fresh petticoats she also found, and over them the pretty dress, and finished by tying its sash in cobalt silk, she saw that from being so long without them she had overlooked the stays, and was forced to repair the omission, and make herself seemly.

Already there were signs of life from other quarters: pots dragged across the surface of a kitchen range, the scent of wood-smoke rising, a man's voice giving orders. She hoped she might avoid discovery, and actually did, even by children. She made her descent through the Commandant's garden by natural slopes and artificial terraces, where shaddocks and lemons, bananas and guavas appeared on congenial terms with cabbage- and tea-trees and the stiff cut-outs of native palms. A palm-leaf cut her hand as the result of her looking to it for support.

On reaching the bottom-most terrace she arrived at a flight of stone steps leading down to the muddy river. A white egret stalking in the shallows rose and flapped into the distance. She heard what could have been the crow-minder's rattle on the opposite shore. She looked about her, instinctively and furtively. At such an hour she might have succeeded in making her escape had it not been for the numerous innocent kindnesses she had experienced at Moreton Bay.

Instead she stood awhile enjoying the moist, palpitating air before returning voluntarily to the prison to which she had been sentenced, a lifer from birth.

Halfway up the slope she encountered a deputation consisting of Kate the eldest Lovell, a white-haired boy, and two younger tottery girls.

Kate informed her, 'We've come to find you, Mrs Roxburgh, and bring you to breakfast.' Her speech had the stiffness of formal composition, the others simpering in time with their sister, until at the end of it, everybody burst.

Mrs Roxburgh again received the impression that they visualized her as the naked survivor, who doubtless the moment before had finished defecating behind a clump of their father's bamboos.

So she smoothed her dress before appealing to them, 'You will breakfast with me, I hope, and give me courage to face the morning.'

It was too strange for them to contemplate for long.

One little girl announced very firmly, 'We had our breakfast.'

'We've got our lessons,' the boy told, 'with Miss Scrim. If we don't do them our father will whip us.'

Mrs Roxburgh heard herself, 'It's right, surely, to carry out the tasks you've been set, and to expect punishment if you don't.'

Her too spontaneous moralizing might have depressed her had not the children offered hands and brought her up the last of the slope. They seemed to take sententiousness as much for granted as the surroundings in which they found themselves.

At the end of the morning, after the school-room had disgorged its rabble of relieved children, Miss Scrimshaw came to Mrs Roxburgh's door. 'I should have warned you,' she said, 'Captain Lovell is returning early from the Commissariat, and would like the opportunity of talking to you before we dine. He must write the report for His Excellency.'

'I can hardly refuse him, can I?' Mrs Roxburgh replied.

'That is for you to decide.' Miss Scrimshaw enjoyed the dependence of others but saw to it that they did not abuse the relationship.

'How have you occupied yourself this morning?' she asked with less acerbity.

'I have sat and watched the light changing, and listened to the sounds of an unfamiliar house.'

'In that way also, I expect one can learn something.' Miss Scrimshaw laughed. 'In any case I shall fetch you when the Commandant arrives.'

Without expressing active disapproval she left Mrs Roxburgh to her passive pursuits.

The prisoner had in fact experienced twinges of conscience for her own inactivity. She had been roused from lethargy at one stage by the feeling that somebody was about to pinch or even strike her for not having joined in the search for yams or the chopping of fern-roots. She knew, however, that it was more important to avoid ambush by those endowed with guile. For she heard on and off the footsteps, the voices, of morning callers. Mrs Lovell was entertaining the ladies of the garrison, all of them doubtless kind, and at the same time inquisitive.

And now the Commandant.

He received her standing in the centre of a room which might have impressed had she been more impressionable, and had she not suffered the same fate as the furniture, of covering great distances and ending up battered, scratched, dusty, though still with a hint of having enjoyed more pretentious circumstances. There was a smell of must from a worn, dust-impregnated carpet mingling with the scents of citrus and guava which strayed in from beyond the veranda. Bars of sunlight prevented her distinguishing the less aggressive, original design woven into the threadbare carpet, just as gilt grilles would have deterred her had she been inclined to investigate the rows of rigidly aligned books. But dear life, she had never been bookish unless to please others, and the Commandant would not have been pleased. He frowned, and closed his watch. The family dined at three, she had heard. He would have a good two hours in which to torture his victim if he chose.

At the beginning he was out to charm. 'I trust you are rested,

Mrs Roxburgh?' He smiled at her from under sandy eyebrows, and manoeuvred a heavy, claw-footed chair.

She thanked her adversary. The chair was so wide across its crackled seat that she now sat stranded in the middle of it, gripping for support at carving which she felt had been polished by hands sweating as nervously as hers.

If the Commandant was not exactly nervous he appeared more hesitant than one would have expected in a man of his authority. 'As you must understand, I have my report to write for the Governor, on the circumstances of the wreck, your survival, and recovery. So,' he sighed, digging an elbow into his desk, 'I'd be glad to hear your account, if it will not open wounds which have healed. I would like to think that this can be – *achieved* without causing you unnecessary distress.' He was looking somewhat congested for the effort, and although he had renewed his smile it was directed at the blank sheet of paper before him.

'Nobody – nothing – could distress me – not by now, Captain Lovell.' If her claim was brazen, at least she would not look in his direction; it was the line of his cheek, his rather coarse wrists, which might open old wounds.

'Then,' he said, 'tell me in your own words what happened.' She could scarcely accuse him of not being liberal.

'Well,' she considered, lowering her head, tasting her underlip with her tongue, 'we were shipwrecked as you know – as you have heard from this other survivor.' She felt herself perspiring intolerably. 'What can I tell you,' she gasped, 'if you already know?' It was not an argument to satisfy a man.

She must not look at the Commandant, but reserve her eyes as weapons in some passage at arms which called for greater subtlety. Instead she sat staring at her own hands held at the level of the cobalt sash, amongst the heart's-ease, as though she had the stomach-ache, and no matter if he thought her feeble-minded.

The Commandant was contained by patience. 'It's by hearing different versions of the same incident that we arrive at the truth, Mrs Roxburgh, in any court.'

'Oh,' she cried, 'I was never in court. Perhaps that's why I was never sure whether I'd arrived at the truth – whatever the incident, Captain Lovell. For all that, I survived.'

She would have liked to glance at him, but thought that she might not have the strength.

She continued, while hanging her head. 'My husband was killed. Yes, that is truth – a wound which perhaps will never heal. The blood gushing as I pulled the spear from his throat! I shall always remember the glare, the flies.'

The Commandant was making judicious notes.

'Then the blacks marched the crew away.' She wet her lips; she could not resist asking what hitherto she had not wished to know, 'I wonder who is your other survivor?'

But the Commandant was conducting the court martial of a woman, one as disturbing as she was disturbed. 'The blacks – did they treat you kindly?' He spoke with what amounted to delicacy in anyone so exalted, and at the same time, coarse-boned.

She must not look at him, as she had decided in the beginning.

'Well,' she began afresh, but paused, 'they were not unkindly – considering they had been fired on. Oh yes, poor Mr Courtney opened fire – the first mate. Several members of the tribe were killed. So they killed Captain Purdew – and Mr Roxburgh – in retaliation. No,' she added, 'I would say they treated me – reasonably – well. Of course they beat and pinched, and held fire-sticks under me, to frighten me into climbing trees for 'possums and maggoty old honey. There was also a disgusting child they wanted me to suckle, but I could not. I was dried off. I could not have fed the one I lost at sea.'

It was the Commandant who was disgusted; she could sense that.

'Oh, I don't blame the blacks! The child died. It would have done, even had it not been disgusting. So I was not to blame, neither. Now was I?'

He kept a silence through which she heard the action of his quill.

'No one is to blame, and everybody, for whatever happens.' Further than that she could not lumber.

'What else?'

They had arrived at the tortuous part of the journey.

'Oh,' she raised her head, her throat, in which the veins would be standing out she suspected; she drew in her nostrils until they must be looking all gristle, 'the black children! The children were not as spiteful as they had been taught by their elders. We would play at *purru purru . . .*'

'*Purru purru?*' Captain Lovell sounded his gravest, his most official.

'Ball,' she answered. 'We used to skip, too. I sang to them.'

'What did you sing?' It was as though he were determined to commit an indecency.

She could not remember, so she resolved to forgive him. 'Some nonsense or other.' (Not *Go, deceiver, go!* that was later, surely? and to someone else.) 'It was while we were crossing to the mainland, and the children were frightened by the rough sea. Yes,' she decided, 'it must have been then.'

'And when you arrived?'

By now it was the middle of the day. The Commandant was sweating; it trickled down over the neck of his tunic, which he was too correct to unhook. Mrs Roxburgh's muslin was damp; the cobalt sash showed a high-water mark.

'Well, you see, Captain Lovell,' she hastened to appease him while it was still easy, 'it was the gathering of the tribes – for corroboree.'

'Did you take part in their corroboree?'

'As much as a woman is expected to. It is the men who perform. The women only accompany them, by chanting, and by slapping on their thighs. Oh yes, I joined in, because I was one of them.'

'Did you understand what you were supposed to be singing?'

'Of course not. I was not with the tribe long enough to pick up more than a few words in common use. But surely it is possible to understand what words are about without understanding the words themselves?'

The Commandant more than likely did not understand, but was writing. Mrs Roxburgh suspected that what she understood had little to do with words, in spite of tuition from Mr Roxburgh and his mother. So it would be throughout her life.

'There was one morning,' she remembered, 'very early, when I came across some of the members of my tribe, in a forest clearing. I never understood so deeply, I believe, as then.'

'What were the blacks doing?'

'It was a secret ceremony. They were angry with me and hurried me away.'

'Because you saw what they were at?'

'It was too private. For me too, I realized later. A kind of communion.'

'If it made such an impression on you, I should have thought you'd be able to describe it.'

'Oh, no!' She lowered the eyes she had raised for an instant in exaltation.

The Commandant threw down his quill, and sat back so abruptly the chair and his heels grated on the threadbare carpet.

'To return to our more factual narrative, it was at the corroboree, was it not? that you first saw the escaped convict who, according to my informants, rescued you.'

'Yes,' she said, and added, 'I am sorry that friends I hold dear should have informed against me.'

The Commandant could not suppress his irritation. 'Isn't it natural for human beings to exchange information on matters of importance?'

'Yes, and I am unreasonable, I know. Mr Roxburgh often suggested that.' She smiled at her hands as they tightened on each other against the sash.

'This man – the convict,' Captain Lovell suggested, 'would have told you his name – or *a* name – I don't doubt.'

'Yes. Chance. Jack Chance.' She pronounced it softly because she could not remember ever having spoken it before in its entirety.

The Commandant echoed it, little above a whisper. His quill engraved, then embellished it, but in the margin, because he might not have accepted the name.

'Don't you believe in him?' she asked sharply.

'There was a man called Chance who bolted, but before my time. I have it in my predecessor's record.'

Captain Lovell continued embellishing the name 'Chance' with curlicues. 'How did he treat you?'

'With the greatest kindness and consideration.'

'His reputation is not of the best.'

'Oh, I know he is a crude man. But I am used to crudeness, Captain Lovell.'

She looked at him to reinforce her assertion, and his blue eyes snapped at her.

'Haven't I lived among the blacks? But had I not, to live is to experience crudeness.'

'From what I have heard of the Roxburgh family, I should have thought, Mrs Roxburgh, that you had led a sheltered life.'

'The mind is not always sheltered, Captain Lovell, from its own thoughts and imaginings.'

It must have sounded eccentric. She could read distaste in the expression of his mouth; he was only used, no doubt, to sweetness and compliance in a woman.

'The man Chance,' he asked, 'how is it that, after accompanying you on this arduous journey, in what can be termed a gallant rescue, he ran back into the bush on reaching the Oakes's farm?'

'He was frightened, of course.'

'But could he not imagine that his action might weigh in his favour, perhaps even earn him a pardon?'

'I promised him a pardon.'

The Commandant frowned.

'But he was still frightened, naturally,' she said, 'after all he suffered. The scars are in his back.'

'Those were from the old days,' Captain Lovell grumbled.

Then he looked at his witness and asked, 'You did not by any chance discourage him, did you? I have known men frightened by forceful women.'

'He is a forceful man. He cannot have been discouraged by any action on my part. I promised him a pardon,' she insisted.

'My dear Mrs Roxburgh, the pardon is for His Excellency to grant, upon my own recommendation.'

She had begun twisting her hands. 'But I promised it, Captain Lovell! I have nothing left in life, not even my wedding-ring, which I preserved till the last day – and lost. Nothing, I tell you! It is for this reason – and surely I deserve some reward for all I have undergone? for this that I insist on a pardon for my rescuer.'

After she had subsided into unhappy silence the Commandant seemed to be listening for reverberations.

'Perhaps you do not realize, Mrs Roxburgh, that the man was convicted for the brutal murder of his mistress, herself a slut of the lowest order.'

'Oh, Captain Lovell,' she cried, 'most of us are guilty of brutal acts, if not actual murder. Don't condemn him simply for that.

330

He is also a man who has suffered the brutality of life and been broken by it.'

She could hear, she could feel herself, gasping with the desperation of the farmyard in which she was reared: the calf with the knife at its throat; the hissing goose whose neck she herself had severed; more relevant, and worse, she could see the terror in Jack Chance's eyes, and the mouth on which her own had failed to impress that loving-kindness which inspires trust.

The Commandant poured his prisoner a generous quantity of brandy. 'You are carried away by a tender heart,' he decided with approval, to which was added the slightest dash of irony.

'Duty,' she protested, 'will not allow me to keep silent.'

Would his sense of irony persuade him to question her claim? She was almost too shaken by emotion, as well as too fogged by brandy, to care which direction her defence took. The tumbler with only the dregs left was hanging aslant in her hand.

When suddenly she asked, because it had been nagging at her, 'Who is the other survivor?'

'A fellow named Pilcher, the second mate, who was in command of the pinnace when it became separated from the longboat in a storm. Do you remember?'

'I remember Mr Pilcher the second mate.'

'But the circumstances in which you last saw him?'

'Yes, I expect I do. But it was all storms for weeks on end – and dreams – or nightmares. I believe I was delirious for much of the time, from drinking sea-water – and the birth of my little boy. Had not Mr Roxburgh sustained me throughout, I would not be here.'

She had stood the empty tumbler on the desk, and sat twisting the invisible band on her ring-finger.

'I think,' said the Commandant with cruel persistence, 'I should bring you together with your fellow survivor. He is a little unhinged, poor wretch. He is working at present as a clerk at the Commissariat, and shows no inclination to proceed south or be forwarded home. Yes, I think you should meet. The exchange of common experiences may exorcize some of the ghosts in your recollections.' The Commandant was standing above his victim, looking down upon her with what could have been scientific detachment or vindictiveness, though if taken to task, he might have professed solicitude.

'I am willing to see Mr Pilcher and hear his story.'

The Commandant sprung open his watch, and at the same moment, a gong sounded in the outer regions. 'Excellent!' he declared. 'I hope you are as ready as I for dinner. I am told there is a suckling pig. Or chaudfroid of fowl if you prefer it. And sillabub.'

'Thank you, I have no appetite. I would rather go to my room.'

'But will receive Pilcher this evening?'

'If you and Mr Pilcher wish it.'

Mrs Lovell herself tried to tempt their guest to a very small helping of the chaudfroid, or at least a glass of sillabub, both of which she refused.

Mrs Roxburgh might have dozed had she not been lying so straight and tense in anticipation of the threatened visit. There were intimations of thunder besides, followed by a plashing of rain, a sluicing of leaves in the darkened garden. As aftermath, a scent of citrus and laid dust invaded the room. Even the light seemed to have been washed: it wore a pronounced, lemon gloss; the shadows were a bluer black.

Presently Miss Scrimshaw came to suggest she join them at the tea-table. 'Your spirits will be lowered,' she warned, 'lying here alone in the dark.'

But Mrs Roxburgh declined tea. She casually remarked that she was still 'half-expecting a visit'.

Miss Scrimshaw's discretion was severely taxed, but she thought to reply, 'Perhaps the person did not care to set out through the storm, and now that it is late, has decided to postpone coming. Your friend's company should be doubly agreeable to-morrow.'

Mrs Roxburgh did not enlighten the spinster on her friend's sex or the nature of the visit, and Miss Scrimshaw, who flourished on mystery, went away burgeoning.

The day following the visit that failed to materialize, Mrs Roxburgh rose even earlier than on her first morning at Moreton Bay and dressed herself in her black Paramatta, which those who served her had returned brushed and decent to her room. During the night she had conceived the notion of taking a solitary walk to acquaint herself with the neighbourhood before human activities influenced its character. That her own mind might influence what she saw and heard was a possibility she easily dismissed.

All was much as she had experienced already in company with Jack Chance the convict: the dust, the stones, the ruts over and against which she was soon toiling; the native trees scrubbier and more deformed for their contact with intrusive man; stone and brick houses in sturdy imitation of a tradition, together with more slapdash hovels in currency daub-and-wattle. It was the hour before arthritic age and inquisitive innocence begin to stir; the humblest dwelling still buzzed with the respectability conferred by sleep. Catching sight of the stranger, a sow with a string of squealing piglets galloped for safety, and a red, cankered dog snapped at the folds in a trailing skirt.

Upon climbing the hill she reached the inactive wind- or treadmill, round about it a litter of corn-cobs stripped of grain, near by a hand-cart which had lost a wheel. Children might have left off playing here had the scale of things been a lesser one and her knowledge incomplete. She crossed the trampled grass separating her from the stationary mill, to touch nail-heads which feet had polished in the worn boards, and become re-acquainted with some of the stations of purgatory.

A bird was calling; or was it warning?

It did in fact call her attention to voices at the foot of the hill, their volume amplified by morning stillness. They were men's voices, growing louder, more cacophonous, as they approached the summit. Sometimes the babble was cut by the terser tone of orders, or again, by curses, in a different key. Mrs Roxburgh should not have felt panic-stricken; it was what she had wished in her heart, she realized: however painful the collision might prove, she was drawn to the companions of the man she may have wronged.

The gang mounting the hill through the scrub were now so close she distinctly heard the clanking of irons, the rustle of chains. Her impulse was to draw aside and remain the unseen observer, but fear, remorse, or some hellish desire to participate again in what she already knew through the experience of suffering, caused her to stand rooted to the track where the men would pass.

Heads were bowed as they struggled on towards her, so that they were not immediately faced with what must at a glance appear an illusion. The two guards preceding the chain-gang were the first to catch sight of the woman in black. They stiffened and gasped, jerking their muskets to the ready as though preparing to defend the prisoners against a rescue. Then the leaders of the convict file threw up their heads like so many dun-coloured animals. Startled into an abrupt halt, they could not avoid jolting their dependants into disarray; curses flew as body thumped against body and head cannoned off head.

Mrs Roxburgh roused herself to draw aside. All down the line, faces were feeding on the apparition. The mouth of one bumpkin of a guard was quivering in his fiery cheeks; another, of less sanguine cast, had buttoned up his lips in disapproval or disbelief. The prisoners' expressions showed them either devouring the present with overt lust, or else exhuming the buried past with despair for what they re-discovered. As for Mrs Roxburgh, she was united in one terrible spasm with this rabble of men, their skins leathery above the unkempt whiskers, eyes glaring with hatred when not blurred by cataracts of grief, hands pared to the bone by hardship. She recognized it all, and over it, that familiar stench of foxes. If there were scars, at least they were hidden by the felons' dress; nor would she feel their bodies shudder while asleep in her arms, though the rustle of never-motionless chains conveyed a distrust which no passion or tenderness of hers could ever help exorcize.

Then she realized that an uproar had broken out around her; the bush kindled, crackled and spat beneath the shower of oaths, ribaldry, laughter, and gusts of frustrated desire to which it was being subjected.

One fellow shouted, 'I jobbed it inter better than 'er at 'Ounslow, an' got the pox for it.'

'Ay, you can never tell where the pox lies.'

'It could lie with me, I don't mind tellin' yer, Billy, if there was any chance uv runnin' the colours up the bloody flagstaff.'

One of the guards had taken his musket-stock to the prisoners.

'This is no place, ma'am, for a lady,' the corporal-in-charge advised her in a wavering voice. 'Better go down to the settlemen'.'

334

Mrs Roxburgh regretted having forgotten her veil. She hardly knew what she murmured in reply to the corporal. Whatever her feeble remark, it was drowned in the torrents of abuse, warnings, simulated farts, and above all, the sound of blows. She started walking as quickly and smoothly as her skirt and the sticks littering her path allowed, but had not escaped the length of the linked prison file when one of those she was passing, turned and spat. She felt his spittle trickling down her cheek.

The increased hullabaloo might have humiliated her worse had it not been partly her intent to submit herself to humiliation as punishment for her omissions and shortcomings. She was punished and humiliated none the less. As she dragged her skirt over the stones and tufts of uncharitable grass, it saddened her to think she might never become acceptable to either of the two incompatible worlds even as they might never accept to merge.

She went on, wiping the man's spittle from her face, and after negotiating a sluggish creek, regained what the inhabitants doubtless regarded as the streets of their township. By now she should have felt liberated from her own morbid thoughts and intentions, free to return to the Commandant's hospitable house, its citrus groves and pretty children, had she not sensed the approach of a second trial, as unavoidable as the first in that it was of her heart's choosing.

What she presently perceived could only be the party of women prisoners marching from the female factory towards the hospital where they worked by day. Their progress was less regimented than that of the male felons. The soldiers accompanying them were but token guards. In one instance she suspected the man's compliance to be the return for services rendered. The fellow strolled rather than marched, chatting to the girl beside him with the familiarity and lack of further expectation which informs many a marriage. There was no immediate evidence of the rampant hatred and despair which distinguished the male prisoners from human beings, but as the women drew closer, in their dust-toned, ill-fitting uniforms, their appearance grew more slovenly, their pace ragged and out-of-step. Their laughter was doubtless directed at the stranger; an individual giggle, rising shrill above the general mirth, made it more pointed.

Mrs Roxburgh bowed her head. Her meeting with the women

could prove more disturbing than her brush with the men, since women, particularly those who have been persecuted, are more resentful of another woman's intercepting their thoughts and mingling with their fantasies. The women would no doubt dread that she, a stranger and a *lady*, should visualize their more obscene dreams, their substitutes for frustrated love, the tenderness shared with a husband in his absence, or their ploys to attract a current lover.

The distance separating her from the women was so diminished that neither side could avoid appraisal. For her part, she could see that some of the faces had died, while the life which remained in others showed every sign of hopelessness, brazen defiance, or passive depravity. The women stared back at their accuser (she could only be that) from eyes bolstered on pouches of skin, in bloated cheeks, their mouths hinged on incredulity and bitterness. Any remnant of sweetness or beauty looked as though it depended on hypocrisy for its continued existence.

One young woman of noticeably Irish countenance, black, frowzy ringlets, and lashes so thick they could have been beaded with flies, greeted the stranger jauntily. 'Mornun, mum. The freedom of a walk is somethun I reckon we all of us can share and enjoy, on such a day.'

The others, with the exception of those who had died, hooted in appreciation of their companion's audacity. The guards laughed with them. Though her words had the sting of irony, she spoke with such immense good humour no one could accuse her of insolence.

Mrs Roxburgh hesitated at the side of the road. She would have liked to speak to the questionably cheerful Irishwoman, to have taken her hands and held them in hers, and after some fashion conveyed to her, how they had both aspired and lost; when the loose ranks were jostled forward, and the woman's last glance, bereft, yet curiously consolatory, suggested that they might have understood each other.

The prisoners marched on in the awful abandon of their coarse frocks, wrinkled boots ploughing the dust, while Mrs Roxburgh humbly turned in the direction of the Commandant's 'residence'.

Here an immediately recognizable figure was emerging from the gates. True to her nature, Miss Scrimshaw was investigating

336

something or other. In her brown gown, her padded hair, her bobbled shawl, she stood looking out from the lee of a straight hand.

'Oh,' she cried on sighting her renegade friend, 'you should never venture out unaccompanied at Moreton Bay. If you wish to take the air Mrs Lovell will have them harness the horses to the carriage, provided the hour is a reasonable one.'

'As you must see, Miss Scrimshaw,' Mrs Roxburgh pointed out, 'I have come to no harm.'

Appropriating her friend's arm the spinster may have remained uncertain. Probably no part of Mrs Roxburgh was actually broken, but Miss Scrimshaw herself had sustained many a spiritual bruise in spite of the toughness of seasoned leather.

'In any case,' she said, on guiding Mrs Roxburgh into the safety of the grounds, 'I am glad you have come. I have good news for you. Your acquaintance is bound to be here this evening. Whatever made him postpone his visit the Commandant will see to it that Mr Pilcher pays his respects.'

Then she looked at Mrs Roxburgh, to receive approval, or to see her suspicions justified by the latter's reaction. But Mrs Roxburgh did not utter, while her expression remained so withdrawn the face might have been sheltering behind the widow's veil, which, Miss Scrimshaw noticed, her friend had omitted to wear.

After the profuse dinner customary at the residence the Commandant approached their guest, smiling as though for a secret between them, 'The individual of whom we spoke will be here by half-past five, I'd say,' he opened his repeater and frowned at it, 'or six at the latest.' He closed the watch, and smiled again, gratuitously it seemed to Mrs Roxburgh. 'He'll not shirk his duty on this occasion.'

One of the smaller girls inquired, 'Is Mrs Roxbry goin' to whip Mr Pilcher?'

'What a thing to imagine!' The mother blushed for her child's supposition.

'Then why does he have to be forced?' wondered Totty.

'But they're old friends. There's no question of his being *forced*!'

Mrs Lovell was so embarrassed she lowered her voice to inform

Mrs Roxburgh, 'You shall receive him, my dear, in the *little* parlour.' Although intended as a kindness, it made the situation darker and stimulated curiosity. 'There you will be both comfortable and – private. Unless you would care for Miss Scrimshaw to be present.'

Mrs Roxburgh politely implied that she would rather dispense with Miss Scrimshaw's presence.

She might have wondered how to pass the time before the visit had she not realized the distasteful event must soon take place. So she arranged herself in the little parlour, and hoped that Miss Scrimshaw would not come offering advice beforehand.

The discreet lady had taken her cue, however: when the time came she simply announced, 'Here is your visitor'; and left them to it.

Mrs Roxburgh had decided not to rise as her caller entered, but did so at once when the moment occurred, for she could hardly condemn an individual whose past was not more dubious than her own.

So here she was, every bit like a gentlewoman afflicted by some nervous disorder, wetting her lips and dabbing at them spasmodically with one of the handkerchiefs provided for her. 'Won't you sit down, Mr Pilcher?' the uneasy gentlewoman invited. 'I am so glad you have been able to come. This is perhaps the most comfortable chair. Or do you prefer something more upright?'

She winced for the rheumatics in her shoulder, which had not bothered her since her recovery from the inordinate journey, and which no doubt were the result of sleeping naked on damp ground. Of 'all that', Mr Pilcher could not have known, although on the other hand he might. There was no knowing what her eyes might have given away.

But the mate did not seem aware of any imposture. His own condition was more important, the inner life he must be living; and then he more than likely saw her as one who would become his accuser.

'Thank you,' he said when they were at last painfully seated opposite each other.

Pilcher had aged, to put it kindly. It made her touch her hair, and look for a glass which did not immediately offer itself. He was so thin as to look transparent in places, and even more deeply lined than before. She was not sure, but he might have suffered a seizure.

'At least one can see,' she said in a tone adopted from some patroness or a mother-in-law, 'you're in excellent health, Mr Pilcher. I am so glad – so very glad.'

He hung his head, the hair cropped short, like a convict's, down to a pepper-and-salt stubble.

He admitted formally, 'I can't complain,' his voice without any of the venom she remembered.

'I would like to offer you something, but am myself no more than a guest of the house.' Thus absolved, the great lady dangled a wrist over the arm of her chair.

'There is nothing,' he assured her, 'nothing I need.'

Now that both had done their duty by society, and established their bona fides as far as is humanly possible, Mrs Roxburgh looked at her caller and made the decidedly brutal request, 'You must tell me all that has happened to you since last we met.'

She meant to encourage her visitor, or anyway, in some measure, but on hearing her own voice was reminded of the black swans encountered while living with her adoptive tribe. It was the same hissing as when the birds arched their necks, and extended their bills, spatulate and crimson, making ready to protect themselves against the intruder.

Although Mrs Roxburgh felt, and must have looked, pale in her black, she wondered how Mr Pilcher found her, but could not tell since he had launched into a narrative.

'You'll remember after we put out from the cay – after our attempt at caulking – the storm got up and separated our two boats.'

Mrs Roxburgh realized he did not intend her to answer, but she did. 'Yes,' she said gravely, 'I could not easily forget.'

Like a good navigator, Mr Pilcher would not allow himself to be distracted. 'Well,' he continued, 'we was blown south at such a bat I'd not of been surprised had we landed up on a second reef. Particularly with the crew I'd got – all the rawest from *Bristol Maid*.'

Mrs Roxburgh remembered the hairs bristling on the humps of the bosun's great toes, but decided against resurrecting the bosun. She saw that Mr Pilcher chose to manipulate the details and the persons in his life, at least since the parting from the sluggish long-boat. She rather envied the mate for having become his own guiding spirit. The details of her life had been chosen for her by whoever it is that decides.

'Without charts and in such a gale, it wasn't possible to navigate. I can only say,' Mr Pilcher said, 'we must of been favoured by Providence.'

Becoming conscious of her stare, he lashed his hands round one of his emaciated knees.

'We were lucky enough to find ourselves, when the storm abated, off a part of the coast where the pinnace could be easily beached. And glad I was to be rid of 'er. The sea, too. Never no more will I go to sea.'

He coughed, and hid the result in a handkerchief. He could not have been sure whether his audience was frowning at his decision to renounce a vocation, or simply disapproving of a dirty habit.

His voice grated and wavered. 'From then on, we lived off the land so to say, and times was less lean, though often we went short. You get to hate one another when you're hungry.'

'Yes,' she agreed, while thinking that only a man could be so self-absorbed and boring.

But because her mother-in-law had taught her that a lady's role in life is to listen, she leaned sideways and propped her chin on a receptive hand.

'Some was for droring lots, to decide which of 'em 'twould be, but I wouldn't have no part in that.'

'And what about your companions? Did they favour eating one another?'

Mr Pilcher swallowed. 'Some of 'em was eaten.'

Mrs Roxburgh might have been thinking the mate had never looked so loathsome.

He told her confidentially. 'The blacks consider the hands are the greatest delicacy.'

'Did you try?' Mrs Roxburgh asked.

Mr Pilcher became so agitated he rose from his chair and began patrolling the room. 'I ask you,' he said at last, 'Mrs Roxburgh – would you?'

'I don't know. It would depend, I expect.'

Since she was caught in her own net, and Mr Pilcher had subsided again, she found herself struggling to her feet. Pain in one leg, or the root of an invisible tree, all but tripped her.

Looking up from the vantage of an easy chair the mate ventured to suggest, 'I bet you had a tough time yourself, Mrs Roxburgh – before the rescue.'

She answered, 'Yes.' As though the rescue ever takes place!

'They say you lived among the blacks.'

'That is so – and learned a great deal, of which I should otherwise remain ignorant.'

She was standing with her back to him after finding the lookingglass she had known must exist in Mrs Lovell's lesser parlour. Thus stationed, she could watch Pilcher while hidden from him, seated as he was at a lower level. Yet in the end the disadvantage was hers: she was faced with her own over-watchful reflection.

'And was brought to the settlement by some bushranger, or bolted convict, I am told.'

'I was so fortunate.'

'Who bolted again, just when he might have expected justice.'

'He became frightened. That – I hope – was his only reason for running away. Though the truth is often many-sided, and difficult to see from every angle. You will appreciate that, Mr Pilcher, having experienced the storm which separated the pinnace from the long-boat.'

She would have expected a wave of malice to rise in the man she remembered aboard *Bristol Maid*, and again, the evening on the cay, but he only murmured, 'That is true,' looking old and ravaged.

'So,' she said, after she had turned, 'I hope we can accept each other's shortcomings, since none of us always dares to speak the truth. Then we might remain friends.'

His eyes, watery from the moment when he entered the room, had started running.

'Friendship is all I have left since my husband was speared to death on the island. I forget, if I ever knew, whether you have a wife, Mr Pilcher?'

From snivelling, he hardened, as though frozen by a vision of the past. 'Yes,' he said, 'I had. But did not love her as I undertook. I was ashamed, I suppose, by what I must have thought a weakness. That is how she died, I can see.'

He sat rocking in recollection.

'Love was weakness. Strength of will – *wholeness*, as I saw it – is what I was determined to cultivate. That is why I admired you, Mrs Roxburgh – the cold lady, the untouchable.'

'I believed you hated me – and for what I never was.'

'So I did – your gentleman husband too – and was glad at the time to see you both brought down to the same level as the rest of us. And stole your ring.'

'I gave it to you.'

'Look,' he said, feeling in a waistcoat pocket, 'I've brought it back, the ring I took.'

There it was, glittering in the half-light, the nest of all but black garnets.

'Keep it,' she said. 'I have no use for it.'

'Nor me neether,' the man insisted, as though the ring disgusted him.

So she took it from between his tremulous fingers and, going to the window, threw it into the nasturtiums below, where the broad leaves closed over it. 'A child will find it,' she said, 'and value it as a plaything. Or it could be of service to some gardener – after his release.'

She laughed to ease the situation. 'Thank you, Mr Pilcher, for coming to see me. I hope we shall meet again before I sail from Moreton Bay.'

But she did not believe either of them truly wished it.

In the absence of prisoners, guards, witnesses, and inquisitors, early morning was an extenuating benison, especially when the young Lovells broke in, climbed upon the bed, snuggled against her, and insisted on tales of the black children she had known. Innocence prevailed in the light from the garden, and for the most part in her recollections; black was interchangeable with white. Surely in the company of children she might expect to be healed?

'Were they good?' asked a Lovell boy.

'Well, yes – not always perhaps, but at heart.' Was it not the truth behind the scratches and pinches they administered in accordance with their parents' orders? She remembered the eyes of the black children.

Their Lovell counterpart rippled in the bed with what might have been suppressed giggles. 'We're not good,' said Kate.

'Miss Scrim thinks we're abominable,' young Tom confirmed.

'Praps we are!' Totty giggled some more on her own.

'Nobody is good all the time,' Mrs Roxburgh allowed. 'I am not. But hope to learn.'

It sounded so curious, they looked at her, and left soon after.

Almost every morning they materialized in her room. She was perhaps mad, but a harmless diversion, and unlike their parents and Miss Scrimshaw, undemanding. They would stroke her arms, her shoulders, her cheeks, the skin of which, although superficially soft, concealed a rough grain. Had their parents known, they might not have appreciated rituals of such a subtle order that the children themselves would have been at a loss to explain; the pleasures they enjoyed early in Mrs Roxburgh's bed possibly remained a secret.

The morning after Pilcher's visit they did not appear. She wondered at it no more than casually while yawning her way into her clothes in the correct order, as she did by now instinctively. She was wearing her muslin with the heart's-ease pattern, the gift of an officer's wife who constantly attempted to express her admiration of one whose moral courage and powers of endurance had helped her survive what amounted to infernal trials. Mrs Roxburgh, on the other hand, was made to feel light, frivolous, implausible, when dressed in the earnest young woman's gift.

As on practically every morning, she took her walk in the garden, the light twirling round her with appropriate frivolity. I am unworthy, it recurred to her, of anybody's faith, least of all the trust of the children who confide in me.

She looked to see whether somebody might have discovered her secret, and there was the barefoot Kate, her hair and gown transformed by light, walking entranced it appeared, her gaze concentrated on whatever she was holding in her hands.

'Kate?' Mrs Roxburgh called, the exquisite child's purity rousing in her the sense of guilt which was only too ready to plague her.

Kate might have taken fright; in any case her trance was broken.

Upon reaching her Mrs Roxburgh asked, 'What is it you're holding?'

'Nothing!'

The child was carrying the corpse of a fluffy chick, the head lolling at the end of a no longer effectual neck, the extinct eyes reduced to crimson cavities.

'*Nothing!*' Kate screamed again, and flung the thing away from her.

And ran.

It seemed to Mrs Roxburgh that this bend in the brown river, with its steamy citrus plantation, garden beds too primly embroidered with marigold and phlox, and beyond a hedge, cucurbits of giant proportions writhing on mattresses of silt, was designed for revelations of evil, as was the low-built, rambling, deceptively hospitable official residence presided over by the fecund Mrs Lovell and her authoritarian spouse.

Or was she attributing to her surroundings emanations for which her own presence was responsible?

Her speculations made her shiver uncontrollably.

Since the children were started on their lessons, Miss Scrimshaw had come out, and could not help but notice.

She began feeling the guest's hands. 'How *cold* you are, Mrs Roxburgh!' She fetched a shawl. 'Do you not feel well? I imagine you could have contracted a fever, exposed as you were to an intemperate climate, and are not fully recovered.'

'No,' Mrs Roxburgh answered, 'I am well. But oh God, I must escape from here!'

'So you shall. Though it is not a matter of escape. His Excellency is sending the Government cutter, which should arrive any day to take you to Sydney.'

'I don't know why I should be pardoned before others who are more deserving.'

'I would advise you to forget.' Miss Scrimshaw spoke scarce above a whisper, as though it were an issue which affected only themselves.

She seated her patient in a cane chair, there on the veranda, before leaving for the kitchen offices to order beef tea with sippets; not that Miss Scrimshaw was simple enough to believe in any kind of panacea, but had a respect for conventions which are believed to console others.

While she was gone, Kate Lovell slipped out of the school-room, and she and Mrs Roxburgh clung together for a short space.

'Yes,' Mrs Roxburgh whispered, 'yes. I understand. And so will you.'

Kate had run back and Mrs Roxburgh composed herself by the time Miss Scrimshaw returned tasting the bouillon for temperature and seasoning.

Mrs Roxburgh refused her dinner (three o'clock by the Commandant's repeater) to the distress of Mrs Lovell, who came out to coax and fuss, and draw the cocoon of shawl closer still about her friend's shoulders.

Surprising in one so innocent, Mrs Lovell suggested, 'You must not be so merciless, my dear, towards yourself. Whatever is past, you have so much to look forward to. A woman can look to the future, don't you see? However unimportant we are, it is only in unimportant ways. They will always depend on us because we are the source of renewal.'

Mrs Lovell's faded looks were illuminated, her harassed manner dispelled by her moment of inspiration. She was so surprised at herself, as well as pleased, that Mrs Roxburgh might have shared her pleasure had she not observed the Commandant emerging from the dining-room.

Captain Lovell was noticeably suspicious of whatever secret his wife and her confederate were enjoying. Over and above the natural jealousy at work in him, he was made impatient by a shred of mutton stuck between his teeth, and yet another duty to discharge.

He informed Mrs Roxburgh, 'I've asked the chaplain to pay you a visit this afternoon. Nourishing food is not everything, is it? Let no one accuse us of not giving thought to your spiritual welfare! You'll find, in any event, that Cottle is not a bad fellow.'

'It's unnecessary, thank you,' Mrs Roxburgh replied. 'I mean, I would hate to waste anybody's time.'

Mrs Lovell gave her friend's shoulder a push. 'Oh, go on, Mrs Roxburgh! Again you're doing yourself an injustice. And Mr Cottle is not the fate my husband makes him sound. It will be good for you, besides.'

She was one of those practical women too distracted by their daily responsibilities to give overmuch thought to religion, but

345

who will recommend a helping of moralistic pudding to any they feel in need of it. Deprived of humour by a sense of duty and his own handsome features, her husband might have disapproved of his wife's mundane translation of his more sententious advice had he not also been her lover.

As for Mrs Roxburgh, she accepted once more the fate or chains that human beings were imposing on her. It was not altogether weakness on her part: surely her survival alone proved her to be possessed of a certain strength?

None the less, she awaited with foreboding the chaplain's visit, which was to take place like the second mate's in Mrs Lovell's lesser parlour. As the day had been a sultry one the shutters were stood open at evening to admit the faint gasps of a breeze. A coppery light lay to somewhat baleful effect upon the carpet and the furniture. Because of the heat Mrs Roxburgh had not exchanged her muslin for the weeds the chaplain might have expected.

The members of the household were most likely strolling or playing in the shrubberies, or dallying in the kitchen garden, for she was aware of that attentive silence which prevails in houses temporarily abandoned by their occupants. It was not so much the unwanted visit as a sense of rising hostility and emotion which prevented Mrs Roxburgh enjoying what should have been peace and quiet. Through the aching emptiness of martyrized scrub and rutted streets, she became conscious of a thudding from metal being hammered into wood, men's voices shouting instructions, and at last a deep threnody accompanied by concerted rapping, as of spoons battering on tin plates, but muted by confinement and distance.

If at this point silence seemed to fall in the lesser parlour, it could have been because the chaplain walked out of the garden, across the veranda flags, past the open shutters, and into the room, unannounced. Her attention was necessarily distracted by the presence of Mr Cottle, a small man, bright-lipped, eager-eyed, perhaps not entirely happy in the honorary tunic which had displaced his frock, but which did not disguise an abundant spiritual energy. The nervous cocking of his head and plaiting and unplaiting of fingers failed to suggest that the rebuffs he had received would deter him from continuing to exercise that energy in the rescue and cure of souls.

'Mrs Roxburgh!' He smiled, and if his smile too, was nervous, he had fired his first, tricky shot in a siege by enthusiasm. 'I believe – according to my wife – that you and I come, more or less, from the same part of the Old Country.' The dimple in a shaven, pointed chin appealed to her out of its blue surrounds.

Poor Mr Cottle, he was so small, his army boots were too large for him, his tunic inadequately patched where the right elbow had worn through (only vaguely could she recollect a small, but eager wife as one of Mrs Lovell's morning callers).

'From which part?' it was Mrs Roxburgh's duty to inquire.

'From Somerset – Withycombe, to be precise.'

'Oh,' she replied, and with a sad look which doubted his credentials, 'there's the river between us. You are from England.' She laughed, not unkindly, but to dispel any illusions he might have about their consanguinity. 'I was born to poor country, and perhaps for that reason take more than usual notice of pastures. I admired your fat fields, Mr Cottle, as I drove with Mr Roxburgh, after our marriage, into Gloucestershire.' Again she smiled amiably enough, and the chaplain grew dewy with relief, if not actual gratitude.

'I hope you will not be disinclined to listen,' Mr Cottle was becoming every instant more nervously ardent, 'if I remind you of the comfort your faith could bring – in a bereavement which the circumstances must have made doubly painful.'

Mrs Roxburgh lowered her eyes.

'Others have clothed and fed you since what all of us see as your miraculous escape. I would offer you the Gospels,' Mr Cottle patted his pocket to give his statement shape and substance, 'and an invitation from your fellow believers to join them in bearing witness this Sunday, and any other on which you find yourself at Moreton Bay.'

'Oh,' Mrs Roxburgh moaned, 'I don't know what I any longer believe.'

'I can't accept that your lapse in faith is more than a temporary backsliding,' Mr Cottle asserted, and ventured to add, 'that of a truly Christian soul.'

'I do not know, Mr Cottle, whether I am true, leave alone Christian,' Mrs Roxburgh murmured.

The chaplain was halted.

'If I was given a soul, I think it is possibly lost,' she said.

Mr Cottle appeared to poise himself on the balls of his feet inside his large-size army boots. 'If that is the case, I suggest you might be recovered for the faith here in our Moreton Bay communion.'

Mrs Roxburgh confessed, 'I was never able to live up to all that others expected of me.'

'Humility has its peculiar rewards, as you will realize if you join us. It will rejoice your heart only to hear the men doing justice to the hymns.'

'Have you a church at the settlement? I've not noticed one on my walks.'

'No,' he told her, 'we haven't, as yet. Our services are held in a hall at the prisoners' barracks.'

'I could hardly worship under the eyes of prisoners, some of them condemned for life.'

'You would not see them, Mrs Roxburgh. You would sit at the front of the congregation, with the Commandant and Mrs Lovell and the officers of the garrison. The prisoners are ushered in after the arrival of the official party, and are seated at the rear of the hall, where the guards keep a close watch on them. You will have nothing to fear, I assure you.'

'Only my conscience, and that can be more terrifying than any unseen criminal.'

The chaplain's lips moved wordlessly until he managed, 'In case you might find it more to your liking, I ought to mention a small unconsecrated chapel built by an unfortunate individual with whom you are already acquainted – Pilcher of *Bristol Maid*, now employed at the Commissariat. Soon after his arrival here, he started working, in his own time and with his own hands, to build this chapel, which some might call a folly. It is not commendable as architecture, but I do not doubt the sincerity of the builder's intention. It might appeal to you, Mrs Roxburgh.' His eye grew hectic as he thought he might have penetrated this Cornishwoman's opacity and reached the quietest inside.

But Mrs Roxburgh said, 'I would not care to break in upon Mr Pilcher's prayers.'

'It can be arranged, if you wish. He'll be flattered to feel you take an interest in him and his creation.'

Mrs Roxburgh smiled, but her expression had more of sadness in it. For a moment, but only a moment, Mr Cottle feared he might have floundered out of his depth. Then his faith flung him a lifeline, and he sprang to, and stationed himself in the centre of the carpet, determined to effect the rescue of a fellow being bent on spiritual immolation.

'Mrs Roxburgh,' he announced, 'I am going to ask you to join me in a short prayer. Let me but guide you, and like many others, you will find that Jesus is expecting you.'

Mrs Roxburgh sat looking petrified. 'I've forgotten the language!' her stone lips eventually ejected.

Now that the spirit was working in him the evangelist was not to be discouraged. He had got down upon his knees, from where his military boots, the best fit the Commissariat could provide, looked more noticeably roomy, his fluttered eyelids whiter and more exposed in their closure.

Still seated, her hands on her sash, Mrs Roxburgh could feel herself looking desperately brutish.

But the chaplain had begun to pray, 'Our Lord and Maker – you who have shown mercy to one whose life was most grievously threatened, lighten I pray you, a heavy heart, and spare the soul its torments real or imagined . . .'

Suddenly it was the chaplain who found himself most grievously threatened: the other side of his devout eyelids the Cornishwoman had started to scream.

'What – yes, it is! Don't let them, for God's sake! They'll flay the skin off 'is back. They'll beat the soul out of 'n – and that's worse, a thousand times, than killing a man!'

Still on his knees, Mr Cottle had opened his eyes, to see the woman who was also Mrs Roxburgh screeching like a peacock in Mrs Lovell's lesser parlour; while out of the distance, from across the creek, through the humid ranks of lemons, shaddocks, citrons, and guavas, the voice of a human being answered or appealed in such unearthly tones the chaplain might not have realized had his intended convert not drawn his attention to them.

'Go!' she screamed. 'Do! Do! We can – surely? Oh, we must!'

The chaplain could feel her nails eating into the wrist she had torn from its prayerful attitude. Her insistence allowed him little dignity as he tottered to his feet in his wretched boots.

349

'Dear Mrs Roxburgh,' his voice trembled from arriving at the upright in double time, 'this is a penal settlement for hardened criminals. Captain Lovell is humane by comparison with his predecessor. But punishment must be administered, in certain cases, when it is due.'

He could feel the blood trickling down his wrist where she had seized him.

'I advise you,' he continued, but need not have bothered: she had slipped from him, and was lying stretched on the parlour carpet.

So the chaplain at least was freed, and went, mopping his forehead, his eyes, his hectic cheeks, in search of ladies who might take charge of the hysterical female who had frightened him not only at his prayers, but also almost out of his wits.

It was Miss Scrimshaw who informed Mrs Roxburgh a while later that she had gone off in a faint. The latter lay on her bed looking up at the white ceiling. Miss Scrimshaw herself was white-lipped within her brown complexion, for the scene she had recently witnessed had been a most distressing one: sobbing children, flustered servants, her friend Mrs Roxburgh stretched out cold in her rucked-up muslin. In calmer circumstances the picture might have appealed to the spinster's cool eye and aesthetic sense as a somewhat unorthodox Dormition. Now the chaplain alone, twitching inside his shabby tunic, prevented her appreciating what she saw.

Miss Scrimshaw could not care for this small cleric of an evangelical persuasion. She admired large men, handsome officers in His Majesty's Services, and those other officers of the cloth, if large too, and destined for the purple. She had exchanged vows as a girl, it was known, with a naval lieutenant who died of a fever at Antigua, and remained more or less faithful to his memory, though she might have accepted a certain bereaved bishop had he proposed.

All this passed through Miss Scrimshaw's mind as she supervised the gathering up of Mrs Roxburgh from the carpet, and afterwards, as she stood bathing her friend's temples, a sibyl as it were, broody with the fumes of eau de Cologne.

But that which Miss Scrimshaw did not care to recall as she

pursued her ministrations was the screaming of the man they had strung up to the triangle in the gateway of the prisoners' barracks. She must banish it from her memory, along with anything else too naked or too cutting, which her upbringing and undefined social position had taught her to ignore. She only hoped her friend Mrs Roxburgh would not make it too difficult for her.

But Mrs Roxburgh, again in possession of her mind, appeared to have chosen Reason as her mentor. 'Don't you find him a tiresome little man?'

'Whom?' asked Miss Scrimshaw, as always careful of her grammar.

'Mr Cottle.'

'Yes indeed!' Miss Scrimshaw agreed with such heartiness her rather yellow teeth were exposed.

'But well-meaning.'

'If well-meaning is ever enough.' On second thoughts Miss Scrimshaw added magnanimously, 'We should be thankful, I suppose, for minor virtues when vice is so often in the grand manner'; while hoping she had not regressed too far in the direction of the incident which had been the cause of Mrs Roxburgh's collapse.

But the latter spent a fairly cheerful evening, helping little Kate with a watercolour, and accepting to take a hand at whist with the Commandant, Mrs Lovell, and Miss Scrimshaw herself, after the tea-table had been cleared.

Early morning, once the source of innocent joy, had become for her a breeding ground of dread. The children no longer came to her since the fright they got on finding her lying, as they thought, dead, a deception which could not be soon or easily forgiven. But she continued to waken as the first tinge of grey was filtered through the darkness surrounding her, the hour when she felt most isolated, and consequently, induced to explore the labyrinth of conscience. As the light grew more substantial she appeared abandoned even by her shadow, and however ecstatic the choir of birds, silences were inevitably appended, through which she would find herself tramping rather than walking in bush featureless and listless enough to have been a reflection of her hopes.

On such a morning, thrusting her way through scrub grown denser, the going rougher, still within sight of the brown, sluggish river, though well beyond the confines of the settlement, she was arrested by a glimpse of something which at first suggested floating, flickering light rather than any solid form: it was such a refractive white, and her thoughts had withdrawn far from her surroundings into the obscure recesses of her mind.

Then she saw that here among the dusty casuarinas she had come upon a small rustic building in crudely quarried, but whitewashed stone, and realized that this must be Pilcher's folly, the unconsecrated chapel the ordained minister had mentioned. Her heart was beating uncomfortably, her breathing strained, as she trod carefully, lifting her skirt to avoid stumbling over rocks and breaking sticks in her cautious approach to the open doorway. What she feared was that Pilcher himself might be inside and catch her in the act of trespassing, for trespass it could only be, from her experience of the architect's mind – not unlike certain pockets in her own.

So that to set foot upon the whitewashed threshold was in some sense for Mrs Roxburgh a regrettable action. *Ellurnnnn*, she heard her name tolled, not by one, but several voices. Yet nobody barred her entry into the primitive chapel. The interior was bare, except for a log bench and a rough attempt at what in an orthodox church would have been the communion table, on it none of the conventional ornaments or trappings, but an empty bird's-nest which may or may not have reached there by accident. Above the altar a sky-blue riband painted on the wall provided a background to the legend GOD IS LOVE, in the wretchedest lettering, in dribbled ochre. Nothing more, but the doorless doorway through which she had entered, and two narrow, unglazed windows piercing the side walls of the chapel.

Mrs Roxburgh felt so weak at the knees she plumped down on the uneven bench, so helpless in herself that the tears were running down her cheeks, her own name again mumbled, or rather, tolled, through her numbed ears.

All this by bright sunlight in the white chapel. Birds flew, first one, then a second, in at a window and out the opposite. There was little to obstruct, whether flight, thought, or vision. If she could have stayed her tears, but over those she had no control, as she sat re-living the betrayal of her earthly loves, while the Roxburghs' LORD GOD OF HOSTS continued charging in apparent triumph, trampling the words she was contemplating.

At last she must have cried herself out: she could not have seen more clearly, down to the cracks in the wooden bench, the bird-droppings on the rudimentary altar. She did not attempt to interpret a peace of mind which had descended on her (she would not have been able to attribute it to prayer or reason) but let the silence enclose her like a beatitude. Then, when she had blown her nose, and re-arranged her veil, she went outside, to return to the settlement in which it seemed at times she might remain permanently imprisoned.

She looked back once in the direction of the chapel in spite of a warning by her better judgement against wilfully revoking perfection. There she saw a figure which became that of the lapsed seaman and dedicated architect. Although she restrained herself from acknowledging his presence, he started scrambling up the slope, causing saplings in his path to shudder, dislodging minor rocks, one of which bounded to within inches of the intruder's feet.

She hastened away, and upon reaching the settlement, sensed at once that something out of the ordinary had happened to dispel apathy and relieve tension.

One of the assigned servants ran out of the house and announced from the edge of the veranda, 'Oh, ma'am, the cutter is in the river. They've sighted 'er from up the mill.' The woman was so elated by an occurrence which could not ease her own lot, but which she regarded none the less as an event, that Mrs Roxburgh experienced a pang of remorse.

'And when will they sail?' she dared inquire.

'Who knows?' the woman answered. ''Tisn't for me to decide, is it?' and was brought down to reality and the leaden soles of her boots.

Mrs Roxburgh would have liked to restore the woman's spirits, but in the absence of inspiration, could but murmur, 'Thank you, Mary,' and bow her head, and go inside.

The morning was full of coming and going, slammed doors, voices raised but never enough, laughing and scuttling through the passages (lessons were evidently waived). Mrs Roxburgh's cell seemed the only corner of the house to remain untouched by the cutter's arrival.

Of course she should have gone out and joined in the excited confusion. If she hesitated to celebrate her longed-for release becoming actual fact, it was because she could not ignore a future fraught with undefined contingencies. Had the walls but opened at a certain moment, she might even have turned and run back into the bush, choosing the known perils, and nakedness rather than an alternative of shame disguised.

It was close on dinner-time when Miss Scrimshaw burst into the room in a state of high importance. 'You will have heard the news,' she began somewhat breathily, 'but perhaps not every detail of it, because I myself have been kept in the dark until almost the last moment. Mrs Lovell is so fatigued the Commandant, in the kindness of his heart, is sending her to Sydney for a change of air. The children, who are most of them too small to be left behind, will accompany her. And I shall go to enforce a little necessary discipline!' The governess actually performed a stately step or two. 'We shall sail the day after tomorrow depending on a favourable wind.'

Then Miss Scrimshaw, remembering, turned a deep maroon, which mounted by way of her scrawny neck into her brown, downy cheeks. 'Oh,' she cried, 'how I run on, when it is you who have most cause for rejoicing at the cutter's arrival!'

'I hardly know,' Mrs Roxburgh blurted back. 'Yes, I am glad, of course, but shall be the happier for your company – for my return to the world. I have been so long out of it, I may not easily learn to adapt myself to its ways.'

Dissolving in the emotions of the moment the two women were carried away to the extent of embracing. 'I expect we shall make our blunders,' Miss Scrimshaw predicted, 'but would you not say that life is a series of blunders rather than any clear design, from which we may come out whole if we are lucky?'

Then she laughed, and detached herself, and adjusted her fichu, and sternly resorted to practical matters. 'If we are to be ready, we must start at once to *systematize*. The children alone! Poor Mrs Lovell is too distracted, and then, you may not know, she is expecting.'

354

With some diffidence Mrs Roxburgh offered Miss Scrimshaw her services.

But the spinster remembered she had not included in her recitative a detail not at first sight related to the practical. 'We shall have with us on board a passenger not of our party, a Mr Jevons from London, who has taken advantage of the cutter's mission to Moreton Bay to look up his connections, the young Cunninghams.'

Miss Scrimshaw glanced at her friend, it could have been to see whether the latter might accuse her of irrelevance, but finding no indication of this, she gladly forged on. 'Mr Jevons, I gather, is a merchant of substantial means, but let us not condemn him for that.' Miss Scrimshaw was so indulgent this morning. 'A widower,' she added, to allow the man a modicum of virtue. 'I happened to be passing the Cunninghams' cottage, and in this way made their connection's acquaintance. I dare say we shall find him agreeable and helpful company.' With this prediction, Miss Scrimshaw left to compose a list of 'material necessities'.

Mrs Roxburgh's own possessions and needs were so immaterial and few that she soon followed, and under Miss Scrimshaw's command, set to work collecting spencers, booties, blankets, shawls, button-boots for pairs of feet descending in the scale from small to smallest, 'Kate's old bonnet with the primroses; she looks so pretty in it', pencils, primers, cutlery, bedding.

'And potted meat!' the quartermaster almost shouted. 'And six – at least – four-pound loaves!'

'My dear Miss Scrimshaw,' Mrs Lovell sighed from the sofa where she was prudently resting, 'we are not embarking on the voyage home, and at Sydney shall be staying with the Huxtables.'

'It's as well to be prepared,' Miss Scrimshaw advised, 'for any and every eventuality.'

When at dinner-time the Commandant appeared he made an immediate point of congratulating Mrs Roxburgh on her speedy departure for civilization. Captain Lovell had benefited by his magnanimity towards his wife and family; he had never looked (nor in all probability felt) handsomer, as he sat at table after saying grace, hands folded on his tunic, the wedding-ring exposed, or chucked Kate under her chin, and complimented Miss Scrimshaw on her downright military efficiency. The world was for the moment, if not always, Captain Lovell's.

During dinner his wife, stirring the barley broth Mr Cunningham had prescribed for her, inquired as a matter of course, 'Are they leaving you in peace, my love?'

'Fairly so. I cannot complain,' Captain Lovell answered. 'There is always the tobacco question. And Bragg has made his third attempt, this time with a kitchen fork.' The children's presence did not allow him to elaborate.

All attacked their dinner, and some complained that the mutton was tough, not to say black and nasty. Little Totty was sent from the room. But Mrs Roxburgh had to presume that the Commandant was what the world holds to be just.

When they rose from table she approached him and said, 'I must remind you of my petition, sir.'

'Your petition, Mrs Roxburgh?' His eyebrows started up, while his smile appeared the more brilliant for a slight dash of mutton fat.

'For the convict,' she said, 'the man Chance – to whom I owe my survival.'

'And why must I be reminded? My purpose at Moreton Bay is to see that justice is done.'

Endowed with official integrity and domestic virtues, this imposing gentleman should have convinced her more easily.

'Do you not trust me?' he asked.

'I should,' she mumbled, 'but no longer know,' and broke off.

He tapped her on the wrist. 'You should have more confidence in yourself.'

After which, she left him, and allowed herself to be burdened with all that Miss Scrimshaw considered necessary for the voyage.

Later in the afternoon her commanding officer reported on returning from a personal reconnaissance of the immediate approaches, 'I do believe we have callers, and that it is Mrs Cunningham, the surgeon's wife – with her relative – Mr Jevons – from London.'

For one of her rank and experience Miss Scrimshaw appeared flustered. 'I should tell you, Mrs Roxburgh, that he wears a ring with a diamond in it. But of course a diamond, though not to my taste – on a man – need not make him morally reprehensible.'

To reassure her friend Mrs Roxburgh said, 'Mr Roxburgh – my husband – wore a signet ring.'

'Ah,' Miss Scrimshaw approved, 'that is what one expects, surely, of a gentleman?'

There was no time for more, since Mrs Cunningham and her suspect cousin were already mounting the veranda steps.

The surgeon's wife was a heavily built, swarthy young woman who would have appeared plain beside her spouse had he been present. Perhaps she had brought from the Jevons side some of its 'substantial means'.

As for Mr Jevons, he too was large and dark, well-fleshed, but solid in his fleshiness. Mrs Roxburgh was fatally drawn to look for the ring with the diamond in it, and in doing so noticed the wedding band on the next finger but one. Whereas this same token seemed to stimulate the self-satisfaction inherent in the Commandant, it made Mr Jevons's hand look curiously vulnerable. She hastened to dismiss her thought as a foolish fancy, probably conceived as a result of her own unfortunate experience.

Both Mrs Cunningham and her cousin avoided reference to the events which had brought Mrs Roxburgh to Moreton Bay, except that Mr Jevons remarked in a general way, 'You can't be sorry, after your ordeal, to be quit of the Colony, and start the long voyage home.'

'What else?' she replied evenly enough. 'Though I cannot say there is anything which takes me there.'

There the matter rested, while Mr Jevons expressed appropriate sentiments on the future of New South Wales, and went so far as to hint that he was preparing to drive in a stake of his own and profit from the development of Sydney.

He was the proprietor, it seemed, of a hardware business in Oxford Street, London, to which he drove himself every weekday from his little place at Camberwell.

'Little place? Why, Cousin George! I'm sure, Miss Scrimshaw, if you was to see it, you'd find it a positive mansion.'

Miss Scrimshaw composed a smile which could only be described as forgiving, and apologized when the cousins had left.

'Mrs Cunningham is an inexperienced and somewhat tasteless

young woman. But Mr Jevons is in no way boastful. How did he strike you?'

'I'd say he is kind. His hands look kind.'

'What a curious observation! I never thought to look at his hands, except to notice the diamond ring, and that I prefer not to see.'

Mrs Roxburgh felt that Miss Scrimshaw would dispose of the diamond ring as soon as she was in a position to do so.

For her part, Mrs Roxburgh was glad of such diversions during the hours left to her at Moreton Bay, when she dreaded hearing the renewed screams of the prisoner at the triangle, and almost dared not sleep lest Jack Chance the convict appear in a dream and offer her his love. Her briefest snatches of sleep became dreamless nightmares perhaps by strength of will.

If Captain Lovell on the other hand did not sleep, it was not from thought of separation from his wife and children, but the report for His Excellency, which he was still composing the night before the cutter sailed. To give the Commandant his due, he was scrupulously just within the limits history had imposed on him.

So he scratched away by candlelight, rounding out his periods:

. . . a woman of some intelligence, but given to concealment, or confused I shld rather say, by the ordeal she has recently undergone. It is difficult to arrive at the truth either in the account offered by Mrs Roxburgh, or that of Pilcher the unfortunate second mate. It may suit both, while still too close to the events, to cultivate delusion as a shield or comfort.

Pilcher for the moment shows no inclination to better his lot but seems prepared to end his days as a clerk at the Commissariat. When off duty he devotes himself to the chapel to which I have already referred, doubtless built in expiation of whatever sins he may have committed.

Mrs Roxburgh, while vague about the past, has no definite plans for the future. She is only roused when the fate of Chance, the bolted convict, comes in question. Then she grows most passionate, demanding a pardon for him on his recovery by us, and for which no doubt she will petition Yr Excellency soon after you receive this dispatch. There is no reason to disbelieve her story that the man brought her to a farm on the outskirts of the Settlement, though the lady is unwilling to contribute any but the barest details of their journey, probably out of modesty, for she was discovered by Sergt. and Mrs Oakes without a stitch of clothing after the convict had turned and fled back into the bush, either from delicacy on his part, or fear of retribution.

I propose to send out search parties for this probably deranged wretch, and if, as I hope, we recover him, I wld add my own recommendations for clemency to Mrs Roxburgh's petitions. Granted the man committed a foul murder in a London slum, and was sentenced for life, but it is my humble opinion that he will have been broken by what he has endured and that he has redeemed himself by delivering the lady into our hands, alive and subsequently restored to health.

I have the honour to be

Sir

your most obedt . . .

Captain Lovell was so relieved to have got this deucedly delicate matter down on paper that he could not resist adding an extra flourish to his normally florid signature.

The morning was more limpid, less equivocal, than the emotions the cutter's departure provoked. The captain had gone on ahead in the skiff with some of his crew and his passenger Mr George Jevons. They had already boarded *Princess Charlotte* when the whale boat with the larger party consisting of the Commandant and his lady, their children either shouting or crying, Miss Scrimshaw, Mrs Roxburgh (it must be she, hidden inside the widow's veil) their formal luggage, and a great variety of less orthodox bundles, rounded the last bend separating it from the cutter.

More than anybody Mr Jevons was of assistance in the ticklish operation of hauling the ladies and children aboard. Mrs Lovell, who had been rendered quite weak and tearful at thought of the approaching separation, could only hang on her husband's arm until Miss Scrimshaw produced her smelling-bottle. Miss Scrimshaw herself, breathing deep to inhale the 'ozone', declared to anybody interested that she 'never felt so free as when embarking on an ocean voyage'.

Mrs Roxburgh was silent, but raised her veil for a clearer view of the mangrove banks and the brown river, the latter of which had come out in blue for the occasion.

'Is it not a picture?' Miss Scrimshaw remarked approaching her friend.

'Yes,' Mrs Roxburgh agreed. 'A picture.'

For that was what it looked, a canvas painted in turgid oils, as opposed to the iridescent watercolour of Hobart Town, each in its particular way remote from reality as she had experienced it.

Evidently partial to the company of ladies, Mr Jevons the merchant strolled to where the two were standing at the bulwark, 'I would say that a more valuable picture, to Mrs Roxburgh's mind, will be the view of London River when she first sets eyes on it.'

Mrs Roxburgh remained so strangely silent that Miss Scrimshaw felt it her duty to take a hand and pat the conversation onward. 'Ah, don't be unkind, Mr Jevons, to those who will be left in the Colony! You will have me homesick.'

At the risk of ignoring Miss Scrimshaw Mr Jevons hoped that Mrs Roxburgh would allow him to introduce her to his family circle at Camberwell, over which his sister presided as housekeeper, and foster mother to his three young daughters.

He seemed most anxious to soften what might be the harshness of her arrival, but Mrs Roxburgh was only embarrassed that her friend should be excluded, though inevitably as things stood, from an invitation she must so much desire.

Instead Miss Scrimshaw showed every sign of unaffected approval. 'There! What a ready-made home-coming!' It could, of course, have been an excess of ozone making her sound ebullient.

Mrs Roxburgh was somewhat put out by the spinster's unreluctant acquiescence. She drew away, and at once saw her opportunity for addressing the Commandant in private, a move she had postponed till the last.

'Captain Lovell,' she said, 'I cannot thank you enough for your kindness, and for what I know will be the outcome of your interceding with the Governor.'

Never averse to a bout of moral coquetry, he tapped her on the arm with the sealed dispatch he would shortly deliver into the hands of Captain Barbour. 'You trust me, then?'

She stood as though still considering. 'I hope I do.'

The light glancing off the river struck at the scarlet seal, which glittered like blood only recently clotted.

The Commandant could not help but notice the pulse beating

in the throat of this woman who moved and disturbed him more perhaps than domesticity and his official position warranted.

Soon after, the company was summoned to what Miss Scrimshaw described as a *déjeuner à la fourchette*, which they gladly demolished, and Captain Lovell took leave of his tearful wife and excited children.

But as he stood in the moored skiff his attention may have been concentrated rather, on the woman in black.

Mrs Roxburgh was standing alone at the bulwark, staring it seemed, at the foreshore of grey mangroves, at their oily reflections in muddy water, for the sun had gone in and the sky removed the last of its blue twitching streamers from the brown surface of the river. So the Commandant observed, so too, Mr Jevons, so Miss Scrimshaw, more closely than any. She would always remember what sounded like a sudden cry of pain, as quickly suppressed as it was briefly uttered.

She went forward to offer sympathy and support, but Mrs Roxburgh had veiled herself; her step was firm, her voice dry and steady. 'Let us go below,' she decided. 'We have said good-bye. I have done my duty, I hope, by everybody.'

During the afternoon the two ladies rested in the cabin allotted to them. Mrs Roxburgh, in the end, must have fallen into a heavy sleep. When she awoke, her companion had removed herself, no doubt to attend to the duties for which she had been engaged.

In the diminishing light the narrow cabin was yet so neat, so admirably accoutred in teak and brass, the sound of water on the vessel's timbers so unrelated to the terrors which the more demoniac side of the ocean's nature can rouse in the voyager, she should have had fewer qualms for her re-entry into the rational world of civilized beings. If misgivings persisted, they were occasioned more than anything by her friend's capricious behaviour of earlier that day. What seemed like Miss Scrimshaw's renunciation of the kindly, but rather boring merchant, together with the spinster's uncharacteristically indiscreet treatment, if not actual patronage, Mrs Roxburgh ventured, of herself, was something which frankly puzzled her.

But she continued only vaguely puzzling as she rose in the dusk, and soothed by the sea sounds, the rattling of brass handles, the voices of the crew muffled by distance, refreshed her face and hands with eau de Cologne, and changed her dress. Not until then did she light a candle, the better to attend to her still fairly scanty hair, and was seated at the glass coaxing a ringlet or two when her companion returned.

'Not in the dark, but almost!' Miss Scrimshaw accused. 'Oh,' she exclaimed, 'you are wearing the gown I always thought would suit you!'

'I put it on,' Mrs Roxburgh replied, 'because it is my only change of clothes.'

'It sets you off, if I may say so.'

Mrs Roxburgh did look unwillingly resplendent in the garnet silk. As for Miss Scrimshaw, if she had changed her dress during Mrs Roxburgh's nap, it was for yet another brown, to which she now added as finishing touch a string of onyx recklessly dashed over her head.

Having satisfied herself in the glass that she looked to her best advantage, Miss Scrimshaw turned, and Mrs Roxburgh saw that she was to be subjected to interrogation by one whom she had considered an ally.

'Have you observed,' the inquisitor began, 'that Mr Jevons takes an uncommon interest in you?'

'In me? Absurd! Why should Mr Jevons take an interest in one who is in no way interested?'

'Men,' Miss Scrimshaw seemed to savour the word, 'are constantly attracted to what is difficult and possibly unattainable.'

'Oh, but I am appalled!' Mrs Roxburgh protested. 'And in any case would not want to trespass on another's interests.'

'Oh, my dear!' At pains to absolve her friend, and to administer extreme unction to any resigned passion of her own, Miss Scrimshaw laughed. 'To be candid, Mrs Roxburgh, I could not bring myself to share my bed. I do so love stretching out in comfort.'

Mrs Roxburgh suspected that her re-instated friend had verged on what she most deplored – the vulgar.

Miss Scrimshaw saw her slip. 'Now you will think me immodest. But candour is a natural pitfall – you will surely agree – when pioneering in the bush.'

Mrs Roxburgh loved her.

'If you will forgive me,' the spinster pleaded, 'let us go on deck and take the air together.'

'Let us!' Mrs Roxburgh assented.

So the two ladies groped their way to the companion-ladder, and when they had arrived above, and steadied themselves, linked arms and strolled in the dark.

There was a jewellery of stars such as Ellen Roxburgh believed she might be seeing for the last time before a lid closed, and persistent, if in no way malicious, breezes, as well as a creaking of cordage, a straining of canvas, which for an instant halted her in the steps of memory. She might have staggered had it not been for her companion's arm.

When it was Miss Scrimshaw who did not exactly stagger, but exclaimed most vehemently, 'How I wish I were an eagle!'

'An eagle. Why?' Although she could see for herself the curved beak cutting the semi-obscurity, the fixed eyes glittering by starlight, it would have been impolite of Mrs Roxburgh not to have sounded mildly surprised.

'To soar!' Miss Scrimshaw wheezed. 'To reach the heights! To breathe! Perch on the crags and look down on everything that lies beneath one! Elevated, and at last free!'

Mrs Roxburgh felt dazed by the sudden rush of rhetoric.

Once launched, Miss Scrimshaw was prepared to reveal still more. 'Have you never noticed that I am a woman only in my form, not in the essential part of me?'

Somewhat to her own surprise, Mrs Roxburgh remained ineluctably earthbound. 'I was slashed and gashed too often,' she tried to explain. 'Oh no, the crags are not for me!' She might have been left at a loss had not the words of her humbler friend Mrs Oakes found their way into her mouth. 'A woman, as I see, is more like moss or lichen that takes to some tree or rock as she takes to her husband.'

Had either of the two women parading the deck between the stars and the swell of canvas felt sufficiently moved to fight for her own tenet and convert the other, it was not the moment to proselytize, for a human form had emerged out of the companionway and was bearing down, large and black, ominous but for the voice of Mr Jevons which preceded him by several paces.

'Mrs Lovell is at the tea-table, and invites you ladies to join her if you are inclined.'

'How I neglect my duties!' Miss Scrimshaw cried. 'The sea has badly gone to my head!' Detaching herself from Mrs Roxburgh to an accompaniment of onyx cannoning off onyx, the eagle flumped across the deck, reached the companionway, and disappeared.

The merchant was at liberty to offer Mrs Roxburgh his support, and she to accept. 'Thank you,' she murmured, taking his arm (what else could she have done?).

As on the other occasions of their meeting he gave an impression of solid worth, a quality she was happy to re-discover at night, at sea, but must remind herself that the solid is not unrelated to the complacent, and that Mr Jevons might assert rights she would not wish to grant, she thought, even had she been free of a past in which honourable allegiances conflicted with her own discreditable passions.

'According to the omens,' Mr Jevons informed her, 'we can look forward to a smooth and uneventful passage to Sydney.'

'I do not believe in omens,' Mrs Roxburgh replied, which was scarcely truthful, as she knew.

'I do,' said the merchant with a confidence greater than hers.

Did he, imperceptibly, squeeze the arm linked to his? She could not be sure, and must not, in any case, allow herself to feel comforted.

When they entered the saloon Miss Scrimshaw was presiding at the tea-kettle, for one of the younger children had brought up some biscuit-and-milk on his smocking and the mother was engaged in repairing the damage and soothing him.

Kate and her eldest brother were in a tangle at cat's-cradle.

'Look, Mrs Roxburgh! We're stuck. It's Tom.'

'It ain't!' growled Tom, giving her a kick under cover of a chair. 'That's how girls go on when they've got themselves into a mess.'

Mrs Roxburgh stooped, and after some slight manipulation transferred the string back to Kate in the shape required for the game's logical progression. Kate was entranced. She adored Mrs Roxburgh, and did not doubt that her love was returned. The incident of the mutilated fledgeling seemed to have bound them more closely together.

It was Mr Jevons who brought Mrs Roxburgh her tea, together with a slice of cake so moist with fruit it might have been studded with precious stones. Mr Jevons was advancing, all manly authority and calm, when by some incredible mischance he stumbled, whether against child or chair-leg, or over a ruck in the carpet, nobody saw. Or was it by infernal intervention? Whatever the cause of his downfall, Mr Jevons saw the cake flying off its plate, the cup shooting out of its saucer.

On his knees, he watched the tea-stain widening, darkening, in the folds of Mrs Roxburgh's skirt. Needless to say, the uproar was immense, so much so that Mr Jevons got the shakes. There was no disguising it as he mopped the stain with his ineffectual handkerchief.

Mrs Roxburgh sat looking down at this troubled bull-frog of a man with what almost amounted to languid acceptance of her due, until she made an effort, and returned to the human situation.

Sitting forward, she charged him, 'Dun't! 'Tis nothing.'

'But I spoiled yer dress!' the bull-frog croaked wretchedly.

''Tisn't mine, and 'tisn't spoiled,' she insisted.

She may have touched his hand an instant, for the trembling was stilled, more by surprise than by command.

'It is nothing, I do assure you, Mr Jevons,' she repeated in what passed for her normal voice.

Because their exchange had been spoken so low and only for each other, and because of the children scrummaging after pieces of cake, and Miss Scrimshaw's squawks as she retrieved the fragments of smashed cup, and sponged the stain, probably nobody heard or noticed strangers sharing a secret.

When calm had re-settled, Mrs Roxburgh accepted another cup, offered by Tom. Her eyes grew moist, her vision blurred, but steam was rising out of the tea, and if she felt breathless, restless, her stays, she told herself, were not yet broken in.

Mr Jevons, again the substantial merchant, was no longer conscious of the stain, worsened though it was by his and Miss Scrimshaw's attentions. He could not give over contemplating the smouldering figure in garnet silk beside the pregnant mother in her nest of drowsy roly-poly children, a breathing statuary contained within the same ellipse of light.

He did not see that Kate kicked Tom, and that Tom retaliated with a punch; they were in a different orbit. Nor did Miss Scrimshaw attempt to enforce the discipline she advocated: she was too engrossed, her onyx going click click, shooting down possible doubts; for however much crypto-eagles aspire to soar, and do in fact, through thoughtscape and dream, their human nature cannot but grasp at any circumstantial straw which may indicate an ordered universe.